KILLER DELIVERY

A DANA CAPONE MYSTERY, BOOK 1

CLAIRE FEENEY

ISBN: 978-1-7367289-7-0

Cover by L1 Graphics

www.clairefeeney.com

Author photograph by Anna Monette

CONTENTS

LEGACY KILLERS
(A Dana Capone Novella)

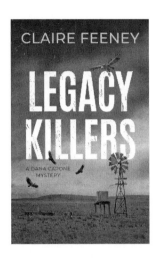

What happens when the protectors become the predators?

Homicide Detective Dana Capone comes from a legacy of death. So when a body turns up in a field just outside of Austin, Texas, she senses a familiar evil lurking.

Substantiating her suspicion won't be easy, and she suspects it won't be well-received by the department, either. Not when all evidence points to the worst-case scenario: the predator she's hunting is someone she trusts.

Read this prequel novella for free when you sign up for Claire Feeney's email list, the Unsubs.

Go to: www.clairefeeney.com/freebie

ONE

Austin, Texas
June 6th, 2018

It felt incredible to absolutely kill it. She'd tried the same material on stage at The Bungalow right before that club shut down and earned tepid laughs at best. Audiences were like that. Fickle. Sometimes just downright sexist or racist. The sum of the parts was hard to predict. It made the nights like this one feel even better, though.

She pulled her cigs from her back pocket as she slipped backstage and pushed open the creaky steel door into the alleyway behind the club. It stank of piss back there, like every nook and cranny of downtown, but the smoke would help drown that out.

She hadn't expected much from Laugh Attack tonight —the comedy club had been especially full of testosterone lately, which could go either way for a female comedian. Sometimes it meant she took the mic and was met with skepticism, and sometimes it meant the audience was thirsty for a refreshing drink of fresh, feminine-infused material. Tonight, the place had been thirsty. Nights like tonight were the reason she'd kept up the frantic pace, hopping from club to club, scrounging up new material on the bus each day, paying to live in this expensive city on the off chance that she would rise to the top. Austin wasn't so bad, but it was hot, and it wasn't where the real comedy was happening. It was like a feeder city, the comedy minor leagues. She'd work her way up to New York or Chicago someday. She was still young, despite what her deep sense of urgency tried to tell her.

She coughed against a rancid whiff of the dumpster a few feet away as she stepped onto the slab and heard the door clatter shut behind her.

Slipping an unlit cigarette between the ruby red of her stained lips, the woman patted her pockets for her lighter. There was her phone, the stiff outline of her ID and debit card, but no lighter. Maybe she'd slipped it in the pack absent-mindedly. She checked. Nope. Shit. Must've been in her leather jacket, which she'd left draped over a barstool inside. It was too hot a night for outerwear. June in Austin? Brutal. Chicago would definitely be a nice change whenever she could afford to move upward and onward.

The shriek of the old metal door opening behind her caused her to jump, and she whirled around.

"Need a light, Cheryl?"

The door whined closed behind him again.

He was still here? For some reason, she thought he'd already taken off. The open mic had wrapped just after nine, and the regulars had left after a half-hour of their usual standing around and trying to out-funny each other. She'd stuck around, as she usually did, to help Heidi close down the place. Someone had to, and the goodwill it engendered from the owner of the club wouldn't exactly hurt her chances of a solid booking in the future.

So, where had he been hiding the whole time?

"Yeah, thanks," she said. "I left my lighter inside."

He plunged his hand into the breast pocket of his black button-down shirt. The long sleeves of it made her sweaty just looking at them. The heat must have been suffocating him in those cowboy boots and jeans, too.

Hold on. He wasn't wearing that earlier, was he?

She thought she would have noticed sooner. Maybe he'd changed for a night on the town.

Her gaze jumped to the wound-up mic cable slung over his left shoulder. He must have been inside, breaking down the sound equipment in some dark corner or finishing off his last drink. Easy enough to overlook him on her way out the back door, especially with her mind racing like it'd been.

He held out the lighter. "What are you doing out here?"

She accepted the offering, flicked it, inhaled, making the tip of her cigarette glow a violent orange. "Needed a smoke, and I didn't feel like being out front. Too many drunks and homeless looking to bum one off me. I only have a couple left in this pack."

He shot her a grin, the intensity of his gaze growing. "And then you're quitting?"

She wished he'd look away, even just for a second. His stare felt indecent, aggressive.

Why is he even back here?

He wasn't a smoker, as far as she knew, and he wasn't taking out the trash. Had he followed her?

She returned the lighter. "Nope. No plans of quitting. Just don't want to have to make a stop for more tonight. Oh, but if you want one..."

He held up a hand. "Nah, I don't partake."

She'd been right, then. Not a smoker. Something was off about him tonight. Anxiety stirred inside her chest, a ball of energy urging her to move.

Then it hit her: *Oh, Christ, he's gonna make a move.*

She angled her body away from him, hoping to break the intensity of his close inspection, his unblinking eyes. God, what a creep. She'd never considered him one before, but things like that could change quickly.

"Not your best performance tonight, but it was okay," he said.

She shot him a sharp look for the unwelcome slight, but when he didn't show even the smallest sign of embarrassment, she cast her eyes down to the dirty pavement.

Had she misjudged the audience? Maybe it had only been the folks closest to the stage who were laughing. Mostly people she knew, people she liked, and who, for the most part, seemed to like her.

Damn.

She scrubbed the toe of her sneaker over a dark splotch on the ground. "Practice makes perfect."

"It wasn't you," he added. "You were on point, and your material was great. It was just the audience. Don't worry about it."

"I'm not. It felt pretty good. You're right, not my best show, but I had a good time up there."

"I could tell. You looked relaxed. First time I've seen you let your guard down. Harvey's anatomically inaccurate abortion material shouldn't have gotten bigger laughs than your joke about the H-E-B express lane. That one was gold."

She tried to take the compliment, but... Harvey's awful joke had gotten more laughs than hers? Really?

No comparing, Cheryl.

"I tell you," he continued, "one abortion joke from Louis CK, and all these guys think they have permission to joke about it."

She shrugged. "They could be mimicking worse behaviors from him."

He laughed, and when their eyes met again, she was struck by something. Or rather, by *nothing*. There was a blankness to his eyes. A void.

She aimed her attention at the wall over his shoulder instead and cleared her throat.

"True," he said once his laughter had stopped. "You should be thankful they're not pulling their dicks out in front of you." His expression tightened then, and his voice lowered. "But I don't know. I think you might like it if they did."

She whipped her attention back around to those darkened eyes. The energy in her chest spun frantically as she searched his features for signs of a poorly executed joke —embarrassment, shame, anything. "Uh, no thanks," she said.

Finishing the cigarette wasn't worth it. He was a creep after all, and this was going nowhere good, and fast. She'd be lucky to get out of there before he could whip out his dick.

She turned and tossed the butt on the ground, a few embers jumping loose on impact, and crushed the thing under her toe. Maybe she could write a joke about this turn of events on the bus ride home. Men using Louis CK's creepiness to advance their own creepiness. Something meta like that.

She whirled back around at the sound of rubber cables slapping the cement slab behind her, and his hands wrapped tight around her neck before she could scream.

Beneath the wet blanket of cars honking, people shouting, live music pulsing from the open doors of downtown bars, no one could hear her gurgling cry for help.

He shoved her back, and she scrambled to keep her feet underneath her, clamping on to his wrists, steadying herself on the same man who was squeezing the life from her.

A knee to his balls, and she might slip free. Just a single thrust, and she would run. Run and not look back. The police station was close by. She would run until she made it.

But the moment she regained her balance was the same moment the heel of his boot crashed down onto her left shin. A pop and crunch in her knee. Her lower leg snapped beneath her.

Another strangled scream that didn't make it past her throat, but she didn't go down. His grip on her neck was too strong, and he held her up by it.

It was all she could do to keep her good leg underneath her. It was her last hope.

She pried away at his hands, trying to loosen even a single one of his fingers. Her eyes bulged and throbbed; tears formed; her brain screamed for oxygen. Why was he doing this?

Her back hit the wall of the adjacent building a split

second before her skull cracked against the bricks. Searing light shot across the inside of her eyelids. She fought the pain to open them. Her vision narrowed to a tiny pinprick. His dead eyes overflowing with a cold fascination, he pressed his lips together in a thin grimace of strain—that was all she could see.

She dug her nails into the flesh of his wrists, tried to turn her head, to look down the alley for help. She'd release her grip on him to wave her arms, but only if there was a chance someone might see it, might stop this.

Any remaining hope dropped out from under her like a trapdoor. The dumpster. It was blocking the view. No well-timed passersby would be able to see her. She was alone. This was it. This was how it ended.

Why? Why? Why?

She let go of his wrist to take a swipe at his eyes. One painful scratch, and maybe he would stop.

She lashed out, but his arms were too long. She swiped at the air.

He tightened his grip sharply, and she felt a sickening crunch in her throat.

Though she still clutched at the last remnants of her life, there was no going back now. Not yet dead, but too late to be saved.

TWO

I swirled my sweaty pint glass on the bar top, expanding the circle of condensation while keeping the splotch as close to round as possible. It was one of my harmless tics that emerged whenever I was anxious or contemplative or, you know, *conscious*. If I'd learned one thing in my life, it was that there were far worse compulsions to indulge. I'd give myself small quirks like this.

The night's quiz host was atrocious. He was a sub for the regular guy, and he seemed to be under the impression that those of us who'd gotten dressed and shown up to compete were just there to listen to his self-deprecating quips rather than play pub trivia.

Just introduce the next category. No one here wants to follow you on Twitter.

I swirled my glass quicker, lifted it, wiped the surface clean with my napkin, and started all over again. It was late, already ten till eleven, and there was one more round to get through, plus going through the answers, before I could collect my winner's gift card and go home. That sounded cocky, but my assumption of victory was based on pure data—I'd won the last five times I'd played at McNelly's, the dingy faux-Irish pub, and I'd only played five times.

It was a Wednesday night. I had to be at work at eight tomorrow morning. Not that a full night of peaceful sleep was something I ever had much hope of getting, but my impatience was starting to bubble over. If this had been an earlier round, I'd have been fine with asking for my tab and taking off, but I was too close to the end. I could smell blood. I just couldn't let it go.

They'd probably put that on my gravestone: *Dana Aisling Capone. 1982-2018. She just couldn't let it go.*

Or why not play it optimistic? 2028.

Over the sound system came: "I'll play a mash-up of songs from the album, and you give me the name of the album and the year it was released, one point for each."

Finally.

The first clue of the round played, and I had it pegged by the fourth note. I downed the rest of my pecan porter while the mash-up finished the first time through, then a second time for those a little slow on the uptake. Leaning forward with my forearms braced against the edge of the bar, I caught the eye of Sean, the bartender, and pointed to my empty pint. He tossed me a thumbs-up.

Something about his expression and the way he moved his head reminded me of my brother. Except Sean still spoke to me.

"Okay, question two!"

Even this host's intonations were grating on my nerves now. It was like he watched way too much Game Show Network as a kid. Probably raised by divorced parents. Both worked full-time. Or maybe they were married, and his mother stayed at home, but he was such a little twerp that she did whatever she could to get a break from him.

Ease up. You don't know anything about this kid. Generous assumptions when you're off duty.

I jotted down the answer for question number two, and the man on the barstool next to me, who was *not* playing trivia but had been sneaking furtive glances at me that, yes, I'd noticed, finally made his move and leaned in. "It was 1988," he said, gesturing to the year I'd written down on my answer sheet. When I dragged my gaze up to meet his, he grinned and winked.

Observing him from a purely objective standpoint, he was probably handsome. He had a Tom Hardy thing going on with his mouth. Tom Hardy's soft lips could carry an otherwise lopsided face a good distance, in my book. But this guy didn't need that. His face was mostly symmetrical, with the exception of a nose that looked like it'd seen knuckles at high speed a few times. Nothing inherently wrong with that. I'd been punched in the face before.

I was happy to report that I'd earned it every time.

But I could never go for a man, Tom Hardy lips or not, who was so confidently wrong about Mötley Crüe. Or one who thought it was his birth right to correct a total stranger on trivia.

"No," I said, mustering the detached patience I usually reserved for uncooperative witnesses. "You're wrong. *Dr. Feelgood* came out in 1989."

"Eh." He tilted his head back as if trying to cushion the blow he was about to deliver. "*Pretty* sure it was 1988."

I smiled because I knew it would put him on his heels. "Then maybe you should've grabbed a trivia card. I wouldn't mind beating you."

He straightened his spine and rotated toward me on his barstool as if I'd finally earned a scrap of his interest. Oh, joy.

"Ah, you're good at this?" he asked.

"I have a strong memory for facts."

Sean dropped off my fresh pint. I ignored it for the moment.

The man tried to catch the bartender's attention, but he was too slow then waved it off like he hadn't cared either way. He turned his attention back to me. "You're sure of that?"

"Sure of what?" My mind had already drifted to a report I needed to finish first thing the next morning. There had been discrepancies in one of the witness statements, and I thought there might be something to it.

"Sure you have a good memory," he said. "Everyone thinks they do."

Bless his heart. "I'm well aware. I deal with that every day."

"With work?"

I ignored him as the third mash-up began. I jotted down the answer. I'd been terrible at music memory in middle school, but my life had changed since then. Now, I remembered all kinds of tidbits. Scraps, really. The most important moments from those years still eluded me. The useless facts, though, I'd gotten those down pat. I'd had to anchor myself to something.

I tended to my memory like a bonsai, now, worshipped it like the tree of life. Because for me, it was that and more.

My barstool neighbor leaned over to check my work. "Yep. Got it."

"I know." I raised my drink to my lips, telling myself to detach from my annoyance.

Generous assumptions, Dana.

Maybe this guy had gotten in a terrible car accident, and his brain's ability to take a hint had never recovered. There. That seemed pretty generous.

He leaned closer, craning his neck to get a better look at my answer sheet, and—poof!—my generosity evaporated. I needed some space from this guy. Quick. He was going to make a move soon; I just knew it. And I was plenty familiar with what happened when a woman openly spurned the up-close advances of a man like this bozo. Things escalated. And I had no desire to explain to Popov why I'd made a man's crooked nose even more crooked at an Irish pub on a Wednesday.

But when I scanned the stuffy space, I realized it was standing room only at McNelly's on trivia night. Nowhere to go.

He leaned further to intercept my gaze. "So, what do you do?"

I glared at him. "I play trivia."

"And you're pretty good at it," he said cheerily.

I took a deep breath and tried unclenching my jaw. I'd been told I could be a little rough around the edges, too blunt for some folks. I was never criticized for being wrong, mind you, only for not putting enough effort toward making people feel *good* about the truth I was dispensing.

I could conjure up all kinds of sympathy for the true victims of this world, easy. And I was perfectly able to tolerate the natural imperfections of my fellow man without going ballistic.

It was just so obvious what people really meant when

they told me to "ease up." What they were really saying was *"Be nice so I can get what I want from you."*

It was cynical and, truth be told, exhausting to believe, but someone had to keep it in mind, or else the manipulators won.

The man beside me just wouldn't quit. "But what *else* do you do? Besides trivia."

The next mash-up played, and I used it as an excuse to ignore him.

"Ninety-seven," he said.

It'd been one hell of a day, and the last sinewy bit of my patience snapped. "You think *Odelay* came out in *1997*? Did you spend the nineties with your face in a pile of cheap coke or something?"

He shrank away, and I regretted my words immediately. It was a little harsh, the kind of cutting comment that would've rolled right off someone at the station, but not the Average Joe looking to get laid at a bar.

"Never done a drug in my life," he said. "I just remember that it came out my freshman year of college."

I sucked air in through my nose and ordered the muscles in my shoulders to relax. "Then you forgot what year you started college." I shrugged. "I dunno what to tell you. It came out the year I moved to Austin, which was *1996*." As soon as I said it, I knew that I'd erred. I'd just given him something to pursue, a foot in the door to my personal life.

Rookie mistake. I blamed the beer.

"What brought you to Austin?" he said, bracing his elbow on the bar.

I glared a hole in my answer sheet as the host played the *Odelay* mash-up again. "My mom."

"So you were young?"

"Fourteen."

"Where'd you move from?"

"A little place called the Dallas-Fort Worth metroplex. Heard of it?"

A deep crease formed between his brows. "You're pretty hostile, you know that?"

He was mad I wasn't giving him what he wanted. Attention, praise, the hope of getting laid.

I softened my tone anyway. I couldn't keep him from being like he was (obnoxious), but I could take it down a notch without relaxing my boundaries. I had control over that. "Not hostile," I said, "just exhausted after a long day of work and hoping to wind down with a beer or two while I play some pub trivia. Alone."

"And what do you do for work?"

That brain-addling car accident of his must've really been a doozy. Why he'd singled me out, I'd probably never understand. I was about as forgettable as Caucasian women came. Brown eyes, brown hair, no curves to speak of, and a "resting bitch face" that just wouldn't quit, I'd been told. But men like him usually singled me out anyway. Probably assumed I'd be grateful just to be noticed. Easy pickings.

Fine. I'd give him the scoop he was digging for, but he wouldn't like it.

I summoned my most disarming smile, just for him. "I'm a Homicide detective. Today, I responded to the scene of an eighteen-month-old who was found dead in his crib." His Hardy-esque upper lip hitched in disgust, but it was too late for him to go back now, to un-ask the question and to un-learn the answer. "Didn't immediately strike me as homicide, but it definitely looked like a dead baby. And parents going through the worst moment of their entire lives." The next mash-up began, and I scribbled *Automatic for the People - 1992*.

When I looked up again, he was staring fixedly at my paper. "Yep," he said weakly. "That's it."

I felt an unwelcome twinge of remorse. I'd gone too far. Again. This guy was a douche, but dropping the dead baby call on him hadn't been fair. No one knew what to do with that kind of information, mostly because there *was* nothing to do with it. No silver lining to a cold, stiff, blue-in-the-face baby. No personal growth narrative to follow. No deeper meaning to assign it. It was just garbage. Emotional garbage that should be dealt with by already ruined people like me and then allowed to fester and rot far away from civilized society.

My phone vibrated in my back pocket, sparing me the brutal task of apologizing to a man who I still very much wanted to punch in the nose. The caller's name appeared on the screen, and I answered, "I just got off four hours ago, Sarge."

"I understand." Sergeant Popov's stern voice was nearly drowned out by the muddled background noise of the city. "But you're going to want to see this, Capone."

"You're on scene?" I asked.

"I am."

That told me plenty. Sergeants didn't respond to every possible homicide, just the most unusual ones. My interest was piqued, sure, but it wasn't like I was the only Homicide detective in this city.

"Who's on duty right now?"

"Towers and Krantz."

"Oh, Jesus. Can't you call up Escobar instead?"

"Not this late," said Popov. "He has Audrey tonight."

I stared forlornly at my fresh pint of pecan porter. I was already two drinks in. If I mentioned that, I might be let off the hook.

But Popov had called *me*. And my intuition was already tingling as to why.

"What are we looking at?" I had to plug my other ear to hear him as the next musical mash-up blasted over the speakers.

(*Abbey Road* - 1969)

Popov only had to relay a few details from the scene before I dug my wallet out of my bag. "Yeah, I'll be there in fifteen."

I ended the call, pulled out a twenty, and tossed it onto the counter next to my nearly full pint. What a waste.

"Here." I shoved my answer sheet toward the nuisance next to me. "You take it from here. I'm already far enough ahead that even you'd be hard-pressed to blow the lead. Just don't change any of the answers I've already put. Enjoy the gift card."

He pouted his luscious lips. "You're leaving?"

"Gotta. People don't stop murdering just because I want to have a drink." *Although it would be nice if they did.*

"See ya, Dana," called Sean from behind the bar.

I tossed him a friendly wave and departed for the crime scene.

THREE

Parking downtown was always a cluster, even on a Wednesday night. Rapid growth and not enough infrastructure will do that. Since I'd come straight from the bar, I didn't have the luxury of driving a city vehicle and parking wherever the hell I wanted, so I pulled into the garage on Eighth Street and walked the few blocks over to Laugh Attack on Seventh.

Following the homing beacon of blue and crimson lights, I headed around the side of the club to where the back alley was cordoned off. The scene only attracted passing glances from those still out this late on a weeknight. Two off-balance men with their arms slung over each other's shoulder slowed down on the sidewalk opposite, rubbernecked momentarily, but didn't stop.

I'd already sweated through the back of my shirt by the time I ducked under the tape. It was humid as hell, and there was no way it'd dipped below eighty degrees yet, not with the heat still radiating from the asphalt like it was. This summer had felt especially brutal, and it was only going to get worse before it got better. Still, I was usually more acclimated by June.

Here's hoping the body is fresh.

Old remains plus the heat were never fun, and it was a shock I'd remained in this line of work for so long with how sensitive I was to smells.

Popov spotted me first as I approached the small huddle of cops. The term for a group of police officers was generally "a squad," but in my experience, "a huddle" more accurately described our kind. Or maybe a copse. A copse of cops.

"You got here quick," Sergeant Popov said.

"I was just on South Lamar."

The question passed behind his eyes, but he was merciful enough not to ask it until we were separated from the group and couldn't be overheard. "You been drinking?"

"Two beers over three hours." I thought back to all the blackout drunks I'd pulled over during my days on patrol who would swear on their grandmother's grave they'd only had two drinks before vomiting all over themselves during the standardized field sobriety test.

I was telling the truth, though. Just two.

"You good to be here?"

"I'm not going to trip over my feet or barf on the body, if that's what you mean. But I'm not exactly *thrilled* to be called in on my time off."

"It's not a pretty one, Capone." The old sergeant's pinkish face was ruddier than usual. I would need to get him out of the heat as soon as possible.

"Sheesh. If you feel the need to prepare *me* for that, you must not be kidding. How long has she been out here?"

"Haven't started interviews, but it's fresh."

"Small blessings. Let's see it."

He nodded and led the way further down the alley toward a dumpster. "Who found her?" I asked.

"One of the managers," he said. "He was taking out the trash before closing up the place, and he found her as she is."

As she is. And how was that?

I found out in just a few more steps.

"Jesus, Pops." I despised the first look at this kind of grotesqueness, but it was also an immense relief to know that even after seeing so many horrific things in my thirty-six years on this earth, I could still feel such intense repulsion at untimely death. There was a lot in me that was broken, but *that* mechanism, at least, remained intact.

My brain projected the stench of the trash onto the mangled girl in front of me, and the beer in my gut roiled.

They'd been right to call me. The reason Popov wanted me instead of Towers or Krantz or any of the other Homicide detectives hung unspoken between us, and I'd keep it that way. It didn't need to be said. Not with a scene like that.

The decedent's body was posed. I recognized that immediately. The positioning wasn't a matter of where each limb had fallen when the killer was done with her. The vic's wrists were bound with the same thick black cord that wound around her neck like a boa constrictor. One long loop of it was slung over the handle of the dumpster so that she leaned against the gangrenous metal, her head lolling forward as much as the constrictive confines allowed.

She dangled with her backside a foot above the ground, her legs outstretched, the toes of her ruby-red high heels pointing skyward in a macabre rendition of the Wicked Witch of the East after the house landed on her. All she was missing were the striped stockings, then I'd have half expected her legs to shrivel and roll up onto themselves.

Her jeans were on and zipped, which would usually indicate no sexual penetration, but when it was staged, all bets were off. If her killer had been willing to take the time to tie her up, he could have dressed her in a completely different outfit, for all we knew.

The thin straps of her shirt hung off her shoulders, and the top of the garment was down below her breasts. Her bra remained in place but offered little support, as the straps had been slipped down as well, and the cups barely clung to her.

Once it was clear enough that the victim had been placed this way, my mind not only looked for what was, but also for what wasn't. You couldn't claim whoever had done this would go to all the effort of tying her up only to then stop caring about details, and one in particular stood out to me: her shoulders were bare. Why?

I gloved up, borrowed Popov's flashlight, and squatted down next to her. Mouth breathing was a given in a situation like this, but that didn't stop the fumes from hitting the back of my throat and gagging me just as I leaned toward her. I turned my head away in a hurry to suck in some fresh air. Almost coughed right on her. Bleach, that was what it was. And not just a little, but a strong enough whiff that seemed to scrape all the way down into my lungs.

I laid a gentle hand on her shoulder. She wasn't yet cool to the touch, but her skin had that papery feeling to it, even through my nitrile gloves.

Bodies have a stillness to them after death that has nothing to do with rigor mortis. We forget about the effect of blood moving through the veins, the way our heartbeat rocks us back and forth, the vibrational energy that pulses from us every moment we're alive. We don't notice any of it in ourselves or in the other living people we come into contact with as we go about our day.

But you sure as hell notice the absence of it. That first touch of a dead body always felt like someone just threw a stick in my bike spokes. That jolt, the reminder of the momentum I'd taken for granted, and then a face full of asphalt. I might as well have been poking at a cellophane-wrapped steak for all the vitality I felt in this woman.

I pushed her torso forward, creating slight separation from the side of the dumpster. The earliest stages of rigor were already setting in, so she couldn't have been out there for more than an hour or two. Relatively fresh. I glanced at my watch. Eleven twenty-four.

Shining Pops' flashlight on the exposed skin of her upper back and shoulders, it was as I'd suspected: her bra clasp was undone. But there was something else. Raw, angry bloodiness. Part of her skin was missing, carved away.

I didn't want to move the body too much just yet, so I couldn't get the full picture of what the skin removal looked like, but then I noticed the stream of darkened blood that ran down her back and terminated in a dried pool on the cement below her.

Next, I went around and checked her other side, as much of it as I could see, anyway. Same thing. Part of the flesh removed. Nothing distinct from that angle, either, only the rough texture of exposed muscle and a glimmer of bone—presumably a rib—just below her shoulder blade.

It'd be a while before we were ready to untie and move the body, but I snapped a few pictures on my department phone to go over later.

"Cheryl Blackstenius," Popov said. "ID was in her back pocket. Lives on Southwest Parkway. Twenty-six years old. Five-foot-ten. One hundred and forty pounds. Regular around here."

"I didn't realize driver's licenses showed what comedy clubs people frequented. That next to the organ donor info?"

"Guy who confirmed her identity told us that last bit."

"He must be a regular, too."

Popov motioned toward the back door to the club. "He's inside when you're ready to have a chat."

"That." I crouched down to inspect the victim's legs. The right shin was bent at a forty-five-degree angle. The snapped tibia hadn't pierced the skin on the calf, but there was a distinct bulge where the broken bone was damn close to it.

"Right," said Popov. "What's your take on it?"

I stood. "My take on what? The shin?"

He nodded.

"Hard to run away if your leg is snapped in half." I took a small step back, adding a little distance between myself and the stench. "Playing the odds and assuming she favored her right side, it's her non-dominant leg that was snapped. Her planting leg if she was gonna try to kick." I waved for the Crime Scene technician to move in and snap further pictures as Popov and I stepped aside.

"That's a smart move," Popov said, "if it was intentional." He led me onto the concrete back slab of the club. Above the steel door glowed a dim security light, the plastic cover clouded with dead bugs.

"It *is* a smart move," I said, glad Popov had already made it this far in the logic. "The kind of smart move someone who's done this before would know to do."

I was tiptoeing close to the unspoken reason why he'd called *me* and no one else. I watched his expression closely.

His lips drew tight, and his wild blond brows lowered over beady eyes. "Nuh-uh. We're not going there yet."

"Then why was I called to this scene?"

He hesitated, squinting his beady eyes. "I know you've got a sixth sense for that sort of criminal, Capone. And god knows I'm not going to begrudge you for it, but there's nothing to support that theory yet."

"But you wanted to see if I'd pick up a scent."

Instead of acknowledging that I'd just nailed his intent, he said, "We conduct our investigations based on evidence, not hunches. If more bodies turn up like this, *then* we'll follow that trail and run it by the FBI. For now, it's an isolated incident."

"Uh-huh. And you know I won't shut up if the evidence *does* shake out that way. Fair enough, Sarge." I surveyed the scene. Only professionals out there. "Where's the guy who found her?"

"Still inside." The steel back door whined as Popov pushed it open for me.

Cool air swirled around me when I stepped inside, making the sweat turn sticky on my skin as I followed the sergeant through the dark backstage and into the seating area, which, by contrast, felt bright. A semicircular stage was surrounded by long tables reaching out like spokes. We cut through the rows and made for the small sound booth at the far end, where two officers were speaking in low tones with a man who blended into the scenery. He was dressed in a black sleeveless tee and black jeans and seated at a black table with a black wall behind him.

In front of him was the soundboard, all knobs and buttons and dials. Nothing on it was lit except for a single plastic square at the corner that glowed blood red. And like a moth drawn to it, the man stared fixedly at the tiny light, all but ignoring the cops in front of him.

Sarge nodded his appreciation at the officers, who looked more than happy to split.

"Mr. Nebojsa?" Popov said, and the young man managed to tear his eyes away from the red light to stare vacantly at the authority figure. "This is Detective Capone with Homicide. She'd like to hear your account for herself."

Nebojsa aimed his bland gaze my way, and I tried to guess his age. He had pronounced cheekbones and the taut skin and lack of wrinkles of a man in his late twenties. But beneath that was the hardened expression of a veteran. Former military, perhaps? Nah, didn't seem quite right, though I couldn't pinpoint why.

His awareness seemed to fill in behind that empty stare, and he inspected me through dark gray eyes. I offered my hand. "You can call me Dana."

He didn't get up, but he took my hand. "Michal. I go by Mike."

Popov excused himself, and I motioned to an empty chair. "May I?" Mike nodded, and I settled in. "You found the victim, correct?"

He picked at a piece of chipped plastic on the side of the soundboard. "Yeah. Found her there when I was taking out the trash."

"You know her?" I asked.

He swallowed hard. "Yeah. Cheryl. She was a regular around here. Not very funny, but..."

I allowed him space to finish. Not very funny, but... what? Jesus. What a time to critique.

He seemed to realize that criticizing the deceased in any way, even a petty one, wasn't the wisest approach, though, and he didn't add anything else.

"When you say she's a regular, what do you mean?"

"An open mic regular. We host them every Monday and Wednesday unless we can book someone bigger."

The "we" didn't go unnoticed by me. Not only did he work here, which I already knew from the fact that he was taking out the trash when he found her, but it sounded like he had some say in the operations, or at least considered himself to.

An overdeveloped sense of importance? Or were the owners just that good at making their employees feel a sense of ownership in the operation?

"And what do you do here, Mike?"

"Lots. Scott and Heidi pay me to manage things when they don't feel like coming in. Booking, running sound for the open mics, scheduling servers, stuff like that."

I smiled and could tell it didn't extend all the way to my eyes. Didn't matter. He was still staring at the soundboard. "Who are Scott and Heidi?"

"The Ruizes. They own the place."

Laugh Attack was well known around town, even to someone like me who never got out in the evenings except for trivia nights. But unlike some of the longtime establishments downtown, the owners themselves hadn't achieved local celebrity status. At least, *I'd* never heard of them. Of course, I generally only knew about individuals who had a propensity for clashing with the law. Owners of an Austin comedy staple? Nah. Not unless they were *especially* weird. And there was stiff competition in this city to stand out in that respect.

Now, Rose Gold, a homeless woman who'd been arrested over six hundred times and was in a race to the bottom with her going rate for an arthritic hand job? I'd have recalled her name and date of birth even after a sufficient blow to the head. She stood out.

Long story short, I needed to learn a little more about the Ruizes. "Have they owned this club for long?"

"Yeah. Scott opened it back in, like, the late nineties. Heidi started helping him when they got married, and now she pretty much runs the show."

"Is that good?"

He shrugged. "I guess. She was already running things when they hired me a couple years ago. I couldn't imagine Scott being in charge."

"Why's that?"

"Have you met him?"

"Not yet."

"You'll know when you meet him. He's technically my boss, so I don't want to..."

I held up a hand to show him I understood. "Right, right. I have a boss, too. I know how it goes."

I'd need to speak with both of the Ruizes soon. Build a rapport with them. They were the gatekeepers for the information I'd need to prove to Popov that my instincts on this were right, that whoever killed and staged Cheryl had killed before.

Was I currently speaking to the killer? Could Mike

Nebojsa have murdered Cheryl in the back alley, calmly left her there, then pretended to discover her only a short time later?

The answer was bitter: if he was the killer, yes, he could. Because only someone who knew how to wear an infallible mask could commit a heinous act like what had taken place less than fifty yards from where we sat. And if his mask was that good, then I'd never even know he was wearing one.

"Mike, do you know anyone who might have wanted to harm Cheryl?"

The words that came out of his mouth carried very little weight for me, but I still searched for any sign of a lie. I watched for micro-expressions, small twitches that don't match up with the emotion he intended.

And I spotted one. The corners of his mouth twisted downward at my question. But not in a grimace. Was that *contempt*? But he smothered it under a mournful gaze in a heartbeat, gone just like that.

"I don't know her that well," he said. "*Didn't* know her. I mean, we hung out a couple times, but I don't know who she spent time with outside of the comedy scene. I don't even know what she did for work."

I craved another small slip-up from him, some twitch around the eyes, anything. But that wasn't how it worked. In an innocent man, that split-second contempt could come from anywhere. It was hardly an admission of guilt. I couldn't assign it a real meaning without more context. The trick was spotting clusters of indicators that he was being deceptive. Couldn't get much out of a single data point, no matter how sharp my eye for it.

One might think that growing up with a man who

destroyed women for sport would give me an advantage in interviews like this, a preternatural sense for it. Sure, I had a slight edge, maybe even an intuition for it, but that couldn't hold much water in a homicide investigation. It could only point me in the direction of the next bit of useful information.

1989. Dr. Feelgood by Mötley Crüe. Discovering the severed finger in the backyard.

I swallowed against the flash of memory. "You said the two of you hung out a couple of times. What was your relationship with Cheryl exactly?"

He crossed his arms over his chest. "I knew her. We sometimes talked. You gotta understand; there's a group of, like, a dozen people here at every open mic. Fresh blood comes in occasionally, and some people drop off, but there's that core group. So I knew her in that capacity, and she was nice enough, but we weren't friends. Like, we didn't hang out *outside* of here."

"Gotcha. Who could I speak with that knew her better?"

He was more than happy to provide a few names to that effect, and I finally slipped out a notepad from my pocket to write them down. I didn't need to. They stuck in my memory immediately, but the act of putting them to paper, breaking eye contact, could help interviewees feel less like they were on the chopping block. They believed my scrutiny was shifting to other people.

Yeah, we'd see about that. "And how do you spell your last name?"

"N-E-B-O-J-S-A. But if you ask any of those people who Michal Nebojsa is, they won't know. I go by Mike Check around here."

"Mike Check?" I looked down at his name where I'd scribbled it, and it clicked. "Oh. You're Czech?"

"Yeah."

"You born there?"

"No."

"But I detect an accent."

"I was born in Bosnia. Why?"

"Bosnia?" I did some quick mental math. "That must have been during the conflict, right?"

"I was born before it officially started, but yeah. My parents moved there for business originally, but I... Is this important?"

"No, no." I looked down at my pad again. "I was just curious. It's unrelated." I closed the notepad and stood, and this time, he got up as well. At five-foot-nine myself, I had an easy inch on him.

Short guy. Could he overpower Cheryl? Her ID had her listed at five-foot-ten. She had the height advantage on him, then, but there was no accounting for the muscle power of hatred, lust, and unsated entitlement, the kind of emotions that would motivate a man to strangle a woman to death behind a dumpster.

"Thanks, Mike. Here's my card. If you think of anything else that might help us find who did this, just give me a call." We shook. "Any chance Scott or Heidi are around?"

"I saw them in the front, by the bar."

I left the main stage area and passed through the double doors, entering a lounge. Against the wall farthest from me was a narrow stage with a single lonely mic stand but no mic. Between that and the bar were an assortment of tables, some with two chairs, some accommodating four.

I located Popov with his back to me, speaking to a man and woman at the otherwise empty bar. The vibe of this space was more like the smoking lounge at a fancy hotel than a comedy club. The overhead fluorescents were off, leaving dark corners where the remaining few sources of light didn't reach. There was a single one on above the stage, aimed at the mic stand, but outside of that, the only glow came from the bar. A long indigo bulb radiated above each shelf of booze, and yellow recessed lighting above the bar top cast long shadows down the features of the three people discussing something that seemed not at all related to the murdered woman outside.

The man, who must have been the owner, Scott Ruiz, leaned back against the counter, one arm draped over it as he clutched a crystal tumbler containing a finger of amber liquid. With his other arm, he gestured animatedly as he spoke.

Despite the Hispanic last name, Scott Ruiz appeared Caucasian. Still, he had the kind of leathery skin I generally only saw on the chronically homeless or the long-timer Austinites, the ones who got here back in the sixties when Janis Joplin was still performing at Threadgill's. Scott wore a turquoise and red bowling shirt, khaki shorts, which had ridden up to reveal knobby knees, and what appeared to be hemp flip-flops. Not the kind of man one might expect to be in charge of *anything* except bringing the pre-rolled joints to the lake party. I was beginning to understand what Mike had hinted at about his boss.

But while Scott was likely pushing sixty, if not already there, his wife didn't look a day over forty. That was, until I moved closer. Then it became clear that a talented surgeon must have been responsible for that deception. Heidi Ruiz's dark roots of otherwise blonde hair were cast into an unflattering relief by the inset lights above her, and her cleavage, served hot and fresh on the platter of a push-up bra beneath her low-cut baby-blue tee, looked like the main event of whatever show she was putting on for Sergeant Popov.

She laughed at Scott's animated story, whatever that was, and the telltale wrinkles around her nose gave away the work she'd gotten done to it.

Scott was about as thoroughly Austin bum as you could find, and Heidi ought to keep a "Made in SoCal" sticker on the bottom of her foot. Quite the pair, those two. Did the comedians get to poke fun at them on stage, or was that considered shamefully low-hanging fruit?

Even Sergeant Popov guffawed at whatever Scott had just said, and it was obvious I was crashing the party as I slipped out of the shadows to join them.

The introductions were quick and to the point, and I didn't miss that Popov introduced the owners by their first names. Chummy already.

"Capone, eh?" Scott said. "Any relation to the infamous—"

"No," I said. Each person I met thought they were the first to make the obvious connection.

Though, to be fair, I *am* a relative of his. Big Al is something like my mom's great-great-uncle twice removed. But I had enough family infamy without adding Scarface to the heap.

Popov eyed me so sharply that I could feel the heat coming off him. Ah, I'd been curt again, hadn't I? "But I can see why you'd wonder," I added, shoving a smile at Scott to salvage the interaction. I decided not to quiz Scott about *his* last name. *"You don't look like a Ruiz."*

Right. The department would love reading *that* complaint. Anyway, just like not all Italians were related to Al Capone, not all Hispanics were descended from Incans. I knew plenty of white Hispanics personally, living in Austin, and every single one of them came from money and acted like their Hispanic last name was something they married into, until they thought they could get a little street cred out of it. Then it was all *quinceañeras* and Spanglish, all the time.

I wondered briefly if Scott Ruiz came from money. It might explain how a bum like him had managed to keep an establishment open downtown. He didn't dress like someone who possessed much business acumen, unless maybe the hemp flip-flops were designer.

"I just spoke with Mike Check," I said.

"Poor baby," Heidi said breathlessly. Or maybe those implants were crushing her lungs, and everything she said sounded breathless. "I can't even imagine the shock." Her hand flew up to grip her throat, and I wondered if she was aware of the ironic gesture. "I can't believe it. Cheryl is— was... Oh, god, the poor thing. We were just chatting with her a few hours ago."

The shock seemed genuine enough, and the fact that Heidi was a woman pretty much scratched her off my developing list of suspects. Yes, I had some biases in that respect, but if men would stop confirming them nonstop, I might've eased up. Until further notice, though, I was looking for a male suspect.

Sergeant Popov subtly excused himself and went to

take a call out front. Just part of our practiced song and dance. He was giving me space.

"Have you two been here all day?" I asked.

"More or less," said Scott. "But our days start late. We got here around four to get things ready with Mike for the open mic, then we stuck around for it. We'd just gotten home for the night when we got the call to come back down."

"Care to walk me through that timeline?" I said, taking out my notepad. "Might help me figure out who all came and went."

Heidi nodded and stepped in. "The open mic wrapped up at around nine, nine fifteen?" She looked to her husband for confirmation.

"About ten after," he said. "We try to end it by nine, but sometimes it goes over."

"Right," she said.

I asked, "You have that out here or on the main stage?"

"Out here," Heidi supplied. "It's supposed to be a steppingstone for new talent, so we keep it casual."

"We can't fill the other room for an open mic, either," Scott added. "Harder to perform to an empty room."

I jotted down *empty room*. "And what happened after the open mic ended?"

"We let people hang out and have a drink and chat for a little if they want," Heidi said. "We're really trying to build a community here, not just a stage, you know?"

I nodded along automatically.

"Scott's chattier with the comics than I am. So, while everyone's milling around, I usually pick up the place— wipe down the tables, flip the chairs, sweep. Cheryl always offers to help. I think she didn't feel like she fit in with the others."

"And she was helping you tonight?"

Heidi opened her mouth but paused, and her expensive face fought back as her brows attempted to pinch together. "Well, yes, but she was also pretty social tonight. I hadn't thought about that. You think that's *significant*?"

Scott appeared embarrassed by his wife's question, but I said, "Maybe. She didn't help you clean up tonight?"

"She did, but it was only after people started to leave. She jumped in and flipped a few chairs."

"Did you see her go out back?" I addressed both of the Ruizes, and both shook their head.

Scott added, "I thought she'd left for the night. She was flirting with Jordan Grossman, and now that I think about it, I just assumed they'd gone home together."

Jordan Grossman was one of the names Mike Check had given me. I'd be checking into him first chance.

Heidi bobbed her head along with her husband's assumption. "Yeah, they were talking a lot tonight. You're right. It hadn't even registered with me until you said it."

"When was the last time you noticed her in the room with you?"

Scott took a swig of his drink as Heidi replied, "Maybe nine forty-five?"

I glanced at Scott, who shrugged. "Probably about that. I wasn't paying attention to it, honestly. Had no idea it would be important, you know?"

"So you cleaned up and left at what time?"

They met each other's eyes, communicating silently in the way I only saw longtime couples do. "Ten after ten?" Scott offered.

"Yeah, maybe ten ten or ten fifteen?"

"No, wait," Scott said, "because I remember we were almost to the highway and we saw that guy fall into the road, and I said, 'Good lord, it's only ten fifteen!' I'd looked at the clock in the car at that point."

Heidi blinked a few times. "Oh, that's right. So, sometime before ten fifteen."

I inspected each in turn. I'd never been in a serious relationship, and I couldn't decide if being this simpatico with another human would make me feel complete or inspire me to suck-start my duty weapon.

I cleared my throat. "Did you know Mike was still here when you left?"

Heidi nodded in a way that caused her breasts to bounce more than her head. "We have a big headliner tomorrow night, and our usual sound guy is in Tulum for the summer, so Mike wanted to stick around and get all set up ahead of time."

"He said he was taking out the trash when he found her," I prompted her.

"Yeah, he does that last thing before he closes. He has a key, so he can lock up whenever he's done, and we don't have to wait around."

"What time did you get home?"

Scott took that question. "A little after ten thirty. Maybe ten thirty-five?"

"You live far?"

"Doesn't everyone now? Austin ain't cheap."

Heidi leaned forward, and even I struggled to keep my eyes off the woman's rack. It *glistened*. "We live in Pflugerville, near 45 and 130."

Dear god. My commute to the station was bad enough,

and I only lived nine miles away. Theirs was more than double that and down congested highways. "That must be nearly two hours in traffic."

"Oh yeah." Scott grinned like it was a badge of honor.

"So you got home just after ten thirty, and when did you get a call?"

Scott said, "Officer Tyber called us just as we were walking in the door. Maybe ten... thirty-seven?"

"Okay, we'll have records of that, don't worry." Tyber must have been the first on scene. I didn't recognize the name, but who could keep track of all the junior officers they stuck downtown?

So, sometime between roughly nine forty-five and when Mike Check phoned the police, perhaps around ten fifteen or ten twenty, counting backward from when Scott got the call, Cheryl was murdered. It was a tight window. But at least we had a window.

I tucked the notepad away, and both husband and wife relaxed visibly.

"Hey," I said, adopting a more casual note, "I noticed you have a security camera out in the back. Or something that looks like it. It was flashing red."

Scott cringed and took a long sip of his drink. "That would be because it's out of tape."

"Tape?"

"Yeah," he said. "It's an older model."

No kidding. "How often do you switch out the tapes?"

"I don't," he said. "We used to, but—"

"But nothing ever happened," his wife finished for him. "Even recording over the same one over and over again, well, you wear it out eventually and have to buy another one. We were spending so much on VHS tapes each month and for no reason. Nothing important ever happened."

Scott continued, "We just left the camera mounted and plugged in so people would think they were being watched. Thought it would deter anything from happening."

I struggled not to make a face. "That's an idea," I said. "Who all would've known that the camera didn't actually work?"

Scott and Heidi exchanged a chagrined glance before he replied, "I guess most of the people who work here. And anyone they told." He rubbed at the back of his neck. "A lot of these kids smoke pot. They step out back to do it." He held up his hands, one still clutching his tumbler, raising it into the air as the remaining slivers of ice clinked around. "I admit, I knew about the marijuana use, and I let it happen. But comedy is hard, and a little puff here and there can help, I've heard."

"We're not concerned about pot," I assured him. "We're more concerned with the murdered woman out back."

"Right, right."

"So, one can assume that a lot of people knew the camera wasn't actually recording anything, is that correct?"

He bowed his head. "That's about right."

None of that was ideal, but it was typical. Murder didn't happen in a vacuum. There were always a few flaky or incompetent people wrapped up in it who complicated the investigation. This time, their names were Scott and Heidi Ruiz. Not bad people, far as I could tell, but unhelpful now. As they say: *bless their hearts*.

After handing them my card and delivering them back into the company of Popov, I let myself out through the back door and into the alley.

"Medical examiner on the way?" I asked the patrol sergeant as she approached. I'd had my fair share of interactions with Sergeant Linda Graves, who ran one of the night shifts downtown. Usually, we crossed paths at a run-of-the-mill shooting stemming from drunken road rage or a drug deal gone wrong. Those were easy enough to clean up, wrap up, and move on from. But this homicide wasn't going to be as simple. There were precisely zero signs that it had resulted from drunken rage. Someone had planned and executed in a particular fashion.

Each of my interactions with Sergeant Graves had been professional at the surface and teeming with a deep commiseration just below. This one was no different. "We called the M.E. a half-hour ago," she said. "He should be here in another thirty minutes. He was asleep. Lives all the way up in Georgetown."

"This is something, isn't it?" I gestured at the body. Evidence markers littered the ground around it. Dried blood here, an empty chip bag there. Almost all of it would be thrown out as unrelated. Maybe some of the blood, too. This close to the bars on Sixth Street? It could be anyone's.

Sergeant Graves kept her eyes on the body, too. "Society doesn't allow harsh enough punishment for men who do this kinda thing."

I shot her a sideways glance. "Jumping to conclusions, don't you think? Who said it was a man that did this?"

The sergeant tossed me a look, and neither of us could resist a glum grin.

"Any idea what kind of cord that is binding her wrists and neck?" I asked. "It's thick."

"Not sure. Maybe some sort of electrical cable?"

In the brief silence between us, it occurred to me how

late it must be. "Shoot!" I pulled out my personal phone from my back pocket. "Will you excuse me for a second?" Stepping to the side, I pulled up Ariadna's number. But when I saw the exact time, I decided it was better to text than call and risk waking her: *Got called in to work. Won't be picking Sadie up tonight. I'll come get her in the morning. Sorry and thanks.*

The message was probably unnecessary, considering it was nearly midnight, and I'd promised no later than eleven. She'd have taken the hint by now. But at least I had a good excuse for it. It wasn't that I'd gotten drunk at a pub and simply forgotten. There'd been a murder.

Cheryl Blackstenius' death was my weak excuse, anyhow.

Sadie would already be passed out anyway. No need to stir her up. And Ariadna had said more than once that she was always happy for the company.

"Sorry," I said, rejoining Sergeant Graves.

"All good?"

"Yep."

"One of my guys just said it's an XLR."

I shook my head vaguely. "And that is?"

"A specific kind of cable. He said it's used for audio."

I gazed at the body where it remained tied up and waiting for the M.E. The flies from the dumpster had realized there was better stuff outside the four metal walls. "Audio like a microphone?"

"I guess so. That's not my area of expertise, though."

I forced myself to keep my eyes on the limp body. "Fair enough. Google will know."

And so will the man sitting behind the soundboard inside.

But I wouldn't get ahead of myself on that. Not yet. There was still a full night's work ahead of me. And if I knew one thing, it was that I needed to pace myself, move with intention, play it close to the bulletproof vest, as it were. I couldn't afford to slip up, but I also couldn't afford to drag my feet.

Because the one thing I knew for sure from this gory tableau was that the killer, whoever he was, was only getting started.

FOUR

He stared at the ceiling in his dim bedroom. The street lamp in front of the house sliced through the closed slats of his blinds, casting slivers of scorching white across the faded paisley quilt. Usually, it was the light that kept him up on restless nights like this, that maddening, unrelenting brightness. But not tonight.

He'd done it; he'd gone through with his fantasy. Not the first time, but the best so far. It wasn't enough to silence the wild craving inside him, but it took the edge off for now. Some small release. He could still smell the smoke in her hair, feel the snap of bone beneath his boot, practically taste his unlimited control over her. Complete. Ultimate. Final.

Had the act served to sate his appetite or only whet it? He'd have to do it again regardless. This one had been flawed, had contained a few key artistic shortcomings.

Nothing to risk him being found out, though. At least, the cops hadn't shown up at his door yet. He didn't expect them to. They were slow, stupid. How many men like him were out there, prowling, hunting, catching their prey over and over again, undetected for decades?

This was only his first bold move, and it wouldn't be his last. Not now that he'd tasted it, felt his heart racing as he tied her up and took his keepsake to pass along. Someone could have interrupted him at any moment, walked up on him in the middle of the act. The risk of it was low—he'd planned this carefully, kept an eye on the comings and goings—but he couldn't have ruled it out completely. And that had been half the thrill.

It had been bold. Courageous. No slinking around, trying to toss the evidence. After all, what was an artist without an audience to appreciate the work? Raymond had taught him that.

He needed more practice before stalking his ultimate prey. The thought of it stoked lightning in his chest. He'd stopped asking himself if he wanted to be her or be inside her. It didn't matter. He deserved neither. The only thing he could do was to obliterate her, and someday soon, he would.

He steadied his mind. Focusing too much on what he didn't yet have would only serve to make him impatient, and in this pursuit, impatience led to sloppiness, and sloppiness led nowhere good. Prison, maybe. Death. But more unthinkable, the inability to create his waking dream.

No one would miss Cheryl. People might pretend like they did, but they'd forget about her completely soon enough and move on with their selfish little lives. Not that it mattered. In a world like this, someone was always winning, and someone was always losing. He was done losing.

He inhaled deeply and brought his hands together, imagining her throat between them again. So soft and supple, clay for him to shape to his desires. With her wrists bound, as if in prayer to him, she was glorious and glamorous. He could have done whatever he wanted to her, violated her in ways unimaginable to most people, tested her body to see how much she could take.

He hardened, and the idea of indulging himself in all the ways he'd resisted earlier that night glistened in his mind's eye like a trophy at the end of a hard-fought match. Why shouldn't he celebrate this way? He'd earned it.

But he'd have to be sure not to rouse the sleeping cunt as he crept across the house. This was what he'd been reduced to in this wretched version of himself: slinking to the guest bathroom to jerk off. What kind of a real man lived that way? He ought to murder her, too. Nothing grandiose, just hands around her throat. He'd make sure to wake her first, so she could stare into his eyes, see the man she'd created with her nonstop nagging.

He'd crept halfway down the hallway when his weight caused the floorboard to moan beneath him. He paused and listened. Silence.

Once the door was shut behind him, he closed his eyes, slipped himself free of his boxers, and imagined for just a moment that his hands were wrapping around her neck again, though it was his own soft flesh he gripped.

His need was too urgent, and he couldn't suppress the whimper that escaped as he finished himself off to memories of her blue lips and tousled hair.

The gargoyle called his name from where she slept, then asked stupidly, "Is that you?"

He cracked open the bathroom door. "Yes, it's me."

"Is everything okay?"

Yes, Mother, he thought spitefully.

He didn't answer her, just cleaned himself up, decided not to strangle the bitch tonight, and then shuffled back to bed.

FIVE

June 7th, 2018

1 day since Blackstenius murder

I hated all-nighters, but I'd known they were part of the job before I ever joined Homicide. Sure, people got murdered in the daylight hours, but that wasn't the prime time. The real action took place at night when shadow selves came out to play.

And when people tended to drink too much.

I lugged my duffel bag from the trunk and slung it over my shoulder before locking up the car. My apartment complex was a tangle of buildings, each in more desperate need of maintenance than the last, but the place always felt more alive than any sparkling new construction ever could. Neighbors just *hung around* all the time, down in the courtyard, on the breezeways, in the parking lot. Some I recognized, some I didn't. My coworkers would call the behavior loitering, but if you just said hello to people as you passed them, even the ones who were most definitely in the middle of a drug deal, you realized it was, in its own way, actually community. Sure, the occupancy turnover was high, as was petty crime, but there was crime *everywhere*. No place was entirely safe from it; the only significant variation from class to class was how safe people *thought* they were.

It was nearly seven a.m., which meant Ariadna would have already left for work. My neighbor owned a taco truck that was a staple, if not an icon, among the construction workers who were up before sunrise to build the subdivisions on the edge of town. I'd interviewed a person of interest once who mentioned the truck by name. When I told him I knew the owner well, his demeanor changed completely. It was like we were best friends. And my new bestie had immediately started naming names for my investigation.

To be fair, Ariadna did make some damn good pork carnitas.

One time, I'd returned home at three in the morning and seen her loading up her truck to start the early rounds. She had music playing softly on the truck's radio and was singing to herself in a graceful Colombian Spanish.

The moment would be with me until I died: my middle-aged neighbor with her hair pulled back in a long braid, a gentle smile on her face, emotion soaking her words. A tableau of complete solitude and total contentment. She was going to feed people, to nurture bodies. Alive bodies.

That had been the first time I ever seriously considered quitting my job.

I adjusted the strap of the duffel on my shoulder and fiddled with my keys as I climbed the stairs to the second floor of my building. The heavy beats of *cumbia sonidera* pulsed from an open window on the first floor as someone got a lively start to their day. Or maybe it was a continuation of the previous night's party. The fact that it was impossible to guess was one of the reasons I stuck around that rundown complex on the southeast side: time wasn't a big deal to my neighbors. Some of them worked, some didn't, and those who did rarely held a nine-to-five. They were entrepreneurs like Ariadna, hustling at all hours, making ends meet despite receiving only platitudes of respect, at most, from the rest of society.

"*¡Señora Capone!*"

I turned toward the sound of the voice and saw Miguel Villarreal sprinting toward me. The four-year-old was rocking a full Winnie the Pooh look—Ninja Turtles shirt and no pants—as he hurled full-tilt at me.

"*Hola Miguel. Qué tal?*"

"*¡No me quiero bañar!*"

"*Ah, pero si no, serás el niño apestoso. Nadie quiere ser eso.*"

"*¡No me importa!*"

He clung to my leg as his mother, Serena, poked her head outside, spotted her son down the row, and rolled her eyes. "*Perdon,* Dana."

I waved that it was fine and then knelt to get a straight look at Miguel. "*Si te dejo ver a Sadie, ¿prometes ir a bañar?*"

The boy grinned wide at my simple offer and agreed to the deal with a fervent nod.

As soon as I unlocked Ariadna's front door with my spare key, Sadie came bowling out, whining and wagging her tail so ferociously that her entire body whipped around with each swing. My dog's tongue was in Miguel's mouth in a heartbeat. He squealed and flapped his little arms in delight, and I grabbed her collar to keep her from absolutely steamrolling him.

"Okay," I said. "Now you *really* have to go bathe."

He giggled again and trotted over to his mother.

"Go on. Go pee." I let go of Sadie, and the brindle pittie hurried down the stairs to mark everything in the courtyard she could find. I'd never had the heart to tell her she lacked the requisite penis for the pastime. Doubt it would've changed a thing anyway. She was just an alpha female. Maybe that was why we'd immediately clicked at the shelter.

From the courtyard below, someone called my name. I looked over the railing, where Sadie was raising her leg on each withered clump of grass, and caught sight of Tara Hernandez, a twenty-year-old low-level weed dealer and a mother of two adorable little boys, waving me down. I hollered a hello, and she replied, "There was a dead squirrel down here earlier."

I thought I'd misheard her. "What?"

She repeated herself, and, yep, I'd heard her right the first time.

"Oh no," I said, trying to inject some sympathy into my words.

It was tricky, the transition from work life to home. I was sure a dead squirrel seemed like a big deal to the average person, but I'd just gotten off an overnight shift with a dead human. Sort of paled in comparison.

Ease up, Dana. It's a beautiful thing that people still care about dead squirrels.

Or maybe Tara had been pointing it out in case Sadie

got it in her head to eat it. That made sense enough, so I nodded my thanks and called my girl back upstairs. She followed me inside our tiny apartment two doors down from Ariadna's.

I flipped on the lights in the entry hall but didn't enter right away. I'd never been a fan of coming home to an empty house. Not for any sentimental reason, like it reminded me that I was thirty-six, unmarried, and childless, but because evil abhorred a vacuum. Leave a place empty, and who knew what would be there when you returned?

I hated to use Sadie as my canary in the coal mine, but the dog's instincts were even better than my own, and she would have known something was off seconds before I might. Seconds always counted.

But Sadie charged in and didn't show any signs of things being amiss. Instead, the dog headed into the kitchen, disappearing behind the counter. A moment later, I heard the familiar lapping sounds that accompanied every return home after staying with her part-time caretaker. I didn't understand why, but the first thing she always did was reacquaint herself with the water bowl. It wasn't like there wasn't fresh water at Ariadna's, but whatever. I wasn't in a position to judge harmless quirks, obviously.

I dropped my bag by the door and locked up behind me before refilling the water dish. I was a creature of habit, too, so it was time to initiate the sequence: microwave meal, recliner, and *Jeopardy!*.

Sadie kept her slobbery hammerhead on the arm of the La-Z-Boy as I flipped through my DVR to pulled up the cache of recorded *Jeopardy!* episodes I hadn't watched yet.

The rubber-band texture of the microwave pad thai

inexplicably soothed me, and soon I fell into a rhythm with my main man Alex.

What is Elba?

Who is Bobby Fischer?

What is a jib?

The answers, or in this case questions, came to me instantaneously, each recollection a delicious shot of dopamine.

I knew my way around a firearm, but memory was my preferred weapon.

It hadn't always been like that. Recollections hadn't always been so clear to me.

Dr. Feelgood, 1989. The same year as the finger. But was it that year? Or was I eight at the time?

I knew about the album release year—that was something I could verify with the internet, a coordinate to anchor myself by. But I couldn't simply Google, *When did I find a Black woman's finger in my backyard?* or even *Which of the fingers was it?*

The closest thing to those inquiries that might've turned up results was *Who is Raymond Lee Dwyer?*

"Who is Buckminster Fuller?" I asked Alex Trebek. Correct again.

It was 1989. It had to be.

And the first time he'd left his studio unlocked was 1995. December twenty-third, 1995, to be exact. Six years after the finger, two days before Christmas.

I had to stop doubting myself.

What I'd learned as a detective was that most people's memories were full of flaws because they didn't *want* to remember the painful parts, the realities that clashed uncomfortably with their personal identity. But my sense of self had already been blown to shit once. After that, I decided to let the facts tell me who I was rather than the other way around. Then, with practice, I'd started to remember.

"What is xenon?"

Right again. And a Daily Double, too.

Cut to commercial break, and as I fast-forwarded, my mind wandered back to work.

Who would be next?

Because there would be a "next" in this case before we could make an arrest. I was sure of that, even if I didn't like the prospect one bit. Despite the gore and spectacle of the crime, there was meticulousness and practiced patience that had gone into killing Cheryl Blackstenius. No one accomplished something like that on their first try, not even the most obsessive of psychopaths.

Was it someone I'd spoken with already?

If only the bad guys wore face makeup like the Joker. If only they spoke in long, sinister soliloquies, expounding on their warped philosophies and troubled childhoods. But that wasn't how it went. The truly malevolent could be relied on for one thing and one thing only: disguising themselves in order to blend in with the masses. It wasn't hard to learn how to act like you cared, and they'd figured that out at a young age. They were such apt pupils, they often came off like the most empathetic people around.

When the public imagined the face of a psychopath, they conjured the Joker. But Two-Face was a closer match.

And Two-Face could be an exemplary scoutmaster or a priest or your child's fifth-grade teacher or even your father.

There was only one way to figure out who had done that to Cheryl, and I couldn't find it through interviewing persons of interest. I may have spotted a strange micro-expression here and there to keep me interested, but it was nothing to put my trust in.

The crime scene was where the truth lay. It was all there, clearer than any villainous monologue could ever be. It was all there.

I just didn't know how to read it yet.

SIX

The earthy aroma of my mother's cooking—oregano, rosemary, simmering tomato—filled my nostrils. I looked around, and there she was at the stove. And there I was at our kitchen table. But this wasn't right. There was supposed to be some sort of strain between us. And hadn't we moved out of this old house already? Yet there we were again, the two of us in the kitchen as if none of the terror had come to pass. It would be a relief if not for the nagging sense that something was monumentally and horrifyingly wrong.

The sound of the basement door shutting and the padlock sliding into place had long since become a single event in my mind, so when I hadn't heard the second half, the rough metal-on-metal of the padlock, I noticed right away. The absence unsettled me, caused me to look up from my homework spread out on the kitchen table.

My mother didn't wonder what he did down there. Or maybe she already knew. Maybe it was more adult stuff that I was too young to understand. Or maybe she didn't *want* to know.

But *I* did. I wanted to see. I had no desire to live in the dark anymore, doubting the strange things I stumbled upon now and again.

Quietly, I stood from my seat at the table.

I turned the knob without making a sound and didn't shut the door behind me as I took one step and then the next, down into the basement. I heard him working; hammering was just out of sight around the corner of the stairs. The savory scents of the kitchen faded, replaced by something else, something that, at first, also registered as savory but also sweet. Was he making food as well?

A step creaked beneath my weight, and I froze. The hammering stopped.

Three more hurried steps, and I made it to the solid basement floor.

From the middle of her shin down to the toes was all I saw. Dark, swollen skin. Dry, callused feet.

And then he was there, bearing down on me, his paternal mask gone, his familiar features laced with monstrous darkness.

He came at me with a hatred I'd never seen before, and my legs flooded with the lava of animal instinct telling me to *run*. He lunged for me—

I jerked awake and looked around the living room. Daylight was still pouring through my curtains, and Sadie lifted her head from where she lay on the floor and obsessively licked the last of the pad thai sauce from the microwavable bowl. She must have swiped it from my lap.

On TV was Double Jeopardy, the same contestants as before I'd drifted off.

I hadn't been asleep long. Only a few minutes. And already I was back at the house? Jesus.

The scene in the basement replayed spectrally as the last remnants of fuzziness left me.

Finally, I remembered: that hadn't been how it happened. We'd never had a basement. With our thick bedrock, no one in Texas did. We'd had a workshop. An art studio out back. And I'd been in the *backyard* before the discovery, not the kitchen. There had been no stairs to slowly reveal the horror. Nothing had shielded me from it once I opened that unlocked door.

My brain had been trying to confuse me, just like all the detectives and agents attempted to do in those days and weeks after. It was trying to muddy my memory with alternate scenarios, water it down. It was trying to protect me, but in a misguided way.

I knew what I'd seen. I wouldn't forget. Not again.

I closed my eyes and ran through the real events as they'd unfolded on that winter afternoon. December twenty-third, 1995. My mind had repressed them once, but I wouldn't let it do that again.

I stared down at Sadie, who was shredding the waxy paper bowl.

It was going to be one of those days, wasn't it? A day when the memories came rushing back again and again, like choppy waves waiting to crash into me as soon as I turned my back to the ocean.

A scene like the one in the alley of Laugh Attack would do that, would jimmy open the stuck doors of my mind and let all the demons run free.

"Fine, fine," I said, putting the footrest down and forcing myself to stand. "No point in doing nothing."

I threw away my trash (much to Sadie's dismay) and tossed my fork into the sink. Coffee first. Iced coffee. It was too damn hot for regular, even if my coworkers liked to use such a preference as an excuse to point out I, despite all attempts to make it otherwise, was still not one of the guys.

I grabbed the doggy life vest and my paddle from the coat closet, then I stuffed Sadie's leash into a waterproof drawstring bag as a formality. The kayak was in my bedroom, but I'd load that up last, so it didn't get stolen from the top of my car.

I turned to Sadie, whose lethally wagging tail could chop a raw carrot in half. "Up for an adventure?"

By the time Detective Benjamin Escobar made it into the office later that morning, I was already lost down a social media rabbit hole.

I felt his eyes on me as he set his wallet and keys on his desk, which was back to back with mine in the Homicide offices. "Death Row," we called the place when we weren't in earshot of a ranking officer, a journalist, or an anti-cop civilian. Ben pulled out his rolling chair. "I thought I was early."

I didn't peel my eyes from my phone screen. "You are."

"Then you're extremely early."

"I am."

He settled into his seat and wiggled the computer mouse to wake up the monitor. "Sorry I couldn't make it last night. Saw it on the news. I assume Popov knew it was too late to call me."

With an effort, I tore my eyes away from the

Facebook profile on my screen. My partner's jet-black hair was still wet with gel he must've applied in his car, and his fresh fade on the sides told me he'd gotten a haircut since I last saw him yesterday afternoon. No shocker. Ben got a haircut at least once a week, presumably to make sure everyone within a mile radius of him could tell he was a cop. No undercover work for that one. He'd stuck with the same hairstyle since we met twelve years before, back when he was doing his field training on my patrol shift. He had a few years on me age-wise, but I had the same on him as a cop. The combination made for a nice, level playing field now that we were partners. "It's fine," I said. "Pops already explained that last night. You didn't need to be there, anyway. All you missed out on was the smell."

He shook his head. "Yeah, I already snuck a peek at some of the photos. Thank god they weren't scratch-and-sniff."

"The body was fresh enough, so it was mostly just the dumpster."

"Not sure if that's a blessing or a curse."

"Me neither." I paused. "I know you have Audrey a lot over the summer, so seriously, don't worry about it, okay?"

He let out a deep breath and bobbed his head before taking me in with a long, appraising look. "You look like you didn't sleep at all."

I tossed him a smile like a hot coal. "I did not. And screw you very much for commenting on my looks." He rolled his eyes. "Decided to go out on the lake with Sadie instead."

"Wish I could start my day off like that. Instead, it's all Pop-Tarts, cartoons, and feeling like the world's worst father for not limiting her screen time or cooking her a real breakfast."

I leaned forward, placing my palm on the edge of his desk. "Don't worry," I said. "There are *much* worse fathers out there."

He bit back a dark grin and shook his head disapprovingly at me, and I was reminded why we worked so well together. He didn't pity me, didn't tiptoe around my past. He knew as well as I did that dark humor beat self-pity any day of the week. "You always help me maintain perspective, Capone." He typed in his username and password in a clattering flash across his keyboard and said, "So what do we got on this?"

"Beyond the story the photos tell?"

"Right."

I'd followed so many leads and hunches that morning, all of which were essentially dead ends, that I didn't know where to start. "DNA tests won't come back until at least tomorrow, but no one in forensics seems too hopeful about them. She was bound with mic cables from the club, which meant that everyone who'd signed up for that open mic, plus everyone who set it up and who knows who else, could have put their anxious and clammy hands all over it. Touch DNA will be more of a wash than it usually is, in other words. She was also out by a dumpster, where god only knows how many homeless people and drunks had been."

"Right," said Ben. "That's a bust. As usual." He pulled out a legal pad from his desk drawer and began scribbling. "Who'd you talk with last night?"

"The owners and the manager-slash-sound guy who found the body. They were the only ones on scene. I made some calls and got in touch with one of the club's cocktail waitresses who wasn't working that night, but was there anyway. She said she likes to watch the open mics."

Ben glanced up from his notes. "Who likes to do *that*?"

I shrugged. "Generally, only the other comedians and whoever they tricked into coming along. My suspicion is that she wants to be on stage but hasn't worked up the courage yet. I arranged to meet her at a bar down on East Seventh, where she goes after the open mic nights. Sound guy tipped me off to that before I left. She seemed moderately coked up when I saw her. Talked quite a lot of shit about Cheryl Blackstenius when I brought her up. All the shit talking was in the present tense."

"Ah. And how'd she act when you told her Cheryl had been murdered?"

I had to suppress an inappropriate smirk. "Lost it. Completely. I had to take her outside because she was making a scene. Suddenly Cheryl Blackstenius was a saint. So helpful. So full of potential."

Ben's upper lip curled. "Typical. Anyone else?"

"Not last night."

"The owners or manager say anything interesting?"

I waved it off. "It's all *interesting*. And all the same. You know I don't put much stock in the interviews."

"Yeah, I know, I know. And what about the vic? What do we actually know about her?"

"That's what I'm trying to find out. Mike Check—that's the manager—he gave me the sign-up sheet for the open mic. If the killer was one of the performers, then we have his name. That's a big if. But it's a place to start. Mike also gave me a list of people Cheryl spent time with. Scott Ruiz, one of the owners, said he'd seen her making eyes at a fellow comedian named Jordan Grossman earlier that night. It was one of the names Mike provided, so I started there."

"And?"

I grabbed my coffee mug and brought it to my lips, only to find it empty. "Nothing immediate jumps out to me. He's active on Twitter, and Cheryl followed him, but he didn't follow back. They weren't even Facebook friends. I put a pin in that one for now. Meanwhile, I've been searching social media profiles of the others on the sign-up sheet, hoping something will jump out at me. Or rather, Jennifer Trout has been searching their profiles." I held up the burner phone I'd been prowling from, the one I only used for my covert accounts.

I paid for the data in cash each month, and it was one of the best professional investments I'd ever made. The IPs of government computers were easy enough to get a hold of, and one login at work would be enough for my sexy cover to be blown asunder.

It never failed to astound me how many men would accept a friend request from a large-breasted woman they didn't know, as if fate had smiled on them, and this goddess was desperately seeking a good time with a two-pump chump. Infiltrating circles of friends was easy enough—just start with the men—and before long, I was past the majority of privacy settings on people's Facebook pages. Because if you had twenty-four mutual friends with someone, it would be a faux pas not to accept that request, right?

Ben hitched a brow at me. "You changed her name?"

"I gotta every so often. Keeps the persona fresh and the 'date joined' distant."

"But aren't you worried people will look at their friends

list and go 'who the hell is that?' when they come to your profile?"

"I'm sure. But that happens anyway. No one knows who half of their online connections are. There were a few years there where all my friends from high school kept getting married and changing their last names. I had to click through to their profile to see who the hell they were."

He squinted at me. "You had friends in high school?"

I grunted away the jab. "I haven't found anything groundbreaking yet. Guy whose Twitter handle matches one of the names on the sign-up *might* be someone to look at more."

"Oh yeah?"

"Lives in Austin, calls himself a comic, asks for people to use the pronouns 'it/that.'"

"Trans?" Ben said.

"Uh, no. Just a jerk. His handle is @dennisrowe, but his name on there is Dennis the Pennis. Real sick sense of humor, lots of dead baby jokes because I guess no one told him those went out of style. Also, lots of tired misogyny."

"That ticks a few boxes."

"For the incel checklist, maybe. But incels, as you know, prefer to blow their load all at once in a mall or a school. I doubt he's our guy."

Ben tapped the end of his pen on the desk, a habit of his that drove pretty much everyone else in Homicide insane. If Sergeant Popov had been around to hear it, his face would've already been beet red. The sound didn't bother me, though.

Ben asked, "Any signs of sexual assault on the vic?"

"Not common ones. Her underwear were on, no signs

of anything on her inner thighs. But her shirt and bra straps were pulled down, and he'd sliced up her back."

"Right. I saw those pictures. Looked like he carved wings into her."

"You thought so too, huh? What kind of wings, though?"

"What kind? Sheesh, hadn't even considered that." He rubbed a flat palm up and down his jaw line, an absent-minded gesture I'd come to associate with him over our years together. "Angel wings, maybe?"

I shook my head. "Typical Catholic."

"Thought this was a crime scene, not a Rorschach test."

"Don't see why it can't be both."

"Fine," he said, "what kind of wings do you think they are?"

I considered it. "I'm leaning angel, too."

He glared at me, then went on, "No signs of sexual stuff, though?"

"Ben," I said pedantically, "the bared shoulders of a woman are considered a *very* sensual place to a lot of men."

"Psh. You don't have to explain that to me. Hell, half the reason I fell for Lucy in the first place was that she was parading around with her shoulders fully exposed on the first night we met."

I held up a hand. "We don't need to go there."

"You're right. And I wish I never had with that psycho. Only took me eight years to realize I'd made a huge mistake."

I not-so-subtly steered the conversation away from Ben's failed marriage. "I've compiled a list of Cheryl's friends who might be able to tell us about her—if she was seeing someone, who she spent a lot of time with, and so on. Her friends list on Facebook was set to private, and for obvious reasons, I can't exactly friend her. But word travels fast, and people are already writing out their long tributes on her wall, which I *can* see." I shook my head. "I wouldn't be surprised if our unknown subject posts one. It'd be like virtually returning to the scene of the crime. And few things in life are more publicly masturbatory than social media goodbyes to a dead person who can't read them."

"You know," Ben said, leaning back in his chair and stretching his arms behind his head, "I hate to ruin your fun, but you keep using male pronouns for the killer and talking about him—or *her*—as if they're exhibiting, shall we say, a *special* kind of criminality."

I pressed my lips together and didn't respond right away. He wasn't wrong. My mind was already ten steps ahead. We only had one crime, sure, but I'd already envisioned the ones stretching into the past that had led up to it and those in the future that would follow. Our unsub, or unknown subject, hadn't exactly been subtle about his skill level.

Expecting Ben to be onboard already was unrealistic. He was a good cop, followed protocol, didn't jump to conclusions. And because of that, he was absolutely terrible at trusting his gut. He'd always rather trust procedures.

I should've expected it. He wouldn't see the crime scene photos and jump from point A to point M like I had. He needed more onboarding before he would be willing to accept this for what it was.

It didn't annoy me as one might expect; this wasn't the first time I'd arrived at a similar conclusion days or even weeks before anyone else. I was under the curse of

Cassandra big time in that regard. Just one of the wonderful legacies I'd inherited.

"First of all," I said, injecting patience into every word, "you *know* it was a man who did this, so stop pretending. Second, limiting your pronouns to him or her is exclusionary of non-binary people anyway"—I anticipated his eye roll and ignored it—"but most importantly, every neuron in my brain is signaling that this *is* that special kind of criminality."

The skin tightened around his umber eyes as he frowned. "Dana. We've been through this."

"And my gut is always right."

"Nooo," he said, "it isn't. You've said so yourself."

I knew what he was hinting at, and I didn't appreciate it one bit. "I never said that." I leaned closer so I wouldn't be overheard. "I said I was wrong on the Rochelle case because I *didn't* listen to my gut. Because I went with goddamn procedure over my instincts. That bastard wasn't a danger to anyone but himself. I should have let him go and stayed with her. We would have caught up with him later on, no harm done." I straightened and breathed in through my nose, trying not to look like a single mention of that incident was enough to get me riled up. It had been months. I'd been cleared, put back on regular duty. I'd gone through the necessary counseling. In a lot of ways, I'd moved on.

But one thing hadn't left me: the high-profile case had put my name in the papers. That happened when you had to take down one of your own. It was sensational. The cop haters struggled to figure out who to root for.

The Rochelle case had, in short, blown up, played into the nation's fears of law enforcement, and, for a few nerve-racking days, stripped me of my ability to keep a low profile. The fact was, the fewer people who knew I existed, the less likely that the media would catch wind of my name change and show up on my doorstep to slap together some *Where Are They Now?* true crime list with me as the headliner.

"I won't be making that mistake again," I continued. "I'm listening to my gut from now on."

But I didn't really believe that, as much as I wanted to. How many times did a woman have to ignore her instincts before she learned to listen to them without fail? A whole whopping heap of times, if my life was any indication.

For a moment, Ben looked like he would keep pushing, but then he shook his head. "Fine. I'll entertain this person being that *special* kind of criminal as a possible theory, but we can't act on it yet."

"So, what do we do with it?"

"I dunno," he said, rolling his eyes. "I guess we hold it in our hearts."

I fought back a satisfied grin as he tapped the space bar fiercely to wake up his monitor again. "And I was having such a good morning..."

I chuckled. "No, you weren't."

It was just as I was slipping back into the flow of my research that a familiar voice yanked me out of it. "If it ain't Pablo and Al."

I didn't have to look over to know who it was, and part of me just wanted to ignore him. But I knew from experience that such a tactic backfired with a guy like him.

Detectives Derek Towers and Jaden Krantz entered from the hallway. Towers was easily one of the hairiest white guys I'd ever met. He had dark, coarse curls like steel wool covering his head and liked to sport V-neck tees that showed off how his unruly chest hair connected through a Milky Way of razor burn to the perpetual stubble of his beard.

As Jaden Krantz loved to remind us all the damn time, he was a "certified Blasian"—mother from the Caribbean, father from Korea. The man was a flirt who was most effective when he didn't speak. If he'd applied half the effort he used hitting on women at crime scenes toward solving murders, he might have made a decent detective. But he didn't.

It was Towers who had called us Pablo and Al. So original. He spoke in a nasally, cocky tone that hinted he might have spent too many summers in Jersey. But I'd learned at a shift happy hour years ago that he'd been born and raised in Orange County. Never even visited the East Coast. It was too bad he hadn't stayed in his hometown rather than joining the Great California Migration and taking up air in my home state.

"Ah, Fawlty Towers," said Ben with an easy nonchalance I could never muster with a guy like Derek, "what's new with you?"

"Same old. Guy shot in the parking lot of Muy Caliente last night. Eight people saw it."

Krantz added, "Not entirely convinced it was homicide."

"Whoa there," I said, "don't overexert yourself, detectives. Shot in front of only eight witnesses? It sounds like an unfortunate accident to me."

Towers smirked. "You joke, but I ask you this: is it really homicide if the guy had it coming?"

"Holy hell," I said. "Spoken like a true mobster."

"You would know, Capone," Krantz shot back, defending his partner's honor.

"Escobar, too," Towers barked, his put-on accent making it sound more like "doo" as he nodded at Ben.

Ben tossed a look my way. "I haven't heard anyone make a lame joke about my last name before," he said. "You?"

"Never." I addressed Krantz. "With genius brains like yours, eight eyewitnesses, and a suspect who undoubtedly spent the last ten hours snorting lines of coke and bragging about what he did, y'all just might crack that case."

"A couple of wise guys, eh?" Towers said.

"Oh Jesus," I muttered.

Towers leaned over to gawk at my screen. On one browser window were the crime scene photos, and on the other, the publicly visible tributes on Cheryl Blackstenius' Facebook wall. "You're wasting your time with that," he said. "I saw the photos already. Probably just some bum high off his ass on K2 who wandered down from Homeless Row and decided to make the voices stop the only way he knew how."

Ben nodded along. "Great thinking. Hey, why don't we switch cases? You can wrap this one up, and we'll do our damndest to solve the Case of the Brazen Shooter you got over at Muy Caliente."

"Not a chance," said Towers, as if the offer had contained a modicum of authenticity. "We got important things to do." He nodded for Krantz to follow, but not before adding, "Don't let her get all worked up just because the murder has a little flair to it. Last thing we need is another FBI task force taking up space."

"Nobody wants the FBI," I said.

Ben added, "Why don't you just worry about yourself, Towers? Sounds like you got enough on your plate with that whodunnit at the cartel bar."

Once they'd left, I focused pointedly on my screen, hoping Ben didn't feel the need to console me for Towers' last pathetic jab.

"Dana," he said, right on cue, "you know they're just trying to get under your skin."

"Yep. Don't worry about it."

He returned to his monitor, clicking the mouse harder than necessary. "Never met two more worthless detectives in my life."

"In their defense," I said, scrolling to a wordy, unpunctuated eulogy on Cheryl's wall, "solving murders is hard."

After a minute of silence, Ben muttered, "'Wise guys'? Jesus."

SEVEN

In the driver's seat beside me, Ben finished off the last of his coffee and stared forlornly at the compostable cup. "I shoulda gotten it on ice like you."

The A/C blasted from the slicktop's vents, but it did little against the June sun. There was plenty of shade in this apartment complex's parking lot from the clumps of cedar trees all around, but none touched the only space we could find.

I glanced over at him as I sipped the last of my icy drink through my straw. "Aah... I woulda been forced to call you a pussy if you had. That's department policy, right? Iced coffee equals pussy?"

He confirmed with a nod. "Definitely on the books. But you could call me whatever you want so long as it kept my balls from sticking—"

I flung open the passenger door and was out and stretching in an instant. Ben followed my lead.

There was just enough of a breeze to make the sweat feel good on my skin, but I wouldn't mind getting indoors somewhere soon. "Let's see what the roommate has to say, and *then* you can tell me all about your personal perspiration issues. Or not. That would be fine, too."

Motion caught my eye as the Crime Scene van appeared around the corner, creeping between the rows of buildings with a furtive air but unmissable in its bulk. The team could take their time finding a spot to set up, since Ben and I wanted to get into Cheryl Blackstenius' apartment first, butter up the roommate a little, and see what information we could glean on our own. It was always best not to swarm the place all at once.

This apartment complex was a nice one, and despite the fact that it had always been my choice to stay in the run-down one where I lived, it irked me when people I had a solid decade on and who probably made significantly less money than I did lived in apartments this nice. Were their parents paying for it? Or were they just doing that Millennial thing of racking up a bunch of debt and then waiting until they were the largest voting bloc and could vote themselves a bailout? Sure, I was technically a Millennial, but just by the skin of my teeth. Some might argue that 1982 was the tail end of Gen X.

But I wasn't a huge fan of *that* generation, either. Not giving a damn wasn't as cool as so many of them thought.

Cheryl Blackstenius' old unit was on the third floor, and even as we climbed the stairs, we were met with stunning views of the Hill Country sprawling for miles. The rent on a place like this must be at least three times what I paid for mine.

Monica Summers answered the door, and Ben flashed his badge. She looked from him to me without any outward signs of comprehension whatsoever. Had no one notified her? Had she not been on Facebook? Seen her roommate's profile already bombarded with self-indulgent tributes?

Monica had straight and silky dark chocolate hair down to the tips of her perky breasts. A curtain of wispy bangs framed big blue eyes that stared wildly at Ben. The moment she took a serious look at his badge, her pupils expanded like a spooked horse's. "What's going on?"

"We're here about Cheryl," he said.

"Oh, god, did she get herself arrested?"

I braced. This wouldn't be fun.

"Can we come in?"

Ben ripped the bandage off once we were seated inside the brightly lit apartment. The place looked like it might have been sponsored by Hobby Lobby. A wooden *Live, Laugh, Love* sign was mounted to an overhang above the kitchen counter, and a string of colorful cloth pennants hung above each window like every day was a baby shower or the summer solstice or, closer yet, a baby shower on the summer solstice for a baby named Summer Summers.

On the rose-colored Papasan chair, Monica Summers cradled her head in her hands and made all kinds of strange, miserable noises that didn't surprise me one bit. I could have pegged her as this type from a mile away.

What *was* surprising was when the girl looked up, a tear-slicked strand of hair stuck to her cheek, her powder-blue eyes puffy, and said, "I'm never gonna be able to cover the rent alone!"

I leaned forward from where I sat next to Ben on the overstuffed plum-colored loveseat and placed a hand on Monica's knee. "There's a lot to think about in this situation, and it will take some time to sort it all out."

Monica sniffled and nodded in an overdone show of bravery.

Should I remind her that someone was dead and that merely needing to find a new roommate was the better side of a raw deal?

No. No point. "You and Cheryl were pretty close, then?" I asked.

I didn't find Monica's indifferent shrug particularly shocking. I was sizing her up pretty quick. She leaned back in the womblike chair, tucking her knees up to her chest to be full-on fetal. "We knew each other okay. I didn't know her before we moved in together. Just put out an ad for a roommate, and she seemed nice enough. I have a cousin who works for a sheriff's department in East Texas, and he ran a background check on her—I've had bad experiences with roommates in the past. But she was clean. I guess you would already know that, though. We get along okay— Oh my *god*! No, now's it's 'got' along." She slapped her hands back onto her face.

The girl had the resilience of a sandcastle at high tide. She couldn't be more than twenty-three, and this was probably the first traumatic thing she'd ever experienced, outside of, perhaps, her parents selling off one of her favorite toys prematurely.

I breathed deep and mustered up some empathy, but it felt a little like scraping burned beans from a cast-iron skillet. "Are you friends with her on Facebook?"

"No. I don't do Facebook. My *grandparents* do that."

"What social media do you use, then?"

"Snapchat. Instagram. I have, like, twenty thousand followers on Insta."

I didn't bother trying to look impressed. "Do you follow Cheryl on either of those?"

"Insta, yeah. But I never really pay attention to my feed, so I didn't keep up with what she was doing, if that's what you're asking."

I nodded and sat back, passing the baton to Ben with a look. "Do you know if she was seeing anyone?" he asked.

"She saw a few people. She'd occasionally switch guys. We've lived together, or we *did* live together"—this time, the verb tense switch didn't cause a breakdown, thankfully —"for about eight months, and I remember three, maybe four different guys. Of course, she might have snuck some in that I didn't know about."

"Anyone you remember from recently?"

She sniffled again and dragged her forearm under her nose. "Yeah. I haven't seen him around in a couple weeks, but it was this white guy—a lot of hers weren't white, which is the only reason I mention it. I'm not a racist or anything. He was sort of sulky, not really hot or even very cute."

"Hair?" I prompted her. "Eyes? Height? Name?"

Monica considered it. "Um. Brown hair, kind of thick eyebrows. I don't remember his eye color because his brows were always distracting. They really could have used a pluck to shape them up, you know? He was... maybe short? I don't know. Cheryl was tall, so a lot of the guys she dated were her height or shorter. She liked them funny, and, well, you know."

Ben shook his head. "Know what?"

"Well, short guys *have* to be funny, don't they? Otherwise, they just get picked on."

I said, "So this guy wasn't tall."

"No, definitely not tall. But I don't think he was as

short as the others. Cheryl was close to six feet, so maybe he was five-foot-nine or so?"

"And do you remember his name?"

"Yep. It was David."

As Ben began to write that down on his notepad, Monica let out a little gasp. "No, wait! David was the Black one. Mike. That was this one."

I felt Ben's coiled excitement beside me, but, calm as ever, he scratched out the D-A-V he'd already written down and scribbled *Mike* instead. "Any chance you know the last name?" he asked.

Her shoulders deflated. "No, sorry."

"No problem. Do you know what Mike did for work, by any chance?"

That perked her up again. I couldn't tell if the girl was more invigorated by the thought that she could be of use or the prospect of posting to her Instagram stories that she was a crucial part of a murder investigation. "He worked at one of the comedy clubs she went to."

I pressed my lips together to maintain my poker face. If this was Mike Check she was talking about, and it sounded more and more like it was, and he'd recently dated the deceased, my hunch about this being only the start of a killing pattern, as opposed to domestic abuse, was going to be a lot harder to prove. Or worse, it might be completely wrong. Ben wouldn't let me forget it if that were the case, if my gut instinct were so off.

I pulled out my burner phone and, in a few taps, had the photo I needed. I held it out to Monica. "This the guy?"

Monica squinted, leaning forward, and then her hand flew up to her mouth. "Yes!" she said, nodding profusely. "That's him!"

I tucked the phone back in my pocket. She'd just IDed Mike Check. Dammit.

"You think he did it?" she asked. "You think he murdered Cheryl?"

Ben slipped his notepad into his breast pocket and held up a steadying hand. "We don't think anything yet. We're just getting a feel for her life at this point. Speaking of which, do you mind if we take a look around Cheryl's room?"

Asking was a formality. We already had a search warrant. But it was always easiest just to get permission and not have to force it.

Monica jumped up. "Yes, of course. Do you want something to drink? I have LaCroix in the fridge. Pamplemousse and coconut."

Ben smiled. "Coconut sounds great."

"Yeah, same for me," I added.

Under other circumstances, I wouldn't have ingested a LaCroix if someone paid me for it, and I suspected the same was true for Ben. But it was just bad investigating to turn down the unsolicited hospitality. Crappy detectives like Towers and Krantz insisted that taking someone up on their offer meant necessary reciprocation later, but accepting the offering *was* the reciprocation. People in Monica's position felt powerless, useless. Allowing them to feel like they could do *something*, even if it was pouring fizzy water into a couple of IKEA glasses, was a gift I could give them that cost me nothing.

I entered the deceased's bedroom first, and it was instantly obvious who'd decorated the frilly shared spaces: not Cheryl.

With the mattress on the floor and only a handful of

comedy club playbills stapled to the wall, it looked more like a college bachelor pad than somewhere a woman in her mid-twenties might call home.

With a cringe, I realized it reminded me a little of my apartment.

Now wasn't the time for judgment, though. The inhabitant of this room had been brutally murdered not even twenty-four hours ago. Cast in that light, the place transformed from unappealing to tragic. The clothes discarded near but not quite in the laundry basket, the top corner of the sheets flung down, the mirrored closet door slid halfway back—all signs of a person who'd intended to return, who'd told herself she had plenty of time to straighten it up later, who'd thought about the long future ahead of her and tolerated the present suboptimal state because of it.

The people I'd talked to so far hadn't painted Cheryl in the most flattering of lights, but being there in that disarray sent a lurching wave of understanding through me.

I slipped on a pair of gloves from my pocket as I approached the overturned cardboard box serving as a bedside table. On it was a small lamp and a stack of three notebooks. I snapped a picture of the setup on my phone then grabbed the notebook on top and flipped through it. Scribbles of words filled the first third of it; jokes she was refining, by the look of it.

I opened to a random page and began to read.

Whenever I'm driving behind someone with a handicapped license plate, and they're going too slow, I think, "If you're this handicapped, maybe you shouldn't be driving." And if I'm behind someone with a handicapped license place who's driving too fast, my first thought is

"Maybe this kind of recklessness is what earned you that license plate."

Dark. Taking a big risk in a culture like Austin's. I wondered if Cheryl had ever tried it on stage, and if so, what reaction she'd received.

I grabbed the next in the stack. It was completely full of writing, too. The corner of a sheet of paper poked out from beneath the bottom notebook, and I slipped it out. On it was a hand-drawn calendar. The heading read *June jokes.* The first six days had an X across them, and I felt a haunting desire to add another one on the seventh day to keep her streak alive.

Dammit. She'd had the drive, the discipline, the willingness to take risks, and possibly enough talent to make it all work. She'd been on an upward trajectory until someone strangled the life out of her.

Of course no one had spoken highly of her. It all made sense now. She had the audacity to be ambitious. Her mind was set on one thing, blinders on. Few people could stand that in the so-called delicate sex.

Monica Summers, meanwhile, was chasing something illusory and hollow on social media—fame with no purpose. Cheryl likely tolerated it, but I could hardly blame her for not engaging more or feeding her roommate's ego. And Mike Check? Had he sensed the potential in Cheryl and felt threatened by it? Was he the envious type who cozied up to those on the rise, only to wait until he had the chance to strike? To bring them back down to earth? To bury them six feet under it?

"I don't know what we're going to get out of this," Ben said, peeking into her messy closet. "It's just sad."

"I think there's plenty to mine here. And they never

found her cell phone. Maybe she left it somewhere in here."

"Doubt it. Have you met anyone under the age of fifty who left their cell at home and didn't go back to get it as soon as they realized?"

I thought back to the night before and then hollered from the bedroom to Monica, "Did Cheryl own a car?" I hadn't found any registered in her name when I checked earlier, but I hadn't thought to check for anything in her parents' names.

Monica called back, "No, she rode the bus."

I looked at Ben and shrugged. "Maybe she didn't have the option to turn around and come back for it."

One of the playbills on the wall featured a few high-profile comedians I'd actually heard of. At least, I recognized the names, even if I couldn't remember a single one of their jokes. Each had performed at Laugh Attack back in March, according to the flyer. Cheryl must have been there. And it must have been a memorable night. Was that because the show was so good, or had something else happened to warrant sticking the moment on the wall as a reminder?

The next poster was also from Laugh Attack, but it was from October 2017. All but one, as I stepped around the various garments on the floor to look, were from Laugh Attack. The odd one out was from a place called The Bungalow.

"We ought to check out this place, too," I said, gesturing at the paper. "The Bungalow. Another comedy club it looks like she went to. If there was an open mic night, she probably frequented it."

A small tap on the door pulled our attention, and

Monica peeked in, two fizzing glasses in her hand. "Find anything good?"

"Do you know if she spent a lot of time at The Bungalow?"

Monica frowned as she handed out the drinks. "No idea. I know she did an open mic night at least twice a week, but I'm pretty sure she did it over at one downtown."

I sipped the La Croix, and the sensation of someone brushing a coconut-flavored feather over my tongue incensed me irrationally. *Just make it coconut or not.*

I tamped down the frustration. "The Bungalow is up north, right?"

"I think so." Monica paused. "Is it— Can I ask you how she died?"

"We're not sure yet," I said quickly.

"But she was murdered, right? Otherwise, you wouldn't be asking all these questions."

Ben fed her the stock non-answer. "We're asking these questions because we're trying to find out if it was a homicide."

Right. Or maybe she sliced wings into her back, cracked her shin, and then hung herself on a fence while her wrists were bound, like a suicidal Houdini.

I downed the rest of the drink quickly to get it over with and felt the carbonation stirring in my chest.

"Will you let me know what you find?" Monica asked.

"We'll let the next of kin know what we find," Ben said. "If they want to share that with you, it's up to them."

I handed her back the empty glass and said, "Do me a favor?"

Monica nodded eagerly.

"Don't post about this on social media. It won't make

you look sympathetic or important. It'll make you look callous. And it could put you in danger." While Monica was still speechless, I added, "Crime Scene technicians are parked downstairs. They need to come up here and gather some evidence for us."

"You think I had something to do with it?" she asked.

"No, but this is where the victim lived. There's always evidence to gather. Standard procedure. If you have somewhere you can go for the next couple of hours, that would help the process move more smoothly."

Ben quickly thanked the stunned girl for the hospitality and handed her his card, and then we headed back down to the parking lot.

Truthfully, there wasn't much for them to gather, but I pointed the technicians toward a few things, including the notebooks. The writing that filled those pages had looked like it was entirely jokes, but you never knew what truth could be found in that. I'd just have to hope no one in Crime Scene thought themselves a comedian and stole her bits. Ripping off the dead was always poor taste.

As I finished giving instruction, Ben informed me that he'd just looked up The Bungalow on his phone, and the club had shut down for good last December. So much for that. Not much investigating to do at a location that no longer existed. Didn't matter, though. We had stronger leads.

Quarter of an hour after we'd left the apartment, I slipped into the passenger seat of our slicktop and closed the door behind me. As Ben slid in on the other side, he shot me a gloating look.

"Oh, knock it off. And start the damn engine. I'm boiling in here."

He did, and once the A/C had finished blasting us with the initial hot air, I said, "I know what you're thinking."

"Is that because you're thinking it, too?"

I rolled my eyes.

"Admit it," he said. "We have reasonable suspicion to call Mike into the station."

"Oh joy, another interview. Can't wait to waste my time trying to wring useful information out of someone who could be an expert liar. While we're at it, why don't we see if we can get Cheryl's corpse to tell us what happened? We'd have about as good of a chance."

"Dana, this could be an open-and-shut case."

I adjusted the air vents irritably, muffling a fizzy belch as I did. "You know *that's* not a thing. Well, maybe the case Towers and Krantz are working on over at Muy Caliente is, but nothing else."

"Great. I'll talk to Popov about getting it scheduled."

I sighed. "Just be sure to book it on my lucky day."

"When's your lucky day?"

"Dunno," I said. "Been waiting my whole life for it to come around."

EIGHT

"How come you never told me you were dating Cheryl Blackstenius?" I sat opposite Michal Nebojsa in the tiny interview room at the station. Behind me, Ben Escobar stood silently, his arms folded across his chest. We'd decided beforehand that I had the best chance of getting information out of this one.

The only thing on the metal table in this sparse and sterile environment was a plastic cup of water, which remained untouched in front of the first official suspect in our murder investigation.

"We weren't dating," he said. The veins in his crossed forearms bulged, but he didn't seem especially concerned with the one-down position in which he'd found himself. Maybe he didn't realize how much trouble he was looking at.

"Sleeping together?" I asked.

He shrugged. "A few times."

"When you say 'a few'...?"

"I dunno. I wasn't keeping track. Maybe eight or nine?"

"That's not a few," I said. "And you told me the two of you didn't hang out outside of the club. Did you have sex at Laugh Attack, then?"

He aped disgust, but when I remained silent, he said, "Only once or twice. The rest was... other places."

"Her apartment?"

"I— Maybe? I wasn't keeping track."

"Your apartment?"

His answer was sharp, like the drop of a guillotine's blade. "She never came over to my place."

"Over how much time did the sexual relationship span? A few months? Weeks?"

He rolled his eyes. "A few months, probably. Like I already said, I wasn't keeping track."

"Were you two sleeping with other people during that time?"

"I can't speak for her, but I was."

"So, it wasn't exclusive?"

"Again, I can't speak for her."

I sensed that he was starting to rattle, but that was what I'd wanted. I didn't let off. "But for you, she was just another lay."

I didn't miss the flash of contempt as his top lip cinched and the corners of his mouth flickered downward. It was the same micro-expression I'd seen on him the first time we spoke. "I liked her just fine. We got along. She was attractive enough. But she wasn't funny. I mean, her material was good, but her delivery was terrible. She came off as angry, not funny."

I leaned back. "That mattered to you?"

"It's why I wouldn't let her open for any of the headliners. She really wanted to. But it would've been cruel to stick her up there in front of an audience who came to see a professional. Not only would it have been cruel, but it would have put the audience in a bad mood for the headliner. My job is to set up the big names to succeed, not to make it so they remember Laugh Attack as the place where they bombed."

"Forgive me, but I don't see what that has to do with you two sleeping—"

"She was just banging me to try to get me to book her, okay?" He uncrossed his arms and leaned forward, gripping the edge of the stainless-steel table. "I didn't feel one way or another about her. She was practically nobody to me. But she was hot enough, and she put out, okay? I'm sorry, I'm a man!"

I held up a hand to calm him. "Let me get this right: you liked her, but you think she just wanted to sleep with you because you had the power to put her on stage for the right shows?"

"Yeah," he said, withdrawing into his slouch again. "A lot of the women—and some of the men—think that'll work."

"You like men?"

A minute pinch at the corner of his eyes. A slight flare of his nostrils. His gaze jumped to Ben then back to me. "Sometimes."

I didn't consider this admission about his sexual orientation damning. If anything, his openness about it worked in his defense. The only reason I'd poked at him there was to see if I could get him to admit something he might perceive as unflattering to the macho image he put off. Sexual repression tended to be at the root of most violence, but Mike didn't seem to be repressing those particular urges.

"Do Scott and Heidi Ruiz know about this added benefit of your position?" I continued.

He scoffed. "They should. It's nothing new for comics to sleep with the right people to get a good spot. It's nothing new for anyone in entertainment."

"But Cheryl, you liked her more than the others?"

"I didn't say that. I said I liked her just fine. Some of the other people were— It wasn't good. They were clingy afterward. Annoying. A lot of them didn't even have good material like she did."

Was that really his criterion for picking a booty call? Their stand-up material? The man could let poor delivery slide, but if the *material* wasn't good...?

"And the men?" I said.

"What about them?" He might as well have spit on me with the way he'd said it, and it was clear he already regretted the previous confession. Maybe he thought we would use it against him. But the truth was, as long as it was consensual, I didn't have two cares to rub together about who had sex with whom. However, if using his sexual orientation against him was what it took to find Cheryl's murderer, I wasn't afraid to go there. Justice, and possibly preventing another slaying, mattered a hell of a lot more to me than his feelings.

"Any of the men you hooked up with into, I dunno, kinks?" I asked.

He pressed his lips together into a thin line, and I wondered if he'd refuse to respond. But I had to try it. Shifting the responsibility for any kinks he might have over to another male meant he didn't have to admit he was into, say, erotic asphyxiation or knife play. It'd allow him to pass the buck along for having engaged in that behavior. He might think he was pushing us toward another lead, but what he'd really be doing was helping us find another character witness against him if we ended up charging Mike.

But when he spoke, he gave me nothing of the sordid sort. "One was into feathers."

I hadn't been expecting that, and I had to bite my lip to keep from laughing. "Feathers?"

"Yeah, he liked... God, do I have to go into it? I don't see how it's relevant. That dude doesn't even live in Texas anymore."

"You don't have to if you don't want," I said. "He liked being tickled on his genitals with feathers?"

Mike Check nodded. "Yeah. It was weird."

Probably some messed-up regression to his childhood. But who was I to judge anyone on their messed-up childhood?

"Any of them into erotic asphyxiation?"

He narrowed his eyes. "What's that?"

"Cutting off the partner's air supply."

He recoiled. "Like, strangling? Ugh, no. Or if they were into it, they didn't try that shit with me."

"Any of the women you were with ever ask you to strangle them during sex?"

"Jesus," he rasped. "No. And if they did, I wouldn't do it."

I pushed my chair back and stood. "Detective Escobar, can I speak with you in the hall for a second?" Ben nodded and made for the door. "Sit tight, Mike. We just gotta speak with our supervisor, then we'll get you out of here."

We relocated to the observation room, watching the suspect sip his water and stare down at the table.

"He doesn't seem into choking," Ben said.

"Not during sex, sure. But we know whoever killed Cheryl didn't have sex with her. It could be the idea of mixing the two that disgusts him."

"But doesn't your theory hinge on some sort of erotic obsession between the killer and the victim?"

I glanced at my partner. "Oh, lord, Ben. 'Erotic' does not necessarily equal 'sex.' They're two different things. Fantasy and reality *can* merge, but they don't have to." I gazed back through the two-way mirror at our suspect. "And nothing can be compartmentalized by the human psyche quite like the physical act of sex. Otherwise, we wouldn't be able to look our partner in the eye after the things we did with them in the bedroom." Ben cleared his throat uncomfortably, and I shot him a sideways glance. "What? Too adult for you?"

"Wouldn't you like to know?"

I rolled my eyes. "You think we've given him enough time to let that imagination run wild?"

"Might as well check."

As we reentered the interview room, Mike said, "Am I free to go now?"

"In just a second," I replied. "A couple more things we want to knock out for official purposes, so we can say we ticked all the boxes." He seemed to buy it as Ben and I took a seat across from him. "You said you were from Bosnia when we first talked."

He jerked his chin back. "Yeah. You remember that?"

"I remember a lot of things. For instance, you said you were young when you came over."

It was clear he wasn't tracking where I was going, but he answered hesitantly all the same. "Came over here in 1995."

December twenty-third, 1995. The unlocked door...

I pulled myself back as quickly as I'd slipped away. "Right at the end of the conflict, wasn't it?"

He nodded, his thick eyebrows lowering as he squinted at me.

"I have an uncle who was over there from ninety-three," I said, "until the end of the war. He won't even talk about it, but I've read stories. You must've seen some truly awful shit."

He reached for his glass and found it empty. Ben jumped up. "I'll get you some more."

"What was it like?" I wasn't going to wait for Ben to return. This was all on tape; he could review it later. But I couldn't get back lost momentum.

"I don't really remember," Mike said, and I saw the first bricks of a stony wall go up between us.

"How old were you when you left?"

Without missing a beat: "Six."

"Seems like you'd remember something."

He glared at me, and the muscles in my shoulder clenched as I got my first full glimpse of the man behind that hard exterior. And what I saw there made my skin crawl.

"I guess I could remember if I had to, but I've done my best to forget."

"I understand," I said.

Ben returned with the refilled cup and handed it off before sitting down again.

I asked, "Did you see dead bodies?"

Mike fixed his gaze on the cup in front of him. "Of course."

"See anyone kill another person?"

"Yes."

"Mutilate the body?"

"Every time." He looked up from his water, and his eyes blazed, full of pain and hatred as he sized me up. "But if you believe I did that shit to Cheryl, you're not as good at this job as you think. I *escaped* that country for a reason. I don't want anything to do with it. It was horrible. I still have nightmares. You can't even imagine the things I saw friends do to each other. I can't even hear a voice outside my window at night without thinking about how my next-door neighbors were dragged out of their house and onto the front lawn by people I went to church with. Family of five, three daughters. They dragged them out by their hair. Raped and killed them while everyone looked on—my other neighbors, my family. Me." I thought he was done as a muscle in his square jaw pulsed, but he went on. "Is that what you want to know about, Detective? You pull me in here to ask me to describe the worst things I've ever seen? You get off on that?"

I didn't react. This was what I'd been working toward. I wanted to see him upset, wanted to stir him up and see what dregs had gathered at the bottom of his psyche.

I said nothing, and Ben knew I was passing the baton.

"I'm sorry you had to go through that," he said, "and at such a young age. No one should have to."

"Yeah, well, I guess all's well that ends well. Seeing Cheryl all tied up was nothing by comparison. I didn't even have a nightmare about it last night."

Neither had I. I could commiserate with Mike Check

on that account more than I cared to admit. Scenes like the one of Cheryl's body the night before were unpleasant, but they were no longer fuel for my nightmares. That tank had been filled a long time ago.

"Can I leave now, or are you going to arrest me?" he demanded.

"You can leave," I said more softly than I meant to. And as Ben got to his feet and ushered Mike out of the room, I remained seated, watching him go.

Was he our man? I'd be a fool to let his actual words sway me one way or another. But the mention of the rapes he'd witnessed... To be able to bring them to mind so quickly, they must have been floating toward the surface of his psyche. Rape and violence were intertwined in his trauma.

But Cheryl hadn't been sexually violated. Could a man like him do one act and not the other? If he had been fueled by his nightmares, could he have killed but not raped?

It seemed unlikely. And yet my mind kept pointing me back to that instant where I'd seen his rage, seen *him*.

As much as I hated to admit it, as it would sway the minds of the department toward a motive that contradicted the one I was pursuing, Mike Check was a solid suspect.

NINE

Forty-five minutes later, after our suspect was fingerprinted and allowed to walk, I stood with my hands on my hips in the hallway just off the station's lobby and watched him leave.

"What do you think?" said Ben, appearing next to me.

His question caught me off guard and ripped me from my faraway thoughts. I'd been thinking about woman twenty-nine, Lucy Hicks, the first body the police had found out in the woods by Lake Worth. Her skull had turned up half a mile away from the rest of her bones. I didn't remember hearing that specific detail in my teens, but I'd read it later, catching up on the crimes, trying to jog my memory. Lucy Hicks had been scattered around.

The mass grave under our studio's floorboards had hit max capacity at twenty-eight bodies. One of the reasons most Texas homes don't have sizable mass graves in the backyard, apart from the low demand for such a thing, is the same reason they don't have basements despite the state's reputation for tornados: caliche rock is a bitch. You get about half a foot down in Texas soil and hit it, and then it's slow going and expensive as hell to keep digging. Raymond didn't want to shell out for that, I suppose. Might've raised too many questions if he'd rented a backhoe for the weekend. Or maybe he was just a cheap bastard on top of every other sin of his.

So, victim twenty-nine and on had needed to be dumped elsewhere.

I turned to Ben. "Huh?"

"You think he did it?"

"Eh."

He stepped in front of me, cutting off my line of sight to Mike Check. "Wait. Are you serious?"

"Yeah. He's solid, but I'm by no means convinced yet."

Ben frowned. "Were we in different interviews just now?"

I relented, dropping my hands to my sides and heading back down the hall toward Death Row. Ben followed. "What makes you think he might've done it?"

As he kept pace, he said, "Just the facts, really. Nothing fancy. Traumatic childhood. Positions himself in a place of power and uses it for sex where he has all the control. The possibility of unrequited feelings for Cheryl." I opened my mouth to correct him, but before I could, he said, "Oh, come on. He said sleeping together was nothing, but you could see it in his eyes. He had a thing for her."

"Even so, you don't know the feelings were unrequited," I said. "No one knows that now."

"Okay, fine." We reached our desks, and Ben sat in his rolling chair, spinning it to face me as I settled in across from him. "Why *don't* you think it's him? I thought you put no stock in interviews."

"I don't."

"Yet your opinion evolved over the course of that one. *Why?*"

I couldn't blame him for his frustration. After all, wouldn't it have been nice if we could wrap this up and stick a bow on it before the end of the day? But that desire blurred the vision of even the best cops. Sometimes we wanted justice so bad, we let our subconscious draw up the blueprint, then manufactured it ourselves.

"The odds, for one. What are the odds we'd grab our guy on the first serious interview? But also, think about the timeline. The window for Cheryl's murder is small. It was a matter of minutes between when she could have been murdered and when Mike said he discovered the body and called the cops. It doesn't make any sense that a practiced killer would stage a body so particularly and patiently then be unable to wait more than fifteen minutes for someone else to find it. If our killer got off on people seeing it, which is very likely, he would have let someone else discover it, even if that meant waiting until the morning."

Ben stared up at the textured ceiling panels. "Or maybe he murdered her in a fit of rage, strangled her to death, and then once she was dead, he figured, *Hey, why not arrange her like one of my screwed-up fantasies rooted in my traumatic Bosnian childhood?* So he did, then his mind returned to him, and he was horrified by what he'd done and called the police in a panic?"

I only just managed to keep from rolling my eyes. "Even someone with seriously screwed-up fantasies doesn't come up with *that* on the fly and pull it off the first time. The missing skin under the shoulder blades? You don't do that in a frenzy."

Ben's broad chest deflated visibly while his shoulders slumped. "Okay, how about this? He's our guy for this murder, *and* he's killed before? Then we're both right."

"You're just saying that to shut me up."

"Obviously. Or maybe I've worked with you enough to know that sometimes your instincts are right."

I held up my hands. "Whoa, Nelly. Don't come at me with so much confidence all at once." I grabbed my water bottle off the desk and took a sip. I'd refilled it at the water fountain only an hour ago, and it already tasted stale. "You just wait, though. Give it a couple weeks. Our unsub has gotten away with murder at least once. He'll be back again. And in the meantime, we sure as hell better get a camera up on that back alley behind Laugh Attack. Anyone who gets within fifteen feet of the scene over the next two weeks gets a coveted place on our suspect list."

"I wish you'd stop calling it an unsub like we have any serious reason to believe this is more than a one-off."

"An unknown subject is an unknown subject," I argued. "You're the one limiting the use to a serial killer."

He briefly shut his eyes for patience, a gesture he did often with me, at hearing the term spoken aloud. "You think he'll return to the scene?"

I cocked my head to the side and grinned. "Look at you using the masculine pronoun. And yes. They always do. But first, there's somewhere else he'll go."

TEN

June 9th, 2018

3 days since Blackstenius murder

"All I'm saying is that you can't go through life wondering if everyone's a psychopath," Ben said, holding an iced coffee.

We'd found a bit of shade to park in underneath a large oak tree, and I'd backed the car in so we'd face the front doors of Hudson-Langor Funeral Home. Cheryl's Saturday service was set to start at nine thirty, and the clock on the dash indicated it was hardly past nine. But already, the first of those looking to pay their respects were starting to trickle in.

"I don't go through life wondering if everyone's a psychopath," I said. "For instance, I know you aren't."

"Huh." Ben stared straight ahead through the windshield. "I think that's the nicest thing you've ever said to me."

"Don't let it go to your head."

A purple Dodge Charger pulled into the lot, and

Officer Tutsu waved it toward him, approached the window, leaned down, and appeared to give the driver specific parking directions. This was all as Ben and I had discussed with him earlier this morning before his overtime assignment. Tutsu's body cam would catch a solid glimpse of the occupants of each vehicle, who we'd review and catalog later.

Ben kept his eyes on the brick facade of the funeral home as he said, "There's a test for it." He groped around the open Bougie's donut box on the armrest between us. He grabbed the glazed blueberry without even looking at it. Damn. I'd been eyeing that one next.

"A test for what?" I asked, trying to forget about the donuts.

"For being a psycho. Doctors use it to diagnose."

"Oh. I know about *that*. It's interview based, though. No good."

He took a bite out of his blueberry donut and made a face before setting it back in the box, eyeing the selection, and grabbing a s'mores one instead. I watched him closely, not judging, but wondering if that meant blueberry was back in play.

"There has to be something, though," he said. "You always talk about micro-expressions. What about those? Yes, psychopaths are good at controlling their outward appearance, but micro-expressions are subconscious, right?"

"Oh sure, they have micro-expressions, but can you always tell what each one means? It's rare you catch one that's definitive."

Mouth full now, he said, "I tell ya"—he chewed further

so I could understand him—"I don't know how you live like that."

I didn't know either.

"Recognize him?" Ben gestured with his half-eaten s'mores donut at a slender white male in khaki slacks and a black dress shirt. The guy was approaching the front doors alone. His hands were in his pockets, his head down, but his gait seemed rushed, like he wanted to get this over with and move on with his day.

The man paused at the door to hold it open for two older women, and as he did so, I nabbed a straight-on view of his face. It clicked. "Dylan Elijah Fowler."

"What do we know about him?"

"His name was on the open mic sign-in sheet the night Cheryl died. And it was on the others they'd kept since mid-May. None before that, though."

Ben wiped crumbs from his mouth with the back of his wrist. "We got the sign-up lists?"

"Yeah, Heidi found the bulk of them in the ticket booth somewhere and passed them along day before yesterday."

Ben turned his attention back to Dylan Fowler, who had clearly gotten stuck on door duty for a string of incoming mourners who must've assumed he worked at the funeral home. They didn't even pretend to help him with the door, just walked straight past him. One older woman nodded her gratitude.

"This guy just showed up out of nowhere a couple weeks before the Blackstenius murder?" Ben asked.

"Looks like it. Haven't talked to Scott or Heidi about him yet, though."

"And you recognize this guy from...?"

"Facebook," I said. "Couldn't get much from his profile.

I gathered from what I could see of his public posts that he does something with kids, but I don't know what."

"Pedophile," Ben said. "Just look at him."

"I am," I said. "I don't see anything that screams, 'I want to have sex with children,' but you never can tell, I guess. I'm sure even child molesters hold open the door for the elderly every once in a while. We're not looking for pedophiles, though, Ben. Cheryl was twenty-six."

A line of vehicles formed, snaking out of the lot and stretching down the frontage road, as Officer Tutsu took his time getting each driver to roll down their side window so his camera could take inventory.

"What about him?" Ben pointed at another man approaching the doors. "Wait, is that Jordan Grossman?"

"Good memory," I said. "Yeah, that's him. Damn, he's fatter in real life."

"Aren't we all?" Ben brought the straw of his iced coffee to his lips. "He's the one Cheryl was flirting with before she was murdered, right?"

"According to Scott Ruiz."

"We haven't ruled him out?"

"I haven't ruled out anyone except *maybe* Mike Check."

Ben shut his eyes and inhaled. "Just because he was sleeping with Cheryl?"

"Like you said, he seemed into her. That psychology doesn't add up."

"You don't know that. Sure, you can guess, but only Mike knows what's going on in his head."

"Oh come on, Ben. The missing skin? The posing? You and I have seen a *lot* of murdered girlfriends, and none of the bodies have ever looked that fetishized. If Cheryl and

Mike had had *no* sexual history then I'd be the first to list him as a suspect. But this is not how angry boyfriends act. This is some other psychology at play."

"You're sure it can't be both?"

"I'm sure."

"Forgive me if I'm not. I don't disagree with you completely, but I'm also not a psychologist, so I'm open to all kinds of surprises."

I decided to let it drop, since we were clearly back at this impasse. Whatever happened, though, I wouldn't ignore that little voice inside my chest. It was becoming harder and harder to explain that to anyone else, though. And I had to admit: statistically speaking, when a woman was murdered in this city, her male partner was the killer.

I didn't like ignoring such stark data trends to go with my gut, but I liked it even less when I ignored my intuition only to realize too late that it'd been steering me right all along.

"What's the latest on Grossman?" Ben asked.

I shrugged and grabbed the blueberry donut from the box, ignoring the bite out of it. "He left a freaking essay on her Facebook wall yesterday, probably in preparation for all the traffic it'll get as a result of the funeral. I wouldn't be surprised if he writes another one in the guestbook."

Ben grunted his disgust.

"Speaking of which," I added, "you talked with the Blacksteniuses about the guestbook, right?"

"Yep. They agreed to let us make photocopies if it helps with the investigation."

A news van hardly got its front wheels onto the funeral home property before Officer Tutsu charged forward, shaking his head and waving the driver back out again.

"There they are," Ben said. "Surprised it took them so long."

"Think he needs help?"

Tutsu continued to gesture wildly and approached the van's driver's-side window.

"Nah. Looks like he's got it locked down."

Ben was correct. Tutsu had the van backing awkwardly out onto the frontage road in no time. Of course media wanted to film the service. Despite the department's attempt to keep the full extent of the murder secret, they couldn't seal it up airtight. Not when Mike Check kept telling everyone what he'd seen. Probably trying to wring as much sympathy sex out of it as he could.

Just because I didn't think he was a killer didn't mean he wasn't an absolute slimeball.

There were a few details about the murder scene that weren't yet public knowledge—Mike had never mentioned the broken leg or missing skin in his official statement, for one—and those few details would likely prove crucial in implicating someone eventually.

Even still, the local news stations had sniffed out enough gruesome details to make a compelling tale of it. But luck was on our side at the funeral. POTUS had been advocating for Russia at the G7 summit, and national news could talk of nothing else. Which meant there was no room on the front page for the brutal murder of a single woman. Not even a pretty, young, white one.

What was bad news for the country, and probably the world, was good news for our investigation.

If there was a second murder, though...

"There's Scott," Ben said.

I thought I'd glimpsed them pulling up in their goofy

Nissan LEAF a few minutes before, but I hadn't been certain it was the Ruizes through the tinted windows.

Scott Ruiz strolled past the front of the building toward the entrance. The bum had really outdone himself this morning, rocking a black bowling shirt and black Velcro water sandals for the somber occasion.

"Where's his wife?" I asked.

Sudden movement on my right made me jump a split second before there was a knock on the car's window.

"Found her," I muttered.

I hit the button, and my window rolled down as I tried not to flinch at the eyeful of freckled cleavage only a few inches away from my face.

"Sorry, I didn't mean to sneak up." Heidi's hair was teased into a large knot on the top of her head, and from that close, it was clear she wasn't one of those women who removed her mascara each night before bed. Just add a little more in the morning. Glob it on. I hoped it was waterproof, or she was at risk of looking like a lost member of Kiss before the service wrapped.

"No problem," Ben said, leaning over the center console to smile up at her. "What can we help you with?"

"I wondered if you would be here. I just want to see if you've learned anything new, maybe get an update."

It was easy enough for me to slap a dumb smile on my face in times like these when I knew Ben would have something polite to say. Left to my own devices, only smart-ass responses would have tumbled from my lips. Things like "We found out who the killer is, but we're just lying low for a while to see if he kills again," or "If you're so interested, why don't you jump on the task force? We could really use the help of a certifiable genius like you."

There was no reason why we would tell Heidi anything. Because, while the odds of the killer being a woman were next to none, we had to assume anyone could have done it until we had a clear suspect.

"We're still gathering evidence and information," Ben said. "These things can take some time."

"Do you think the person who did it will be here? At her funeral?"

"We don't know."

"Sweet Jesus," she said, straightening suddenly and hiking up the front of her black spaghetti-strap tank, which had slipped down to reveal the crests of a crimson bra.

When she leaned over again, her tone carried a jagged edge to it. "You know it's not exactly helping business around the club that a woman was murdered, and *y'all* still haven't done your job and caught the one who did it." She braced a forearm on the open window. "I mean, Christ! How hard can it be to catch a deranged killer? They're obviously not right in the head. They can't be that smart!"

"I understand," Ben crooned. "We're working on it. And I have full confidence that when we finally bring someone in, it'll be the right person."

"Shit, I should hope so. Otherwise, why do my taxes keep paying your salary?"

She straightened again, and I was already rolling up the window as I added, "Nice talking with you, Mrs. Ruiz. I'm sure it'll be a beautiful service."

We watched the woman stomp back to her husband, who was waiting dutifully by the front door for her.

"She lives in *Pflugerville*," Ben said, glaring after her.

"Yeah, I don't think she understands how taxes work.

But then again, she doesn't seem to understand how a lot of things work." I paused. "That was a little abrupt, wasn't it?"

"You tell me. This is the first time I've met her. Is she a *bruja loca* all the time?"

"She didn't strike me that way in Laugh Attack at all. The hot and cold is certainly strange."

Ben sipped his iced coffee until he hit all air in the bottom. "Whatever. Screw her. Who else are we looking for today?"

As I consulted the list again, my phone buzzed in my back pocket. Ben's buzzed a couple seconds later, when I already had mine out and was unlocking the screen. "DNA results are back."

"That was quick," Ben said, tapping away at his screen.

"Guess someone decided it was worth prioritizing." I opened the PDF from the lab and zoomed in, squinting at the report. Holy hell, was I already to the age where I needed cheaters just to see my screen? I zoomed in just a little more and dragged the document around with two fingers until I found what I needed. "I smelled bleach at the scene. Looks like it was poured on her hands and probably wiped under her nails. Well, fuck. That'll do it."

"No shit. Not a single complete profile? We got nothing to go on?"

"Looks like it." I put down my phone. "Hang on, does this mean DNA evidence isn't always a silver bullet? That's absurd."

Ben chuckled and set his phone in the coin holder of his door. "Guess we'll have to do this the old-fashioned way."

"I'm in," I said around a mouthful of donut. "Let's find

the last guy who filed a complaint against one of us and railroad him."

"That's not— Eh, you might have a point." He opened the donut box and stared down at the emptiness inside. "Goddamn you, Capone. I bought those. There were a half-dozen and I only had two."

"So what?" I said around the last bite. "My taxes pay your salary."

ELEVEN

June 19th, 2018

13 days since Blackstenius murder

The sliver of moon overhead reflected off the surface of Lady Bird Lake as he waited on the rocky bank for his date to meet him. Of course she'd come. She wanted something from him.

And she'd been drinking. He'd waited and watched until she was a few drinks in before he approached her. He'd needed her to be compliant but not sloshed. It wouldn't be fun if she was too drunk to comprehend, to be afraid.

People stumbled around their entire lives with the question of their death hanging over them—when would it happen? How? He'd observed the magical thinking that death might wait until a decent moment, might give each person a chance to make something of themselves before swooping in. Watching that hope dashed, seeing the moment it blinked out in their eyes, was a thrill he wouldn't give up for anything.

Death came for each person whenever the hell it wanted.

And, sometimes, whenever the hell *he* wanted.

The crunch of arhythmic footsteps yanked him from his thoughts, and he scrambled to his feet, peeking out from behind the tall weeds. It was her, all right. Showtime.

His heart raced with anticipation, but he wasn't nervous. His was the heightened sense of a predator who already knew his prey's fate was sealed.

Just look at that dress she was wearing, all gold sequins and not much else. Her bubblegum-pink high heels made the blood rush to his groin. He'd brought her a pair, but this was better. Not quite the right color or shape, but more *natural*.

"There you are," she said. A sheen of sweat caked her foundation and faded her lower eyeliner into dark semicircles. The shimmer of her perspiration in the moonlight proceeded down her neck, across her shoulders.

"What took you so long?" he asked.

"Are you kidding me? I had to find the damn place."

She was too loud. Much too loud.

He closed the distance in a few long strides, the gravel of the hiking trail crunching underfoot.

"So?" she said, quieter now. "What's the big news?"

"Were you followed?" he asked, enjoying how little concern he felt for such a matter. He was slipping into the zone. This was where he excelled. Even if she had been followed, he knew he could take care of it.

"Was I *followed*?" She laughed incredulously. "By who, the *homeless*? We're not spies here. No one's bored enough to follow me anywhere." She swatted at a mosquito on her arm. "Ugh, can you just tell me whatever you wanted to tell me so I can get out of here?"

"Not tell. Show. Follow me."

He led her to the spot by the water. Overgrown milkweeds and dry grasses obscured them from the view of anyone on the trail.

"Oh." Her voice fell heavy with disappointment as she took in the surroundings. "I see." She sighed. "I kind of thought it was going to be like this. I figured you were kind of a creep, but I didn't have you pegged for this exactly. Ah well."

When she went to her knees in front of him and reached for his fly, he stopped her. "Leslie, what are you doing?"

She looked up at him from beneath heavy false lashes. "This is why you brought me out here, right? You can hook me up with a big opportunity, but you want to get sucked off first. I mean, I'll do it as long as you actually follow through."

"No, no, no," he said, reaching down and pulling her to her feet. "That's not it at all."

"Oh."

He couldn't tell if her blush was from embarrassment or the alcohol.

"Then why did you drag me all the way out here?" She looked around, and he let her. He wanted her to put the pieces together for herself. He needed her to realize on her own that it was already too late, that she was hopelessly caught in his trap.

"Wait," she said. Her expression morphed, and he knew she'd finally spotted it. He followed her gaze to the thick black cable coiled like a snake on the ground. Her gaze traveled up to meet his, and he saw the final piece click into place behind those glassy eyes. Word had gotten around about Cheryl. Leslie knew what the XLR cable meant.

"What's that for?" she asked breathlessly.

"I want you to do your set for me." He'd string her along if he could. Serve her up alternate endings to this scene to keep her hope for survival treading water.

"Out *here*?"

"Why not? If you're good, I'll pull some strings, maybe get you to open for a big name."

She rose slowly to her feet, keeping her eyes on the wound cable. There wasn't a mic attached to it. He had no need of one.

As soon as she had her legs under her, she took a quick step back from him.

Good for her. She wasn't frozen to the spot. She may dress like a bimbo and use that persona for the stage, but he'd caught glimpses of a quick mind behind it all. He'd known it was nothing but an act up there.

She'd put together a puzzle the police hadn't yet cracked. And now there was only one way this could end.

His way.

As fun as it would have been to chase her down, to allow her the hope of escape only to overcome her and steal that hope all over again, he wouldn't let her run. Maybe if they had been somewhere more remote, but not here, in the small hiding spot in the middle of the city.

"Come on, Leslie. Let me hear your set."

She took another step back up the gravelly slope, and her left high heel caught on a rock and snapped. Her ankle rolled beneath her. She sucked in air but managed to keep her balance. "No, thanks. I'd rather earn my way than have—"

"Fuck it," he said, and then he brought down the heel of his boot onto her shin.

Game on.

TWELVE

June 20th, 2018

14 days since Blackstenius murder

The rising sun struggled to break through the oppressive blanket of humidity overhead as Ben Escobar and I stood shoulder to shoulder on the empty hike-and-bike trail of Lady Bird Lake, taking in the body of Leslie Marie Scopes.

"You can say it," he urged, and I could tell he was bracing himself. "Just say it."

"No way," I replied.

"Dana."

"I just don't think we have enough evidence yet to say whether or not this was done by the same guy who killed Cheryl."

The body of Leslie Scopes, IDed from the driver's license wedged between her cleavage, hung from the dog-bag dispenser where she'd been tied up with an XLR cable and put on display. Her left shin was bent at a nightmarish angle, and the fuchsia heel of the corresponding shoe had snapped clean off.

Her wrists bound, the cord winding up around her neck and then over the doggy waste station, winglike stripes of skin missing on her back, the aggressive aroma of bleach in the air—I struggled to find a way this could've mirrored Cheryl Blackstenius' murder any more. And then I found one: this victim was wearing high heels, too. Not the greatest footwear for a hike-and-bike trail. I filed the incongruity away for later.

I shook my head mournfully. "If *only* there were similarities between the crime scenes. But I just don't see any here. None at all."

"God's sake, Capone," Ben muttered.

Leslie had been found by a jogger just before sunrise. The early-morning call from Pops had made me forgo my predawn kayaking time on this very lake. I'd make it up to Sadie later, but it might be a while before I could head back to the apartment. I'd have to text Ariadna when I got a chance.

Sergeant Popov was already on scene when Ben and I had arrived in separate vehicles minutes before. He finished giving directions to the technician and joined as we gazed at the dead woman baking in the sun. "Already sent word to the FBI."

"I don't know why you would bother them with this," I said. "This strikes me as a totally isolated incident. Unlike anything we've ever seen."

Popov shot me a warning look, and I backed off on the sarcasm. For now.

"We're already looking into the victim," he said. "We

need to see who she might know in common with Cheryl. Could have just been a case of wrong place, wrong time."

I scoffed. I couldn't help it. This charade of keeping all options open was growing absolutely ridiculous. "Women know better than to walk around a place like this at night. Even intoxicated women." I turned to Popov. "I don't mean to throw a bunch of criminology jargon at you all at once, but you *are* aware men like to kill us lady folk, right?"

Popov pressed his lips together and grunted.

"No," I continued, "someone lured her down here. Someone she knew and presumably trusted. Or maybe someone who had something on her and was threatening to spill, but I doubt that. What's a nobody like her got to hide?" I felt a sharp pang in my chest at calling this poor, stolen life a "nobody," but there wasn't any point in taking it back or apologizing. No one home inside that skull of hers to apologize *to*. "And besides, I already know a little something about her."

"Oh yeah?" Popov said. "Enlighten us, please."

"Leslie Scopes, you said. Her name was on the sign-up sheet for the Laugh Attack open mic the night of Cheryl's murder. It also appeared on most of the ones Heidi Ruiz gave us dating back over the last few months leading up to the first murder."

"We got those in a week ago," barked Popov. "You sure you've got the right name?"

"Yes, I'm sure I got the right name. But here." I pulled out my city phone and flipped through the photos until I found it. "I snapped a picture of the list for an instance such as this where my memory was not to be believed." I didn't feel the need to look at the list myself to double-check. Enough people questioned my memory as it was; I didn't make a practice of doing it to myself.

"Damn," said Popov. "I think we might need to contact all the other women on that list."

"And the men," I added. "You should contact them as well."

He narrowed his eyes at me as if *that* would be enough to stop me in my tracks when I was just getting started.

He should have learned by now. Not *my* fault he hadn't.

"Oh, come on, Sarge. Just because we don't know if the unsub has killed a man doesn't mean he hasn't or that he won't. And besides, there's a chance one of the people on these lists is our guy. If he knows we're checking in on everyone who's signed up, the odds of another Laugh Attack comedian being the next target go way down. We'll keep those women safe."

"He'll just move on to some other group then."

I grinned. "So you *do* think it's a serial killer. Good to know."

Popov snapped his mouth shut then grunted again. "Fine. We'll do it your way until the FBI tells us differently." Then he stomped off to make some calls.

"She's a comedian, too," Ben muttered, his arms crossed tightly in front of his chest. "Dammit."

"Yep. Don't tell anyone, but I'm not exactly thrilled about being right. I mean, sure, it *feels* great, but, you know. Circumstances." I let my eyes roam over the sunbaked corpse in front of me. "I wonder if *her* material was solid, but the delivery sucked."

We exchanged glances, and he said, "Does that mean you're boarding the Mike Check bandwagon?"

"Slow down. It's just a thought. I do think we should learn a little more about her comedy, though." I searched around for someone from the M.E.'s department. Someone needed to get Leslie in a freezer before she baked through. The flies from the bagged dog shit had already found their new quarry. It was yet another similarity between the murders. Was that detail intentional? The first one tied to a dumpster, the second to a doggy waste station? Flies? Was that an important element in this macabre routine?

"The missing skin," Ben said. "Still going with angel wings?"

I took another look. "Well, I've never seen angel wings, so I'm no expert. But it's not a stretch to imagine the unsub has some weird innocence obsession with his victims. Nothing to indicate he's picking off virgins or anything. Hell, these could be fairy—"

"Oh, for chrissakes..."

I looked up quickly, thinking Ben's grumbling had been intended for me. Like maybe the guy had secretly hated fairies all these years, and the mere mention of them set him off. I found the spot where he had been just standing unoccupied. He was marching toward the edge of the lake, only twenty yards away, and waving his arms in the air to get the attention of the kayaker. The idiot had his phone out and was taking pictures. Typical. Probably gonna post them on his Instagram Stories. Not quite main-feed-worthy. Not from that distance, at least.

"This is an active crime scene," Ben shouted as the kayaker finished snapping his pics and shoved his phone away like the flailing detective might wade out there and confiscate it. "Have some freaking respect!"

On his way back up the muddy slope, he paused and stared at something on the ground. "Dana, get a tech over here. We have shoe prints."

After tracking down the nearest tech, I met Ben where he stood guard. "Looks like more than just shoe prints." I gestured to the indentation in the mud leading up to the gravelly trail. "Either this place has alligators or Leslie's body was dragged from over here." I surveyed the area. It was a secluded little spot, would provide a good bit of visual shelter at night. If someone had walked up and seen movement, they would have assumed it was an animal or, more likely, a homeless person relieving himself, and they would have moved along quickly.

"None of these looks especially useful," I said, pushing a sweaty strand of hair off my forehead with the back of my wrist. "No sign of tread, each one sliding around a little."

"Just looking at them, though, they look like boots, don't they?"

"Sure do," I said. "And not just any boots."

"Right. With that pointed toe? Cowboy boots for sure."

"Christ. Tell me we don't have a killer cowboy on our hands."

We stepped aside for the tech to come in and get what casting she could of the imprints.

"The Cowboy Strangler is a catchy name," Ben said as we made it back onto the gravel. The tiny rocks clung to the mud on the bottom and sides of my shoes, making my feet even heavier.

"I'll do you one better: the Wrangler Strangler."

"Shit, Capone. That's solid." He paused. "You ever think about moving the hell out of Texas?"

"And what, miss out on this pleasant morning weather? No thanks." I wiped at a fat droplet of sweat inching down my temple as the two of us went back to gathering evidence.

THIRTEEN

June 25th, 2018

19 days since Blackstenius murder

Five days had passed since Leslie Scopes' body had been found. Victim number two. That we knew of.

It'd been a long and fruitless five days.

A lot of good the boot prints in the mud by the lake had done for us. Shoe-print evidence was shaky science at best anyway, especially in a public place. Besides telling us that the unsub owned a pair of vintage cowboy boots somewhere in the size range of men's nine to twelve, it didn't narrow down the pool at all, since everyone we were looking at had a shoe size in that range and could have owned boots like that. We were in Austin, Texas. Even the hipsters owned a pair.

We'd paid Mike Check a visit at his home almost immediately, and that yielded a whole lot of nothing. He claimed he only knew her vaguely, insisted they'd never slept together, and provided about as weak of an alibi as existed: he was home sleeping at the time of Leslie's murder. If we gleaned any important tidbits from that discussion, I sure as hell hadn't noticed them. Maybe he was a good liar, maybe he was innocent, but he was definitely an asshole. He'd described the latest victim as "the chubby blonde who thought she was Amy Schumer." Not that her weight was relevant or that I would have described the victim as "chubby," but the word made me want to use his Adam's apple as a punching bag.

Ben was on his third cup of coffee since lunch when he leaned over his desk to squint at his computer screen. "Just like we thought. Total bust on the DNA."

I tore my eyes from my monitor where I'd spent the last two hours poring over Leslie Scopes' blog. At first, I'd just scanned the comments for anything of interest, but as it turned out, the blog itself was quite entertaining. Witty, pointed, pulled no punches. I had a dozen years on Leslie Scopes (and counting), but I got the impression that I would've enjoyed a happy hour with the deceased if fate had ever brought us together in that way, rather than in this one. Her posts were full of amusing observations and good material overall. Still no clue how it translated to the stage, though, no idea about her delivery.

I sighed and turned my attention to Ben. "Figures. But I might've found another close friend of hers to look into."

"Jesus, another?" He let out a deep breath. "I don't feel like the last few we talked to did us much good. The ones from Laugh Attack knew her, but they didn't give us jack. The others hadn't ever heard of Cheryl. You really think this one's the winner?"

I reached for my coffee cup and found it empty. Damn. "Nah, probably not."

Had any of Leslie's friends read this blog? The way they'd described her in our interviews made it seem like she was all party, like a sorority girl crossbred with an ice shot block. More Smirnoff than sense.

But that just didn't square with the rapier wit of her blog. It occurred to me that Leslie had most likely been an intensely introspective introvert struggling to exist in an extroverted world. I was intimately familiar with how that went, how that mismatch often required alcohol to quiet the inner voice and lubricate conversation.

I flashed to some of my less-wise decisions during my freshman year of college, back when I thought I had a chance of rebuilding a normal life for myself, just after the name change and before Googling potential dates had become commonplace. I was pretty sure my liver was *still* trying to recover from that foolhardy attempt at fitting in.

Ben tapped his pen on the desk, pulling me from a fuzzy memory where some frat guy whose name I'd never learned was asking me to step off the bar at Hemingway's, where I'd been strip-dancing to Britney Spears. *Yeesh.*

"Any progress with mutual friends of the victims?" Ben asked.

"I talked with Leslie's mother, and she's trying to get the login for her daughter's Facebook page. Leslie didn't have a legacy contact set up in case of her death, so Mrs. Scopes has to jump through all the hoops by presenting the death certificate and so on. Needless to say, the woman's got other things on her mind right now, and progress is slow. But she said she'll let me poke around the friends list once she has access."

Ben stopped tapping and brought the clicker end of the pen to his lips. "Why comedians, you think?"

"Comedy is murder." When he shot me a look, I said, "I don't know, Ben. So far, we've only identified two victims with this killer's signature. Sure, both were aspiring comedians, but two dots form a line, not a pattern."

"Said the person who saw one murder and immediately thought *serial killer*. You really think the comedy connection might be a coincidence?"

"Could be. The unsub may be a comedian himself, so he's just targeting women he knows, ones in his immediate vicinity. And because he's a comedian, they happen to be comedians. I mean, have you and I been talking to the same dudes lately? Half of them are programmers at Google or Oracle and only ever encounter women at Laugh Attack. That would be their pool to draw from. But maybe the next vic, god forbid, won't have any connection to the club. If that's the case, and we can find any mutual friends between her and the other two, it won't be too hard to triangulate who we're dealing with." I paused, running down the list again. I just knew there was something we were missing. People always wanted criminals to be masterminds, but that was almost never the case. More times than not, they were stupid and pitiably bad at crime. This guy might be an anomaly, though. Or maybe we were just overlooking something obvious.

"You checked the footage from that new security camera in the back of the club lately?" I ask.

"No, actually. Checked it day before last. Wanna review it now?"

"Might as well."

Ben logged into the shared storage with his credentials, and I moved around our desks to peer over his shoulder at the monitor. The device was motion-activated, and there were a handful of unreviewed records listed with time stamps, all from this weekend.

That we'd covertly installed exterior cameras covering the front and back of the club was our department's little secret. I didn't have much interest in the one out front—it caught too much movement and covered too public of a space for us to expect anything useful to happen there. But the camera hidden in the back, right next to the useless one already there—I had a good feeling about that one.

Ben clicked the first one from Saturday night, and the video window popped open. The equipment was set up to record retroactively thirty seconds before the motion was detected, so he fast-forwarded through the part where nothing was happening. The camera was positioned over the back door, angled down on the stoop, and had a straight shot of the area next to the dumpster where Cheryl had been found.

At first, it was just the top of a head on the screen, but I recognized the scraggly hair soon enough.

Scott Ruiz stepped out onto the back step, and at first, I couldn't believe what I was seeing. He was clutching the side of his head and staring straight at the murder spot. He mumbled something, but I couldn't make it out. Talking to the deceased? Reliving the thrill?

"What's he—"

Then I noticed the cell phone in his hand. "Oh." He turned, angling so I could see him in profile as he stared at the ground and shifted his weight, speaking to someone on the phone. I couldn't hear him well enough to guess who he was chatting with, but there was nothing suspicious about the owner of the club stepping outside to take a call.

Before long, he hung up and strolled back inside

without a second look at the spot by the dumpster. It was definitely creepy that he could be back there carrying on a conversation so nonchalantly while only feet from where someone he'd known was brutally murdered less than a month before. But then again, Laugh Attack had been his home away from home for decades. Maybe he had enough positive memories of the place that one bad one didn't taint all the rest.

The next video, also Saturday night, could be quickly dismissed. In it, two young women stepped onto the back stoop, clearly unaware of being recorded. They passed a joint back and forth. The back door opened, but I couldn't see who was there, only heard a muffled male voice. Mike Check? The women nodded, and one licked her fingers and crushed out the joint, tucking it into a little baggie and slipping it into the back pocket of her pants.

Third in the queue, from late Saturday night, showed Mike Check stepping outside with a giant black trash bag in his hand. He paused on the back step and stared directly at the spot where Cheryl's body had been. Five, ten seconds passed, and then he snapped out of it, tossed the bag into the dumpster, and returned inside without a second look. The video ended.

"What do you think?" Ben asked.

"Couldn't see his face, could we? It makes sense for him to be back there for trash duty."

"He stared at the spot for an awful long time."

"He did. It's something the guilty party would do. But it's also something a traumatized but innocent man who discovered a body there might do. For all we know, he was having flashbacks to goddamned Bosnia."

The next video was from Sunday evening: the door

opened, and Heidi Ruiz stepped out, followed by none other than Jordan Grossman. My instincts told me right away that this wasn't right. And sure enough, the door had hardly closed behind them before he looked around for observers then moved in on her. He grabbed for her ass, but she didn't slap him across the face, as a woman who had no interest might. Instead, she fought back a smile, deflected his arm playfully, and *giggled*. Jordan pulled a vape from his pocket and sucked on it. Heidi snuck a guilty glance around before leaning against the building and striking up a conversation. Nothing about his body language indicated he cared what came out of her mouth. In another couple of minutes, they headed back inside.

"What do you think that's about?" Ben said.

"You know what that's about."

"You think *Scott* knows what that's about?"

I frowned. "I doubt it. Whether he would care is something different, though."

"I'll leave it up to you to advise Heidi not to carry on with a person of interest in a murder investigation," Ben said. "You know, woman to woman."

"Oh gee, thanks." Heidi should've already known better. She'd been there when Scott said he saw Cheryl and Jordan flirting the night of the murder.

A strange possibility occurred to me. Maybe Scott *did* know about the affair, or at least suspected. If that were the case, hinting that Heidi's lover was flirting with someone else might have just been a vindictive move to get at his wife. Or maybe he'd been hoping to get Jordan investigated as payback. Either way, it threw his initial observation about Jordan into question for me.

The next video was from later on Sunday. Mike Check

taking out the trash again. This time, he didn't spare a single glance for the murder spot. Instead, he fixed his eyes ahead as if intent on *not* looking at it. He marched over, tossed the bag, then marched right back in.

Interesting.

The last video was from late Sunday, and the time stamp had it logged hours after the club had closed. Promising.

I gripped the back of Ben's chair tighter as he pulled up the video.

Nothing, nothing, nothing, then a figure walked into the frame from the side. He wasn't coming out of Laugh Attack; he was coming down the alley from the street. He was hunched, moving slowly, and it was tricky to make out much of his face in the darkness as he shuffled straight for the obscured spot behind the dumpster. The exact location where the body had been discovered.

"Oh, goddammit," I said, turning my eyes away as soon as the man dropped his drawers and began to defecate on the cement. Ben didn't click out of the window immediately like I would've done but instead angled his head slightly away, cringing while keeping his eyes on the screen to make sure he didn't miss any possible leads. Like I've said, a consummate cop, that one.

"I can smell it through the video," I said, returning to my desk as he finally clicked out of the pop-up window.

He was still cringing as he said, "Think it could be related? Maybe that's our guy, and he gets off on defecating at his murder sites?"

I narrowed my eyes at him. "No. I don't think that homeless man is our unsub. I think he found a place that was obscured from the view of the street and had to take a shit. And so that's what he did." I paused, bracing myself before asking, "What he do after he finished? Anything strange?"

"He didn't wipe, if that's what you're wondering," Ben replied. "No. Nothing strange. He left the alley."

That had been the last of the videos from the weekend, and I wasn't sorry about it. There would undoubtedly be more in a few hours, once Laugh Attack's open mic crowd began to arrive and step out back for a smoke, but for now, we were all caught up.

"Can't say any of that was particularly helpful," Ben remarked. "Interesting, sure, but nothing much to act on other than keeping an eye on Heidi."

A new thought seeped in slowly. Once it had some bulk to it, I said, "You think that's why Heidi was so aggressive in the parking lot at the funeral the other day? You think she's worried about us finding out about her affair with Grossman?"

Ben's eyebrows lifted toward his dark, gelled hair, and he pouted. "Could be. Yeah, it would make sense."

I shrugged. "Or she's just a bitch."

"Or that." Ben scanned the documents littering his desk. "And you feel good about ruling out a possible romantic relationship between Leslie Scopes and Mike Check?"

"He says it never happened, and no one else has mentioned a thing about it, even when we asked directly." It'd been a long few days of interviews since discovering Leslie's body. Two deaths in a small community like the comedy scene in under a month had made for some real screwball conversations full of paranoia and egocentrism.

But none had even so much as hinted at that particular romantic relationship.

One woman we'd spoken with, one of the few women who was a regular at the open mics, bitterly told us that Leslie had probably screwed someone's boyfriend and gotten what was coming to her. A few minutes further on into that conversation, though, it was apparent that the interviewee was under the impression Leslie had screwed *her* boyfriend. And a few minutes after that, it became clear that she actually had no idea who Leslie was and had confused her with a comic named Lauren Smith, who had moved to New Orleans last April.

Then there was the squirrelly nerd boy who lived and worked at the new Oracle campus. He derailed the conversation with a five-minute screed against "the Mexicans" and how they had been killing white women and trying to frame white men for it since the late sixties to start the next civil war.

And yet another Caucasian male, who was less of a nerd and more of the type who would shoot up a school, seemed *determined* to make us believe he'd murdered both the women without saying so much. Lots of "I didn't do it... but if I had..." and "I bet she looked amazing all tied up" and "Whoever did that must be a real criminal genius." But a few pointed questions about the actual murder scene made it clear he was not our guy. Definitely worth keeping an eye on, though, in case a golden opportunity arose to confiscate all of his guns.

Detective Towers entered the office, marching over to our desks by the window. He slapped a file against the palm of his hand and waggled his eyebrows like he was about to deliver shocking paternity test results.

"Popov asked me to hand this off to you." He flapped the folder in front of Ben's face.

"Great. I'm one manila file short today. Oh wait, is there something *in it*?"

"Course there is," Towers said, missing the sarcasm completely. "Preliminary FBI profile on the killer. Hot off the press. I read over it already. Airtight as hell. If you can't wrap this thing up by the end of the week, I'm gonna have serious doubts about youse guys' ability to do this job."

While his attention was on Ben, I snatched the file from his hand. "Thank you." I flipped it open.

Ben asked, "Did Sarge mention anything about when we can expect agents buzzing around here?"

"He said he hasn't requested them yet, but I have a feeling he will soon. Shit's already hit the news. City's gonna be flipping out in no time. And if another girl turns up..."

"Yeah," I said, "we got it," and dismissed Towers with a flick of the wrist.

Ben pushed past the other detective, circling the desks to read over my shoulder.

"Yeah, well, you two have at it," Towers said awkwardly before showing himself out again.

I only needed to skim it before I formed a clear opinion. I shoved the papers into Ben's hands for him to finish at his own pace.

"Not impressed?" he asked, taking it back to his desk.

"I'm impressed these jokers still manage to get a government paycheck, and that's not exactly a high bar. The FBI might have been helpful with this kind of thing forty years ago. But this report doesn't tell us anything DIY sleuths wouldn't guess from watching a few true crime documentaries."

Ben continued to flip through it. "It's broad, but it doesn't mean they're wrong."

I felt the pinprick of a tension headache spark to life between my eyes as I recited the facts I'd just read. "Caucasian male, twenty-five to thirty-nine, lives with mother or overbearing female relative, loner? They're describing ninety percent of all male comedians in this town. We already suspect it's one of them. They might as well have added that our unsub enjoys dick jokes, can't wait for Louis CK's comeback tour, and believes women are naturally less funny than men."

Ben conceded with a nod. "I hear you. This bit about him watching BDSM porn but not participating in the community himself is..."

"Groundbreaking?" I said sarcastically.

"Right. This, though." He pointed to the page. "They even have his vehicle picked out."

"Please. It just says, 'Similar suspects have been known to drive a Prius or other electric/hybrid vehicle.'"

"Saying he drives a Prius is pretty specific."

"Sure, except it doesn't say that. Maybe he drives a Tesla. Or whatever the hell that thing was that BMW put out a couple years ago. Or maybe he drives a gas-guzzling truck. Saying similar suspects drove a particular type of vehicle doesn't mean our unsub does."

"You think they'd include it if the odds of it were slim?"

"No. The Bureau is chock-full of hubris, but they're smart enough to play their odds. I imagine the fact that the murders took place in the liberal oasis of Austin, Texas, helped them narrow down the eco-friendly car bit." I sighed. "The only useful thing they gave us is that they couldn't match the main elements of it—the signature and MO—to any previous incidents in their database. So, either those parts have changed, or this guy has killed before and we just haven't found the bodies yet." I paused. "Wait, let me see that again real quick." He handed it across our desks, and I accepted it from him before slam-dunking it into the wastebasket. "There."

Ben leaned his head to the side like a patient mother. "You sure about that? We're not exactly overwhelmed with hot leads."

"Yeah. I'm sure. Besides, I have a much better idea for getting the information we want. If we think the killer hangs out around Laugh Attack, then why in the hell are we sitting here and not poking around there?"

He squinted at me. "Are you proposing an official operation?"

I flashed him a pleading and innocent grin. "Unofficial?"

"Nope. Nuh-uh. You have to be wired up at the very least. And the recordings will be official evidence."

"Fine," I said, holding up my hands in surrender. "As long as I don't have Towers and Krantz as an entourage, I guess I can accept all the rest."

FOURTEEN

With preliminary plans for the undercover visit to Laugh Attack knocked out, Ben insisted that we left work at a decent hour. That term had always confused me, "decent hour," especially when referring to any time period between three thirty and six thirty in the afternoon. If there was an hour where people were most decent to each other, it was definitely not rush hour, which was where I found myself as I left the station and headed home.

As I finally pulled into my complex, I was dazed from gridlock and exhausted from yelling at rude drivers. I noticed the time on my dash, and it occurred to me that I could take Sadie for a solid walk and still make it over to Baker's Bar and Grill for the first round of their trivia night.

The courtyard was uncharacteristically empty as I lugged my bags across it, but I chalked that up to it being dinnertime. The stillness in this normally busy area reminded me of a lull in a group conversation: inevitable but also defying the odds.

The community bulletin board was littered with old,

rain-stained advertisements for lawn services and multilevel marketing schemes, but the fresh, crisp white of a new sheet tacked on top caught my attention.

Lost cat. Snowball. 2 yrs.

I didn't know what people expected to happen to their cats when they let them run around outside near a parking lot and a major road. Cats were pretty savvy, but if they got freaked out, their reactions went to hell. You could only dodge so many cars before your number came up. I can't tell you how many cats I'd cleaned up back when I was on patrol. Dogs, too. It's not technically our job as cops, but we do it anyway to avoid people swerving around the big-ass vultures and to allow the poor beasts a little peace and dignity. After all, they might have been someone's family member.

My desire to hold Sadie pulled me away from the bulletin board, and I started to reconsider my plan of leaving her to go to trivia.

Dropping my heavy duffel on the breezeway, I knocked on Ariadna's door. My girl barked protectively on the other side, and a moment later, all five-foot-two of Ariadna greeted me while maintaining a grip on Sadie's collar. The pittie yanked hard, and my neighbor was forced to let go if she wanted to keep all her fingers attached.

"I didn't get a chance to walk her today," she said. "Long day. Flat tire. Didn't get home till late, then it's too hot today."

"*Please* don't worry about that. You fix the flat?"

"Yes, I—" Sadie took off toward the stairs, her usual routine, and Ariadna's eyes opened wide. "Oh, no, no. Sadie. Come back!"

"She'll come back."

"No, there was a dead squirrel down there earlier. I don't want her to eat it."

I leaned over the railing to check, but the dog was just making her usual rounds, so I turned back to Ariadna. "Where was it?"

"Under the stairs across the way," she said. "The Carrera kids were over there poking at it when I came home this afternoon. I told them to knock it off. Maybe someone already cleaned it up."

"I'll check. There was a dead one a few weeks back. Maybe they're sick or something."

I whistled for Sadie, and she came bounding up the stairs, all muscle. I could see how people would be scared of an animal like her. But pits were the Dwayne Johnsons of dogs. They could do some real damage, but they were more into hugs.

Once I let Sadie inside and heard the intense lapping in the kitchen, I grabbed a pair of my latex gloves and a trash bag, closed the door, and made for the courtyard on squirrel duty.

As I approached the stairs Ariadna had pointed out, my mind was already deep into the what-ifs of a rabies outbreak. It just took one case to go public before panic set in, and every hot, slobbery dog was suddenly thought to be a deranged rabies machine, brimming over with deadly froth. We'd had one of those scares eight or nine years before, and by the end of it, I thought I was going to lose my mind every time a rabies call came up on the monitor. Got to pet a lot of sweet dogs, though.

But when I found the squirrel, the cause of death was so clearly not an illness that my breath caught in my chest. The squirrel was on its back, head gone. Any hope that a larger animal could have done this was erased by the fact that the separation point was a clean cut, like the work of a guillotine.

There was a slit up the animal's belly, flaying it, the guts spilling over. Ants were already making a meal out of those.

A squeal behind me made me jump. But it was just Briana and Santos, two elementary-aged neighbors. Santos was flinging one of those sticky hands you get from a machine for two quarters at Briana, who squealed again and dodged it. The hand stuck to the rusted-out community grill instead.

"Hey," I called to them.

They stopped what they were doing and turned guilty expressions my way.

"Do either of you know what happened to this squirrel?"

Briana shook her head emphatically, but her eyes were oddly wide. Her parents must have told her I was a cop.

"I seen it earlier," Santos said, trotting over.

I shooed him away. "I'm cleaning it up. Y'all get on with whatever you're doing."

I slipped on my gloves and stared down at the mutilated creature again. Could it be anything other than what my mind jumped to right away? Could a raccoon have done this? A dog? Hell, a coyote? We were in the city limits, but not far from the southeast edge, and small packs of coyotes still came through sometimes.

My experience, let alone my eyes, told me no. This wasn't the work of a wild animal. Or, in a sense, perhaps it was. But the kind of animal that hunted for sport, not food.

I pushed that hypothesis aside for now. I didn't have

enough data points yet. A couple of dead squirrels weren't enough to get worked up about. Not everything could be something.

But that new poster for the lost cat leaped into my mind again, and I couldn't deny that if there wasn't a pattern yet, one was on its merry way to emerging.

You don't know, Dana. You just don't know.

Yet every fiber of my being said otherwise.

FIFTEEN

June 26th, 2018

20 days since Blackstenius murder

The Scopes family had smartly scheduled Leslie's funeral for a Tuesday evening. The local media's interest was officially piqued by the second slaying, but a weekday service would draw far fewer eyes than a weekend one. It was also less likely to get the usual looky-loos who flocked to this sort of tragedy and thought they could sneak into the service unnoticed.

I hated that a family mourning the loss of their daughter had to consider such factors, but that was how things worked. That was how attention worked. That was how *people* worked.

I had the manifest of attendees from Cheryl's service in my lap as we sat in the car and checked them off one by one as Ben and I spotted them. There were plenty of stereotypes about serial killer behavior that were more myth than reality, but the notion that they liked to be present at the service was a tried and true one. It was an irresistible craving for this type of predator. The power they got from taking a life was only magnified when they saw how many people they'd hurt through the act. And the temptation to relive the scene, to gaze upon the framed portrait of his prey and imagine her dying all over again, was simply too much to turn down.

My father had attended quite a few funerals in the early nineties. He even brought his youngest daughter with him on occasion.

"At least we don't have to worry about Heidi Ruiz coming at us again," I said.

Ben looked up from his cell phone. "Huh?"

"Heidi Ruiz. We don't have to worry about her running up on us again."

He looked around. "Why's that?"

I pointed to the front of the building. "Because Scott's right there. I saw him pull up, and she wasn't in the car."

"Probably holding down the fort at the club."

I eyed Scott's ensemble. It was the exact same bowling shirt and flip-flops that he'd worn to Cheryl's service. "Nice to see he isn't changing for anyone."

Ben shook his head. "Jesus. We ought to arrest him just for that."

"Ben Escobar: Fashion Police." I put a checkmark by Scott's name. Then I crossed Heidi's off the list. "And there's Dylan Fowler. At least *he* knows how to dress."

"Which one is he again?"

I put a checkmark by Dylan's name. "He works with kids."

"A pedo, then."

I chuckled and scanned for another familiar face.

My phone buzzed, rattling gratingly in the center console. I checked the screen and cursed automatically.

Ben glanced over. "Towers?"

Not a bad guess. "Worse. My mom."

"Oof."

Ben was one of the few people I'd ever attempted to explain this dynamic to. I'd never planned on unloading that kind of family garbage on him, but too many stakeouts like this one had eventually greased the wheels.

"What's she got to say?" he asks.

I opened the text message. "Oh, for the love of..."

"Bad?"

"Of course it's bad. She said she heard about the serial killer in Austin and wants me to be careful. And then she reiterates that she doesn't think it's safe for a woman to be working my job."

Ben let out a large puff of air. "You gonna remind her she raised you in the same house as one?"

"No point." I tucked the phone away and stretched out the tightening muscles in my neck and shoulders. "She's rewritten history too many times and convinced herself there was no way of knowing her husband was butchering women in his studio. Her hard drives are totally corrupted."

"Denial's one hell of a drug," Ben said, and that about summed it up.

We fell into an easy silence, and I had a strange impulse to mention the squirrel from the evening before. The discovery unsettled me so much that I'd skipped trivia and stayed home with Sadie.

I couldn't think of what I would want Ben to say about it, though. What *was* there to say? You couldn't arrest kids on suspicion of them becoming serial killers. That wasn't the way things worked. You had to let the budding evil run its course, and then some poor suckers like Ben and me were called in once the psycho took the inevitable next step down his soulless path.

No, there was nothing Ben could say to make it any better or any worse. There was an inevitability to evil, no hope of eventual eradication, but someone had to oppose it.

I'd just have to keep an eye on the situation at home. Maybe tell Ariadna not to let Sadie out of her sight while she was in the courtyard.

I skimmed my list again. "Mike Check hasn't shown up, has he?"

"Nope. Not yet." Ben braced his phone on top of the steering wheel so he could doom-scroll through the news while we worked. After a brief silence, he said, "Oh boy. *Here* it is."

"Here what is?"

"Media just dropped a name for him. The Stand-up Killer."

"Ooh. That's good. Damn, that's *really* good."

"Yep. That one's gonna stick."

This changed things, though there was no need to point it out. We both knew. It was a turning point. Killers read the news. And the news had just given him a brand. Whether or not it was significant to him that Cheryl and Leslie were both comedians or whether it had just been a matter of convenience no longer mattered. He was the Stand-Up Killer now, and I'd bet on my life that he'd stick to that commonality of victims going forward. Why destroy such a solid brand name?

Another comedian would be killed unless Ben and I could catch him first.

SIXTEEN

June 27th, 2018

21 days since Blackstenius murder

He forced a small smile and slipped the mic back into the stand. His new material deserved better than that from the audience. But everyone was too damn morose to laugh, and the crowd was thinner than usual.

His material was solid, and his delivery was killer. He knew how to present himself just the right way, how to read a room and mold himself into what people needed him to be. That had always been his talent. It was how he got to satisfy his urges without anyone suspecting a thing.

But the cops had been sniffing around lately, working with Scott and Heidi, and the police presence was clearly ruining the vibe. How much had they looked into him, he wondered? Wouldn't take much digging before the oddities in his life stacked up, and then everything he built could come crashing down.

Two dead. The detectives wouldn't lie low forever.

Soon they'd kick it into high gear, grilling everyone about where they were when Cheryl and Leslie were murdered. And when that day came, he'd lie. But what if they saw through it? Glimpsed the real him, the person he kept locked up until it was safe to come out and play.

There were other comedy clubs in town, but disappearing from this one would draw suspicion, too. No. He'd stay.

He made his way to the bar as the emcee introduced the next comedian. But halfway there, his gaze found hers. Their eyes locked. A fuse in his memory sparked. No way. There she was. It was *her*.

The blonde wig she had on couldn't fool him. He'd thought about her too often over the years.

There was no mistaking it. *The girl that got away*.

But what was she doing there? In that club? After two murders? Why now?

Dylan Elijah Fowler ordered another pint of IPA, then marched over to find out.

SEVENTEEN

"Dana?"

Well, damn. Days of planning and approvals, and I'd hardly made it three steps into the club before someone outed me. I was never gonna stop hearing about this from Ben. He'd insisted the blonde wig looked fake.

I glanced around as casually as I could and spotted Dylan Fowler marching toward me, a wide, astonished grin on his face. I hadn't spoken with him in any official capacity yet, but Ben had called him to set up an initial interview and learned a few things in the brief exchange, including that he was a teacher at a local Catholic elementary school.

I had no clue how this guy knew who I was.

Dylan had a few inches on me and got a little too close before he stopped, but I fought the urge to take a step back and cede ground. He had a pleasant face, with bright blue eyes and brown stubble around his jaw. And his grin, which was on full display, could have been charming if I hadn't been so caught on my heels.

How had he recognized me so quickly?

"Did someone just say your name?" came Ben's voice through my earpiece.

The comedian on stage began his set with a whimpering joke that fell flat right away.

Even though we were at the back of the room with a bit of distance between us and the stage, Dylan kept his voice hardly above a whisper. "Dana Dwyer?"

My pulse skyrocketed. I sucked in air through my nose to counteract the adrenaline at hearing someone call me by *that* name. "Yeah?" I said.

"It's Dylan. Dylan Fowler."

"Uh-huh." I tried to remain as neutral as possible until I could figure out what the hell was happening.

His eyes narrowed. "You don't remember. We were lab partners in Mr. French's science class."

I shook my head, having only a vague memory of a teacher by that name. "When was that?"

"Seventh grade. Abbott Middle School."

I nodded slowly. Checked out. That had been my school. Still no memory of a Dylan Fowler. Seventh grade existed among some of the biggest gaps in my memory, though, so I went along with it for now. "Right, *right*." I mustered a placating smile. Pretending to remember trivial bits and pieces from those years of my life was not a new game to me. The fear-based memories from that period, the ones my brain worked so hard to repress, then I worked so hard to unearth, tended to dominate now. Benign things like the name of middle school lab partners became collateral damage, buried under the rubble of the mental war.

"Wow," he said, taking me in. "You look great. I've always wondered what became of you."

What *became* of me? I'd moved away, changed my name, gone to a crappy therapist, struggled through every day for the next decade, decided to hunt the hunters for myself, and, most importantly, avoided social media (outside of my covert accounts) like the plague. Of course. What *else* would I have done? What else would *anyone* have done?

"Thanks." It was the only response I could think of for a statement as stupid as that.

Ben's voice buzzed in my ear. *"Capone, is this guy for real?"*

No telling yet.

"Are you going up there tonight?" I motioned to the stage.

"Just did. You didn't see it?"

"No, I just got here." The process of putting on makeup in the visor mirror of the unmarked car had taken longer than I expected.

Since I'd already been on scene here in an investigative capacity, I was probably not the best for this job. But I was the only female in Homicide, and I'd be damned if I handed this responsibility off to anyone else. So that amounted to makeup. Lots of it. And the blonde wig that made my neck sweat and my head feel like it was an expanding hot air balloon. My smoky eye was already smudging by the time I'd adjusted the mop on my head and crawled out of the car. Ben had been kind enough to point that out, but not tactful enough to use words other than "slutty raccoon" to describe it. "At least no one will recognize you," he had added.

Except someone had recognized me. Or the girl I used to be. Thankfully, no one had heard of a "Detective

Dwyer" working the case because Detective Dwyer didn't exist. I'd been Capone for even longer than I'd been a cop. Even longer now than I'd ever been a Dwyer. Fortunately, the few people who might've recognized me in this club— Scott and Heidi Ruiz and Mike Check—probably didn't even remember my first name. People tended not to with law enforcement, even if you told it to them again and again.

Dylan frowned. "It wasn't a great set. I mean, it was, but it wasn't well received. I think people around here are a little too down to laugh."

"Down about what?"

He glanced around furtively. "We'd better go somewhere else to talk."

"Right. Yeah."

We stepped through the front doors, standing awkwardly under the overly bright LED lights below the awning. On the sidewalk just to my left, a homeless man slept like a rock under a faded and tattered Mexican blanket.

"I like what you've done with your hair," Dylan said with a sly grin.

And that did it, somehow. That particular grin. It was like a wormhole that sucked me back through time until I found myself staring into the face of a much younger man. Greasy. Crooked teeth. Breath like he'd never learned to brush. I felt the repulsion carry through the years to the present-day him in front of me. But none of those things remained now. Was that really the same person, or had my hippocampus just conjured up something to fill in the gaps?

"You don't remember me at all, do you?" he said.

"No, I do. I just... That was a long time ago."

"I was a year behind you. We were in that lab together when I was in seventh, and you were in eighth. You probably remember my brother better. He was in your grade. Brady Fowler?"

"Oh. Oh, yeah, I actually do! Played in the band, right?"

"Yep. Trumpet."

"Wasn't he class president, too?" It was a strange relief to feel memories flowing easily back to me now. Like pressing on a knot in your shoulders and feeling the clenched muscles release. Dylan didn't look especially proud of his brother's accomplishment. "He was."

"I'm sorry. Don't take it personally. There's a lot about those years my memory hasn't retained."

He scrunched up his nose. "Right. Yeah. I didn't want to mention..."

"That's kind of you, but it's okay."

"I wanted to say something to you back then, that I was sorry and that it didn't matter to me what he did, but you moved away. And we didn't even have MySpace then for me to track you down."

"Don't worry about it," I said. "There's nothing anyone could have said to make *that* shit better."

Except maybe "I believe you" or "We'll keep searching for the rest."

I forced a smile to ease his tension, and he chuckled on an exhale. "No kidding. Jesus. I can't even imagine."

"We don't need to talk about it."

He nodded. "So, uh, what are you up to lately?"

"Trying to settle into the city. Just moved here a couple of months ago. Bartending at the moment."

He tucked his hands into his jeans pockets. "Oh really? Where at?"

"Julian's. It's a new place over in the warehouse district."

"Not far from here, then. I haven't heard of it. I'm not cool enough to keep up with that scene, I guess."

I smiled but didn't bother challenging that assertion. Not when he was wearing a T-shirt with a drawing of a twenty-sided die above the words *Carpe DM*. "And you? What have you been doing?"

He shrugged, his hands still in his pockets. "I teach kindergarten, so I'm just on summer break right now. Good time to practice my real passion. I hit open mics obsessively during my breaks. You get a fever for it. Wait, are you a comedian, too?"

"Hardly. Been thinking about getting up there but haven't pulled the trigger yet."

"You signed up for tonight?"

"No. Just scoping it out."

"Right. Right."

"Kindergarten teacher," said Ben through my earpiece. *"Told you he was a perv."*

I ignored the color commentary.

Dylan must have mistaken my silence as a genuine lull in the conversation, because he said, "Well, I'm gonna head out, I think. But since you're new and don't know a lot of people in town, would it be okay if I gave you my number? You can give me a call, and we can grab a drink or coffee or whatever and catch up more."

"Yeah, definitely." If only every person of interest coughed up his info that easily.

I got his number, then narrowly deflected a hug from

him, and we said one last awkward goodbye before he left down the sidewalk.

I stepped back into the air conditioning.

"You really don't remember him?" came the voice in my ear.

"I remember him some."

"Just seems strange that you, of all people, wouldn't remember someone."

Not that strange. But I'd try to explain it later. Or maybe Ben would just drop it.

For now, though, I had to play it cool and hope that none of the people I'd already interviewed would recognize me lingering in the back.

I glanced over at Mike Check, sitting at the bar and watching the male performer closely as if trying to activate latent psychokinetic powers. What was he thinking?

I counted five women in the audience of perhaps two dozen people. Three were doting on the men next to them in such a way that I guessed they were plus-ones rather than comedians. That left two—Nicole Acosta and Aurora Fox. One Hispanic and the other Black. The most recent FBI profile would've had me believe their skin color meant they were safe here, that they didn't fit the victim pattern.

If only killers still adhered to rules like that.

I understood it was born of an era where only murdered white women raised society's hackles and sounded the alarms of law enforcement. But I also knew from personal experience that it just wasn't reality. Not now, and maybe not ever.

The ugly truth was that the public and law enforcement expected certain types of people to go missing and turn up dead. And when they did, it was viewed as their own fault—they shouldn't have done drugs, they shouldn't have sold themselves, they should have worked harder if they didn't want to be poor. They should have been *white*.

The men who hunted knew about this bias and exploited it. They lived in a dark fantasy world, sure, but they were keen observers. They knew who they could pick off without the public caring.

The FBI may have seen Nicole Acosta and Aurora Fox as safe from danger, but all I saw was two incredibly vulnerable women. Women who might not have the champions they needed if they went missing.

And now I'd been seen here. Had I caught the attention of the killer? At least I knew what I was up against. But still, I'd have to be more careful from now on.

So long as I maintained this cover—and this annoying wig—I'd have to be Dana Dwyer. The bartender. The little girl from White Settlement, Texas. The daughter of the infamous Raymond Lee Dwyer.

If only I could remember who she was and what she'd done.

EIGHTEEN

"Get this goddamn thing off me." I tugged the wig off as soon as I was in the car. Ben pulled away from the curb, where he'd been parked a block down Seventh Street from Laugh Attack. "It's like wearing roadkill." I tossed it into the back seat.

"You look good as a blonde, though."

I glared a hole in the side of his head until he finally looked over.

"Sorry, had to say it."

"No, you didn't." I reached up the back of my shirt and flicked the switch to my mic. "Dylan Fowler. Jesus. I stared at his name on the lists a hundred times, and it never even prickled at my memory."

To Ben's credit, he didn't pester me about that fact. "I Googled him along with the word 'kindergarten' and was able to find out more about him. He *is* a teacher, and at St. Ignatius Catholic School, no less."

I wiped a makeup remover cloth across one of my slutty raccoon eyelids. "'No less'? What do you mean?"

"I just mean, if he's trying to build up a facade of being a harmless, upstanding citizen, he found the right job working at a private school like that."

"Right." I cleaned off my other eye and chucked the used wipe onto my tactical bag at my feet. "Who would ever suspect that a grown man working with children under the Catholic Church might do terrible things? *Perfect* cover."

Ben shot me a pointed glare.

"Oh, come on," I said. "Don't tell me you're *that* kind of Catholic. Even Papa Francisco admits there's been hanky-panky."

I pulled out my phone and went through my contacts until I found the name I needed. If anyone could help me recall Dylan from those early years, it was Maggie Woods. I sent off a text.

"He fits the FBI profile," Ben said. "Caucasian male in his thirties."

"You're thinking about it in the wrong direction," I said. "It's not that he fits the profile so far. It's that he doesn't *not* fit it yet. There's a big difference."

"You don't think it's suspicious that someone you went to middle school with, who undoubtedly heard about your dad at an impressionable age, suddenly shows up at the same club where a woman was recently murdered out back?"

"Not really."

Ben held up a hand as if bracing himself for what he was about to say. "Okay, that's strange, because it seems like *exactly* the kind of logical jump you would normally make. If you were an outside observer to this situation, you'd already be balls-deep digging up dirt on this guy on some crazy hunch that, as much as I hate to admit it, would have a good chance of being right."

"Psh. I think that's a bit of an exaggeration."

He scrubbed a hand over the stubble of his jaw line. "God, how I wish it was."

I didn't respond and stared absently at a cluster of rowdy tourists hesitating at the corner, trying to decide if they should cross on the Don't Walk sign or not.

Ben wasn't wrong. He knew my mind better than just about anyone, and that *did* sound like a conclusion I would happily pursue. So why wasn't I? Was it because we didn't have enough facts to support that suspicion? Or was it because I'd just bumped into someone who might be able to remind me of the good parts of my childhood, and I wasn't in a hurry to toss that aside? I was plenty aware of my emotional needs. I just wasn't entirely sure if that was what was behind the reluctance.

A few minutes later, Ben pulled the unmarked car into the city garage on Eighth Street. "What was he wearing? Black graphic tee and jeans?"

I thought back to the dorky D&D shirt. He wore it well enough. "Yeah, why?"

"Mm-hm. I thought I recognized his walk and build from the memorials, but I couldn't see his face." Ben sighed, and I had a feeling I wasn't going to like what he was about to say. "I saw him head off to his car after the two of you said goodbye. Wanna guess what kind of vehicle he drives?"

Even in the dim security lighting of the garage, I could make out the lines of smugness around Ben's mouth.

"Are you screwing with me?" I demanded.

"Nope."

"A goddamn *Prius?*"

"Yup."

"Shit." I yanked off my uncomfortable flats one by one and tossed them onto my bag. "If the FBI lucks out on this one, I'm gonna be so pissed."

Ben parked and shut off the engine, but he didn't make to leave the car yet. "What's your gut telling you, Dana?"

A wave of exhaustion descended quickly. "It's hard to say. He's definitely awkward, but he seems nice." I heard the words flowing but couldn't stop them. The embarrassment hit immediately.

I was losing it, clearly. Never once had I arrested a man on a murder charge *without* encountering at least one of his female friends or relatives claiming, "But he's so gentle and sweet! He would never do that!"

I scrambled to backtrack. "I just mean that he didn't... Shit, I don't know what I mean. I'm clearly tired."

"Then don't worry about it right now. Go get some sleep. Maybe in the morning, you'll have a better feel of it. I'll keep digging on him in the meantime, let you know if I find anything that stands out."

My phone buzzed, and I checked it.

It was a text back from Maggie Woods: *Dylan Fowler?! Why do you want to know about Fowler the Prowler? I figured he'd be dead by now.*

"What the hell?" I read it again.

"What is it?"

I told Ben to hold on, then responded to Maggie: *Fowler the Prowler? I don't remember that.*

Only a few seconds later: *You don't remember? He was caught spying on the girls' locker room. They almost expelled him.*

No, I did not, in fact, remember that. But it was certainly something worth noting.

"St. Ignatius School," I said. "Is it co-ed?"

He shook his head. "Boys only. But before you say—"

"No, that's actually good this time. Because we might not have found our killer, but you might be spot-on with the perv stuff."

Yet even after I filled Ben in on Maggie's intel, I felt oddly reluctant to suspect Dylan of something so gruesome as the murders of Cheryl and Leslie. It made no sense. Was it intuition or some other need causing the resistance?

We'd been lab partners, Dylan and me. Had we also sat together at lunch? Had we been *friends*?

Or perhaps all of his memories of me were one-sided. Maybe Fowler the Prowler had set his sights on me in middle school. Had he been a murderer in the making? Had I escaped more danger as a kid than I'd realized?

And now that he knew I was in town, was I in danger all over again?

I kept running into a brick wall every time I tried to remember moments in middle school with Dylan. There had been a moment of recognition outside the club, but that was it. His younger self lacked any sort of backdrop in my mind. It was a blank canvas, like most things I tried to recall between the first time I found a body part in my backyard until the FBI showed up. Years stolen from me that I'd fought to get back, bit by bit. But only the bad bits, really. Because those were the ones my mom and siblings and *Raymond* had said didn't exist. Those were the ones I'd had to fight for just to know I hadn't made it all up, hadn't blown up my family for nothing. The muffled screams, the blood trails over the grass, the strange smells that couldn't be from his acrylics or varnish.

My mind had tried to bury it all in its own mass grave, one decomposing memory at a time, but unlike Raymond's victims, those horrific clues hadn't been unearthed in bulk.

December twenty-third, 1995. The day my world had ended in fire and ice inside our backyard studio. The hellish reds and oranges of Raymond's art surrounding the hidden pit of cold bodies. His fire turning them to ice. Destroying everything I thought I knew.

Why had no one else read the signs? Why had it had to be me who found it?

It was one in the morning as I pulled into the parking lot of my apartment complex, and I was still thinking of him. Of Raymond Lee Dwyer. Dear old Dad. He hadn't made it as a commercial success with his art, so he'd kept his day job of pest control management until my mom was hired at Lockheed in ninety-four, just ahead of the corporation's big, lucrative merger. Reports said the killings increased in frequency the year or so leading up to his arrest. Dramatically. My mother's high-paying job had allowed him to quit pest control and pursue his *real* passion. My family had thought that meant painting his abstract expressionist nonsense.

Not quite.

I grabbed my bag out of the trunk and shut the door harder than I meant to.

Could Dylan be a similar case? Could comedy be that creative passion for him? Murdering women his inspiration? Two murders so far, both while he was on his summer break from teaching. I hated to admit it was a pattern, and I knew that if I hadn't gone to school with Dylan, I would be barking about it to Ben and Popov like a hound that had just caught a jackrabbit trail.

Coming up the stairs and into the breezeway, I didn't notice the thing on the ground by my front door until I nearly stepped on it. My chest seized up, and I only just kept myself from screaming and waking the neighbors.

The security lighting on the ceiling glinted off one of the sharp teeth in the cat's gaping mouth. The feline's belly was slit, its insides gone, but judging from the lack of blood around it, the gore wasn't committed on my doorstep. It had been moved here. Placed. Staged.

I knelt beside the poor animal for a closer look. The gray fur around the slice was stained dark with dried blood. I thought instantly of the missing cat poster. Snowball, though, had been pure white. This poor cat I didn't recognize. I doubted that meant Snowball was safe inside some good Samaritan's home, though. Not when someone was running around who would do this to a cat.

And then leave it on my doorstep.

Someone wanted to send a message. They wanted to scare me.

I steadied myself to show no fear then looked around slowly. Whoever had done this could be watching. It might thrill them to see me scared, so I'd deprive them of that, at least.

I didn't see any eyes staring back at me, but that didn't mean anything. It was dark, and there were lots of hiding places, plenty of apartments facing mine across the courtyard with tiny, prisonlike windows by the front doors. No immediate danger, though, so I put my back to it. It was a bad time to retrieve Sadie, since Ariadna would be up in only a few hours anyway, so I decided I'd get her later in the morning instead.

That left me entering an empty apartment, and I didn't love that, but I had a gun. I tried the handle and was relieved to find it locked. That was some small comfort.

I snapped pictures of the cat on my phone then bagged it up. I knew the system well enough to know there was no point in keeping the body as evidence. Evidence for what, anyway? Just a cat death, and we hardly even had the resources to solve human deaths in the department lately. But the pictures might come in handy later if this happened again.

I hoped to hell it didn't.

Once was enough for me. Message received. I was being watched. Maybe even stalked.

NINETEEN

June 29th, 2018

23 days since Blackstenius murder

"Monday morning," said Sergeant Popov just before lunch the following day. "They're sending a couple of agents over. One from the San Antonio office and one from here. They'll be setting up in a conference room to work closely with us on this."

Ben and I were the only two detectives in the Homicide office; everyone else was either out to a long Friday lunch or following leads.

I leaned forward as Escobar lifted the back of my shirt to clip the small recording apparatus onto my bra. "Good to know," I said.

I'd waited two days before contacting Dylan Fowler and taking him up on his offer to chitchat about the olden days. Appearing overeager wouldn't do me any favors. If he *was* the one committing these murders, I'd have to be careful not to set off warning bells that I was suspicious.

Sure, he didn't know I was a cop, but the internet existed. And if I presented as anything other than a deadbeat with a shitty childhood, he just might search past the first page of results on Google. I happened to know that page eight was where Raymond's crimes stopped taking up all the real estate for my name search and the first mention of "Dana Capone" appeared. From there, it wouldn't be hard to find what I really did for a living. Or if he somehow got a picture of me now and did an image search... cover blown. The Rochelle case a few months back would make sure of that. Picture in the papers was never a good thing for a cop, but one who was also, well, *me*? I suspected a few more people around the station had put the pieces together, and, in true form, no one would just say it to my face. Not something like this. Easier to just log my past away as yet another reason to discredit my decisions on the job.

Appearing overeager to see Dylan again might also have given him the wrong impression about my intentions. That worried me the most, in fact. If he didn't know I was a cop and I'd rung him right away, it would make sense for him to believe I had some sort of sexual interest in him. He wasn't a bad-looking guy—dorky, but that was no crime—and he might make a good friend to have, assuming he wasn't a brutal psychopath, but I wasn't looking for anything beyond that. Period. Having him think I was would only complicate everything.

Popov pointedly avoided looking at me while my shirt was raised in the back and exposing my midriff as a result. He stared down at the crime scene photos spread across my desk instead. "You two say this is a promising lead. So, make it count. This could be our last chance to get something good before the FBI plows in like a wrecking ball."

"Nice to know I'm not the only one who thinks of them that way," I mumbled.

"Hold still," Ben said. "You keep wiggling, and I might accidentally undo your bra."

"That unskilled?"

"No. *Too* skilled. I can get one of these off a woman just by looking at her the right way."

Popov shook his head as if to clear it. "*As I was saying*, I'm sure the chief would appreciate it if we made it clear that the department can handle its own problems without help from the Feds."

"No one wants that more than I do," I said. "It's been more than a week since the last victim. I can't imagine we have much longer until we're one deeper."

Ben lowered my cotton shirt and offered me the wig. I pushed it away. "He knows I'm not a blonde. I'd rather not."

"And what are you gonna say when he asks you why you were wearing one the other night?"

"I'll tell him I was embarrassed to be seen there. He'll understand."

"Will he?"

"Yeah, he will. Because I'm gonna make him. Don't forget, I'm Dana Dwyer, the traumatized girl who found a mass grave under her father's art studio." I pointed at Popov. "See? That expression Sarge is making right now. He wants me to talk about anything else." I shamelessly adjusted the underwire of my bra that was riding up from the receiver clipped on the back. "Everyone's face does that when I mention that unpleasant chapter of my life. I can get out of talking about *anything* if I just toss in a reference to Raymond."

Ben cringed. "Do you really play that card with people?"

I grabbed my purse and checked for my essentials—phone, keys, wallet, gun. "It's among the cards I've been dealt, Ben. I think I've earned the right to play it as much as I want."

Popov frowned. "Whatever you gotta do, Capone. But don't give away too much. We can't burn you as an asset yet. You're the only woman we have in Homicide."

"Oh really? I didn't notice."

The sergeant grunted. "If you weren't good at your job..." But he didn't finish, just marched out of Death Row.

I turned to Ben. "How do I look?" I'd donned civilian clothes, rather than my usual off-duty cop clothes, as best I could. Khaki capris, a charcoal-gray V-neck tee, some strappy sandals, and I even put in my pearl earrings, just for this.

He leaned back, studying me. "You look like a serial killer's daughter."

"Perfect. Shall we?"

Dylan Fowler's home was in a quiet, established neighborhood in South Austin. A modest two-story with a tan brick exterior and a metal railing around the porch, the house had probably been standing since at least the seventies. The lawn was a patchwork of dirt and crabgrass, and the garden in the front was wild with weeds jutting from unkempt shrubs.

I checked my rearview mirror before pulling into the driveway. Ben Escobar's unmarked Explorer was hardly more than a speck behind the loaner car I was using for this occasion (not a chance I'd hand over my actual license plate number to a murder suspect). The fact that I'd been able to borrow an unclaimed Toyota Prius, of all makes and models, from the impound lot was just a fun bonus, a little flourish. Had to get my humor where I could.

I knocked on the metal front door and waited. Maybe we should've planned to hang out somewhere public the first time, but I suspected meeting him on his home turf would be better for getting beneath his defenses.

And it wasn't like I got into this line of work to be safe. I did it to keep others safe. And with the clock ticking down before the unsub got itchy for another plaything, I didn't have time to work this lead slowly.

So, I'd suggested coffee at his place and chalked it up to us being a bartender and a teacher wanting to save a buck.

As I waited for him to answer the door, I recalled the hesitancy in his voice when I'd suggested his place. It hadn't struck me at first, but now it was taking on a bit of a foreboding color. At least I wasn't visiting at night. It was the middle of the afternoon, bright, hot, unsexy. Unless he had something to hide, my being there wouldn't be a problem.

Or maybe his house existed in a similar state to the yard. I'd given him a few hours' notice in our plans. He could've cleaned up. It wouldn't hurt him.

The door opened, and only a screen stood between me and an older woman with a bob of matte-black box-dyed hair and narrowed eyes.

"Oh, sorry. I was looking for Dylan Fowler. I must have the wrong house."

"No, you have the right house, Dana," the woman said, pushing open the screen. "Come on in. I'll holler up to him." She led me through a time capsule of a living room and into the kitchen. "I'm Francis Fowler, Dylan's mother. We've met before, but you probably don't remember, what with all the..." She waved her hand vaguely, and it was a fairly concise way to sum up serial murders. She snuck another sideways glance at me. "I guess he didn't tell you that he lived with his mother. I don't know why he'd be ashamed of it, honestly. Lots of boys his age do that now." She was a squat thing, but I could already tell she was a force. Overcompensating for size, perhaps. Or maybe a zealot. People didn't have to be tall or strong or even have particularly good aim to wield shame as a deadly weapon.

Francis gestured to a chair at the kitchen table, and I took a seat just as she disappeared through the door on the other side of the space. *"Dylan! Your lovely friend is here!"*

Lovely friend? Yikes.

Francis didn't return, leaving me alone, and I folded my hands on the plastic floral tablecloth and surveyed the cramped kitchen. It wasn't dirty, but it wasn't exactly tidy. There didn't seem to be enough storage in the cupboards. Various appliances—coffeemaker, blender, juicer, toaster oven, and slow cooker—made the minimal counter space even more limited.

A window above the sink faced out onto the front lawn, and I wondered if Mrs. Fowler had watched me through there from the moment I pulled into the driveway, sizing me up. Felt about right.

Footsteps down the stairs, and then Dylan entered the

kitchen, wide-eyed. "Hey." He glanced over his shoulder, clearly checking to make sure we were alone, then whispered, "I didn't know she'd be home, sorry. You sure you don't want to go out somewhere for coffee?"

Before I could respond, Mrs. Fowler was back in the kitchen. "Nonsense! I've already started brewing a fresh pot! You two have a seat, and I'll serve you. It'll be just like a café. Your generation wastes too much money on fancy coffee anyway."

Dylan shut his eyes against the embarrassment but took a seat.

What Mrs. Fowler had said was an obvious lie, though. There was no coffee brewing yet. And that was made even more obvious as the woman shamelessly pulled the can of Folgers grounds from the cabinet and set to scooping it out.

"It's good of you to live with your mother and help her out," I said, helping him save face.

He stared at the tablecloth and scratched the side of his head. "Yeah."

Damn, maybe this wasn't going to work. Francis was making him clam right up. I wouldn't get anything good out of him so long as the woman's stifling presence loomed over us.

"I'm so excited to see you, Dana," Mrs. Fowler said, her back to us as she turned on the brew and tucked the coffee can away again. "When Dylan said Dana Dwyer was coming over, well, I just couldn't believe it. It was like you vanished off the face of the earth after all that stuff with your father came out. I'm sure you were terribly embarrassed by it."

"*Mom*," Dylan said.

She swiveled to glare at him. "What? We can't talk

about what happened? She has nothing to be ashamed of, and I'm sure she'll be relieved to know not everyone said such nasty things behind her mother's back like Janet Baumbauer used to. You remember her, right, dear?"

She addressed the last question to me, and I smiled politely. "Of course."

Janet Baumbauer? Who in the hell was that?

"I'm just saying, I'm just saying," continued Mrs. Fowler, "women of Dana's age don't like dancing around the truth, Dillie. They like blunt talk. They're not scared of reality like my generation was raised to be. Isn't that right, Dana?"

Usually fast on my feet, I found myself unsure of how to respond. Agreeing with Mrs. Fowler meant uniting against Dylan, and I needed to keep him from shutting down. But disagreeing with her seemed like a surefire way to ignite a truly hostile environment.

Play the middle ground. "I don't know. I've never been like other women my age."

"Can we talk about something else?" Dylan blurted.

"Only if your *guest* wants to," Mrs. Fowler said, her eyes glued to the coffee pot as it spit out the last hacking coughs of brew.

"You mentioned we had science class together," I said. "I hardly remember that. Or really anything about school that year."

Dylan opened his mouth to answer, but Mrs. Fowler jumped in. "That was biology, right? He was supposed to be in natural science, but he'd whizzed through that over the summer. Always loved science and was especially good at it. It was the one thing his brother wasn't great at, so I think he saw the opportunity to be the best at something for once."

Jesus, what a nightmare she was.

As Dylan and I fell into an uncomfortable silence, Mrs. Fowler poured our cups and brought them over. She set down three mugs, not two.

Almost as soon as her backside had hit the chair, she jumped up again. "Oh! I got the cream and sugar out and forgot to bring it over! I know you can't drink your coffee without it, Dillie."

"No, I like it just fine black, Mom."

"No, you don't," she said. "Stop trying to act tough in front of Dana. Women like sensitive men now." She set the white porcelain sugar bowl on the table and scooped out a spoonful. As she moved the spoon toward his mug, he pulled it away and lurched to his feet. "I have some old yearbooks upstairs if you want to look through them."

I recognized a not-so-subtle plea when I saw one. "Yep. Sounds good."

Mrs. Fowler wasn't entirely deterred yet, though, and she moved the spoon toward my coffee. I said, "I'm watching my sugar intake, thanks," and followed Dylan out of the kitchen.

I made it to the top of the carpeted stairs without sloshing my beverage. When I looked up from the mug, Dylan was already disappearing into a room on the left.

"Keep the door open!" Mrs. Fowler shouted from downstairs.

As soon as I followed him inside, he shut the door. "I'm sorry," he said. "She's a lot."

"No kidding." I sipped the coffee. It tasted like the

grounds might have been partially fossilized. I smacked my lips against the stale bitterness.

"It's fine if you don't drink it," he said, setting his cup down on a wooden dresser and heading for the closet. I took in the sight of his bedroom, and... wow.

If I hadn't known better, I would've said this was the room of a high school boy. The only exception was that it didn't smell like jockstrap, and wrinkled clothes weren't flung all over and collecting in drifts in the corners. But the bed—a mattress without a box spring or frame—and superhero posters on the walls spoke of someone obsessed with boyhood, not a thirty-five-year-old man.

Fowler the Prowler.

And yet Dylan still didn't strike me as a pedophile or a serial killer.

I needed to stop thinking about it, but I couldn't seem to. Fact was, there weren't telltale signs for either one, outside of catching the person in the act, and I should've known better than to base my assumptions on the song and dance someone put on for me.

But even still, there were often those glances one got behind the veil, moments when the wearer of the mask didn't know he was being observed or felt confident in the lack of suspicion cast his direction and allowed himself a moment to relax. For most people, those split seconds, those easily overlooked anomalies, only seemed curious in retrospect. But I had enough experience taking stock of all the small, seemingly insignificant things adding up to one horrifying conclusion that I liked to think I'd learned to spot them for what they were in the moment.

It was the constant pull I lived with. Experience, gut

instinct, training, and self-doubt, each with their own agenda, rarely pointing in the same direction.

"Sorry," he said, returning with his arms full of books. "I didn't make my bed this morning." He set the books on his dresser next to a framed photo of the Fowlers—Francis, Dylan, and Brady. I couldn't make out the faces of the boys clearly enough to guess their ages, but the quality of the image had me place it in the late nineties. Definitely one taken on film, not digital. There was no father or father figure in sight. I understood on an intellectual level that being fatherless took its toll on young men, but all I felt was that they might've dodged a bullet.

All those talking heads who said any father was better than no father needed to come have a chat with me.

Dylan grabbed a handful of the sheet and quilt, tossing them up toward his pillows. "Good enough. Have a seat."

We settled next to each other on the foot of the bed, and he placed the stack of yearbooks between us, taking the first one off the top. "This was my seventh-grade year, your eighth." He flipped through the first few pages of sponsorships, mostly from car dealerships and dental practices in the Fort Worth area, and landed on the teacher pictures. "There's Mr. French. You remember him?"

I inspected the spectacled man on the page, and his bristly blond mustache did start to bring back the days spent staring glassy-eyed at him. "We dissected frogs together, didn't we?"

Dylan beamed. "Yes! And you insisted on doing all the slicing. You got mad at me for handling the intestines too much."

I didn't remember it *that* vividly. And though I knew my childhood memories weren't what they ought to be, it still struck me as an especially odd detail for anyone to remember.

"Here," he said. The yearbook was spread between us, and he inched it more his way to flip through the pages. "There. That's me."

A greasy-haired boy with a unibrow and severe acne on the lower half of his face grinned up from the page. "Yep," I said, more memories returning. "That's you." When I'd imagined his greasy face before, it hadn't been just my memory supplying a placeholder. I'd actually remembered.

Which meant the rest of my memories could still be down there, somewhere, the ones I'd never had to testify about.

A knot in my stomach loosened.

"You really don't remember much, do you?"

I kept my eyes on the page, letting them roam over the sea of under-groomed faces. "No, I don't." Admitting that to Dylan felt natural. I wasn't defensive about my loss. Was that because I'd just discovered that it *was* still there in my mind, waiting to be gently nudged forth, or was that because I trusted him not to use the knowledge against me? The latter would've been crazy, unfounded at this stage. "I've never really tried to remember this part of my life. I mean, I remember some things like they happened yesterday, but school, social life... With that stuff, I hardly remember a thing."

He nodded, and though I could feel his eyes on me, it wasn't long before he turned them back to the yearbook. "Crazy how the mind works."

Crazy indeed.

I breezed through to the eighth-grade classes, and my eyes homed in instantly on my own youthful face.

I could only just make out the top part of that blue and orange striped shirt that I'd loved so much, but the glimpse of it transported me back in a heartbeat, and another moment came crashing in on the heels of it.

My mother sitting on the couch, staring at the dark screen of the TV, smoking what was likely her twentieth cigarette of the day. The beeping of the excavator backing up and the indistinct hollering of the men I didn't know in my backyard. The detective calmly reminding me that this was my last chance for a long time to get what I needed from the house.

And the scent on the air as we stepped out front to leave—fresh dirt and a hint of something like garlic, sweet onion, and rotten eggs.

I'd kept the blue and orange shirt I wore that final day for years and years without meaning to. Then, long after I dropped out of college, I'd returned home to purge my belongings, and there it was, wrinkled, forgotten, soaked in guilt and shame and grief.

"Oh! There's Maggie!" I said, pointing to the only Black student on the entire yearbook page. Our hometown hadn't been named White Settlement, Texas, for nothing. Only ten, fifteen miles east, though, and I would've been the only white girl in my class.

Maggie stared up from the glossy page with her usual sideways grin, exhibiting way more confidence than any fourteen-year-old girl should. Her hair was pulled tight against her scalp in a high ponytail, and her hazel eyes shot the camera a glance that seemed to say, "I'm onto you."

"Y'all still talk?" he asked.

"Yeah. She's about the only one I keep up with," I explained.

"Is there a reason for that?" Then quickly, "I mean, you weren't bullied or anything, right?"

"No, I don't think so. Not before it all broke, at least. And after, there wasn't an opportunity for anyone to bully me before we skipped town. Lord knows I did my best to lose touch with everyone."

"But not her? Not Maggie?"

"Nope, not Maggie. She just kept sticking around." I needed to call her. She'd moved to Philadelphia after college, and I hadn't gotten to see her nearly as much as I would have liked. I had an urge to call her right then, until I remembered that this wasn't just a friendly visit I could blow off whenever I felt like it. I had a job to do.

And it was all being recorded.

Shit. Without Ben jabbering in my ear, I'd momentarily forgotten that bit, lost myself in this Memory Lane nonsense. I hadn't just been showing vulnerability to Dylan. I'd been showing it to the whole damn department.

I tried to replay everything I'd said, inventory what sort of mortification I could look forward to back at the station, but before I could, Mrs. Fowler hollered something incomprehensible from downstairs.

"What?" Dylan hollered back.

Mrs. Fowler yelled again, and Dylan grunted. "One second." He marched downstairs, leaving me alone.

The moment he disappeared, shoving the door mostly shut behind him, I jumped up from the bed, careful not to topple the stack of yearbooks, and tiptoed over to his closet. I looked around but didn't see anything out of the ordinary. As it was with porn, so it was with incriminating murder evidence: tricky to define, but I'd know it when I saw it. But nothing there stood out. Half the closet was graphic tees, the other half collared shirts. Jeans and slacks were folded and stacked on the floor beneath the tops. Some old shoes. A stack of three-ring binders caught my attention, and I flipped one open. Lesson plans.

I had a pretty good idea that the closet was a bust. At least so far as I had the time to search it now. Maybe a more thorough investigation would turn up something, but I didn't have that luxury.

I slipped the closet's accordion door shut again before heading over to a slender door on the opposite side of the bed. This, too, looked to be some kind of closet, probably reserved for linens, considering how narrow the door. I'd spotted it earlier and made a mental note, but now was my chance. I had to see.

I tried the handle. It didn't budge. Maybe it was stuck. But no. Not stuck. Locked.

There was something behind that door that he didn't want anyone to see. Was it a porn collection he kept away from his overbearing mother? Every grown man deserved to have some privacy for *that* sort of thing.

Or could it be a specific type of porn? The kind that showed woman tied up and beaten, like the FBI profile suggested? Or worse, a little knife play pushed too far, where entire chunks of skin were pulled from below the shoulder blades?

It seemed unlikely that I'd catch that much luck, but this job was occasionally weird like that.

The carpet muffled Dylan's footsteps on the stairs, and I didn't hear him until he was almost to the top. I scrambled back to the bed but was pretty sure he caught my last lunge just as the door opened. He paused on the threshold, eyeing me suspiciously. Rightfully so.

"What are you doing?" His eyes darted from me to the narrow closet and back.

"Nothing. Sorry."

And there it was. Only for an instant, but I didn't miss it. The light went out behind his eyes, and I'd have had to be blind not to notice.

It was the look of someone who thought he'd been found out. The pupil dilation of fight, flight, or freeze.

Then I saw it. The rage.

His body had chosen to fight. It'd sized me up, decided it could take me, and now it sent the necessary chemical signals through him. Adrenaline was surging to his extremities, blood pulsing away from all nonessential functions and into his arms, legs, and head.

The rage might morph to contempt, and then I'd truly be in danger. Because contempt carried justification on its back. Justification for *any* action.

I couldn't give him the space to let his mind go there. I had to derail his suspicions. Now. "What'd your mom want?"

He continued to inspect me as I determinedly kept up the facade of innocence. Whether he finally bought it or not, the muscles in his arms appeared to relax, his posture softened, and he shook his head. "She wants you to stay for dinner."

"It's only four thirty."

"We eat early here. My mom says it helps me stay fit to not eat after five thirty."

"Dylan, I hope you don't take offense, but your mother's a real trip."

Redirect the focus, the aggression.

His shoulders softened further. "That's one word for her. No offense taken."

"I'm always up for a free meal."

Did I want to spend a second longer in the stifling toxicity of this household? Not a chance. But I still hadn't found anything definitive, and the last thing I wanted was to leave totally empty-handed from an operation I had spearheaded.

"I eat whatever I want once she goes to bed," he blurted. "Sometimes I go out for Whataburger."

"Good. You should. Your house, your rules."

He looked like he was about to say something else in defense of his independence, but instead, he leaned out of the room again to holler my answer down the stairs.

In those few seconds, while he shouted down to her, I tried to swallow but found my mouth completely dry.

Something strange was going on with these two, and until I could figure it out, I wouldn't be safe in the Fowler household.

TWENTY

"I keep telling him that if he ever wants to find a good woman and settle down, he needs to move out, but he just insists on staying with Mommy." Mrs. Fowler had hardly put a single strand of spaghetti in her mouth since we'd sat down to dinner ten minutes before. There'd been no opportunity for it with the way she kept on.

I, on the other hand, hadn't stopped stuffing my face with the mediocre pasta and canned meat sauce, hoping Mrs. Fowler would keep going until she said something useful or simply ran out of steam. At that point, I might be able to conduct a meaningful conversation with my person of interest.

It didn't look like either would happen anytime soon.

"Mom," Dylan said, "this is *my* house. I let you live with me."

"Just because you pay the mortgage doesn't make it your house. The head of household is whoever lives in the master bedroom, and that isn't you." She pressed her lips together, and her eyebrows rose in a challenge, like she'd finally pinned him with his back to the wall. More like she had his balls in a vise. I hadn't seen anyone quietly take that kind of abuse in a very long time. Not even from a parent. It couldn't last. He had to have some way to blow off steam after a humiliating thrashing like this.

"If you're going to be spending serious time with Dana," Mrs. Fowler continued, "she should know the truth about your living situation. And about you. You're not yet the man of the house. She has a right to know."

I crammed more spaghetti into my mouth than was advisable and couldn't help but sneak a glance at Dylan to observe his reaction to that appalling comment.

His face turned the color of the Ragu, and he smacked the table with a flat palm. Hard. But the cotton-backed plastic tablecloth muffled the noise. "Jesus *Christ!*" he snapped, and I hastily covered my mouth with the paisley-patterned linen napkin to keep from accidentally spitting out my food.

His nostrils twitched as he met his mother's eyes. He didn't blink. "She was just supposed to come over for coffee to catch up! It was just a casual thing! You're the one who invited her to stay for dinner, not me!"

Mrs. Fowler's mouth snapped into a thin line, and the fire in her blue eyes spoke of severe future consequences for his behavior. I wouldn't put it past her to try to spank him later on, but the way he was glaring at her told me it might be the last thing she ever did if she tried. He'd crossed a line. I suspected even he knew it. But it didn't look like he cared.

When Francis spoke again, it was hardly more than a whisper. "I did not raise you to use the lord's name in vain. Especially at your mother."

As his fury collided with her scorn, filling the room with toxic fumes, my mind jumped briefly to the gun on my belt. I hadn't thought I'd need a Taser for this visit, and I'd had nowhere to hide such a bulky thing, but I was starting to wish I'd found a way to bring one along. Who would I have to use it on, though?

Then suddenly, Dylan's anger collapsed in on itself, and his shoulders slumped. "Sorry, Mom. I'm sorry."

Oof. I hated to see it.

Francis had won the standoff, but that wasn't enough for her. Not even close. She grinned smugly. "You should also apologize to your special guest."

"No, no," I said around my unchewed food. "It's fine. I deal with much worse on a daily basis."

Mrs. Fowler turned to me politely. "Worse than *that*?" She paused. "And what do you do for work?"

"She's a bartender." Dylan delivered the information like a whip crack.

"Ah." And just like that, any esteem Francis Fowler had held for me vanished into thin air. "I imagine you're great at that. Speaking of which, how's your mother?"

I blinked. My mind made the leap between the two seemingly disparate topics immediately, but I struggled to fathom anyone besides this lodged splinter of a woman juxtaposing those two things so brazenly.

Generous assumptions, Dana...

Maybe she hadn't meant it like that. Maybe.

I swallowed down the last bits of my food and composed myself. "My mother?"

"Yes. I heard she had a bit of a hard time with, well, you know. *Events.*"

Screw generous assumptions. This woman used my

cover as a bartender as a segue into gossiping about my mother's well-known drinking problem. If Dylan *was* the one behind the murders, all he'd need to claim insanity was for his attorney to bring Francis Fowler to the stand.

I forced a smile anyway, reminding myself that this was all business. And yes, it was also personal, but I hadn't been kidding when I said that I dealt with much worse people on a daily basis.

However, when I tried to recall said worse people, I came up empty. "My mother is doing great. She struggled with her *illness*, but she's better now."

"Illness. Right, I've heard it called that. I imagine it was hard for everyone in your family. You have siblings, right?"

"Older brother and sister. My sister was already out of the house when Raymond's crimes came to light, so."

"Mom, I don't think Dana came here to talk about that." Dylan's tone was restrained but hinted at the same rage I'd witnessed a moment ago bubbling under the surface.

Mrs. Fowler was all salty sweetness when she said, "Why don't you let her speak for herself, Dillie? If she's uncomfortable, she can say so." She looked to me for an indication.

"I don't mind talking about it," I said. "But it's not great dinner conversation."

I was speaking Mrs. Fowler's language. Politeness. Pretense. She smiled, and it didn't reach her eyes. "Of course not. Maybe you'll stay for dessert, then? There's some Jell-O in the fridge."

I ignored the repulsive offer, turning instead to Dylan. "Hey, I heard about what's been going on at the Laugh Attack. Two comedians were killed?"

He set his fork down on his plate and shook his head. "It's terrible. The community is all torn up about it."

"Oh yes," Mrs. Fowler said, "I read about that in the paper. I—"

"Did you know either of the victims?" I asked.

Dylan sighed. "Yeah, but not super well. I mean, we knew each other and got along at the open mics, but we weren't friends. Hell, they might not have even liked me."

And yet you went to both of their funerals. "What makes you say that?"

Mrs. Fowler said, "He's always thought that about people. Needs extra reassurance."

I kept my eyes locked on Dylan to let him know I didn't care what his mother had to say. It worked, and he didn't engage with the jab. "There's this guy who runs the sound and puts together the open mic rosters. He also does a lot of the booking. We don't get along. He knocked me off the list one night to make room for one of the girls he was hooking up with, and I called him out on it in front of a few people. He didn't like that." Dylan swirled noodles on his fork, an almost imperceptible smirk on his lips. "He wants to pretend he's not getting that benefit from his position, but everyone knows he is. It's probably the only way he knows how to get any." He shrugged. "He likes to talk shit about me to the people he sleeps with from the club. The ones who were killed, Cheryl and Leslie, they bought into it completely."

"This guy was sleeping with *both* of the victims?"

He nodded emphatically.

"Seems like something the cops might want to know."

"Yeah, no kidding. I'm sure they do. It's probably the first thing anyone told them. That guy's a creep."

I could feel the stifling maternal presence stiffen next to me with each curse word from her son's mouth, but I did my best to block it out. "That sucks," I said, "that people believe him."

"Not everyone does. Most of the dudes don't. It's just the women. He gets them under his spell with that devil-may-care vibe he's working so hard on. But the guys know he's a douche." He held up a hand. "No, maybe that's not fair. Some of the women can tell he's a douchebag. There was a girl who was hanging around for a while—Stephanie something? Stephanie Lee, maybe? She stopped coming a month ago. I assume she figured it out, ya know? Saw through his bullshit. I'm pretty sure she slept with him for a while because she hated my guts from day one. Let's just say I don't miss her, but I gotta give her credit for growing tired of Mike's power trip. She wasn't even a comedian, just lurked around the club. I mean, the only thing more depressing than being an aspiring stand-up is being a groupie for aspiring stand-ups."

Mrs. Fowler leaned forward. "I keep telling him it isn't a healthy way to spend his time, but he won't listen."

"It does sound like a lot of drama," I agreed.

"I won't argue there." Dylan scooped the forkful into his mouth. Now that his mother had taken a back seat, his appetite seemed to have returned full force. "A lot of clubs are healthier, have a much more, I don't know, *positive* vibe. But I've always liked the setup of Laugh Attack. Anyway, it's worth it. You'll understand once you get up on stage. There's nothing else like it. You're totally at the mercy of the audience. You put yourself out there, and they have all the power. But each time you make them laugh, you take that power back."

"I hadn't thought about it like that. In terms of power, I mean."

"Everything's about power, right?"

I nodded noncommittally. He wasn't wrong, but that wasn't the conversation I wanted to get into. "Were you at the club the night the first person was killed? I heard it happened, like, right after the open mic or something." I took a sip of water from the blue plastic cup and tried to keep the question casual.

"Yeah," he said. "I can't even believe it. I mean, I left early that night—I usually just peace out after my set because the other acts are so bad—but depending on what time it happened, I could have found her, you know?"

"What do you mean?"

"She was in the back alley. If I don't leave immediately, I usually go out back after my set to get some air."

I recalled what the owner, Scott Ruiz, had said about the comedians going out back to smoke weed. No doubt Dylan would get in on that action with dear old Francis waiting back home for him.

I feigned shock at the information he'd just relayed. You know, like a person who didn't see a lot of dead bodies might. "Oh wow. Yeah, that would have been awful."

"Shyeah," he replied, eyes wide. "Horrifying. Do you know how she was found?"

"Nuh-uh."

"Dillie, I don't think—"

"She was tied up with a mic cord. Apparently, her shin was cracked in half, and her wrists were—"

"Enough!" Mrs. Fowler declared. "That's enough of that talk at the dinner table."

I hardly noticed the woman's bold display, though. I

was too hung up on the fact that Dylan knew about the broken shin. That detail hadn't made it to the press, as far as I knew. "Where'd you hear about all that?"

"Papers, mostly. And people at the club talk. Well, Mike Check talks. He never stops, especially when he has something this good to talk about. I'm sure the bastard has already used it to get him pity-laid."

Mrs. Fowler made a show of clutching her heart.

"You think there will be more?" I asked.

"More what?"

"Murders."

Just before he scooped a chunk of ground beef into his mouth, he said, "Jesus, I hope not."

Mrs. Fowler mumbled, "I hope you don't talk like that at work."

"Of course I don't, *Mother*." He spat the last word like an insult. "Who talks the same way around five-year-olds as they do around adults? Give me a little credit."

I let the conversation shift away from Laugh Attack, even though I was eager to get more from him, and I stuck around for another ten minutes as Dylan told me about his job at St. Ignatius. Feigning interest became more difficult as the carbs set in, and to be honest, kids bored the hell out of me. Kids were cute, sure, and obviously, my job included protecting them. I was all for that. But my eyes glazed over, and my mind wandered any time I had to spend more than a few minutes actively engaging with them. I didn't even bother to see my own nieces and nephews. Not like my sister was huge on that anyway.

The point was that the conversation was slowly lulling me into a cloudy and dull mind, and that was not the way to be when I was working a case. I needed to get gone before I made a slip I couldn't explain away.

I thanked Mrs. Fowler for the coffee and dinner and agreed to come back to see her soon, though I couldn't imagine the woman wanted that. Not from a bartender. Maybe she hoped to wring more gossip from me later. Or more misery. Schadenfreude was one hell of a drug, and I'd learned to spot an addict like Francis from a mile away. People like her could easily become hooked on my childhood. By the sounds of it, she might already be.

"It really is my house, you know," Dylan said as he walked me out onto the front porch.

"Huh?"

"It's my house. I just let her live in it."

"I hope this doesn't come off as rude, but *why*?"

He chuckled. "She's been through a lot. My dad was a real piece of shit. He left us when I was six, and my brother was seven. Brady lives up in Denver and never comes to see her. He hates her guts."

He paused before the driveway and gazed toward the street. "Is that your car?"

"Yep. I see you got one, too."

"Great minds," he said. "Figure I drank out of enough plastic straws back in college; I should make up for it by being fuel-efficient."

"Math checks out. I just like the way it drives. And the hatchback. Lots of space in the back."

He stuck his hands into his jeans pockets and sighed. "Yep. Definitely that." Then he went in for a hug before I could stop him, and I tried not to lock up when I felt his hand brush against the microphone's receiver clipped to my bra strap.

It was a quick hug, though, and I didn't catch any hints that he thought anything of the hard protrusion. He probably didn't know what the back of a woman's bra normally felt like, not so long as Francis had his nuts in a jar on her cramped kitchen counter.

"Maybe I'll see you around Laugh Attack," he said.

"Yeah. Thanks for the walk down Memory Lane." I forced a smile and waved goodbye.

No sooner had I shut the car door than Escobar's voice blasted into my right ear. *"Well, that was all kinds of weird, wasn't it?"* He'd been so silent that I'd almost forgotten he was listening.

I started the quiet engine of my loaner and exhaled, letting myself relax. "You're telling me. This debrief is gonna last all night."

"For the last time, Capone. We're not spending the night together, no matter how much you beg."

I bit down a grin and watched Dylan in my rearview mirror as he disappeared into the house.

"You wouldn't last a night with me, Escobar. Now shut up, and if you beat me back to the station, put on a pot of coffee like a good boy, would ya?"

TWENTY-ONE

June 30th, 2018

24 days since Blackstenius murder

It was just past three a.m. before we'd processed and annotated all of our recordings, and I'd typed up my report. Not only was it late, but my mind was exhausted from running in the same circles over and over again.

Dylan had believed both victims were sleeping with Mike Check. I wasn't under the impression that he and Mike talked much, and yet he'd known about Cheryl's shin. Had Mike really gone into that sort of detail about the scene in a public setting, or did Dylan know about the broken leg by way of the more sinister scenario?

Dylan Fowler certainly fit the FBI profile to a T. He was the right age, drove the right car, lived with an overbearing mother, and had turned up around the club right before the murders began. He ticked the boxes, no denying it.

So the question became: *How much do I care about the*

FBI profile? The answer was, still, *not very much.* They'd been right before, I'd give them that, and their criminal psychologists had certainly learned from the best, but the bureaucracy wasn't exactly known for its ability to evolve with the times, and, boy, had society changed since the sixties and seventies. Even since the nineties. In some ways, at least. In others, well, nothing had really changed.

So that was where I found myself in those early-morning hours, wondering exactly where I fell on the Dylan Fowler theory. The evidence so far had nothing to say about it because there was no evidence connecting him.

Technically speaking, that was all I should have concerned myself with: collecting facts. Follow the trail to a likely suspect, not the other way around. Then, once I felt like I'd collected enough, my job was to present it all to the assistant district attorney. Forming my own opinion wasn't required and did little more than cloud my judgment to the point of being unable to do my job properly. I knew that well enough. The only thing that truly mattered in the course of law was what the judge or jury decided, not what some screwed-up Homicide cop suspected.

Sergeant Popov had held over with the George sector evening shift, and the old Russian was no doubt in a hurry to review our findings and get a few hours' sleep before his regular shift in Homicide began.

He entered the conference room with a drum-sized 7-Eleven mug full of steaming coffee and lowered himself gracelessly into the chair closest to the TV. "Let's cut to the chase. Is Fowler our guy?"

"We can't tell," Ben said, taking the lead.

"You can't tell?" Popov echoed. "Is that the summary?"

"We don't have any evidence, but..." Ben shot me a

look, and I motioned for him to go ahead and say it. He'd made his position on the matter clear to me over the last half-dozen hours. "He fits the preliminary profile from the Behavioral Analysis Unit almost to a T. White male in his thirties, loner—"

"That part's up for debate," I interjected just to make sure *someone* said it. "He seems like a loner right now because he's a teacher on summer break. You meet enough teachers, you know they have no life outside of school during the year, and friends don't suddenly pop up the second the final bell rings for summer."

Ben waited until I was finished then continued. "He lives with his overbearing mother. I mean, she's one of the *most* insufferable, emasculating humans you could imagine. And, of course, he drives a Prius."

"Which we already knew," Popov added. "Anything else? I'd love to hear that I didn't authorize a total flop."

If I stood a chance of being taken seriously in my hesitations, I also needed to present the whole story. What I said next didn't work in Dylan's favor, but it had to be said if I gave a shit about getting to the truth. "He seems emotionally stunted." That got Popov's attention, just like I knew it would. "If you could've seen his bedroom, it looked like a child's. Band posters, very little mind paid to decoration. It was like he'd moved back home, and his mother had just kept everything the same as when he left for college. So that's weird that he wouldn't update, but people get busy, right? Especially teachers. Except that's not exactly how this went down. He claims to own the house himself, so we looked up the records, and it shows that the house was purchased by its current owner, Dylan

Elijah Fowler, only five years ago. He decorated it like that *as an adult.*"

"Was emotionally stunted in the profile?" Popov asked.

"It doesn't have to be when it comes to the type of criminal we're hunting, sir. Yes, our unsub appears to be an organized killer, so you might expect a more pristine home environment, but that's not always the case. Killing is so intermingled with the DNA of—"

"Okay, get on with it. What else we got?"

I blinked away the exhaustion that was setting in hard and fast. "There's a locked closet in his bedroom. There are actually two closets. One doesn't lock, and when I had a minute alone, I checked it—legally, don't worry—and didn't see anything in it that would arouse suspicion. But the other one, which was smaller, possibly a linen closet, was locked. I don't know why he would do that when it's just him and his mother there."

"Porn," said Popov flatly. "Or, hell, maybe it *is* a dead body. It's anyone's guess and, quite frankly, irrelevant, since we can't get in there without more evidence to grant us a warrant. Was he at Laugh Attack the night of both murders?"

"Yes," I said. "But I don't know about after, during the time frame when Leslie was lured from the bar and murdered. I couldn't quite steer the conversation in that direction without it being obvious. We'd need to bring him in for questioning before we could get that information, I think."

"Also," Ben added, "he has a beef with Mike Check. And he seems to be under the impression both Cheryl Blackstenius *and* Leslie Scopes were sleeping with him."

Popov's bushy, translucent eyebrows pinched together.

"I thought we ruled out a relationship between Mike Check and the Scopes girl."

"We have," Ben said. "No one we spoke with seemed to think it was a real possibility, and Mike Check flat-out denied it. But if the killer is picking his targets based on any sort of *revenge* motive..." He shrugged. "Who knows? Maybe the killer covets any woman Mike Check touches. And if Dylan *thinks* he touched both women—"

"The crimes weren't sexual in nature, though," Popov said.

"All due respect, sir," I replied, the pinprick of a tension headache forming between my eyes, "when a straight man murders women, it's always sexual in nature."

Popov grunted. "Fair enough, Freud. So, here's my question: after all you've just told me about this Fowler guy, why in the Sam Hill would you conclude you're *not* looking at a viable suspect? Lack of physical evidence aside, he fits the profile and then some. He was hanging out at the comedy club both nights. He believes both vics were sleeping with a guy he hates."

"We haven't even mentioned the outburst at the dinner table," Ben muttered.

Popov tossed the hand not holding his giant coffee into the air. "What's the mental block, then?"

Ben crossed his arms and stared fixedly at the conference table. "I'll let Detective Capone take this one."

I knew my audience, and I understood this would *not* be well received, but I had a duty to say it. Because if I didn't, no one would, then we might continue on down a path to the wrong conclusion. And in the meantime, more women would die.

Some lessons we learn the hard way. I had to speak up.

I braced myself and spat it out. "The FBI profile is wrong. Some parts are too specific, and some are way too general. Adhering to it too literally is just going to blind us. I don't know how else—"

"It's both too specific and too general?" Popov set down his coffee and put his head in his hands. "I'm too tired for this shit, Capone."

"I knew you'd say that, and it's fine. I understand you have to proceed according to what you have. But I can't get behind Dylan Fowler being our guy. Not yet."

He lifted his head again, dragging his fingers down his pink face as he did. "What would it take? I ask that genuinely because I can't even guess."

I remembered the glare Dylan shot me when he'd returned to his bedroom and spotted me lunging for the bed. And the way he'd slapped the table at dinner *was* a strange aberration from his usual demeanor, almost like his facade had slipped.

Two parts of me were locked in battle, and I couldn't see clearly through the fog of war. "I don't know, sir. I guess I'll know when I see it."

"Okay. Fine, fine." He took a long sip from his plastic coffee cup. "At least I know where you stand on it. Escobar, do you share her opinion?"

"No, sir. I'm pretty sure Fowler is our guy."

"Over Mike Check?"

"Mike's not off our list, but I would put Fowler ahead of him. Either way, I think each begs for more investigation to cover our asses and keep on the DA's good side."

I knew Ben would apologize to me in short order for disagreeing in front of the sergeant, but there was no need. It wasn't his job to trust my hunches. Wagering your job on someone else's gut was a great way to find yourself without a pension.

"Send your report to the Bureau," Popov continued. "They'll want to know we have someone who fits the bill. Agent Wicklow from the San Antonio office and Agent Turner from Austin are the ones coming on Monday morning. You can direct your report to them."

I didn't know a Wicklow, but I'd worked with Agent Turner a few times before and always found the woman to have a balanced view of the world. If we had to have the FBI crowding us, she would be my first pick.

It was nice to know that, occasionally, even *I* could catch a bit of luck.

Sarge stood. "Anything else you need from me?"

"No, sir," Ben and I said together.

The moment the door shut behind Popov, Ben turned to me. "I'm sorry, Dana. I hate to—"

I held up a hand to stop him before gathering the copies of the written brief that we hadn't bothered using with Sarge. "No hurt feelings here. I know what a lost cause looks like. I just hope Dylan has a good lawyer. Once the FBI hears about all this, they're not going to wait to snatch him up for something."

"Something like the murder of Cheryl Blackstenius and Leslie Scopes?"

"They're not going to get him for that. I'd put money on it. There's no physical evidence connecting him. They would have to find his blood on one of the victims to make a case out of that, since we already know he saw them both prior to the murders. They don't have that, though, according to the medical examiner's report. But it doesn't really matter. We saw that with the Juventus case. They couldn't prove he was the one killing those migrants, so they got him on minor drug charges in Williamson County and had one of their judges give the poor guy the max sentence."

"And the killings stopped."

"It was *marijuana*, Ben. They arrested him for intent to distribute."

"But the killings stopped."

"You really buy that? The theory that Juventus was also the killer leaked to the press. It was everywhere. The real killer got a free pass, probably changed his MO and moved out of state. And even if, say, the FBI *did* get the right guy, what happens when marijuana is decriminalized here in five or ten years, and they decide to make it retroactive?"

Ben opened his mouth but never got the chance to respond because the door opened again without a knock preceding it, and Popov stuck his head in. "Everybody properly caffeinated?"

I froze. His stern tone sent my heart racing. "Why? What's up?"

The sergeant opened the door wider and nodded for us to follow him. "Just got word. Lady Bird Lake. A woman's body just washed up."

TWENTY-TWO

Ben and I rode together to the scene. The body was on the other side of the lake from where Leslie Scopes had been found tied to the pet waste station.

"Good lord," Ben breathed as we crossed the open field toward the caution tape. "Of all the places to wash up."

"Good thing someone found her before sunrise," I said. "Could have been a kid that made the discovery."

"Or a dog."

Auditorium Shores was arguably the most popular spot on the lake to take a picnic, kick around a soccer ball, or throw a Frisbee. It was also one of Austin's go-to off-leash areas for dogs. The sun hardly had to glow in the east before the place was crawling with disturbingly limber people on their yoga mats. And since it was the summer, the mornings also meant a wave of parents trying to tire out their kids first thing so they could get a little peace and quiet in the afternoon.

Popov had smartly bowed out to go home and sleep, putting us in charge of catching him up to speed later on.

I could've gone for a nap myself, or at least a quiet moment out on the lake with Sadie to reset. That the killer had made my favorite spot in town his dump site didn't sit well with me. I knew the location shouldn't make these killings feel personal, but it did. What little optimism remained in me kept hoping I'd eventually find someplace that felt like a home should: no predators prowling, just safe and secure. So far, no dice. I was the lightning-struck tower. Nothing around me was built to last.

As we crossed the manicured field down toward the lake, I spared a thought for the dead animals around my apartment complex. Specifically, the cat on my doorstep. There felt an inevitability to it, really. Like I had been marked as a child, or perhaps even at birth. Evil had a way of finding me.

But maybe that talent went both ways.

The body was already covered in black plastic when we arrived. I recognized Sergeant Graves and approached her. "Sergeant."

The woman turned and acknowledged me with a small tilt of her head. "Detective Capone. Wish I could say it was nice to see you again."

"I've got a real Grim Reaper vibe going, huh? This is my partner, Detective Ben Escobar. Escobar, Sergeant Graves."

"We worked the murder at Laugh Attack together," the sergeant explained to Ben. "Just seems right that we should be on this one, too."

Ben said, "You think it's related?"

"I have thoughts, but you take a look for yourself."

She led us over to the black lump, and one of the officers pulled back the plastic.

My stomach clenched as the victim's face was revealed. I wasn't usually squeamish, but the bloat of a waterlogged body always tested my stomach's mettle. IDing was going to be a bear. "Any idea how long she's been dead?"

"Not yet," said Graves. "If I had to guess, a few weeks. Maybe more." She motioned for the officer to pull the sheet back farther.

The victim was tied up with black nylon rope, hardly visible beneath the bulging bloat. It left her looking less like a human and more like a grotesque honey-baked ham.

I leaned close, getting hit with a strong, regrettable whiff of lake sludge as I did. Bits of the vic's bound arms were missing. Fish food now.

While only a few scraps of her clothing clung to her body, that held little importance compared to what was happening below the knees. And what *wasn't* happening.

"Has the rest of the right leg turned up yet?" I asked, shifting my weight to inspect the mangled mess of the knee.

"Nope," said Graves. "And I don't expect it to. It looks like she's been in the water a while. You'd expect her to have shown up much sooner unless something was holding her down. I don't see any obvious punctures to the lungs just looking at her, so I think that leg was attached to something heavy."

"Concrete boots?" Ben said, raising a skeptical brow. "That's not something we're used to seeing here."

"Exactly," said Graves. "I don't think it was that elaborate. More like whoever did this tied a heavy rock to her leg and threw her in."

"Then the ligaments tore, and she surfaced?" I said.

Graves cringed. "That or the snapping turtles found her."

I didn't bother with further speculation. Because the foot that was still attached to the rest of her, or rather what was on that foot, now *that* was interesting. "She was in the water for weeks—let's say turtles ate one of her legs off, her clothes have seen better days, and yet *somehow* that single high heel stayed on." I gestured at the mossy thing. Only small bits of a faded, ruddy color were visible beneath the tangles of green and brown vegetation. But there was no mistaking what it was—the sharp toe poking up toward the stars, the spiky heel still intact.

"I was thinking the same thing," said Graves.

Ben said, "Bodies are found with shoes on all the time."

Graves and I exchanged a look, and I decided to take mercy on him. "Not shoes like this. The thing doesn't even have a strap on it. She'd be hard-pressed to keep it from falling off just walking down Congress Avenue."

"The bloating might have something to do with it," Graves suggested.

"Well, *now*, sure. But she wouldn't have become waterlogged immediately." I crouched beside the shoe. My attention snagged on a strange dimple in the center of the victim's remaining foot. I leaned closer and aimed my flashlight at it.

Oh, sweet Jesus.

As quickly as I could without losing my balance and toppling onto the dead woman, I moved around to get a clear look at the sole of the heel. Sure enough, there it was, sticking out only a quarter of an inch, but unmistakable. "There we have it."

Ben joined me low to the ground. "There we have what?"

"I think I figured out how the shoe stayed on." I waved

Sergeant Graves closer before pointing my beam at the spot again.

"That is a large nail," said Graves, bracing her hands on her thighs. "Yeah, that would do it."

I'd always appreciated Ben's open displays of disgust. He didn't feel the need to pretend he was immune to the horrors humans inflict on one another like so many other men I worked with. And this was no exception.

"¡Dios mio! Why would anyone nail a high heel to someone's foot?"

"Because they wanted it to stay on," I replied. "Duh. Thought that would go without saying."

Ben and I both stood.

"Why'd the rooster cross the road?" I asked.

He arched an eyebrow at me like I might've gone off the deep end sometime in the last three seconds, but he humored me nonetheless. "Why?"

"Because it was stapled to the chicken."

"Jesus, Dana."

"What, you haven't heard that one?"

Sergeant Graves said, "I've heard it."

"See?" I jabbed a thumb her way. "It's not like I made it up. It's a classic."

Ben shook his head.

Fine, no jokes. I wasn't comedian material anyway.

"Can we roll her?" I asked. "Just onto her side will be enough."

Graves took the shoulders, leaving Ben grimacing as he placed his gloved hands on the victim's hip.

I tilted my head to the side, aiming my flashlight at her back.

Ben adjusted his grip to get a look for himself. "You seeing wings?" he said. "Because I'm not seeing any wings."

Her shirt was in tatters, but the state of her bloated skin was even worse. "I'm not seeing much of anything," I admitted. "Lots of missing skin, but if any of it was carved intentionally versus what's happened to her in the water since... I couldn't say." I stood again. "Doesn't matter. This is the same guy."

Ben still appeared green in the gills as he and Graves moved the victim onto her back again. "You can't say that yet, Dana. I mean, you *can,* and you do, unsurprisingly. But too much is missing. Yes, she's tied up, but it's with nylon rope, not a mic cable. And no wings."

"You can't say there *aren't* any wings, Ben. You can only say we can't tell if there are." I rested my chin on my fingertips and thought it over. "It's entirely possible our unsub hadn't fleshed out the whole scene, pardon the pun, when he killed this woman. She looks like she's been in the water a long time. I would bet you that once forensics and the M.E. take a look, we're talking three weeks at least. That could mean she predates Cheryl Blackstenius. It's not uncommon for a killer to add new flourishes as he goes, amplify the fantasy."

For whatever reason, Ben still seemed reluctant. "She's also missing a broken shin to tie her to the others."

"She's missing the *entire* shin, Ben."

Sergeant Graves quickly excused herself and ordered around a few patrol officers, leaving Ben and me to have it out.

"Okay," he said, jamming his hands into his pockets. "I admit there are some similarities. I *might* even agree with your hunch here. But someone has to be the devil's advocate. People don't want three bodies from the same killer turning up in a matter of weeks. The city won't like it, which means the chief won't like it, which means Popov won't like it."

"The FBI will like it," I said. "They'll *love* it. This is their wet dream. Maybe I should call them right now and have them send the agents early."

He gripped my shoulder and gazed fiercely into my eyes. "You're *clearly* sleep-deprived." He let his hand drop and looked down at the body again. Silence hung between us before he said, "Honestly, she looked vaguely Asian to me. And Asians don't fit the victim pattern."

I sucked in air. "Yikes. First off, the fact that you see her eyes swollen shut and say she's Asian is... pretty racist." Ben opened his mouth, but before he could get a word out, I held up a hand. "I know, I know. You didn't mean it like that. Whatever. I know you're not racist. But also, if her race doesn't fit the pattern, then we might have the wrong pattern."

"That is"—he narrowed his eyes at me—"not police thinking. I mean, hell, how many people have died in Austin in the last three weeks? If you wanted to, you could say they all fit the pattern of being Austin residents and tie the deaths together."

I checked the time on my watch. Just before five. "Don't murdersplain to me, Ben, I have a full year on you in Homicide. Besides, I see your point, but that doesn't mean it's the right approach here. Her high heel was *nailed onto her.*"

"*Exactly,*" he said. "And that wasn't the case for either Cheryl or Leslie. Their shoes weren't nailed on. Ergo, it's not a pattern."

I was done pleading my case. Ben was one of the few people in my life I genuinely liked, but if I didn't get some space when I was this tired and he was this contrarian, I would end up liking him a little less.

I wandered to the edge of the water and gazed out over the city. It was still quiet, and there was a pleasant breeze coming off the lake, shushing the world as it sifted through the dry grasses and Mexican sycamores around the banks.

Where had he dumped her? How had nobody seen him? Or perhaps someone had, but who would expect to see a man dumping a woman's body in the heart of Austin? Who would recognize what they were actually witnessing?

People only ever saw what they expected to see. And as much as it stung like an infected wound to admit it, I was no exception. Was that what I was doing here? Seeing all the similarities and ignoring the obvious deviations between crimes?

I could suffer from tunnel vision when I believed I had a natural-born predator in my sights. But that kind of focus and fixation was the only way to catch them. You took your eyes off for a second, and they slipped away.

So, what if this body *was* unrelated? I let the scenario play out.

The nylon rope binding the vic's arms to her body was pretty standard for anyone who wanted to secure a prisoner. It was also available at any home and garden store. Easy to get a hold of. And while the cement boot, or whatever had been used as an anchor, was more elaborate than what we usually saw, it would only take watching one mafia movie to get that idea.

I scanned the expanse of the lake.

The interstate stretched right over the water to the west

of Auditorium Shores, and it didn't take being in law enforcement to know I-35 was a trafficking highway. Cartel could have tossed her over. It would've made a large splash and risked someone seeing it, but leave it to the cartels to have brass balls like that. And leave it to Austinites to assume nothing bad could happen in their safe city.

That left the high heel to account for. A nail driven through the foot could be to hold on the shoe. But what if that wasn't it? What else could be the reason? Stigmata? Could it be some sort of religious statement? Maybe the nail had gone through both feet originally, but once they bloated, the missing foot was forced off. Or the turtles got to it.

There weren't stigmata marks on the hands, as far as I could tell, so that might rule out the already paper-thin theory. Stigmata meant holes in *both* the feet and hands, even though it'd long since been established that the nails went through Jesus's wrists, not his palms.

I dragged a hand down my face and fought against the weight of my eyelids. I needed sleep, assuming I could survive the drive home without taking out a guardrail. These all-nighters had carried a taste of thrill when I first made detective, but a decade later, and the novelty had worn off.

Debating myself was getting me nowhere. Asian or not, this poor girl was one of *his*. I was sure of it in every part of my body that *wasn't* my overtired brain.

TWENTY-THREE

Sadie was curled up on the handwoven rug, snoring rhythmically next to me in our dark living room. The dog seemed to enjoy the meditative state I slipped into when I had my cards spread in front of me on the coffee table.

I'd long ago decided that I could never tell a soul at work about this hobby of mine. They already thought I was a little off my rocker, and learning I read tarot wouldn't do to my reputation any favors. Especially with the Catholics like Ben. Never mind that I didn't believe there was any magic in the process of shuffling a deck and flipping cards over one by one.

Or maybe I did.

Sometimes it was hard to completely refute the notion of magic when the story the cards told was so damn accurate. But the idea that there might be some invisible force at work when I shuffled and created my spreads didn't fit with any of my other beliefs about how the world worked, so I never took it on as truth, no matter how convincing the evidence might be in isolation.

There were two prominent stigmas against reading cards. The first was that it was a nonsense way to pass the time, all statistical odds and psychological projection, a parlor game for the illogical. Accordingly, anyone who practiced it was of low intelligence or otherwise playing fast and loose with reality.

The second stigma was more insidious, though. Strong tides washed through every culture, and once the water subsided, the debris on the bank might be the only reminder we had of how close we came to danger. I grew up during the Satanic Panic. The fear had roared through the collective American consciousness, a backdrop upon which all evil acts could be put in a nice, neat context.

Satan worshippers, witchcraft, heavy metal—all of it was said to corrupt the youth and create monsters. When Raymond had made the news, those buzzwords colored headlines for weeks, and I felt the insidiousness of the label firsthand.

But in the end, it was all just a flash flood of hysteria. The FBI debunked the connection between the evilest men in modern times and actual satanic worship. Turned out that the ones who took lives so easily, so gleefully, so gruesomely worshipped no one but themselves.

Still, once the flash flood had passed, among the detritus on the shores were things like earth magic and tarot, practices that hurt no one, that were as far from evil as Christianity. Or perhaps even farther, if my basic knowledge of the Crusades held.

I'd learned as a teenager what evil really was, and it wasn't found in a deck of cards. Nothing was found in my deck except bursts of clarity and fresh ideas, and only if I was lucky. When the stakes were so high, like they were with this string of murders, I'd take help wherever I could get it.

The five-card spread on my cleared-off coffee table slowly brought me into the right state of mind to locate the fine threads that connected these three murders. The flicker from my Santa Maria de Guadalupe candle cast long strips of light dancing over the arcana. I relaxed, breathed, began the turn.

The Seven of Cups. The Four of Swords. The Five of Wands. The Lovers. The Devil.

My phone buzzed on the couch behind me, and I jumped as the rattling of it tore through my calm like a bullet.

"Dana Capone."

Ben's voice greeted me. "How'd I know you'd still be up?"

I glanced at the clock by the TV. "It's only ten thirty."

"She said after an all-nighter. You're a real-life zombie, you know that?"

"I do. Is that what you called to tell me? Because if you're up too, it's not just me who's the undead."

"I only get to crash out early when Audrey is at her mother's house, but I have her tonight. I just got her down to bed an hour ago. And *then* the nanny wasn't happy about staying late, so I had to make it up to her."

"You don't mean..."

There was silence on his end, then, "Oh, *god*, no. She's, like, twenty-three, Capone. Sheesh. Give me some credit here. I'm not to my midlife crisis yet."

I glanced down at my cards absent-mindedly, my eyes fixing on the Lovers' vibrant colors and twisting lines. "I dunno, Ben. Madison was pretty young, and you went after her."

"We hooked up for two weeks. And you were seeing her younger brother."

"That makes me a cougar. It makes you a creep. Anyway, I assume you got something for me."

"Yeah, what I was *gonna* say before your vulgar implications was that Detective Chan in Missing Persons just called me up about ten minutes ago. They were able to ID her."

Sadie shifted in her sleep, snuggling closer against my crossed leg, and a sudden and welcome wave of tiredness swept over me. "Must've been good if you couldn't wait till morning to call. You know I don't usually accept calls from single men after nine p.m."

He ignored the last remark. "Turns out she *is* Asian like I said. Her dad's Korean."

"Okay? And what else?"

"What do you mean? That's it. I needed you to know I was right."

"Fine, you're not a racist."

He was slow to respond, and I could imagine him on the old sectional in his living room, feet kicked up onto the coffee table, the phone in one hand, a bottle of Pacifico in the other. It'd have a lime slice floating in it.

"I don't have any of the Laugh Attach sign-up lists on me," he said, "but I figure asking you is as good as looking up the vic's name. So, do you remember seeing the name Stephanie Lee on any of the rosters?"

I stared down at the cards. "No. She wasn't on the list. But the name rings a bell. I dunno why, but it does."

"I won't hold it against you that you can't remember. It's late at night, and it's a pretty generic name."

"Gee, thanks."

He paused again, and my mental picture of him was all but confirmed when I heard the distinct sucking sound of him taking a swig from a bottleneck. "I'll ask around tomorrow morning," he said, "and see if anyone around the club has heard of her. But I gotta tell you, I think it might be unrelated."

"I know you do. And I guess it doesn't matter if it is or isn't. When it comes down to it, she's still dead."

"Ah, yeah, there's that."

We signed off, and I tossed the phone back onto the couch. Stephanie Lee. Where had I heard that name recently?

Or maybe Ben was right, and it was just generic and sounded like some other name I was familiar with.

I returned my attention to the spread and tried to relax my mind again.

Seven of Cups. Four of Swords. Five of Wands. The Lovers—

"Holy shit."

There it was in a flash. The timeline even matched up. I knew where I'd heard the name Stephanie Lee before.

From Dylan Fowler.

TWENTY-FOUR

July 1st, 2018

25 days since Blackstenius murder

It was seven in the evening before I made it into the office the following day. My insomnia was somewhat famous around the station, and my colleagues had long ago stopped giving me shit for showing up at odd times. They knew I had to get my sleep wherever and whenever I could. Most seemed to assume it was the cases keeping me awake until sunrise.

Right. Like working Homicide would disrupt my delicate feminine constitution. Investigating murders didn't horribly affect any of the others in my division, but that estrogen-laden Dana, she was really struggling.

What was it to me if they believed that, though? I'd always enjoyed being underestimated. It left room for surprises.

As far as I knew, my past wasn't common knowledge. I'd changed my last name before applying to the department, and I'd made it clear to those who needed to know that it was no one else's business.

That didn't mean it hadn't gotten around. Cops gossiped with what could only be described as excessive force. Usually, the information that spread was all kinds of wrong. What kernel of truth there might be was saddled with the worst fears of each person it passed through. Just a side effect of a profession where a solid performance required overtaxed adrenals, topnotch worst-case thinking, and a healthy dose of paranoia. And all while maintaining a calm exterior to represent the department well. The tension had to come out somewhere, and the rumor mill was it.

With the exception of Ben and a few others, mostly direct superiors who needed to know for one reason or another, no one else in the department had firsthand intel on my childhood. There was a scare a couple years in when one of my shift mates on patrol had put two and two together and started digging, but my sergeant at the time put a muzzle on that before it made the headlines.

I'd been around long enough now that I liked to think people saw me for my successes and failures for APD, not for who I'd been and what had happened to me prior to the academy. That may or may not be true, but the bottom line was that if anyone had heard whispers about me, they certainly didn't let me know it.

And so, they assumed my insomnia was work-related. They didn't know about the ancient nightmares at the root of my deprivation. They didn't know that cases like this one only woke that sleeping terror that was already there, with its snarling face and stench of death.

But I hadn't spent the afternoon catching up on sleep. I'd been busy. And productive.

"There you are," said Ben as he hung up the phone at his desk. He was smiling smugly. As much as I liked and respected the man, it'd be fun to wipe that look off his face when the right moment presented itself.

"Here I am." I unburdened myself of my bag then swiveled in my chair to face my desk. "You got something?" I'd keep a poker face about my hand until he showed his. Gotta get your thrills where you could.

"Sure do. And I just got off the phone with Agent Turner, and she agrees with me."

"Just tell me what it is. You don't need backup if it's a sound theory."

"The very *Korean* Stephanie Lee was reported missing two months ago, last seen leaving a bar with her boyfriend at the time, Roger Smart. Then Smart moved to Sacramento the same weekend she disappeared. Her friends say she was a talented pianist but *not* a comedian. No evidence so far links her to the other two victims, kinda like I was trying to tell you at the scene." He leaned back in his chair, clasping his hands behind his head. "What do you think?"

"I think you're right."

His eyes popped open. "Really?"

"Hell no. But I understand why Agent Turner agreed with you, given *that* information. However, I collected different information this morning, and it's going to prove you wrong."

"For once," he said, "*just for once*, I'd love if we could be on the same page."

I woke up my monitor with a tap on the mouse. "Then flip to the right one, my friend."

After logging into my inbox, I let my eyes roam down the list of unread messages. Jesus... how many people thought it was necessary to copy me on every correspondence? I clicked on one that looked relevant to my actual job and read through it. "Huh. Seems the ballistics report came back on the shooting down on Eleventh Street the other night, and it matches a gun supposedly stolen from Jeremy Johnson's home on April twenty-ninth." I turned to Ben for a reaction only to discover him glaring at me unblinkingly. "That's good news," I added. "We knew Johnson was the one who did it, and the fact that he never reported the gun stolen until someone was shot is plenty to get a search warrant."

"Great, great," Ben said dismissively. "But are you going to tell me why I'm wrong about Stephanie Lee, or are you going to punish me and go behind my back to build your case and then hang me and the FBI out to dry?"

I frowned at him. "I would never hang you up to dry on purpose, Ben. But if you decided to side with the FBI when they were especially wrong, then it might happen *accidentally*."

He squinted at me, and his lips pressed into a sharp line. The pissed-off skepticism was quite handsome on him, actually.

"Okay, fine, I'll tell you. No, better yet, I'll show you. Get up."

He grunted. "Where are we going?"

"Sixth Street."

He patted his pockets then held up his empty hands. "But I don't have any cocaine on me."

"Don't worry, I brought enough for both of us. Let's go."

We left the station and entered the muggy evening air. It was only a few blocks to get to where we needed to be, but by the time we did, Ben's dress shirt had dark circles under his armpits and a blob on the back that looked unfortunately like a target.

The streets weren't packed yet, but they would be soon. Even though it was a Sunday night, it was the first of the month, and you couldn't stop people from drinking hard on the first if you tried. Bills paid, money gone—the credit cards would take it from there! All the coke dealers had Venmo now anyway.

But I didn't need the streets to be absolutely flooded with drunk tourists to make my point. I only needed a handful of wobbly women. "Pizza?" I said as the glowing sign for Roppolo's loomed down the sidewalk.

"I'm more interested in learning why we're out here."

"You will," I assured him. "But do you *also* want pizza?"

"Well, *yes*. Of course."

We grabbed a slice each, and I led him to a solid vantage point to take in the scene. We leaned against the brick exterior of one of the bars, beside its large open windows overlooking the street. Establishments like this were known around the department as crack shacks ever since the two brothers who'd owned several of them were busted for a drug-trafficking operation that began in Juarez and ended in little baggies that could be purchased at a reasonable price from said crack shacks if one knew the right way to ask.

The traffic barricades that allowed the Sixth Street

partiers to stumble around freely only went up on Friday and Saturday nights, which meant that on this unusually busy Sunday, cars crept through the intersection, drivers doing their best not to hit the pedestrians who buried themselves in their cell phones or lawlessly whizzed through the crosswalk on electric scooters.

I wiped a spot of pizza grease from my cheek with the flimsy white napkin crumpled in my hand. "Look at these women," I said to Ben. "Particularly, focus on the ones coming out of the bars and clubs. Is there anything in common so far as what they're wearing?"

To his credit, Ben actually observed them for a silent moment, eating his folded slice and pondering. "Women's clothing?" he said, finally, then added, "But no, not even that."

"Exactly," I said. "Now, turn your attention to the footwear. How many women are wearing high heels? And I don't mean a little bit of a wedge. I'm talking full high heels."

He didn't need as long the second time. "Maybe half?"

"I'd say closer to a third." Ben granted me that with a nod. "You know why?"

"Nope."

"Because it's not the fifties anymore, and high heels are uncomfortable as shit. And we're in *Austin*. Live Music and Sloppy Dressing Capital of the World. Women here have their 'going out' flip-flops."

"All right, fair enough. But what's your point?"

"Cheryl Blackstenius was five-foot-ten. Mike Check, who she was very likely still trying to impress in the days leading up to her murder, was five-eight. I called up Monica Summers, Cheryl's roommate. I asked her to check

Cheryl's closet for any high heels, since we didn't think to while we were there. She didn't find any. Fair enough, though, right? Maybe Cheryl was wearing her only pair the night she was murdered."

Ben nodded. Good. I still had him hooked.

"But if Cheryl was five-ten and the man she was hooking up with and trying to impress was five-eight, she wasn't going to wear heels around him. Mike Check has an inferiority complex if I ever saw one. He uses his position of power to get sex. I mean, thank god he chose to work in comedy and not politics or religion, but that's beside the point. Cheryl would know that wearing heels, making herself a brush over six feet tall, wouldn't play well with someone like Mike. And yes, all women have an awareness of this sort of thing. People would make jokes about the height difference between them, *especially* in a place like Laugh Attack. Mike was probably touchy about her height as it was—maybe he'd made comments before; wouldn't put it past him. I'd even venture to guess that she slouched when she was around him. And if you remember, Monica said that Cheryl generally went for short guys. She wouldn't be in the habit of wearing heels.

"So, I called a few of the people on the sign-up list from that night—don't worry, we've cleared all the ones I spoke with. Unfortunately, most of them were men and couldn't remember what footwear she had on. But then I got a hold of Heidi Ruiz, and she said she was almost sure Cheryl was wearing Converse on stage the night she died. That's usually what she wore, apparently. It was more her style. And yet she was found at the crime scene in heels. Could she have changed shoes after the set? Sure. But there's no clear reason why she would. None of the people we've spoken with have mentioned any plans she might've had to hit the town after. And as you can see, heels are by no means a requisite for hitting this town."

I snuck another glance and was pleased to see that familiar expression he wore when new information was actually getting through and wreaking havoc with his existing theories.

I pushed on. "I called around about Leslie Scopes. And it turns out that the friends she was with said she was wearing heels when she left them at the bar on the night she was killed."

Ben held up a hand to stop me. "Okay, so I *thought* I knew where you were going, but it sounds like you just disproved your own theory."

"Not necessarily. Because I also called around about Stephanie Lee."

He sighed exasperatedly. "We don't know she's related."

"You might change your mind when you hear this. I confirmed with *three* people that two months ago, she was dating none other than Michal Nebojsa."

His head whipped toward me. "She was dating Mike Check? Are you shitting me?"

"I wish I was." Not true. I was thrilled to have unearthed that little tidbit today. It made it harder to pretend her death wasn't tied in with the others.

"Goddammit." He stuffed an overlarge bite of pizza into his mouth and moaned despite the unwelcome news.

"Turns out, she was never on the sign-ups because she never got on stage. But she came around the club a few times. She was just a weird comedy groupie, like Dylan Fowler mentioned."

"Hold on. Dylan Fowler?"

"It's all on the recording from his house," I said. "Go check the tapes."

"No need. I'm sure you already have."

"Obviously."

He wiped grease off his chin with the heel of his hand. "So we definitely have a connection between Stephanie Lee and Laugh Attack, then."

"And Mike Check, yes. But there's more. Until her disappearance a month ago, not a single one of Stephanie's friends I spoke with had *ever* seen her wear high heels. And definitely not any as flashy as the one nailed to her foot."

Ben shoved the last of his crust into his mouth and licked his fingers. "Let me get this straight. You think the killer, what, brought his own shoes to the murders? Then he killed the vics and put the heels on them? You telling me we have the BYOH Strangler running around?"

"In two of the cases, yes. For Cheryl Blackstenius and Stephanie Lee, I think he brought the shoes with him, which opens the door to all kinds of interesting pathologies and theories."

"And he didn't put the heels on Leslie Scopes because she was—"

"Already wearing heels, yeah. I described the ones we found on her to her friends, and they confirmed she was wearing those that night. And they weren't *that* different from the style and color of the pair on Cheryl and the one found on Stephanie. I think the killer might have brought heels for Leslie and then realized he didn't need them after all."

"Shit," he breathed, his gaze flowing over the

thickening sea of bodies. "And you're sure Lee was dating Mike Check?"

"Yep. He fits the description. Guy named Mike, works at a comedy club. So, when I called the Ruizes to speak with Heidi, I asked about that, too. She wasn't sure if she remembered a Stephanie Lee, but Scott said he remembered her."

"Of course he does. What is it with white guys his age and Asian chicks?"

I decided not to let the rhetorical question derail me. "Scott described her, and it was a match. For obvious reasons, I haven't verified the story with Mike Check yet."

"Shit," he said again.

"I won't tell anyone how wrong you were," I said. "It'll stay our little secret."

He sighed and ran a palm back and forth over his gelled black hair. "Too late for that. The FBI already knows, remember? You talk to Dylan?"

"Huh?"

"I just mean, this pretty much seals it, right? I know you weren't convinced before, but now you know about the shoes and the fact that Dylan mentioned Stephanie Lee even before she was a known victim. Doesn't get much more suspicious than that."

I felt the pizza make its way back up my esophagus. All I'd meant to do with the theory of the heels was tie Stephanie Lee into the equation. But Ben had a point. It was hard to ignore that the string which tied her in also wound itself around Dylan. Goddamn insomnia. Goddamn tunnel vision.

A little less enthusiastically, I said, "No, I didn't speak to him."

This was not the conclusion I'd hoped Ben would come away with from our excursion, but it was clear that this was the one crystallizing behind his dark eyes. And why not? Objectively speaking, it made a hell of a lot of sense.

"What do you need from me now?" he asked.

"I need your help convincing ol' Pops that we should bring Mike Check back in for questioning."

"And Dylan Fowler, too, right?"

I shut my eyes. "No, I don't think we need to go there just yet. But Mike Check, yes. We need to confirm he had a relationship with Lee. He's the connection between these three women."

"He's *one of* the connections. We already know he didn't date Leslie."

"But he knew her. He knew all of them."

"Dana, he's not the only one." Ben inclined his head toward me, and when I made it clear I got his meaning, he relented. "Dylan Fowler aside, Laugh Attack is the connection. And there are plenty of other men who've been hanging around there for a while who we still haven't fully cleared."

"It's not Dylan." The words were out before I could stop them. I didn't even know if I believed them anymore, and I certainly didn't understand why I felt the need to defend him from suspicion. It wasn't like I had a ton of fond memories of him from my youth. I hadn't even known who he was or what past we shared until he told me.

Fowler the Prowler.

"Help me out here," Ben said, "because you were resistant to Mike Check as a suspect when we started out. I said he seemed like our guy, and you wouldn't get on board. Now that Mike Check seems much less likely to me, and Dylan Fowler is looking promising, you're suddenly Team Mike. Are you just doing this to screw with me?"

Three men on electric scooters, weaving recklessly between those on foot, came zooming by us on the sidewalk, and Ben had to jump back to avoid the last one running over his toes. Once he was done cursing, I explained myself.

"When it was just one girl, and you were taking the line of intimate partner violence, yeah, I couldn't get on board. But once we added Leslie, who we don't assume had a sexual relationship with Mike, that takes intimate partner violence off the table. Now I can start to really get on board."

"And Stephanie Lee? He had a relationship with her."

"Yeah, but a man who murders three women in a span of a couple months isn't just an abusive boyfriend. He's a serial killer."

"You also said the friends and family of serial killers were usually safest."

"Maybe he didn't consider Stephanie or Cheryl a friend. He slept with them, but who hasn't slept with someone they loathe deep down?"

Ben squinted judgmentally at me.

"And I've said from the start," I added hurriedly, "that Mike Check could fit the bill for a serial killer."

"It *could* also be Dylan," Ben persisted. "The Fowlers are just too weird, and he fits the pro—"

"I know." I still had the crust left—the best part of the pizza, in my opinion—and I tore off a chunk.

"Be real with me here. Are you actually pro-Mike Check, or are you just playing defense for Dylan?"

"There's no reason why I would do that." I popped the crust into my mouth and headed back toward the station.

Ben hurried to catch up and stepped in front of me, bringing my momentum to an abrupt halt. "You're not being straight with me, Dana, and I don't like it. Why are you resisting this theory?"

I held back my desire to square off with him. "I don't know, Ben. I just... My gut is telling me no."

"You sure it's your *gut?*"

"What else would it be?"

He stuck his hands in his pants pockets and shrugged a single shoulder. "He's a connection to your past and not a bad-looking guy. One might even say he has a certain Ted Bundy appeal." I glared at him. "Sometimes I wish you would really get a clue, you know? I was listening to the conversation y'all had in his bedroom. I heard the tone of his voice. I know pining when I hear it, and you're the kind of woman a man would carry a torch to the ends of the earth for."

"Oh, please. You sound like a jealous boyfriend."

Ben scanned my face in a way that made me supremely uncomfortable. I met his eye, though, refusing to let my discomfort show.

"You know how you come up with all your wild theories, Capone?"

"They're not wild, but sure."

"Well, I got one for you. And you're not gonna like it, but I think you need to hear it."

I planted my feet firmly and crossed my arms over my chest. "Go for it."

"I think Dylan Fowler somehow found out you were in Austin and followed you here. I think he's been obsessed with you for a long time. And maybe he learned a trick or two from your old man, or maybe he just found inspiration in it, and those sick fantasies have been swimming around his mind for a few decades. Now he's here to show off for you. Flaunt his feathers. It's no secret that women go for men who remind them of their father."

The insinuation was a knife to my stomach until I breathed in and faced it straight on. And then the sheer lunacy of it cracked through.

I clapped a hand on his shoulder. "You're all right, Ben. Your theory is *completely* bonkers, but you're my kinda crazy. Keep thinking outside the box." I shoved the rest of the pizza crust into my mouth and headed back to the station.

TWENTY-FIVE

He drew closer, his hunting ground now in sight. Cops swarmed this area on the weekend, but that didn't matter. They were smart enough to stick to the main drag of Sixth and turn a blind eye to bars like this one.

The giant neon sign above the front door flashed *Sheep's Clothing* in pink, then white, then blue, drawing him in like the scent of a roast in the oven. Maintaining a low profile was key, but he was in good company; most people kept a low profile when they came to this place. Until they didn't. Then they went big; they dressed to be seen.

He'd tried it once, back when he was little. The beating he received from the monster who raised him had been so severe, he'd never tried it again.

So now he just watched them. Dreamed about them. Strength and compassion. Confidence and inclusion. True belonging. He longed to possess it, not in himself but through someone else. All those things he never got, he craved, but only to crush them slowly.

He had no intention of making a kill tonight, but the hunt would do him good, hone his mind, help him identify his next target. It was time to attempt a stronger quarry, to advance his skills.

The process of vetting and stalking could take days, weeks. And if his prey noticed him, grew suspicious, he'd have to abandon it and move on. Patience was critical. The only ticking clock he faced was the growing hunger inside him, but he could manage it if doing so meant he stayed a free man until the end.

But he wouldn't move on from *her*. His painted butterfly. Never. She had it all, everything he wanted to destroy. Her neck in his grip would be ecstasy, but he understood there were bigger plans in store for her, better uses in the grand scheme.

She would become the bait to lure a different kind of predator, one who had yet to be fully awakened. He would see to it, though. He would use his butterfly to draw her in, force her hand, and realize who she truly was.

It was a sacrifice on his part, yes, but one that would guarantee his place in history. He would suss out that latent instinct in the huntress, one that had been awakened decades before and stoked again earlier this year. She was the ultimate prize—not prey, but predator. If it was the last thing he did, he'd get to her.

The shrill voice of some candy-and-bubblegum pop singer piped through the cramped bar's speakers and ricocheted around the black interior walls. He kept his sunglasses and ball cap on even after he entered. In other places, such a thing would be considered so out of the ordinary as to be suspect. But not here. Here, everything was suspect in one way or another, and that made it ordinary.

He approached the bar. There was no shortage of beautiful women in this place. He could easily convince one to leave with him. It might take the offer of money to accomplish, but not much. Probably wouldn't require more than an offer to buy the next round.

How many in there were just waiting to whore themselves out? To pretend they were reluctant while in reality craving it hard and fast and rough? They didn't dress that way because they were shy. They might play the part, blushing and giggling over his advances, but if he flashed some cash and told them to follow him, at least one of them would before the end of the next song. He was sure of it.

But there was no glory in picking off the sickest of the herd. No true satisfaction.

He scanned the claustrophobic space. A dark hallway branched off from the dance floor in the back corner, leading to the bathrooms. There was an emergency exit that way as well. Could he and his prey slip back there unnoticed?

He'd had no intention of striking on this territory until the final blow, but it wasn't a terrible idea. No authorities poking around, plenty of noise to cover up any squeals, booze flowing freely.

Plus, some fresh air might be nice. He couldn't stand the thought of doing it again by another fucking trash can, though. It'd almost ruined Cheryl for him, that stench, swatting away the flies as he tied her up.

The pet waste station with Leslie had just been a stroke of inspiration, not of any particular personal enjoyment.

Make the cops think it might be an important element to the killer. Throw them off his scent, so to speak.

He didn't want to linger and draw eyes to him, even though he'd learned from a young age that his was about as forgettable of a face as there was. Everything about him was forgettable, insignificant. His younger self had hated the fact, but he'd since learned the advantages of it. He could be caught in the very act, and a witness would be hard-pressed to recall much more about him than "white male." That wouldn't get the cops very far.

The bartender addressed him as he slid onto an open stool. "What can I get you, handsome?"

He grinned. She almost reminded him of the one he was hoping to see tonight, to *watch*. "Whiskey neat."

She arched one of her over-penciled eyebrows. "Any whiskey in particular?"

"Wild Turkey sounds fine."

Her upper lip curled. "It's your hangover, sugar. That'll be five."

He slapped seven down on the counter and turned back toward the crowd while she fixed the drink. The tinny music grated on his nerves, and even more so the longer he went unsuccessful in spotting his quarry. She should be there. This was her regular spot. Her regular night. Where she came to let loose and spread her wings.

And then he saw her. He recognized the back of her head immediately. And that ass. God, he might even break his own rules to bury himself in that once he had her under his control. Such an act might leave forensic traces and get him caught, locked behind bars, but what did he care? She was his ticket to the end of the line.

He'd never flirted with her. She couldn't know he came

there specifically to watch her. She'd probably recognized him around the place already, but she wouldn't think much of it so long as he didn't approach her and recognize her back.

"Here you go, hon." The bartender slid him his drink.

He took it and, before she could slip the money away, asked, "What time do you get off tonight?"

She rolled her eyes and held up her hands, wiggling her manicured fingers. "Sweetie, I get off whenever I damn well please thanks to these babies. And it's not ever gonna happen with you, so put that straight out of your mind."

He chuckled and raised his glass to her. "I had to try."

TWENTY-SIX

July 2nd, 2018

26 days since Blackstenius murder

Popov peeked his head into Death Row early Monday morning. "Escobar? Capone?"

I looked up from the files spread across my desk.

"Conference room in five," he said. "Agents Wicklow and Turner just arrived."

I'd had plenty of warning that this was coming, but that didn't mean I was looking forward to it.

They'd call it a joint task force, but I suspected APD would be shut out of it once the agents got a handle on our intel.

At least it was Agent Turner. And maybe Agent Wicklow wouldn't have his head up his ass.

Ben caught my eye across our desks as we wrapped up what we were working on and got to our feet. "If you behave yourself," he said, "I'll buy you ice cream afterward."

"And if you don't hang me out to dry, I'll put in a good word for you with your barely legal nanny."

"You're sick, you know that?"

"Sick of you not getting laid. Might loosen you up a little. I think we could all benefit from that." I logged out of my computer. "I'm gonna need two crush-ins. Three if they have that pecan praline syrup in stock."

"You got it."

"And served in a waffle cone. The kind with colored sprinkles on the outside."

"Whatever you want, Capone. Just be good."

I gathered up the case files that I'd spent a good part of this morning printing and organizing. I was certain my theory about the heels was correct, and even Ben seemed about eighty-five percent on board with it. But that just meant he couldn't find any major flaw in it *yet*, not that he had stopped looking for one.

And that was probably for the best. *Someone* ought to keep poking holes, and I was way too keyed into it to see much else.

We hadn't spoken to Popov about my theory yet, and that was also probably for the best. A long, sleepless night had me even more turned around about where I thought the heel theory led: Mike Check or Dylan Fowler? I couldn't remember the last time I'd felt so conflicted about suspects. Most homicides that weren't simply random acts of violence usually had a blindingly obvious suspect, and the trick was simply making sure you got enough evidence off the sloppy criminal so the DA's office could put them away.

"Detective Capone, great to see you again," said Agent Turner. She circled the conference table as we entered the meeting room. We shook, and her grip was nice and strong, so I didn't end up crushing her hand. Always a pleasant surprise.

"Good to see you, too, Agent," I replied. Ashlynn Turner had rich, dark skin and a commanding presence that didn't so much demand respect as simply establish that respecting her was the natural order, and you'd be wise to fall in line. If her cheekbones weren't registered as weapons somewhere, they ought to be. I suspected that if she looked at someone just right, the object of her attention might keel over from internal injuries. But there was also a kindness that radiated from her, the type that I'd only ever witnessed in people with deep confidence and genuine pride about who they were. I would do just about anything to feel that way, as if there wasn't a crucial cog of my basic machinery that had rusted out and for which no replacement parts existed.

Turner greeted Ben next and then introduced Agent Wicklow, who didn't bother to walk around from the other side of the conference table but instead extended his hand across, forcing us to reach. We took turns leaning awkwardly over to shake.

"Please have a seat, everyone," Sergeant Popov said, gesturing toward the open chairs.

It wasn't lost on me that Turner stayed on our side of the table while Wicklow and Popov settled in opposite.

Agent Wicklow was hard to look at for long. It wasn't just that he was unattractive—though, yeah, there was that. I didn't mind looking at people who weren't blessed with a symmetrical face or clear skin; that was all fine by me. You were dealt what you were dealt. But you could wear it in a lot of different ways. It was something else about him that made him unpleasant. Or maybe a combination of features. His skin was the color of a power-washed street curb, and he had no chin to speak of. Perhaps it was just his unfortunate facial structure that made him look like he'd just smelled something rotten.

Or maybe he was an asshole.

My guess was that he was either borderline genius or extremely well connected to make it into *this* job with a face like *that*.

Some cops claimed looks didn't matter in law enforcement, but that was just willful ignorance. Appearance mattered an awful lot in this line of work. It could be the difference between people trusting you enough to give you the information you were after or immediately taking a disliking to you and clamming up until someone more to their taste showed up. Not only did the latter situation waste time, but it was one hell of a humiliation. I'd seen it happen. The other officers didn't miss it, and then the cop gossip started. Group texting like you wouldn't believe.

I wasn't a fan of Wicklow's face *or* the way he held himself, chest out like a middle school girl before she got her breasts in. The FBI might try to take over the investigation, but I'd be damned if I let Wicklow speak to a single witness or suspect in person.

Popov said, "The FBI has been kind enough to send us two of their best from the Austin and San Antonio offices to help us look into the murders of Cheryl Blackstenius and Leslie Scopes."

I kept my mouth shut about the obvious omission; I'd get to it when the time was right. (I could afford my own damn ice cream cone.)

"They're offering their manpower and their resources," Popov continued, "including access to the VICAP database to search for similar signatures and MOs across the country. It's all at our disposal. They'll be setting up in this room and staying until we get this sorted out. I discussed it with the assistant special agent in charge out of San Antonio, and ASAC Grissom and I agreed that in-person would be easier than all the back and forth via email and phone."

That all sounded tolerable so far. Maybe even encouraging. Access to the Violent Criminal Apprehension Program, or VICAP, was not only useful, but yet another small admission that I'd been right all along and we *were* looking for a serial offender who might have been doing this sort of thing for a while now, just not in the Austin area.

Naturally, after that morsel of good news, I waited for the other shoe to drop.

"And in return—"

Ah, there it was.

"—we're going to let Agent Wicklow take the lead on this. We all seem to be in agreement that a third victim will show up before long, so we'd like to prevent that. Escobar, you got anything to catch us up to speed on?"

Of course he called on Ben and not me.

Ben stood and cleared his throat, and my heart began to race. Strange.

I knew what *I* would say in this situation, but the odds were about fifty-fifty that Ben took it that direction.

"Yeah, actually, we do," he said. "After further investigation, we believe that Stephanie Lee, the woman that washed up in the lake, was, in fact, victim number three—chronologically, victim number one—of the unsub who murdered Cheryl and Leslie."

I didn't cheer, but hot damn, did I want to. Forget about putting in a good word with Ben's nanny. I'd hire him a new, age-appropriate one and pay for her myself.

Sergeant Popov's face transitioned from a delicate dusty rose to maroon in a heartbeat, and Agent Wicklow's scowl deepened.

Agent Turner kept a solid poker face, though. "What brought you to that conclusion?"

Ben's eyes darted down to me on his left. I nodded for him to keep up the good work. "Stephanie Lee had her remaining shoe nailed to her foot," he said. "We believe it was important for whoever killed her to make sure the high heel stayed on. We think high heels, specifically red ones, are significant to the unsub's fantasies."

"But I thought we agreed the XLR cable was the signature," Wicklow said.

"It could be, or it could fall more under his MO—he needed something to tie up the women, and the XLR was available for two of the three murders. Additionally, the M.E. said Lee was killed *before* Blackstenius and Scopes. Maybe the unsub didn't have access to any of Laugh Attack's XLRs at the time of Lee's murder, or maybe he hadn't incorporated that element into the fantasy yet. Signatures can develop over the course of the killings."

Wicklow remained scowling, and I was becoming more convinced that his face was stuck that way. "You're telling me you think the unsub's defining signature is... women wearing women's shoes?"

I kicked my feet out in front of me, settling in as Ben

launched into the cultural education I'd given him the night before. I'd see how good a student he was.

"Not as many women in Austin wear high heels around as you'd think," he said, and I only barely suppressed a satisfied grin.

When I looked past him, I was relieved to see that Agent Turner, at least, seemed receptive to his reasoning and was nodding thoughtfully along.

Well, damn. We might not have to fight the FBI on it after all. Wouldn't that be something?

By the time Ben finished laying out the evidence, I was ready to get a word in. "We think Michal Nebojsa, a.k.a. Mike Check, is a solid suspect. We know he doesn't fit the profile completely, but with all due respect to the FBI, the profile was garbage." Popov opened his mouth, but I cut him off at the pass. "What I mean to say is it hasn't been updated to account for Stephanie Lee and is so broad that it's essentially useless."

Ben took his seat in a hurry, and Turner cracked a smile, but Wicklow said, "So broad, and yet Michal Nebojsa doesn't manage to fit it." His scowl twitched at the corners as if he was attempting a smirk. "I understand there's a suspect who *does* fit the profile, though. Completely. How come we're not talking about him?"

"If we're really married to the profile, Mike Check fits it close enough," I said. "He doesn't live with his mother, but he does share an apartment with an older female cousin. Under the right circumstances, it could amount to the same basic pathology. Sure, he drives a Land Rover instead of a Prius, but if we get too attached to the profile, take it as scripture, we're more likely to let our unsub slip away than catch him."

Wicklow remained unconvinced, if his shit-sniffing expression was any indication. "I've reviewed the file, Detective Capone, and I listened to the recording. Oh yeah, even the part where Fowler mentions the name Stephanie Lee. I wonder if you or Detective Escobar were planning on mentioning that bit."

I could feel Popov's gaze flicker between Ben and me, but I refused to acknowledge it.

"Doesn't mean she could be included as a third victim," Wicklow continued, "but if we do decide to go that way, it puts Fowler at the top of our list. He sure didn't act like an innocent man during that visit. And that's going purely on your noted suspicion in the debrief. I understand you found a locked closet that piqued your interest."

"Fine," I said. "But 'not innocent' doesn't necessarily mean 'murdered three women.' It's my job to be suspicious when I'm gaining intel on a person of interest, Agent Wicklow. That doesn't mean every bit of my suspicion is warranted. For all we know, that locked closet had his winter clothes in it. Or, hell, maybe it's full of gay porn he doesn't want his mother to find. If he's not out yet or confused about his sexuality, that might cause a similar suppressed rage to what we saw in his outburst at the table. And if we're looking *specifically* for a man who lives with his mother, we also don't have that with Fowler. Francis Fowler lives with Dylan. He owns the house and could ask her to leave at any time. It's in the power-up position."

Wicklow scoffed. "His mother may live with him, but she's the one who wears the pants."

"I am curious," Turner said, "why you seem so keen to eliminate Fowler, Detective Capone."

"I'm not keen on it. I just... Okay, fine. I am keen on it.

And I can't explain why." I settled back in my seat, trying not to visibly deflate at the admission. Maybe I should just let it drop, admit that Dylan was a smart choice to focus our attention on. After all, it *could* be him, just like it could be Mike Check.

And yet, if I had to pick one, my money was *still* on the sound guy with the traumatic Bosnian past.

Turner addressed her colleague from the Bureau. "I'm inclined to agree with their theory on the high heels. I think we should look further into Fowler, but I think we need to put a little more pressure on Nebojsa, too."

"Fine," Wicklow said. "As long as we have enough resources to look into both, it sounds like that'll keep everyone happy."

It wasn't exactly a victory, but it also wasn't a defeat. I'd take it.

Now all I had to do was get my mind straight on who I thought was behind the murders and why. "We should also remain open to a third option."

"Of course," Turner said.

"Obviously," muttered Wicklow.

As Ben and I left the room and made our way down the hall toward our offices, he shot a sideways glance at me. "You happy?"

"Not really," I said. "Which is weird, because I thought working Homicide was supposed to be uplifting."

He chuckled darkly. "If you wanted to feel inspired, you should've stayed in the Sex Crimes division. You could always request a transfer."

"What, and leave my partner behind? Never."

"Yeah, you'd have to find some other *estúpido* to stick his neck out for you to the FBI."

I stopped him before we entered Death Row and tried not to cringe at the sound of Towers talking loudly on the phone at his desk. "About that," I muttered. "Thanks. I owe you one."

Ben flashed a half-grin my way and, stepping closer, cradled my cheek in his palm like we were a moment away from an HR complaint. "You owe me *way* more than one." His warm hand dropped, and he left me standing like a dumbstruck fool in the hallway.

He wasn't wrong, though. I may never be able to pay him back for all the times he'd had my back, but damn, it sure was nice to know there was someone in my corner from time to time.

TWENTY-SEVEN

July 3rd, 2018

27 days since Blackstenius murder

Sadie kept watch at the front of the kayak, peering through the gray predawn air as I counted my strokes. Twenty then rest. Twenty then rest. I made it to the middle of the lake, far enough from the bridges that the *thunk thunk* of cars over the ridged asphalt joints was drowned out by the chorus of cicadas.

It was peaceful there. The current pulled me along gently. A skin-and-bones man with white hair slicked by sweat passed me on a stand-up paddleboard without saying a word. There was almost no one on Lady Bird Lake at this time, when the only hint of an impending sunrise was a faint tangerine glow tickling the pitch sky to the east. I came here for the solitude. That was the only incentive for being out this early, but it was plenty. If you wanted companionship, you had to wait another hour for the so-called early risers, each of them hopped up on matcha smoothies, marching out in their Lululemon and Under Armour to take the lake by force. But before they arrived, there were people like me and the silent, skeletal paddleboarder.

And a serial killer.

I shut my eyes tight. It wasn't the time for that. The whole point of being out there was to clear my mind. I would *not* let him take this place from me. I was so sick of monstrous men stealing my peace.

I opened my eyes and leaned forward, giving Sadie's soft rump a pat.

When my mother and I had first fled to Austin, we didn't live anywhere near this lake. Instead, we settled in Pflugerville, a suburb just north of the city limits. It was a town of graveyards, white flight, and SUVs with stickers of *Caitlin* or *Grant* above a soccer ball or baseball bat on the rear window. It was a land of unnecessary "pf"s to show pride in the town name. Strip malls full of Pflugerville Pfamily Chiropractic and yard signs advertising Pflugerville Pfarm Pfests.

First chance I had, I'd moved south. College at UT for two years before I was sick of that nonsense. In those years, nothing drove me to rage more instantly than people my own age. They didn't have a clue about life. Not that I did, either. I'd had *less* than a clue after my world was turned upside down. But what I did have, and what others my age lacked, was some awareness of how little I understood.

Sadie sniffed the lake air, and I gazed at the banks through the dim light of the waning gibbous moon. He'd been there, maybe only yards from where I was, when he dumped the body of Stephanie Lee. And I might've been first to find Leslie Scopes if I'd been out with Sadie that morning instead of cooped up in the office. That might not have helped catch him, but it would've spared the person who *did* find the victim a little unnecessary trauma.

Those were the kinds of memories that were the hardest to process. The violence you could neither prevent nor fix that had nothing to do with you yet was so personal, so intimate. That violence wasn't yours, except now it was. Always. And there was no greater purpose behind it, no greater reason. It didn't have to exist, but some evil had made it so.

At least good old Raymond Lee Dwyer had been courteous enough to hide his bodies rather than put them on display where a child could've stumbled across them.

But a child did, I reminded myself. A child did eventually discover his destroyed bodies. Not just the ones found underneath the studio workshop, but ones no one else believed existed. The ones that predated the mass grave. Bits and pieces of them, at least. *Their* skin was too dark to be his victims, I was told. I hadn't seen what I thought I'd seen. I was confused. My memory was hazy and trying to fill in the gaps.

And so, some of the women were still unaccounted for, years later.

How many unseen and unnamed people had this killer already erased in Austin? Were their bodies in the lake, waiting, begging to be found and named? Stephanie Lee had her name, but she'd almost joined their ranks, misclassified, shunted to the side for Missing Persons to file away.

Did knowing her name change a single goddamned thing? It didn't undo the horror of her last moments, whatever those were. It didn't change the loss her family must feel. And naming her certainly didn't bring her back from the dead.

The sky glowed brighter, and I stared down into my reflection on the water's surface. My vision softened. Something ghastly floated just below, reaching up. Hair flowing passively with the currents, arms groping toward the heavens, mouth lolling open and begging to be seen, fingers grazing the bottom of my craft.

"*Help.*" Her pleading word, lodged deep in the marrow of my spine, traveled out through the decades.

She was reaching as if a single touch might undo all the damage wreaked upon her. But I knew it was too late. She was a mutilated ghost. She'd end up down below with the others.

Alive but doomed.

Begging. Crying. Bleeding.

I needed to save her. To flee. To help, somehow.

My legs no longer worked.

The studio door slammed shut behind me.

It's him.

"Nice day!"

I jolted from my tunneling memory and had to act quickly to steady the kayak with my paddle. A man in his early twenties passed me on a stand-up paddleboard and shot me a thumbs-up. He grinned like he'd injected nitro coffee straight into his jugular.

"Jesus," I muttered, casting a glance down at the water again. There was nothing reaching up but weeds. As always.

It was time to get off the lake, clearly. Drop Sadie off, shower, then I had a quick visit to make before I hit the office for the day.

The serial murders and reappearance of my old classmate were reawakening parts of me I thought I had gotten a handle on long ago.

I needed some answers, and only one person I knew could provide them.

The fact that he was a prime suspect in serial murders hardly even crossed my mind.

TWENTY-EIGHT

I was thinking about fireworks as I turned off the shower and reached for my towel. It was July third, and they'd been popping off at random intervals for the last week. I'd just heard what I thought was a small string of Black Cats go off while I finished rinsing the conditioner from my hair. It was hardly seven a.m.

Stepping from the shower and onto the bath mat, I wrapped the towel around me and headed to the dryer to grab clothes from the load I'd just moved through. But the moment I entered the hallway, I could tell something was wrong. What it was, I couldn't say. Something was off. Something was missing.

Then it hit: Sadie.

She usually waited outside the bathroom door for me, her nose pressed to the crack at the bottom.

Maybe she was getting into the trash.

I called to her. Nothing. No sound of her collar tags jingling. No slap of her tail on furniture.

The searing image of the flayed cat jumped into my mind.

"Sadie? Come here, girl."

Still clutching the towel around me, I padded into the living room.

And then I saw it.

The front door. It was wide open.

The hair on my arms stood on end. Someone could be in the apartment.

I hurried to the coat closet to grab a gun. Once my fingers wrapped around the grip of a .40, I was able to breathe again. But clearing the apartment would have to wait. First things first: I needed to find my dog.

I aimed the barrel at the ground and held on tight to my towel as I stepped outside onto the breezeway. "Sadie?"

"Ay, miss!"

The call came from down below, where a kid named Ronny Mondragon was scratching Sadie behind the ears in the courtyard. She was wagging her tail, and Ronny, no more than twelve years old, was waving. I relaxed, but only slightly as he gawked at me in my towel, and I tried not to step too close to the balcony to avoid giving everyone and their cousin an eyeful.

"Can you grab her collar and hold her?" I asked, and he nodded as I held up one finger to indicate I'd be right back.

I cleared the apartment haphazardly on my way to the dryer to slip on sweat pants, a sports bra, and an old white tee before heading back out in bare feet.

"Thanks," I said, as Sadie spotted me coming down the stairs and wagged her butt ferociously. The muscular dog tugged free of the kid's weak grip and ran up to me like she hadn't seen me in ages. "Where'd you find her?"

He shrugged, clamming up (no doubt because he'd just seen me in a towel). Water dripped from my hair onto my shoulders and back, but it felt good in this heat.

"She was just out here, Miss Dana."

"Where? Doing what?"

He pointed. "Over there. Just sniffing that trash can."

Sounded about right. "Did you see her leave the apartment?"

"Nah. I just seen her out the window and came to play."

"You didn't see anyone leave my apartment? Or maybe come by and leave the door open?"

"Nah, miss."

He gave Sadie one last scratch behind the ear and then ran home. My tone must have made him think he was in trouble.

A man and woman were sitting at a graffiti-ed picnic table in the corner of the courtyard by the grill and cemented-up pool. I recognized the woman as a neighbor, though I didn't know her name. I'd never seen the man before, and I would have remembered someone like that. He wore a baggy white T-shirt and sported a distinct neck tattoo. Just the name Derek in calligraphy. I had questions about that, but now wasn't the time.

Sadie stuck close by me, perhaps sensing the tightness of my posture, and I approached the two at the table. "Excuse me. *Disculpe*."

The man leaned over, and the woman turned. "Yeah?" he said.

I glanced up at my apartment to check the angle. The man would've a hard time *not* seeing someone leave through the door. "Did you by any chance see someone come in or out of that door?" I pointed.

They exchanged a glance, then he said, "I saw... you."

"No one else?"

"No, but we just come out here, like, five minutes ago."

My shower couldn't have lasted more than ten minutes. Okay, maybe fifteen. Was he lying?

I flashed him a smile. "Thanks."

"Everything okay?"

"Yeah, yeah, it's fine. My door was just open when I got out of the shower."

His brows pinched together with concern. "Ah, *una hermosa gringa* like you should make sure to close your door."

"Thanks," I said, already leading Sadie back toward the stairs, "great suggestion."

I made her sit on the doorstep while I cleared the apartment more thoroughly. No one there. Nothing obvious missing. But I could feel the fear creeping in, the unease that took root and functioned so quietly it almost went unnoticed, even as it seeped into everything.

I called Sadie inside and closed and locked the door behind us.

The obvious question now was whether I should call this in.

I'd responded to a handful of calls of a similar nature in my five years on patrol. If I'd arrived on this particular scene, learned the facts—resident returned from a long day on the lake, had her hands full as she entered the apartment, hadn't slept much the night before, and never heard her dog barking while she was in the shower—my conclusion would be obvious: she didn't close the door behind her all the way when she entered her home. The dog had noticed, pried the door open, and escaped.

Maybe that was all this was. Sure, closing the door and locking the bolt had become a single motion for me, but I wasn't infallible. And I'd been more preoccupied than usual with work.

Or maybe...

Nothing happened in isolation. The dead squirrels. The cat on my doorstep. It sure felt like someone was sending me a message. And today, the message would have been: "I can get to you."

The idea of reporting it to the FBI flashed in my mind. It could be useful intel for their database.

But no. I had nothing to go on but gut and experience, neither of which mattered much in this system. And what would I say? *Hey, there have been some dead animals in my complex, and I found my front door open when I got out of the shower. No, nothing was taken. Yes, my dog was fine. In fact, everything was just fine.*

Popov, Escobar, Turner, Wicklow—they'd all think I'd cracked under the pressure of this case, and my credibility would be shot. And I knew all too well that credibility wasn't just useful; for women, it was a matter of life or death.

I took a deep breath, let my pulse settle, and decided to file this away, just forget about it if I could. It was probably nothing anyway.

Even still, Sadie was coming with me today, so maybe I wasn't completely convinced there was nothing to worry about.

TWENTY-NINE

The overhead slats of the pergola under which I sat did almost nothing against the sun rising quickly toward its zenith. Sadie had the best spot of the two of us, lying in the shade beneath the coffeehouse table. Her sharklike mouth hung open as she panted out the summer heat.

Droplets of cold, slopped water from the dish I'd set beside her dripped down my shin, but I didn't wipe them away. I'd take whatever I could get. This sun was brutal.

I reached beneath the table and scratched her behind the ears, flapping them around. "Don't worry, we won't be here long. I'll get you in the A/C soon." I leaned over to see her face and sensed open judgment in it. It was also possible I was projecting. "Trust me," I muttered to her, "I'm not trying to lose my job today." She continued panting steadily. "Okay, maybe there's a little bit of an ulterior motive to this. But I know exactly what I'm doing."

She leaned forward and slopped up some more water from the metal dish, not giving a good goddamn.

When I looked up again, Dylan Fowler was approaching our table.

"Thanks again for meeting me," I said as he took a seat across from me. Sadie rose from her position in the shade and sniffed him around the knees. He eyed her cautiously, as most people did when a pit bull of her size moved toward them in a hurry. But he relaxed almost instantly and offered her a hand to sniff. In his other, he held an iced coffee.

While he was preoccupied with Sadie, I tapped the screen on my phone then set it facedown on the table. Typical behavior, but not for a typical reason.

The steadying sounds of morning traffic on Manchaca Road filled the air, creating a sense of calm I wanted to soak up and store for later. Dylan looked as calm as I felt as he slipped his sunglasses onto the top of his head and settled in. The table was in a shaded area of the coffee shop's patio, which was good, because it was shaping up to be another hundred-plus day.

"Thanks again for suggesting a place to meet where my mom isn't," he said.

I kept my mouth shut on that one.

"It's fine," he said. "That's not a setup. You can agree she's horrible, and I'm not gonna turn on you."

"She's not horrible, but she's pretty... invasive?"

"You don't even know the half of it. I've caught her looking under my mattress for porn when she thought I was gone. I mean, what the hell? I have every right to look at porn in my own home."

"Maybe she wasn't judging you," I said. "Maybe she just wanted to borrow it for herself." Part joke, part test. I hadn't met or read about a single serial killer who didn't have a whole mess of strange sexual feelings trapped in the web of his maternal relationship. A joke like that could set one off.

But to Dylan's credit, he only cringed and pretended to gag. A fairly standard response for anyone. "Is that why you wanted to meet? To make me think about my mom— No, I can't even say it."

"Sorry, sorry. No, I just..." My two reasons for arranging this battled for position in my head. I shut them both out and let my gut take the lead instead. Best not to overthink this, or else I might realize how dangerous of an idea it was. "There are... a lot of things I don't remember from middle school. There are some things I remember that I wish I could forget, but then there are mundane things that just have no home in my memory. And my memory is good. It's sharp. I just have these... these gaps. And I wonder if I filled them, if that would help cushion the blow of the other memories. Because the terrible ones are all I have of that time. I can't think of anything from my childhood without them coming back."

He nodded, and with tender concern etched across his face, I realize that Ben was right: Dylan wasn't a bad-looking man. This was absolutely not the time to be noticing that, though. I forced myself to think of Ted Bundy. That did it.

"What do you want to know?" he asked.

"You say you knew me in middle school. I only keep in touch with one other person from that time, and she's already told me what she remembers from those years. But you recognized me the moment you saw me at Laugh Attack, so you probably remember even more. That's what I wanted to talk about. The simple stuff from that time of my life. What was school like? Did we sit together at lunch? Who did I sit with at lunch, if not you? What was Mr. French's class like? Anything funny you remember from it? Did we have other classes together? What *time* did school let out?" I paused. "Actually, I know that one: 3:18 p.m." I shook my head. "And see, the only reason I know that is... Well, it doesn't matter. Start with the other ones."

"Is this because of your dad?" No shyness in his question, just a factual curiosity.

"Yes."

To his credit, he didn't ask further questions but inhaled deeply. "We did *not* sit together at lunch, that's for sure. You saw that picture of me in the yearbook. You think a kid like that would be allowed to sit with a girl like you?"

"Good point."

"Mean."

"What?"

He laughed. "Okay, fine. You're just agreeing with me. But no, you sat with Dennis, Gabrielle, and Maggie."

I sipped my iced latte and leaned back in my seat without disturbing Sadie's head, which rested on my left foot. "Who'd you sit with?"

Fine wrinkles appeared around his eyes as he squinted. "No one, usually. Sometimes the other kids who sat with no one would sit at my table, and we'd all sit with no one together."

"But your brother, wasn't he kind of a big deal?"

"Yeah, and he disowned me the second he saw I wasn't going to be a huge hit." He forced a pained smile. "Kind of a douche."

"Jesus. No kidding. Have you always been a loner?"

His eyebrows jumped up his forehead. "A loner? Shit, that makes it sound like I had plans to shoot up the school."

"Nah," I said, "that was pre-Columbine. Back before shooting up a school had crossed anyone's mind."

"Except Charles Whitman."

It took me a second, but then the trivia clicked. "Right." I leaned forward and whispered, "I don't think you're supposed to talk about the UT Tower shooting when we're only a few miles from campus."

He winced guiltily.

"Relax," I said, "it was over fifty years ago. I was kidding."

Our conversation took a natural break, and I gazed around, taking in the smattering of open laptops and strained expressions on the tables around us. Then he asked, "Do you remember your thirteenth birthday party?"

I immediately ceased the sip I was taking. "No. Why? Do *you* remember it?"

"Yeah. I was there."

"You were?" Not to be a snob, but I couldn't imagine inviting him. But then again, I didn't even remember having the party.

"Yep. I think your mom invited the entire seventh grade. I was in sixth, but Brady was invited, so I got to come, too. I just remember counting down to you blowing out the candles. 'Three, two, one, blast off!' I didn't really understand it until later on."

He said something else, but I was no longer at the table. I'd blasted off through time. I was back in my childhood home.

I could see Raymond clearly, his smiling face, those deep dimples that engendered so much trust from complete strangers. This was the father he was most of the time. Kind, loving, charismatic, a twinkle in his Irish eyes. Every year: "Three, two, one, blast off!" Then I'd blow out the candles. Three, two, one... March twenty-first. That would have been 1995.

Dylan's voice cut through my thoughts. "Can I say something?"

"Of course."

"I hope this doesn't come off as weird or insensitive, but you seem fairly, I dunno, well adjusted about this whole thing. Anyway, I always liked your dad. He was always really nice to me."

"Yeah, he was nice to me, too."

Except for that one time.

"I just don't understand how he managed to be like that while he was, you know, killing women on the side."

I grunted a heavy sigh. I couldn't even begin to count the number of times I'd puzzled over the same thing in the years that followed his arrest. But, as usual, the simplest explanation was the best. "He's a psychopath, Dylan. The fact that you don't understand him speaks favorably of your mental condition."

"I guess so. I've just never met anyone else like him."

"I sure as hell hope you haven't."

He stared vaguely at something in the distance behind me. The sun had already added color to his cheeks. "Do you still talk to him at all?"

"Nope. No point in talking to a psychopath."

He squinted at me. "What do you mean?"

Was it even worth the effort of explaining? Their behavior ran so counter to how the healthy, non-psychopathic brain worked that most people I mentioned this to merely nodded along like they understood. Then the next sentence out of their mouth verified that they did not understand.

But I was curious how Dylan would respond. He might get it like only a certain type could. One way to find out. "There are only three reasons to talk to anyone." I counted them off on my fingers. "To increase intimacy, to share practical information, and to use them as a sounding board to develop your own ideas. Psychopaths like Raymond are useless for all three of those. To start, they use another person's sense of intimacy with them as a weapon. They can't experience true intimacy, though. The more you believe they can, that they can bond in any meaningful way with another human, the easier it is for them to manipulate you.

"As far as sharing information goes, you can't gain any useful information from them because you can't trust a word they say, not even with a lie detector. Lying comes so naturally, none of their biometrics change when they do it. They have no fear of being caught, no conscience to put up resistance. When it comes to swapping information, it's not a fair exchange. They just leech useful information out of you and give nothing useful in return. The less informed a psychopath is about the people around them, the better for everyone.

"And lastly, you can't use them as a sounding board to develop ideas because they love nothing more than screwing with your head, so you'll walk away even more confused and unsure of yourself than when you came to them. Or worse, you'll have arrived at a completely insane conclusion and feel entirely sure about it."

Dylan nodded. "Like the Manson Family."

I narrowed my eyes at him. "Yeah, like that." I hadn't been expecting the first sentence out of his mouth to mention *that* whole shitshow, but he wasn't wrong. "Charles Whitman and now the Manson Family? You, uh, sure know your psycho trivia."

"Who doesn't? It's fascinating, isn't it?" But as soon as the words had spilled from him, he cringed. "Well, I guess you wouldn't think so. And with good reason."

"No," I said, "I agree. It's fascinating, all right."

Or else I wouldn't have a career in murder.

It wasn't a pretty truth, but there it was. I did enjoy learning about the darkest of our species. My trauma hadn't immunized me against that fascination. My roommate sophomore year of college was a psychology major, and everyone had teased her that it was the major for women with daddy issues. I wouldn't argue with that. But I also couldn't judge because until I dropped out, I'd majored in criminal justice. Everyone's daddy issues were different.

"Go back to my birthday, though," I said. "What else do you remember?"

"Which one?"

"You were at more than one?"

"Yeah, I was at your fourteenth, too."

March twenty-first, 1996, or whatever weekend had fallen closest to it. The FBI was already watching my house at that point, though I hadn't learned that fact until much, much later.

"Okay, either one. What do you remember?"

As he launched into the vivid details, from the color of the cake to the other kids who were there, and even some of the presents and activities, my mind began to slip away.

The details didn't come spilling back to me in a deluge

like a part of me had hoped they would, but he remembered enough to help me fill in some gaps. How in the hell did he remember so much about it? So much about *me*?

My fingertips found Sadie's head, and I stopped fighting to recover memories that probably weren't there and never had been. It was looking more and more like my mind had never stored them in the first place, that it had already barred the doors to happy memories to make room for the fear, the doubt, the shame.

Because by the time I turned fourteen, I *knew* the dark horrors lurking in the Dwyer household, that my father murdered women in his studio and buried them under the floorboards, that my mother did everything she could to pretend he didn't. Of course I couldn't remember my fourteenth birthday. Not after I, the youngest of the three Dwyer children, had discovered Raymond's secret months before. And kept it.

And because of that, I'd let more women die.

The rest of our conversation was a blur, but that was fine—I could review it later.

As I loaded Sadie into the car, I wondered if I'd gotten what I came there for. Had I gleaned anything useful to the investigation? Anything meaningful to my personal mission?

It was hard to say while those seemingly benign words of Raymond Lee Dwyer rattled around my brain.

Three, two, one, blast off.

THIRTY

Despite the eerie jaunt down memory lane, I left the coffee shop energized. Maybe it was just the caffeine, but I suspected it was more a sense of liberation after learning that those memories I'd flagellated myself for losing hadn't been missing for lack of effort on my part. No amount of prodding would shake them loose because they seemed to be entirely gone. Maybe I could stop trying to find them in the dark silence of my bedroom when my mind spun after another abrupt nightmare.

I brought three coffees along with me to the station after dropping Sadie off with Ariadna. I considered getting Agent Turner an iced coffee, presuming no one would be stupid enough to even *think* of calling her a pussy for it, but I ultimately decided against that assumption. Folks around Death Row could be pretty damn stupid. We were in the air conditioning anyway, so hot coffee wouldn't kill us. And the gesture seemed like the least I could do as a peace offering after Turner and Wicklow actually listened to my high heels theory (albeit through Escobar's lips) and accepted it for the solid one that it was.

Who knew, maybe I was just one unexpected coffee gift away from Wicklow not being such an insufferable bastard. A girl could dream.

"There you are," said Ben, looking up from his computer screen. His eyes traveled to the three cups of coffee. "Whoa. Long night?"

"Nope. Just feeling generous."

He eyed me, not bothering to mask the suspicion, as I offered him a cup. He accepted it in the end and set it next to his keyboard. "And who are those other two for?"

"Our besties from the Bureau."

"Huh. Okay. Um." He glanced around the clutter in front of him and drummed his fingers anxiously on the desk. "Okay, yeah. You'd better come with me. We'll deliver them their coffee together."

Then he stood abruptly, neglecting to grab the thermal cup I'd just handed him from the desk.

"What's this about?" I asked.

He spared me only a glance. "Come on. Bring the coffee. Actually, let me carry that for you."

The chivalry could only mean one thing: he was legitimately worried I might throw scalding coffee on someone. "No, I think I got it just fine."

"Nope." He grabbed one side of the cardboard tray, and I let him have it without a fight. I had no desire to scald *him*.

Not yet, at least.

We entered the conference room, and Ben announced our presence immediately with a loud clearing of his throat.

Wicklow was on the phone, and Turner looked up from her laptop, eyes darting between us. "Morning, Detective Capone."

Oh yeah, something was off. "Morning, Agent Turner." I scanned the room, first focusing my attention on the evidence boards taped to the wall. I discovered almost immediately what was amiss.

"Um." A disproportionate rage for this particular battle rose inside me, and I swallowed it down. "Why are there only *two* victims and crime scenes listed on that board?"

Wicklow appeared exaggeratedly put out as he told the person on the other line that he'd call them back. He ended the call and answered before Turner could. "We've decided, upon further review, that only Cheryl Blackstenius and Leslie Scopes match as victims of the same killer. It was a stretch to include Stephanie Lee. You must have known that. And we don't want to pollute the data."

"So, *if* you catch him," I said, "you won't charge him for Lee's death? Do *not* tell me you think it's that boyfriend of hers who left town instead."

Wicklow's mouth tightened around the corners, and his spine went ramrod straight. "What I think doesn't matter anymore. That's a separate investigation independent from the Bureau. It's all yours to close out now."

"You have *got* to be kidding me." This was beyond stupid; this was dangerous. Plain and simple.

Ben made a brave (and foolish) move to hand out the coffees.

"Nuh-uh." I extended an arm to stop him. I wasn't looking to make nice anymore. "Stephanie Lee hung out around the club. She was, at the very least, sleeping with Mike Check."

While Turner continued to look embarrassed, Wicklow showed no signs of shame. The abuse only seemed to buoy him. "We know that. But Mike Check has been eliminated as a suspect."

A white-hot calm washed through me. The shapes in my periphery wobbled and blurred. My next question came out hardly more than a whisper, which should count as fair warning. "*Why* would you eliminate him as a suspect?"

Wicklow shrugged smugly. "He has an alibi for the second murder. He was over at the apartment of another female comedian from the club. I read that in *your* report."

"And my report *also* called that into question. You actually buy that?"

"Yeah."

"Christ!" I threw my arms into the air. "His account was totally uncorroborated. The girl he was supposedly visiting couldn't tell one day from another." This was an even bigger mess than I'd thought. "She claimed they passed out drunk by eleven. Leslie was murdered after that. He could have snuck out without her noticing, easy. If she was sleeping with the greaseball for a good slot on the schedule, she'd lie for him, too, no doubt."

Turner stepped in. "We have him on surveillance video entering her apartment before Leslie is reported to have left the bar that night, and he doesn't leave the unit until the next morning. Cell phone records support that."

"So he snuck out through the patio. It was a ground-floor apartment. There wasn't a camera covering the back of the building. And he left his cell phone behind.

Everyone knows those things are traceable." I could feel a headache coming on. "Shit." I turned to Ben and nodded for him to go ahead and hand out the coffees. But he'd been burned once before, so he proceeded with caution.

I took a deep breath and refocused. "Who do we have left as suspects? Anyone new turn up?"

"Nope," said Wicklow, reaching across the table, asking for his coffee with a groping open hand. "Just Fowler."

"Oh, for the love of... Don't even think about it, Ben."

Ben froze then returned the coffee cup to the cardboard tray.

"We've already contacted him," Wicklow continued, "and his alibi is weak. He said he was likely on his way home from Laugh Attack when Cheryl Blackstenius was murdered, and he was already at home by the time Leslie Scopes was last seen at the bar."

"He lives with his mother. She can vouch for him being there."

"Except she can't," Wicklow said. "We spoke with her on the phone this morning. She doesn't remember when he got home on those specific nights. In fact, she spent half the time complaining to us about how he doesn't get home until two or three in the morning lately."

"I take it you didn't tell her that her son was under investigation for a double homicide, then?"

"We made it clear he was under investigation," Wicklow said. "I mean, why else does the FBI call you up asking for your son's whereabouts on two specific dates? But we didn't even make it to the crime before she was ratting out his late nights doing god-knows-what."

I massaged my temples. What an absolute nightmare that woman was. So caught up in her need for drama that she might've given the FBI what they needed to put her son away for life, whether he was guilty or not.

"Have we definitively ruled out all the male comics around the club?" I asked. "There have to be more that fit this garbage suspect profile if we're so set on adhering to it. I mean, we have *no physical evidence* linking Fowler. Besides, I was *just* talking with the guy, and I know you hate to hear it, but I promise you: nothing about him says he's capable of killing three women."

And now Turner rose to her feet. Meeting her eyes felt like staring down the barrel of a loaded gun. "Why were you with our main suspect without letting us know ahead of time? You should have been wearing a wire."

"It wasn't about the case," I said. "I didn't even bring it up. We talked about other things."

"*What* other things, Detective Capone?"

"I went to middle school with Dylan; you know this. And not to be *that girl* who unloads her emotional baggage, but I had a pretty zany childhood, as I'm sure you've already heard. I don't remember a lot of what happened, and I was hoping a conversation with him might jog my memory."

Agent Turner's expression didn't soften, but it also didn't harden. In fact, it gave away about as much as a titanium wall. "Did Dylan Fowler know your father personally?"

I didn't want to answer because I knew where she was going. Ben had already gone there. But Turner wasn't someone whose questions you didn't answer. "Yes. That's part of what we discussed. They met at a couple of my birthday parties."

When the agents exchanged a dark look, I couldn't stay quiet. "No, no, no... It's not that."

"He could have seen something," Turner said.

"And if he did," Wicklow added, "and he was already thinking about doing something..."

Turner asked the room, "Do we know why he moved to Austin?"

I opened my mouth to respond but realized I didn't have a clue to that one. "No, but I assume it was for work."

Wicklow jotted down a note on his pad. "Detective Escobar, can you look into that? See when he moved to town and verify his employment records at St. Ignatius. If he didn't move just before starting there, we might have something. If the dates don't match, see where else he was working—a restaurant, retail—if it's something trivial, then it's likely he moved to Austin for another reason before he had a promising job offer."

"Him and everyone else in this city!" I hollered. "You know how many people move to Austin without a job lined up? Everyone, that's how many. Last count I heard was 150 people a day moving into town. You think they're *all* possible serial killers?"

Wicklow glared at me. I tried to take it seriously, but it was hard when staring at a weak chin like his. The feature only made his doughy lips extra punchable. Or maybe the things that came out of those lips made them extra punchable.

"I have to note that you spoke with our prime suspect one on one without recording the conversation or letting anyone know," he said. "I don't want to have to do it, but it's protocol, and you left me no choice. I didn't make you meet up with him, after all. That's on you. It's up to Sergeant

Popov to determine your reprimand for it, but in the meantime, you *cannot* do that again and possibly compromise our investigation."

"Read you loud and clear." I turned to Ben for some backup in storming out of the room, but his feet stayed planted as he continued to clutch the cardboard tray and two remaining coffees. I'd drink both of them myself as soon as we got the hell out of there.

His expression was strange enough that I couldn't dismiss it. "What?"

It was no secret I was beyond pissed, so his next words proved just how brave he was. And how goddamn infuriating. "Don't do it this way, Dana. Just give them the recording. There's no point getting in trouble if you don't have to."

Maybe if I glared at him hard enough, those words would magically be unsaid.

Turner's and Wicklow's eyes burned holes in the side of my skull, but I kept my eyes on my partner. He knew me too well, knew that I was reckless, but never without a way to cover my own ass. In that moment, though, I didn't want to cover my ass. I just wanted to storm the hell out.

With a great effort, I closed my eyes and took a deep breath. Why had I set my phone on the table if I wasn't going to use that when push came to shove?

The idea of Wicklow listening to it repulsed me, though. He didn't deserve to know as much about those birthdays as I did.

"Just give it to them," Ben urged again. "Then they have a record of the conversation and can't claim you spoke to a suspect outside of the investigation." He turned to

Wicklow. "If she hands over the audio file, will you label it as official intel gathering?"

Before he could reply, Turner said, "Definitely. That's what it was."

Ben turned back to me. "Agreed?"

This deal felt like a betrayal of the worst degree. Ben was the only person I'd told about my habit of recording virtually every conversation I had, logging the files, reviewing them later to test my memory. It was how I'd strengthened my ability in the first place. What was on record couldn't later be denied, after all.

The only person I didn't record my conversations with was Ben. I used to, but for some reason, it stopped occurring to me to bother with it on our stakeouts and lunch breaks. And when I noticed that, I realized that I had no impulse to start it up again. Not with him.

With everyone else? Definitely.

My mind raced over my conversation with Dylan. I hadn't said anything that could get me suspended, but once I handed over the file, it wouldn't just be Agents Wicklow and Turner who heard Dylan's retelling of my birthday party, moments from my childhood that were news even to me. Anyone at the FBI could hear it. And if they arrested Dylan and took him to trial, everyone there would hear it as evidence as well. *They'll know,* screamed a voice inside of me. *They'll put it together, that you knew and didn't say, that you don't deserve to live after those other women died, that you could have stopped it so much sooner.*

But it didn't seem like I had a choice. Ben had set up a fair trade, objectively speaking. Now that they knew the recording existed, if I refused to hand it over, they'd just find a legal way to confiscate it, but only after Popov fired my ass. "Yeah. Fine. I'll send the file."

"And no editing," Wicklow said.

"Of *course* I won't edit," I snapped. "Not looking to be sent to prison for tampering with evidence." I grabbed both coffee cups and raised one in a toast to the station's lovely guests. "Better get to it." Then I marched from the conference room without looking back or waiting for Ben to follow.

THIRTY-ONE

July 4th, 2018

28 days since Blackstenius murder

I was going to get my ass chewed out for this. But all I needed to do was find one compelling bit of evidence why Dylan Fowler wasn't our unsub to open up the investigation so that we didn't miss the real killer. Accomplishing that would make the ass-chewing worth it.

And it seemed only fitting that I should free Dylan from suspicion on Independence Day.

Why I was so set on this was muddy even to me. Maybe it was my gut. Or maybe it was something less flattering. Either way, I was ready to see this thing through. The agents could keep digging from afar, but I had a way in to get up close and personal without attracting Dylan's suspicion. If he was guilty, I would be the one to find that out. And if he was innocent, I would get to rub that shit in Wicklow's face. I didn't see a real downside here except the risk of an ass-chewing. But when was I not at risk of one of those, really?

As soon as I pushed open the heavy door to Laugh Attack, though, it became obvious that I should have at least told Ben where I was going. I considered it prior to leaving my apartment, but it'd seemed best not to take him down with me if this all went to hell. This way kept his hands clean.

And there was that tunnel vision again. I only ever noticed it once I'd inched outside of it. By then, it was usually too late to do anything about it. I was too committed. In this case, I'd been so focused on proving Dylan's innocence that the subsequent question had slipped my mind: if he wasn't the one, someone *else* around the club probably was. Someone I was about to rub shoulders with. Without backup.

Even just the short walk from my car to the front door had been enough to start sweating underneath the stupid blonde wig. Dylan would believe I was wearing it to hide my identity as Dana Dwyer, daughter of Raymond Lee Dwyer. The main purpose, though, was to hide my identity as Detective Dana Capone, stubborn crusader.

I'd reaped the benefit of having a generic appearance many times in my life. When I was a kid, I'd hated it. I'd hated thinking of myself as a forgettable face. Of course, all scrawny white, brunette little girls kind of look the same unless something sets them apart, and that something, whatever it turns out to be, is just fodder for bullying anyway.

Then Raymond's crimes came to light, and I'd learned just how useful it could be to blend in; being more recognizable would've only led to more misery.

As a cop, my fairly unremarkable features were akin to the ability to shapeshift. I never wore makeup in my daily life, so a little bit went a long way toward deflecting recognition from all but the ones who knew me best.

And Dylan Fowler, I supposed.

But with the wig, makeup, and civilian clothes, I should go unnoticed by virtually everyone. My goal when I prepped for something like this was to know that I could leave the scene, return *without* the wig and makeup but with my badge and gun, question the people who were there about the blonde woman with too much makeup, and have no one even remember her, let alone make the connection that it had been me.

Even still, the plan was to keep a low profile—stay in the back, watch, then disappear before the end.

The open mic hadn't started when I arrived. I passed the ticket booth and made for the bar.

The aspiring comedians stood around, drinks in hand, chatting in small groups. I ordered a tonic with lime, and as the bartender made it, I glanced around and recognized a few of the faces from my investigation so far. There was Mike Check, whose alibi I'd spent yesterday afternoon trying to crack but to no avail. I was beyond annoyed by that fact.

Jordan Grossman stood with both Heidi and Scott Ruiz in the corner—a ballsy move, I had to say. Chatting away with the man whose wife he was most definitely screwing? I hadn't thought he had it in him, mostly because I wouldn't tell *what* he had in him. Not after internet-stalking him as thoroughly as I had. While our camera footage told a story of a sordid love affair he had going with the club's co-owner, his online presence told a much different tale. My discovery of a few of his self-deprecating jokes on Twitter about his inability to get laid had led me on an afternoon-long wild goose chase that had ended on a subreddit called /r/asexuals, where Grossman was an active contributor.

While his posts had made it clear that he was struggling with the question of his possible asexuality, that alone hadn't eliminated him from my list of suspects. It had been finding that he was actively engaged in a three-hour-long Reddit fight with someone during the window of time when Leslie Scopes was murdered that had crossed him off my list. I was comfortable with that elimination. I'd never heard of an asexual serial killer anyway. Seemed near enough to an oxymoron.

I paid for my drink with a five and told the bartender to keep the change, and then I returned to my regularly scheduled lurking.

Sipping my drink through two stir straws, I identified face after face from my online prowling, each one appearing in my mind with a thick black Sharpie line through it. Not him. Not him. Not him.

Tomas Ramirez was chatting animatedly with two women I didn't recognize on the far end of the room. He had been signed up for the open mic the night of Cheryl's death but hadn't been on the roster the night of Leslie's. That wasn't an exoneration by any means, though, because I'd gone through weeks and weeks of other sign-up sheets for the open mics, and his name was on all of them. That made the omission more suspicious than anything.

Sergeant Popov and Agent Wicklow had initially questioned keeping Ramirez on the list due to his race, but Ben supported my argument that it was too soon for that. He knew as well as anyone that Hispanic racial identity functioned on a continuum. Ramirez's fairly light skin meant he could pass as white in most major American cities if he just anglicized his first name and didn't mention the last. Not that the unsub even *had* to identify as white, but there was something to be said for the statistics leaning that way.

But Tomas Ramirez, the round-faced man-boy that he was, had turned out to be just another dead end. His Instagram told a story of a man fully comfortable with platonic physical contact. Maybe too comfortable, but not in an aggressive way. Definitely not in a repressed way. And he seemed especially fond of throwing an arm around the shoulder of other male comedians. A few photos even featured him planting a big, wet, and "comical" kiss on the cheeks of other men who either pretended to blush or simply looked like unwitting participants in the joke.

Long story short, I had my suspicions that Tomas was among the men who'd offered Mike Check sexual favors in return for a booking.

It wasn't just that Tomas Ramirez didn't fit the standard psychological profile of a man who would kill three women. That wasn't what got him kicked off my list. What did it was that he had been among the group of friends out with Leslie the night she was murdered. And he'd reportedly remained with the group even after Leslie left to meet up with the unsub on the hike-and-bike trail. When I called and asked him why he hadn't been at the open mic that night, he'd explained he had car trouble and had broken down on the side of the road. Records from the body shop confirmed that, and a friend had picked him up and taken him out on the town once his car was squared away.

And soon, if I had my way, Dylan Elijah Fowler would have a line through his name, too. I'd pull his picture down from the suspect board right in front of Agent Wicklow, and we'd start over with new theories. Not a great place to be almost a month after the first murder, but better than nabbing the wrong man and letting the right one go free.

If only Dylan had an alibi, I wouldn't have to be there. I didn't dwell on it too much, though. The truth was that most of us lived our lives without strong alibis. I knew I did. If I was not at work, it wasn't unusual for no one to be able to account for my whereabouts. Just part of living alone and having no social life. Didn't make me a murderer.

If it wasn't Dylan or Mike Check, who the hell was it? Who had we missed? Or who had we wrongfully eliminated? Could the unsub have been a woman?

Seemed so unlikely. The physical strength needed to pull off two murders like Leslie's and Cheryl's was extraordinary, and a woman with that kind of strength would stand out. As I looked around, no one in the club fit the bill, not even me, and I was no delicate flower. All I saw among the women were potential victims.

Heidi Ruiz glanced in my direction, and I turned my head away quickly. She of all these people would be able to place me if she got a direct look.

Although Heidi's husband had founded the club, by all accounts, she was now in charge. I doubted Scott minded all that much, but I also got the sense that it wouldn't matter if he did. Heidi may present like a bimbo with her nose job, fake tan, and silicone breasts, but that didn't preclude her from being sharp, and she possessed an air of authority Scott couldn't match.

When I snuck another look in her direction a minute

later, she was absorbed in a conversation with a man named Pete Gilford—not present on either of the murder nights—and she didn't seem to care who the new girl with the platinum-blonde hair was.

Next to her, Scott was feigning interest in the conversation, but poorly. He was wearing the same leather flip-flops he always did, and was rocking a tie-dyed *Keep Austin Weird* shirt that looked to be about three sizes too big for him. Of course I'd looked into him, too. Couldn't find a trace of him on social media at first, but that wasn't abnormal for a man his age, and one who generally seemed more interested in whatever far-out mantra had led him to open a comedy club in Austin in the nineties, back when the comedy scene in town consisted of little more than Esther's Follies and The Velveeta Room.

An image search of Scott had led me to a picture posted by a cousin of his on Facebook. A holiday photo. There was Scott, all dressed up in his finest flip-flops and a tacky sweater, standing next to an older couple identified in the caption as his parents. They were *not* white Hispanics like Scott. They appeared fully Latino. Scott was either adopted or a child from a previous marriage. That had answered the question of his last name for me, but that was about all that photo was good for. I hadn't found more outside of the occasional newspaper write-up on Laugh Attack where he was mentioned.

No big deal, though. Scott had been easy enough to eliminate from my list of suspects. For one, his well-established reputation around Austin included none of the usual indicators of a serial killer. No murdered animals, no strange signs of aggression or reports of domestic violence. He was known as an open-minded guy, beloved by the

LGBTQ community, no stranger to the gay bars or Pride parades. No record outside of a few misdemeanors for possession of marijuana.

All to be taken with a grain of salt, of course. John Wayne Gacy was beloved in his community, too, before the good people of Illinois learned that he'd murdered dozens of men and boys.

Then Scott's wife had verified a timeline that placed them both in bed for the night in their home in Pflugerville at the approximate time of Leslie's death.

Sure, wives had been known to lie to cover for their husbands, but when I thought about how Heidi accosted Ben and me in the parking lot of Cheryl's memorial, I had a hard time imagining she would stick with a man she suspected of murder. No, she would tear that bum of a husband a new one.

I searched the room again. Still no sign of Dylan yet, and my drink was almost gone, so I ordered another one.

The bartender was a small, curvy woman with ruby-red lipstick and purple hair pinned in a quaff on the top of her head. She looked about as jaded as a bartender could, but she nodded at my order, made me another, and told me she wasn't charging me for this one. I didn't fight her on the point. It was just tonic and a lime wedge, after all.

How many hours of bad comedy had she endured this week alone?

I stuck another five into her tip jar then put my back to the bar to scope out the rest of the crowd. There were maybe thirty people in total now. Each night allowed for eighteen sign-up spots, which probably meant that most of these people were here to perform, and the rest were the plus-ones suckered into coming.

And one Homicide detective.

The heavy front door opened again, and Dylan stepped in from the blinding late-afternoon sun. By the time this show was over, it would be dark outside, but the long summer days meant even an open mic that started at eight would, unfortunately, take place during the cold light of day. Something about that seemed inappropriate, even cruel.

Dylan paused by the empty ticket booth to put his name on the roster, and I seized the opportunity to get him alone. Without another thought, I cut across the small lounge, making a beeline for him.

He glanced up and caught sight of her immediately. It was like his eyes were drawn to her through the clusters of other useless bodies.

But she didn't look like herself tonight. Too much makeup and that stiff blonde wig. Who did she think she was fooling? The rag looked like it came from the clearance section of a party store. No one's hair was like that.

God, the things he could do to her.

But no. Not her. There were other plans for Dana.

And after the way she'd been smugly prowling around his turf as if she wasn't a predator just like him, she had it all coming. She thought she could disguise who she was? Fat chance. He knew why she was there. It wasn't to get on stage.

He'd let her keep pretending, though. It didn't hurt anything. And so long as she believed she was safe, he could make that final move with her whenever the opportunity presented itself. No doubt she thought herself tough shit. He'd show her otherwise.

And he'd enjoy every second of it.

But not yet. Not tonight. The timing had to be right. Best not to rush. After all, the stalking was all the fun.

Although that wasn't entirely true, was it? Killing was also a damn good time. But he could drag this process out as long as he needed, so long as it got him what he wanted. And he would get all of what he wanted in the end.

THIRTY-TWO

Dylan's set was surprisingly good. A little edgy, as they say, but it never quite crossed the line. The bit about unisex bathrooms might have poked a toe over, but he'd managed to jab at Austin liberals in just the right way to force everyone to laugh at themselves. In short, he might have a talent for comedy. Or maybe his set was just a welcome relief from the absolutely dreadful performers who had gone before him. Perhaps it was only good by contrast. Either way, he made me laugh, and I hadn't been expecting that.

I sat at the back of the room, watching with a curious interest. I wasn't funny, myself. Most people told me I approached things too seriously. I always took that as a compliment, though.

Even so, after a string of five unfunny people in a row to start the show, I'd found myself thinking, *I could do this better than that.* They'd treated it like a therapy session, confessing their neuroses and talking about their sad lives while lacking any spark of self-awareness to take it from tragic and pathetic to humorous and cathartic.

Dylan's set was different. He finished off with a story about his kindergarten students outsmarting him and the parents of the kids undermining him with insane parenting theories. It struck me as a healthy release of his stress. No wonder he went to these things religiously during the summer. I'd known a few elementary teachers, and they all seemed on the brink of a complete mental breakdown, and never more clearly than in the month leading up to summer break.

Could a well-adjusted mind like Dylan's murder three women? Dammit, I just couldn't see it. But I knew better than to think that being funny excluded the possibility of also being a psychopath. They could be some of the funniest people around when they wanted to be.

A few years back, a cult leader from Tyler, Texas, had set up shop in west Austin. He'd been charming, hilarious, and possessed the *amazing* ability to make other people funnier as well.

Although, come to think of it, he might not have been as funny as everyone made him out to be. What his admirers-turned-followers didn't realize at the time was that he was slipping psilocybin into their food and drink to keep them impressionable and in awe of his wit. Weak material, but expert delivery straight to their system.

I'd helped nab the asshole before the mass suicide. Maybe I did lack a proper sense of humor.

The crowd applauded, and a few people even shouted their *woos* from the crowd as Dylan concluded his set.

Then Mike Check slid up to the microphone to introduce the next comic.

I grinned at Dylan and clapped emphatically, feeling genuinely thrilled for his success... until I heard the next bit out of the emcee's mouth.

"Next up, we have a newbie. Let's give a warm welcome to Dana Dwyer."

My stomach dropped.

Nope. No way. There was just no way I was getting onstage.

Dylan winked at me and shrugged theatrically, and I wanted nothing more than to slug him in the jaw. He was the only one who could have signed me up under that name. He didn't know how much danger he'd put me in by forcing me into the spotlight, literally, while I was supposed to be undercover.

"Dana?" Mike Check said, shielding his eyes against the stage lights to search the crowd.

Dylan motioned for me to get up, and I shook my head furiously until I felt my wig start to come loose.

He reached me at the back and said, "Come on. You can't keep coming to these without getting up there. I know you want to, or else you wouldn't be here. Now or never! Just do it. You can't be worse than the dead pony guy."

The dead pony guy was Kevin Brobosia. I'd eliminated him from the list because he had been in a psychiatric ward the night of Cheryl's murder. And judging by his set, they shouldn't have let him out.

"I can't," I said. "I—I don't even have any material."

"Dana Dwyer?" Mike said again. "Oh, don't tell me we have another newbie chickening out."

Dylan whispered, "You don't need to have material. Just go tell a funny story for a few minutes." He stood to his full height and pointed down at me. "She's right here."

Funny stories? All the funny stories I had were from work. Drunk, naked transients throwing electric scooters into Waller Creek while the other officers and I begrudgingly called, "Don't. No. Stop. Not the scooters." Or drug dealers trying to evade arrest without realizing a trail of coke baggies had fallen out of their ass and were now the breadcrumbs leading us right to their hiding spot.

I had no life outside of police work. And what had come before wasn't funny. There wasn't a chance in hell I was getting up there. Not. A. Chance.

"Ah, there she is," Mike said, still squinting. "Come on up here, Dana."

There was only one thing I could do.

I ducked my head and tip-tapped my way out of the club. My low profile was blown. People would remember the blonde in the red heels now, but I could still keep them from getting a good look at my face.

Either way, I'd burned this location. I couldn't come in as a detective without letting on, and now I couldn't come back as Dana Dwyer without facing personal humiliation for chickening out.

Though Dylan couldn't have known it, he'd just burned his best chance of staying out of jail.

THIRTY-THREE

Dylan returned with drinks, sliding into the wooden booth opposite me at the Irish pub down the block from Laugh Attack. "Feel at home here?" he asked.

I was still rattled from being called up on stage, but I was less upset with him after the wide-eyed apology he'd offered me outside the club. And the free drink didn't hurt. Maybe I could still salvage this fact-finding mission. "Why would I feel at home here?" I asked.

"It's an Irish pub. Dwyer is, like, the most Irish name there is."

I waved him off but accepted the pint, taking a sip from the overfull glass. "You owe me at least three more rounds after this," I said.

"I'm sorry, Dana. Like I said, I really had no idea you genuinely didn't want to get up there. It was your second time at the club, and I've seen people who come twenty times and never get the nerve. But they always have some material ready if you give them a little push. You always came to class prepared, so I thought it would be the same tonight."

"You were wrong," I said, trying to keep my tone from letting on how mortifying the experience had been.

It shouldn't have felt this sharp, the humiliation. I had been at the club undercover. Dana Dwyer was as much of a fiction nowadays as any alias I could've made up. But when all the eyes had turned to me, wanting something, expecting me to put on a show for their entertainment...

Dylan kicked his feet out underneath the table. "I admit it. I was wrong. I think I said that already. But you gotta understand, that's how I got up there for the first time. A friend I was with signed me up and didn't tell me. He knew I could think of something good and that it didn't matter what it was, so long as I got a single laugh. He was right. I think I got one single laugh out of the whole five minutes. But that was enough. I was hooked. I'd hoped the same thing would happen for you."

"I hear you," I said, "but goddamn, it's presumptuous."

"Is it that I used your real name? I thought about putting a fake one, but I wasn't sure it would put the pinch on you enough."

"Yeah, it was partly my name. But it's mostly that it was an asshole-ish thing to do to someone you hardly know."

He flinched. "I guess you're right. I do feel like I know you, though."

"I came over to your house *once*, Dylan. And then we knew each other in middle school. I'm an entirely different person now." It was probably the most truthful thing I'd said to him all night, and when he cringed again, it was clear I'd found a way to recover this one-woman operation.

I'd exposed the tenuousness of our relationship, a

relationship he clearly wanted to strengthen. He'd divulge anything I asked of him now.

Goddamn, I could be a real chip off the old manipulative block when I needed to be.

"We're both different people than we were," he said. "But I want to get to know you more, Dana."

The meaning of those words while it was just the two of us in the booth, drinks in hand, wasn't hard to decipher. The neon Guinness sign on the wall beside us might as well have been flashing, *Let's Bang*.

Maybe it was my settling adrenaline, but for the briefest of moments, my mind entertained the thought. Would I lean across the table and press my lips against his? Would he meet me halfway? I thought he would. Or maybe I'd walk around to his side of the booth and shove him onto his back, climb on top. He'd like that, I thought. Would I? Dylan was handsome enough, and it'd been so long since *anyone* had kissed me.

Escobar's disapproving expression popped into my mind, and I blinked away the sordid thoughts in a hurry. I'd have never heard the end of it if Ben had read my mind just then.

I wasn't here to fantasize. I shouldn't have accepted the beer. It needed to remain all business. I could pretend otherwise for information, but it had to stay an act. I was better than that. I was the queen of compartmentalization.

I leaned forward. "Okay, then tell me about who you are now. What do I need to know?"

As Dylan began, I did my best to listen in between the words for anything that might prove helpful, but it became clear quickly that this was somewhat of a prepared speech.

The odds of extracting anything related to the case were essentially zero.

I glanced over his shoulder at a table three rows behind us. The man in the booth pretended to read a book, but I knew FBI when I saw it. I'd noticed the same guy in the parking lot of Laugh Attack when I hurried out fifteen minutes before. He'd been sitting in his car, leering over the steering wheel. Not creepy or obvious *at all*.

It was probably Wicklow who'd assigned me a temporary tail. Of course, now that I was proving he'd been right to mistrust me, it wouldn't be temporary.

But I had to do this. There wasn't a choice to be made. I was in for a penny, in for a pound with proving Dylan wasn't our guy, and so long as I could keep the department and Bureau from looking foolish by arresting the wrong person, my indiscretion might be swept right under the rug. I would need to win over Popov as my champion, but that red-faced teddy bear had a soft spot for me. I just knew it.

Or maybe not. We'd soon find out.

"Are you even listening to me?" Dylan said.

I blinked and forced a smile. "Of course."

"And what was I saying?"

"That I've filled out nicely."

He shut his eyes. "Not even close."

"You *don't* think I've filled out nicely? Rude." But before he could escape from that trap, I added, "Hey, I gotta ask you something."

"Yeah?"

"Do you have any *other* good memories of my father? I mean, were the two of you close at all?"

"I wouldn't say close, no. But I remember him coming to speak to our class once."

My pint hovered above the tabletop as I forgot all about the sip I was about to take. "He *what*?"

"You don't remember that? Huh. It was biology. He came to talk about entomology."

"Entomology? The study of *insects*?"

"Yeah. He told us all about how ant colonies work and the hierarchy of a beehive."

I couldn't help but laugh, trying to imagine it. I had no memory of it. None. "Why would they bring him in to talk about that?"

"I think he said he'd studied it in college."

"Oh, god," I said. "He never went to college."

"Huh. Well, I remember that he knew a lot, and it was actually a pretty fun class. He brought a huge ant farm with him."

"He worked for a pest control business before he decided to quit and pursue his real passion full-time. He probably read a few encyclopedia entries before he came to speak."

The obvious next question was: why would he come to my class at all?

It didn't exactly strain my mental resources to answer that. Raymond would've wanted to see how I behaved in school. He was probably watching me the whole time, looking for signs that I would tell someone his secret.

"Ah. I guess it *has* been firmly established that he's a liar," Dylan said.

I chuckled darkly into my lager. "True."

He leaned forward and almost looked afraid to speak. But something compelled him. "Did you know?"

His bluntness stunned me, but I didn't see the point of

hiding it. "Did I *know*? You mean did I know he was killing people?"

"If you did, it makes perfect sense to me that you wouldn't tell anyone. I bet it was terrifying. And you were just a kid."

It wasn't an accusation, then. That was unusual for this topic, but not unwelcome. Since the fastest way to get juicy details from him was to give some, I went for it. I told him something I'd told almost no one. My dark shame. The evil legacy I carried with me.

"I knew, but I also didn't know. It's hard to explain." He nodded just enough encouragement for me to go on. "Raymond chopped them up in the workshop out back. You probably know that, though. It was all over the papers. It was his art studio, and we weren't allowed in there for some bullshit reasons about ruining his concentration and disturbing his muses. He usually murdered on the weekdays when my mom was at work. But sometimes he did it while she was in the house. He'd drug the women and smuggle them into the studio at night when no one would see him. Then he'd go on about his business the next morning. He'd leave women bound and terrified while he fixed us scrambled eggs before school. My mom still swears to this day that she didn't know. But, well, willful ignorance and all that. I don't see how she *couldn't* know just as soon, if not sooner, than I did."

"God, that's horrible."

"It's worse than that." I paused to take a sip of my beer, keeping it small so I didn't down the whole thing too quickly, but enough to keep me forging on. "I found a finger once in the backyard when I was seven. Raymond explained that away as soon as I told him what I'd found.

He said I shouldn't tell anyone about it; they'd think I was a liar. So I forgot about it for a long time. Then I found blood on the kitchen floor when I came home from school. I might have been nine or ten. Doesn't make a difference. Leaving blood around seems sloppy and out of character for him, so maybe that bit never happened? Hard to say. One thing after another like that, little slip-ups. Little clues."

"You can't expect a preteen to imagine what it all adds up to, though, Dana."

"You're right. And I don't expect that. These were strange but explainable occurrences spread out over a matter of years. Years that were, from what I understand, not too bad otherwise."

I paused, wondering if I should continue. I couldn't say what ultimately decided it for me, but maybe it was just nice to be able to talk about it without feeling as harshly judged as I judged myself for it. "Then it was late July during my summer break. In 1996. I was fourteen. I don't know if Raymond forgot I was out of school, or he thought I'd be at the mall or something. Again, a strange slip-up from him when he was so careful otherwise. Anyway, I'd put on my bathing suit and grabbed a towel and some baby oil and had every intention of burning the ever-loving crap out of my skin. Maggie said I'd gotten it in my head to start school the tannest white girl there, like I was trying to make her feel less alone as the only Black girl."

I almost smiled, thinking of the way Maggie described it. She called it "Mission: Melanoma." I didn't remember setting that tanning goal for myself, but that was just as well, since I'd spent the rest of that summer hiding indoors from reporters and looky-loos.

"So, I took it all into the backyard to get some sun, and

at some point, while I was lying on the towel, I heard a woman's voice in the studio. And this is where people usually stop believing me. If they've even lasted this long." Dylan was hanging on to my every word, though, making it clear by his expression he believed it all. For once, I wouldn't have to fight for my credibility. "I'd discovered the bodies in the workshop months before, right around Christmas. And I didn't tell anyone. I forgot about it, actually. Blurred it out, I guess. But I'd found a trapdoor beneath a tarp Raymond kept over the floor of the art studio and... He'd left the door open then. That time around Christmas, I mean. Sorry, the timelines can get a little confusing when I tell it."

"It's fine," Dylan said quickly.

"I guess my curiosity got the better of me. I knew Raymond was lying about something, and I wanted to find out. Well, I found out, sure as shit."

"This was Christmas?"

"Not on, but two days before, yeah. I found the bodies first. Then I found his half-finished project. A woman. She was already doomed. Too far gone, but I don't know if she knew it yet. I did instantly. She was... missing parts and open in places. The best she could hope for was mercy. Just a swift end. As you can imagine, it scared the shit out of me, the doom more than the gore, I think. But before I could run, he found me there." A flash of his wrathful expression forced me to shut my eyes, to blink it away, but the horror of it had already flooded my system, standing the hair on the back of my neck on end.

"Jesus Christ," Dylan breathed. "I'm surprised you survived."

"You and the FBI."

"What happened?"

"When he found me in the studio? I wish I could tell you. I just remember his face, then... nothing. Maybe he threatened me. But more likely, he pulled some other sort of mindfuckery. He was always a fan of that. Either way, he wiped it from my memory. I think my mom knew, but I can't be sure. I just had a lingering sense that something bad was happening in his studio and never to go in there.

"But when I heard the woman moaning while I was out getting some sun—and this was months later, remember— my mind tried to fill in the blanks. What it filled in there wasn't murder but an affair. It kinda fits when you think about it. Raymond sneaking around, my mom sleeping in a separate bedroom and drinking a lot, the rule never to enter his studio, the woman moaning.

"So, despite all the rules and my reluctance, I decided to sneak into the studio and catch him in the act." I took a deep breath and another long drink. "He wasn't in there, but another poor woman was. She was naked, moaning on the floor, both of her legs gone below the knees. He liked to cut them up over time. He'd tourniquet and cauterize the wounds so they wouldn't bleed out before he could have his fun. She had only been captured the night before, so she still stood a chance."

"And did the first time come back to you then? Did you remember what you'd seen in there before?"

I'd been making condensation circles on the table without realizing it. I rotated my pint glass one last time to even out the edges. "Beats the hell out of me. Memory about my memories? That's a tall order for a moment like that. All I knew was that I needed to get the hell out of there before he found me. But was it 'before he found me' or 'before he found me again'? I don't know which was going through my mind. God, I was scrambled. Years of it." Again I paused, this time to sneak another glance at the agent a few booths over. Was he recording this conversation? Had he managed to bug the table?

Didn't matter. Everything I was saying could be dug out of old FBI files anyway. "I still don't know how she managed to shake free of the gag. It was the closest thing to a miracle I've ever seen. Because if she hadn't, and if I hadn't heard her moaning... She was begging me for help. At length. Not like the first woman I'd found at Christmas. The first one could only say one word: help. That was it. But this woman... I was frozen solid. For minutes, it seemed. I couldn't move a muscle. And then I heard someone shut the back door, and let me tell you, that shit snapped me right out of it. I thought it was him. But it wasn't. It was my mom. I told her to call the cops, and... I don't know what it was about that day in particular, but she listened. And that was the beginning of the end for the Dwyers."

Dylan's mouth hung open. "The woman you found the second time, was that Rita Gibson?"

My stomach clenched at the mention. "Yeah. Yeah, it was. You remember that?"

He winced. "I have a confession to make. I was kind of obsessed with the whole thing when it came out." He hurriedly added, "I know it's gawking and terrible, and I regret it, but I was a thirteen-year-old boy who just discovered a man I knew was a *serial killer*."

"Don't worry," I said. "I get it."

"Did you ever talk to Rita? I mean, after the trial and everything?"

That memory had stayed fresh, though I wished it wouldn't. "She came up to me after the trial and hugged me. She was in a wheelchair, obviously. We didn't say anything." I didn't tell Dylan how sure I was that I hadn't deserved the hug. That if I'd just said something the first time I entered Raymond's studio, Rita never would've been in that wheelchair, never would've ended up with the trauma for the rest of her life.

He stared vaguely at his glass. "I wonder what she's up to now?"

"Not a lot," I said. "She lasted four years post-conviction then wheeled herself right in front of an oncoming bus." Dallas PD had ruled it an accident, but I knew that was nonsense without even looking up the case file. DPD surely did, too. As far as police cover-ups went, though, it had been a merciful one. Life insurance didn't pay out for suicide, and Rita's kids had college on the horizon.

"I have to ask," he said. "Your mom. What's it like for her? That must be something to find out you're married to someone like that."

My laugh came out bitter, despite the years of chipping away at this particular resentment. "Queen of Denial, that one. She made the original call to the cops when I showed her what was inside the studio, but after that? She didn't believe the FBI when they presented her with all the evidence. I mean, it's full-on Crazytown in that mind of hers. Sometimes she'll straight up say, 'My husband is in prison for killing women.' But then other times, she'll deny the evidence. She's said things to me like 'He couldn't have killed Jenny Wilson because he was with me that day. The FBI just wanted to catch their man and close the case.' It really goes on a day-by-day basis. The woman is a pro at rewriting history. Especially since all her excuses about why he couldn't have murdered this woman or that are complete fabrications."

"Damn, Dana," he said. "That's some heavy stuff."

"Yeah. Sorry."

"No need to apologize. I asked."

True.

"Don't you have an older brother?" he asked.

"Older brother and older sister. But they're a minefield in their own way. They'll spend a solid ten minutes shouting about how crazy my mom is, and when I so much as agree with them and maybe add another little scrap of evidence to the case they're building, they'll turn on me and tell me I need to stop dwelling on it, that I'm obsessed with Raymond and it isn't healthy. I suspect they both blame me for blowing up the family."

I glanced over Dylan's shoulder again and caught my tail staring at me. He must be a new agent to be caught so easily. His eyes darted down to his book again.

"Do they know what you saw?" Dylan asked.

"Huh? Oh, no. I never bothered to tell them the gory details. And since both were out of the house when I started finding the good stuff, they wouldn't understand. Raymond didn't even build the studio until my sister was gone and my brother was a junior in high school."

"And before that, where'd he hide them?"

"According to the FBI, prior to the studio, he didn't murder women. He was a late bloomer, they said."

Dylan's furrowed brow said it all.

"Right," I added. "It's nonsense. I told the FBI that. The severed finger showed up *before* the studio. They just glossed over that detail. Or maybe it was just a coincidence. Maybe the finger got there some other way."

Dylan scoffed.

"Exactly."

"That's awful," he said. "You know, there's a term for all that."

"For what?"

"For having people tell you that what you've seen with your own eyes isn't real."

"Oh, *that*." I waved him off. "Yeah, I know all about that. I think every woman does, even if they didn't have a situation like mine growing up. I"—I caught myself just before I slipped up and made a quick adjustment— "I read this article the other day from a detective who worked in Sex Crimes. She said the number of women who are raped and then later changed their story would make you want to start rage-vomiting and never stop. Not her exact words, obviously, but you get it. The detective had to work on those kinds of cases ASAP before the people around the victim could convince her that she'd actually wanted it or that it didn't constitute rape because it was with a partner. This detective said she never saw a report she genuinely believed was false."

And I stuck by that. I'd never seen a single one in those few years I'd spent on Sex Crimes before a spot on Homicide opened up.

"Damn," he said. "That's intense."

"It is."

"Austin seems like a pretty safe city, though. It can't have as much of that going on as other big places."

I couldn't fathom why he assumed that, but it also

wasn't the first time I'd heard someone say it. *Oh, but this is a safe city. Not like San Antonio or Houston.*

No city was safe. Not one.

"You'd have to ask someone who knows," I said, trying not to sound bitter. "But from what I can tell, violence against women is pretty universal. Speaking of which, I was just reading the latest on the two murdered female comedians." Seemed as good a segue as I was going to get.

He winced down at the table. "Yeah, I've been keeping up with that, too."

"They still haven't caught the guy."

"Nope."

"I have a theory." I had his full attention then. "I think it's someone at the club who's doing it."

"Mike Check?"

"Oh." I hadn't expected him to have a guess ready, but perhaps I should have. "Mike Check is?"

"The emcee."

"Right. I remember now."

"I just mean, he was dating both of the victims."

Both. He wasn't including Stephanie Lee, then. Maybe he didn't know, and why would he if he wasn't the one who'd killed her? Her name hadn't made it into the headlines while we kept tight reins on what information was released. And considering Mike Check had been her only connection to Laugh Attack, her murder might not have hit the gossip channels, either.

"You'd think," I said, "that if it *was* him, the police would have picked him up by now, right?"

He shrugged. "Yeah, I guess. It's always the ex, right?" His morbid grin faded quickly. "I don't know. I can't see anyone in our community doing something so awful. It would have to be a newcomer, I think. Someone who hasn't been around the scene for long."

"The stranger walks into town," I said.

"Yeah, something like that. Because if it's someone who's been around for a while, why now? Why just suddenly start killing women?"

Because it wasn't sudden, I thought. *We've only recently begun to notice.*

"That's a great point." I considered my next words carefully. I didn't want to taint his knowledge of what had happened, but I also knew that feeding incorrect information about a scene to a killer could drive him mad, make his ego flare up, and that could lead to an involuntary correction of the facts. "I read that Cheryl and Leslie were found with their ankles bound and a gag in their mouth."

He recoiled. "Jesus. Really? I hadn't heard that."

"Yeah, at least that's what all the papers are saying now."

"Huh. Mike said he found Cheryl tied, but he didn't mention anything about her ankles or a gag."

Was that a subtle correction? Had he just used Mike's account as a cover for getting the story straight? Or was he innocently relaying the different information he'd heard through the grapevine?

It reminded me of that old riddle, the one about the man who encounters two brothers in the woods. One always tells the truth, and one always tells a lie, and to pass them, the man has to figure out which is which by asking only a single question.

Was I sharing a table in this Irish pub with the brother who always told the truth or the one who only ever lied? That was the problem when sleuthing out psychopaths.

They often resembled the truthful brother more than the truthful brother ever could.

I couldn't remember the answer to the riddle. I wasn't sure if I'd ever learned it in the first place.

"Do you think another woman from the club will be killed?" I asked.

He cocked his head to the side. "Why, are you worried?"

"Well, I *am* recognizable around Laugh Attack now."

He laughed. "I wouldn't worry if I were you. Everyone's too self-absorbed to remember anyone else for long. Just don't sleep with Mike Check."

"I had no plans of it."

He was the first to break eye contact as his gaze jumped to the wig. "I think you can ditch that thing. Your dad was in the news twenty years ago."

"And so was I."

"No one's going to be able to match that little girl to the woman you are now."

I hitched an eyebrow at him. "You did. And everyone else *will* if you keep signing me up for open mics as Dana Dwyer."

"If you're so worried about it, why don't you just change your name?"

"I'm not worried about it. But speaking of worrying, are *you* worried?"

He tilted his chin up. "About what?"

"The cops. They're probably looking for a man at Laugh Attack as the suspect. You say it's Mike Check, sure. But have the cops ruled *you* out?"

Dylan leaned over the table, speaking in a hushed voice

that managed to carry a heavy load of urgency. "You think I murdered two women?"

"You think I'd be sitting here with you if I believed that? I'm just asking how you can be so sure you're not a suspect."

A muscle in his jaw twitched as he pressed his lips together and straightened in his seat. "Yeah, I guess I can't be sure. They called me. The cops. Well, a detective from the FBI. He was asking about my whereabouts for each murder so he could clear my name."

"And?" I said. "What'd you tell them?"

"The truth, obviously, though maybe I should have lied. The truth isn't exactly convincing. I was either on the way home or already at home when Cheryl was murdered, and I was at home and asleep at the time he gave for Leslie's death."

"Your mom is your alibi, then?"

"Sad to say, but yes." Dylan fell into silence, and I snuck another glance at Secret Agent Man.

"I'd better get going," I said. "It's getting late."

"Gotta wake up early to bartend?" he teased.

"I have a dog. My neighbor usually takes care of her while I'm not around, but I don't want to push it."

"Ah, ditching me for a dog." He paused. "I'm actually okay with that."

The packed street outside the pub left me momentarily puzzled as we stepped out. Wasn't it a Wednesday? Why were there so many people?

A series of sudden blasts caused my hand to fly down to the concealed gun on my hip. But before I completely blew my cover and drew my weapon, I saw the bursting lights in the sky and grabbed the reins on myself again.

"Whoa, whoa," Dylan said, placing a hand on my shoulder. "It's just fireworks, Dana. Look."

I breathed again.

Ah, Independence Day. The time of year when Americans of all ages, races, and creeds came together to trigger the shit out of dogs, soldiers, and law enforcement. I'd almost forgotten.

Dylan didn't remove his hand from my shoulder as we stood there, staring at the display over the tops of the bars and clubs across the street. I suspected he'd forgotten he was even touching me until I felt him slide the hand down between my shoulder blades. He rubbed a few small circles there before breaking contact.

I stuck a hand in my jeans pocket to make sure he didn't try to hold it and kept the other near my gun. My nerves were frayed. Even though I would identify the source of the blasts now, PTSD didn't take orders well.

Once the finale was over minutes later, I realized Dylan was staring down at me with a curious expression.

"What?"

"I'm just sorry, you know?"

I shook my head vaguely because I *didn't* know. I had no idea.

"I'm sorry you went through all that with your dad. And that you can't even enjoy fireworks now."

"Ah." Little did he know, my PTSD stemmed from a wide variety of sources. What I went through as a kid had landed me with my fair share of weird trauma, but my reaction to the explosions was from something else entirely. But for obvious reasons involving my cover, I couldn't tell him about the Rochelle case, the sound of that gunshot on the other side of the door, the fear that we were already too late for all of them.

Even if I were in a position to tell him all about it, I wouldn't. That case was still too fresh. You just didn't speak about things like that.

"Where're you parked?" He pulled his keys from his back pocket.

"Oh, just over there." I motioned as vaguely as I could in the direction of the city parking garage. I'd left my car there on the fool's hope that I could sneak the few blocks over to Laugh Attack without anyone from work noticing. The FBI tail had quashed that hope.

"Where?" he asked.

"A few blocks east."

Dylan frowned and nibbled his lip. "Well, my car is just there." He motioned two cars down by the curb. The Prius. "There was no parking by the time I made it to Laugh Attack. How about I give you a ride over?"

"That's not necessary."

"Dana. You said it yourself. Women are getting murdered. You have to be careful. Just let me give you a lift." When I continued to hesitate, he added, "It'll make me feel better knowing you made it back safely."

Would he even know my car was in a city garage? Probably not. There was public parking mixed in, too. He didn't need to know that I didn't pay.

I couldn't tell if the parking situation was all that was holding me back from getting in the car with him or if the hesitation came from some other instinct.

"Yeah, okay."

We approached the Prius, and as he went around to the

street side, I brushed my hand casually over my right hip. It was there if I needed it.

I rolled my eyes at myself almost immediately. I couldn't help it. I wouldn't need my gun. Dylan Fowler was not our guy.

The bottom of the passenger-side door skidded across the sidewalk on the high curb as I opened it, and I looked around before getting in.

Ah, there he was.

I waved to the FBI agent tailing me and gave him a thumbs-up. Then I lowered myself into the compact car and slammed the door.

I was facing a major problem now: I still didn't have anything that clearly exonerated Dylan. And the clock was ticking. I had to get *something*, or else this whole night was just me punching my ticket at work for going rogue and to no avail. But how to find something in the next few minutes without being too obvious?

This was stupid. The whole one-woman operation. Dylan didn't even have a solid alibi. What was I thinking getting in the car with him?

Nothing, clearly. I'd been listening to my gut. Or maybe Ben was right, and I'd been listening to something else the whole time, that part of my brain that had imagined shoving Dylan onto his back in the booth and climbing on top.

Without a solid alibi, there was only one thing that could exonerate him, and that was his cell data. Even *that* had sketchy legal precedent at best.

Still, if I could just get his cell phone...

No. That was a huge constitutional violation. I wasn't that desperate.

He pulled the car away from the curb. There might be no way to redeem this rogue mission.

"You okay?" he said when we reached the first red light. "You got really silent."

I rolled my head toward him on the headrest. "Just tired."

"You can lean the seat back if you want."

I did, but it reclined only a little farther than an airplane seat. My whole body felt heavy from the adrenaline crash of being called out in the club and the fireworks and the realization that I'd really screwed the pooch.

At least I had it all recorded on my phone. Maybe I could salvage something from our conversation that I'd missed the first time around. I'd be off the case for sure. But would I be demoted? Suspended? Worse?

"You gonna be okay to drive?" he asked.

It was a lame idea, but he didn't *look* like a killer, even with the stoplight casting a bloody glow across his features. Such a stupid and useless thought. "Yep. I'm good."

The light changed, and I was just about to close my eyes when something canary yellow caught my attention behind his seat. I couldn't pinpoint why, but my brain was shouting at me to give this object my full attention. Maybe it was the color. Dylan didn't surround himself with much of it—black jeans, washed-out graphic tees, brown or navy shoes. Or maybe it was pure intuition.

"Is it this one?" he asked, pointing at the glowing blue parking sign.

"Next one down."

My attention jumped back to the spot of yellow. Even

in this darkness, the color was unmistakable. It was only just visible beneath a black windbreaker.

There wasn't much time. We'd be at my car in under a minute. This was my last chance to find something, *anything* to make this evening worthwhile.

I pulled the windbreaker back slowly, trying not to make a sound.

I checked. His eyes were still on the road.

So I pulled the windbreaker back further. My breath caught in my throat at what was underneath.

It was a shoebox. A woman's shoebox.

THIRTY-FOUR

The Prius took a hard left into the next garage, tossing me around as Dylan braked abruptly ahead of the lowered ticket booth arm. "Whoops, sorry. Almost missed the turn."

He rolled down his window and leaned out to grab his slip from the automatic dispenser. It was the last chance I'd have to confirm what I'd just seen.

I lifted the top of the yellow shoebox just enough to get a peek inside.

Holy Mother of God.

A pair of candy-apple red high heels were tucked away inside the box. As far as I could tell from my glance, they were a dead ringer for the ones Cheryl had been found in.

I dropped the lid, but the tissue paper around the shoes didn't allow it to close completely. Shit. I attempted to straighten it out with one hand, but it wasn't happening. I reached over with my other, tucked the tissue paper down, and closed the lid.

When I looked up, Dylan's eyes were on me. "What are

you doing?" His expression held a feverish intensity that made my mouth go dry.

I pulled the lever and pushed the seatback upright again. "Nothing."

The traffic arm was up in front of us, but he didn't pull through. Instead, he continued glaring at me, his nostrils flaring, until a car honked behind us.

He pulled forward, and in that split-second break, I gritted my teeth to keep from showing any signs of what I'd just seen—the high heels *and* the man behind the mask.

This was bad.

This was very, very bad.

I might not make it out of his car if I wasn't careful.

Breathe, I told myself. *You have a gun. You'll make it out, one way or another.*

That thought quieted my mind enough for me to come up with a plan. It came to me suddenly, like someone Upstairs had slipped it in through my ear.

"What level?" he asked.

"Two."

As he crept around the tight turns and honked at a car going way too fast in the other direction, I furtively pulled my wallet from my back pocket, opening it in the narrow space between my right thigh and the car door. From behind a credit card I never used, I slipped the flat electronic tracker that I kept in there. If my wallet were stolen in the next few hours, I'd be SOL in that regard, but my priorities were elsewhere now. I had to hide the tracker somewhere he wouldn't spot it, even if he knew to search for it, so I reached down and dropped it between the side of my seat and the plastic seat frame. Once it was in there, I couldn't retrieve it if I wanted to. Not without tweezers and a whole lot of patience.

Now the only thing that mattered was getting myself out of this car without incident. Once I was safely in my vehicle, I could begin to assess just how deep the shit was that I'd stepped in.

"Just there," I say, and in that instant, it clicked that I'd forgotten a crucial detail to this elaborate lie I'd spun about myself for Dylan Elijah Fowler.

"That one?" he said, pointing at my black CRV. "I thought you drove a Prius."

The lie came naturally. "It's in the shop. This is just a loner."

He accepted the explanation without any questions, but who knew if he actually believed it? Didn't matter. It just had to hold for a few more minutes. Then the lies could crumble to dust for all I cared.

"Thanks for the ride." I flashed him a grin and pulled on the door handle. It was locked.

"Oh, sorry," he said, jumping at the realization. "It does that automatically." He pressed a button, and the mechanisms clicked.

Without another word, I was out of the Prius, pulling my keys from my back pocket. In the span of another breath, I was in my car with the doors locked.

But he didn't pull away immediately, and I watched him closely in my side mirror. The Prius was right behind me, blocking me in. My CRV could take a Prius in a collision like this if it came to that, but I really hoped it didn't come to that.

All I could see was the top of his head as he stared at

something in his lap. Then he straightened, and I realized from the blue glow that he'd just been checking his phone.

His car pulled forward and disappeared around the next tight turn.

With the A/C on full blast, I leaned my head back, shutting my eyes tight, heart racing.

I was such a fucking fool. The very worst there was.

It was Dylan. It'd always been him. I'd gone looking for evidence to exonerate him but instead stumbled upon the single thing that could convince me without a doubt that I'd been wrong from the start. And so, so confidently wrong.

My gut had told me it couldn't be him, but why had I ever trusted that? Everything Raymond Lee Dwyer had done to me was specially designed to tear my intuition to shreds, leave me unable to tell which way was up. The only things, the *only* things, that had ever anchored me were facts. Evidence. The tangible.

And I had just uncovered a lethal dose of that on the floorboard of Dylan Fowler's Prius.

The conversation from the first and only time I'd spoken with Raymond in prison bubbled from my subconscious like an overflowing septic tank. It was twelve years after the FBI had raided our home and scooped him up, ten years after his conviction. The mountains of evidence against him were breathtaking, and I was familiar with all of it. Every woman under his studio had been accounted for, but I knew there were more. I knew it in my bones, even though I had no physical evidence to present. No one did. That was why I went to speak with him. I needed to know that I was right, that what the FBI assured me didn't exist actually did. And the only living person who knew the truth outside of me was him.

I wasn't the little girl he'd last seen. I was five years in with APD and studying for my detective's exam in the fall. I'd encountered evil on the so-called safe streets of Austin day in and day out. I knew any man could be violent, but it took a certain kind of man to commit certain types of crimes against women, and I found a burdensome sort of joy in locking those bastards up. Speaking to psychopaths and sociopaths and narcissists was second nature to me by then. I thought I'd become immune to it.

The trick was not to believe a word they said.

But I was cocky. I'd mastered the art of speaking to evil while at a crime scene, that was all. When I visited Raymond in prison, though, the crime scenes I'd fixated on, the undocumented ones, existed only in my mind. There were no photographs, no DNA evidence, no known victims to interview.

Raymond had been wearing handcuffs and a chain around his waist when I first saw him, and my immediate impulse was to yell at the guard to take those damn things off my father. After all, if he'd wanted to hurt me physically, he would've done it a long time ago.

"Dana, my girl," Raymond whispered. His face had aged far more than twelve years, and the long, handsome dimples that so many of my mother's friends had coyly commented on were now sunken fissures.

His eyes held the same sparkle as always, the promise of a few secrets we wouldn't tell my mother. Not the sinister secrets, though. More like those nights when he'd take me out to dinner, just father and daughter. He'd say it was to give my mom a night off from cooking, and then we'd go straight to the ice cream shop instead, gorging ourselves on scoop after scoop. "A large bowl with four toppings costs the same as a burger and fries," he'd always say with a wink. Then we'd bring my mom home some takeout and lie about what we'd ordered from the restaurant.

I'd forgotten about the ice cream dinners until I found myself staring into his blue eyes in prison. What a strange time to remember a thing like that. A pleasant memory turning up in the unlikeliest of places.

"You never write," he said. "I have to hear about everything from your mother."

"Mom writes you?"

He beamed. "Of course she does. Why wouldn't she?"

Why wouldn't she? The question nearly knocked me onto the dirty concrete floor.

"I hear you're a police officer now," he said. "I'm proud of you."

I felt hot tears push at the back of my eyeballs. "I'm not here to catch up. I have to ask you a few things."

He leaned back and held up his wrists. "I got nothing but time, Bear."

Another detail I'd forgotten. But I couldn't let it derail me. "Why won't you confess to the other women?"

He squinted at me, not unkindly, but with a sense of deep sadness, like I'd just disappointed him. "What are you talking about?"

"You know what I'm talking about. The Black women, Raymond. They have you down for thirty-eight counts of murder. But none of those women were Black. I *know* you killed others. What's holding you back? Another life sentence tacked on? The FBI doesn't have to believe me, but I know what I saw, and the least you can do is confirm that it's true. Anything. Just a yes or a nod or, hell, blink twice."

He did none of those things, only stared at me. "I'm so sorry, Dana. The FBI doesn't believe anyone. I know how frustrating it can be. How do you think I ended up here?"

"How do I think... I think you ended up here for chopping up dozens of women!"

The sparkle in his eyes dimmed, and I had a sick impulse to apologize so it might return.

"You've been reading the news, then." He sighed. "I can't blame you, I guess. I would want to know the truth, too. The father you thought you knew, the one you thought loved you like no one else, is suddenly arrested and accused of all these horrible things. Of course you'd want to know. But do you really think I could do that sort of thing? Me?" He chuckled sadly. "Dana Bear, I drove you to soccer, helped coach your team. I love you and Sean and Shannon and your mother more than life itself. You really think I would risk it all to do those... those *horrible* things? I don't know who did it, but so long as *I'm* in *here*, he can keep on doing it."

"I guess it's just a crazy coincidence that as soon as you were arrested, the killings stopped?"

"They did around Dallas, at least. I assume the man was smart enough to know he could get away scot-free if he just moved somewhere else to keep going."

"Bodies were found in *your* studio. The one you kept locked almost all the time. How in the hell— No. You don't get to do this with me. Maybe other people, but not me. I *saw* those women in the studio. I heard them begging for help."

He nodded, and for a moment, I thought I might get what I came for.

But then he said, "How old were you when you claim to have seen that?"

"Which time? I was seven when I found the finger, Raymond. Ten when I saw the blood in the kitchen. Thirteen when I found the photos in your car *and* the flayed woman."

He tilted his head to the side. "I don't know what photos you're even talking about, Dana. And how come you didn't tell anyone about all of that? How come you only remembered it once I was already in custody?"

I didn't have a good answer for that.

"You gotta be careful, Bear. The FBI is good at planting false memories, especially in scared little girls. I wouldn't put it past them to use you like that to railroad me."

I tried my best not to hear it, not to let the words seep in. "They plant false memories in Rita Gibson, too?" He didn't say anything, so I went on. "Tell me about the other victims. Not the ten they found in the woods, but the others. The Black women. Where'd you dump them? Their families deserve closure."

"I worry about you so much, Dana. You deserved to be protected as a child, and I couldn't do it. I couldn't protect my baby girl from all these lies." The crocodile tears threatened to spill over. "But I've been doing my best to keep an eye on you as you grow up. That's all I can say now, that I'll be keeping a close eye on you, even from my prison cell."

It was a promise that would always chill my blood when I thought back on it.

I'd ended the prison meeting right after that without

saying another word. He wasn't going to talk, and I was done with him. Or at least I wanted to be.

Who was I kidding, though? His specter lived on, always with me, tainting every decision I made. Could I ever be rid of that lingering evil, or had it saturated my blood?

I shivered and turned down the air in my CRV.

Raymond had been charged with murdering thirty-eight women. How many of those could I have saved if I'd simply said something to the right people right away?

And now I'd let my relationship with Dylan mislead me again. Why? What had I hoped to gain?

I cupped my hands over my mouth and nose, trying to slow my breathing, refusing to let self-pity condense into tears. There simply wasn't a strong enough word to describe what a useless fool I was.

You've done it again, Dana.

If I waited for another second to start cleaning up this mess, I was guaranteed to fall apart, so I pulled out my phone, swallowed down the last remnants of my pride, and called Ben.

THIRTY-FIVE

Dylan ate his fries in the dark parking lot of the Whataburger. A car pulled up next to his, and two drunk twenty-something women stumbled out. The one closest to him closed her purse strap in the door and devolved into a laughing fit until her friend came to her aid.

Dana had seen the heels. He was sure of it. Something had happened between the time they got in the car and the time she left that had startled her. No proper goodbye, nothing. And the way they were heading just minutes before at the pub, he'd expected a kiss on the cheek at the very least.

He was an idiot for keeping them in his car, as if he needed them handy at all times, as if he didn't plan out far in advance when he'd actually use them, as if they weren't part of a much larger and more intensive preparation process.

They should have been locked away in his bedroom closet, where he stored all the rest, but his mother, the hag, had been awake when he got back the last time, so bringing them inside was out of the question. He'd managed to get the rest up to his room in the backpack he kept with him, but the shoes hadn't fit.

No way around it: Dana had seen what was in the box and freaked out. But did she actually know what the shoes meant? Had she glimpsed his entire other self in those red heels?

His life was ruined. Why had he let her get so close to him? He should have kept his distance like he usually did.

"*Fuck!*" He tossed the rest of his fries back into the bag and slammed a greasy fist against the steering wheel. He'd worked so hard to keep his two lives separate, and now she could ruin everything. A part of him had hoped he might tell her the truth and that she'd understand, maybe even find his unique form of expression attractive in her fucked-up way, but he could see now that it had always been a fool's hope.

He put the car in reverse. His desire to get the incriminating evidence locked up tight was overwhelming.

By the time he pulled onto his street, his mind was focused solely on damage control. He could always deny it all. No one could prove anything, shoes or no shoes.

It was already past eleven, so he cut the headlights before pulling into the driveway. His mother claimed the light woke her up every time, and he was sick of that crazy bitch tracking his movements. Wouldn't even cough up a solid alibi for him to the cops to keep her son out from under suspicion of murder. Why did she badger him all the time about his whereabouts only to be utterly useless when he needed her to step up? He let her live with him, and she was nothing but a pain in his ass.

He'd had a recurring dream for the last two years of

beating her to a bloody pulp. When he woke up from it each time, all he felt was an overwhelming sense of relief. He wouldn't tell a soul about *that*, of course.

He grabbed the crumpled bag of fries and reached behind him to get the shoebox. The fucking thing was going straight in the closet. There was still a chance, albeit a small one, that Dana hadn't seen them after all, that something else had spoiled the night, something that had nothing to do with him.

Or maybe she *had* seen but wouldn't tell anyone. She'd kept her father's secret long enough. And if he'd learned anything from their conversations, it was that her memory was shaky at best. Easily molded, if need be.

Awkwardly, he pushed himself up and out of the low car, his hands full with the fast food and shoes.

He hadn't even shut the door when the flashlights flicked on, encircling him, blinding him. Dylan shielded his eyes with the Whataburger bag just as an officer yelled for him to put his hands up.

THIRTY-SIX

Predawn. July 5th, 2018

29 days since Blackstenius murder

For obvious reasons, I hadn't been allowed to roll out with Ben and the agents to make the arrest, so I was sitting on my thumbs back at the station, watching the clock tick by and thinking of all the ways I was a total idiot for refusing to see it sooner with Dylan.

The fact that I was starting to feel comfortable around him should have been my *first* indication that something was off. I was FUBAR in the relationships department. It was probably time to call up my old therapist and let her know I had a women's shoebox full of new issues to unpack.

But what really nagged at me was that the FBI was *right*. White male, thirty-five years old, lived with his overbearing mother, loner, drove a goddamn Prius.

What a stupid profile. I still stood by that. And for it to be *accurate*, that was even stupider.

Once Agents Wicklow and Turner returned from the

Fowlers' house, I knew I wouldn't stop hearing about how they'd been right the whole time, and maybe I ought to start trusting the FBI a little more.

My blonde wig flopped like roadkill on the floor next to my desk. I'd forgotten I had it on until I reached the station, and Detective Krantz asked me if I charged by the hour or the service.

Sighing, I reached in the second drawer of my desk and pulled out my face-cleaning wipes. I kept a pack handy to rally on long nights when I worked until the only thing my body seemed capable of doing was pushing grease out through my pores. But now, the wipes proved useful to remove the excessive makeup from my cheap disguise. I needed to rid myself of Dana Dwyer.

I grabbed two and headed to the bathroom.

Staring at myself in the mirror, alone along the line of sinks, I tried not to scowl at myself. Lipstick had always been the bane of my existence. Well, one of them. There wasn't a color in this world that didn't morph me into a clown when I put it on my thin Irish lips.

I scrubbed a wipe roughly over my eyelids to remove the shadow and liner.

I splashed water on my face, removed the remaining eyeliner that washed free, redid my ponytail, and shuffled back to my desk. I wasn't going home until I found out how the arrest had gone, which was too bad, because I could've really used Sadie's head across my lap just then.

They were bringing Dylan in as I passed by the main lobby of the station. Ben spoke with the clerk at the front desk while Turner kept one hand on Dylan's cuffed wrists and another on the back of his neck.

He appeared terrified, disoriented, and in shock, his

mouth hanging open, his eyebrows pinched tightly together as he looked from one authoritative face to the other.

It was solid acting. Raymond would've been proud.

I folded my arms and watched him until he finally spotted me. Here I was with my gun clearly visible in its leather holster and my badge hanging on a chain around my neck. Good. Let him know. Let him see me in my natural state. Let him put the pieces together. A man like him deserved to know the sting of treachery. Let *him* feel betrayed for once. It paled in comparison to the betrayal Cheryl, Leslie, and Stephanie surely felt the moment they realized what was going to happen to them, that they were never going to make it out of their bonds, never going to see their friends or family again.

Dylan's mouth opened even wider before snapping shut. He continued to gape at me, so I forced a smile. *Gotcha.*

I'd caught the killer, but I might've lost my job in the process. Maybe that was a small price to pay, but it didn't make me any more eager to pay it.

Show was over, as far as I was concerned, so I returned to my desk to await my summons to the conference room. It wouldn't be long. It might feel like an eternity, though.

Spinning my chair toward the computer, I attached the file of the unabridged audio recording from the night to the email I'd typed up before I visited the ladies' room, and then I hit send. I'd listened to parts already, and it was hard not to scoff at how obvious the truth was, staring me right in the face with each question he asked about Raymond's life and legacy.

At least I'd figured out which of the two brothers in the woods Dylan was. Lies, lies, lies.

I pulled up the crime scene photos from Stephanie Lee and browsed through them one by one until I found the close-up of the foot. The medical examiner had eventually removed the shoe from her, pulled out the nail, and logged each item as evidence. But in the photo, the shoe was still on. I couldn't be sure of the brand after all the water damage, and the color had faded, but it was clear enough that the original had been something like candy-apple red. It would require a much keener eye for fashion than mine to spot how the style wasn't a perfect match to the ones in Dylan's car.

Cheryl's heels had also been candy-apple red, and shiny like they'd never been worn. Straight out of the box.

And then there was the pair Leslie had been murdered in, and that was where the consistency faltered. But we'd already established that she had been wearing those heels when she left the bar. Dylan must have decided that it was a close enough match and saved himself a step in the horrendous ritual. Perhaps he'd liked it better that way—it felt more organic.

And the biggest question of all: why? Why did he insist on his women wearing heels when he killed them? What did that represent to him? Was it something to do with Mrs. Fowler? She seemed the type to insist that self-respecting women wore heels. Not ones as high as those Dylan was fetishizing, though. Francis would've thought that style was only fit for prostitutes.

I breathed out a curse and ran a hand over my face. Was this a prostitute thing? Had he also been killing prostitutes on the side that we didn't know about? It was an easy crime to get away with if you weren't terribly sloppy. Those of us in Homicide were spread thin, and our higher-ups placed a dead prostitute low on the list of priorities. A few of those *had* come through our office this year, aside from the Rochelle case, which was a whole different matter. Much as I hated to admit it, it would take a lot of dead prostitutes piling up in a short amount of time for it to catch even my attention as a possible pattern, let alone perk up the ears of the press. Dylan was too organized of a killer to make such an obvious misstep. He would've paced himself to go undetected. If I hadn't taken that ride with him, how many more women?

A clank to my left caused me to jump, and I tore my eyes away from a picture of Cheryl's strung-up body to find that Ben had just set down a mug of hot coffee on my desk.

"Thanks," I said, scooting it closer while he took his seat across from me. "I'm screwed, aren't I?"

He shrugged a single shoulder and blew on his steaming cup. "I'd put your odds at about fifty-fifty."

"Fifty percent I'm taken off the case, fifty percent I'm fired?"

"Oh no, you're *definitely* off the case. They'd have to be insane to keep you on. I was thinking more fifty you're fired and fifty you're arrested for interfering with an investigation."

I grunted. "Glad I have your comfort in my time of need."

"I'm mostly giving you a hard time. You know you're too damn good at your job for them to fire you."

I jerked my head back. "Wow. That was, like, a compliment."

"What can I say? No one's forgotten about the Rochelle case, and it *does* look like your interference caught us a serial killer. That should count for something."

Sergeant Popov stomped up to the threshold of the office and glared inside. "You two. Conference room."

Here we go.

I got to my feet and stretched out my neck and shoulders.

"You look like you're getting ready for a fight," Ben said.

"Aren't I? I'm about to get my ass chewed. A little felony stretching is all I can do."

We walked shoulder to shoulder down the hallway, and Ben held open the door for me to go ahead of him into the conference room.

Not only were Popov, Wicklow, and Turner in there, but so were three other agents from the FBI. It was a packed house. Everyone wanted a ticket to the show.

"This is her?" asked one of the men I didn't recognize. He was lanky, pale, and kept his head shaved. Looked to be in his early fifties, so he was probably just ashamed of his balding rather than any sort of badass. His green eyes pulled together the look in a way that was almost, but not quite, attractive. Or maybe I was just exhausted and delusional.

Either way, his blunt question almost made me laugh. *Is this her?* Wow, I'd never felt so notorious.

"Yep, that's her," Agent Wicklow said. "Detective Capone, this is ASAC Steve Grissom from the Bureau."

The assistant special agent in charge didn't make a move to shake. "You're the one who ran the rogue op tonight?"

"Yes, sir." Clutching my coffee mug in both hands, I suddenly felt like an old maid of a librarian. It didn't help that Ben had given me the Austin Public Library community cup.

This whole situation felt silly. I wished they'd just reprimand me and get it over with.

But no, even if they fired me, there would be a long, torturous debrief. Ah, bureaucracy.

"Let's have a seat, shall we?" ASAC Grissom looked around the room, and each person scrambled to find a chair. Ben sat to my left, and I took some small comfort at having him by my side for this. "Detective Escobar said he had no prior knowledge of you going to speak with the suspect tonight, is that correct?"

"Yes, sir, that's correct. He only found out about it when I called him from my car."

Grissom accepted that with a nod. "And Agent Wicklow tells me you were adamant that Dylan Fowler was *not* the man behind the double homicide."

Double homicide. For chrissakes. They were still taking that line, were they? Two steps forward, two steps back. "He's correct. I didn't think it was Fowler."

Grissom nodded curtly again. "So, you went out to meet the suspect at the scene of the crime to, what, disprove the theory?"

"Yes, sir. I truly believed we had the wrong guy. In all fairness, everything we had, and even what we have now, is circumstantial at best. I hope you'll understand my concern when I saw how myopic the investigation had become. If our attention was on the wrong man, the right man would be able to keep killing. I knew I didn't have anyone who shared my opinion on this task force, so I decided not to wait around for another body to turn up to collect more evidence." I paused, and Grissom was gracious enough not to jump in. "It was stupid what I did, sir, but I didn't see any other option. If I had found a way to eliminate him, it would've taken the blinders off this investigation, and we'd have a better chance of finding the right person. We'd have to reevaluate persons of interest who we might have crossed off prematurely or broaden the scope of our search."

Grissom said, "I understand your logic, Detective. Do you still stick by it now that we have a pretty good idea that Dylan Fowler is the man who killed those women?"

"I still stick by the logic. With all due respect, I was our best shot at extracting information from him. I went to middle school with the suspect, and I had reason to believe he'd long harbored a crush on me. There was already trust there, and he didn't know I was a cop."

"Why didn't you set up a proper operation, then?" He seemed genuinely interested, but was it a sign of strong leadership and wanting to understand the situation fully, or was he trying to set me up to say something else that made me look unstable?

But, hell, why not go for it? "I knew from previous interactions with Agent Wicklow that he wouldn't have signed off on it."

A muscle in Agent Wicklow's jaw twitched as ASAC Grissom's attention turned to him. But neither man said a thing.

Grissom addressed me again. "And it would have been the right call not to. I've never heard of a female detective acting this way, to be quite honest."

My stomach transformed instantly into a spring-loaded fist. What the hell did my gender have to do with anything? Had he seen *male* detectives act this way? Was he fine with *that*?

"While it's not my call to make," he continued, "I'm struggling to imagine a scenario in which you're not fired or at the very least demoted for what you've done."

The hot coffee clawed its way up my esophagus just as Ben cleared his throat beside me. "Question, sir."

All the eyes in the room shifted, including Grissom's. "Yes, Detective Escobar?"

"Is anyone outside of this room aware that Detective Capone didn't have backup or approval tonight?"

Grissom's nostrils flared. "No, not that I'm aware of."

"And she got us Fowler," Ben said.

The words hung thick in the air. Everyone in the room could sense where this was going. Wicklow looked like he'd ingested recalled spinach, Turner watched Ben with keen interest, and Popov seemed to be holding his breath as his ruddy face crept closer toward maroon.

"She did get us Fowler," Grissom said. "Are you suggesting that the result makes up for the procedural violation?"

"I'm just pointing it out. But there's something else that I haven't heard mentioned yet. I just noticed it when I found Detective Capone looking over the crime scene photos. So I assume *she's* already put it together."

I stayed silent. I was a fool in a lot of ways, as the events of the night had shown, but I knew when it was time to let my partner do the talking.

"And what's that?" said Grissom.

Ben wouldn't look at me. "The heels we found in Fowler's arms. They match the one nailed to Stephanie Lee's foot almost perfectly. Granted, there are some differences caused by the water damage, but I have a feeling forensics will be able to re-create what it looked like, and when they do, it'll look a hell of a lot like the pair in Fowler's possession. Possibly identical. Capone just helped us tie in Stephanie Lee's murder to this case. Triple homicide, not just double."

"We already dismissed that as a possibility," Agent Wicklow snapped.

But Ben wouldn't be deterred. "It looks like we dismissed it too soon. If we include the Lee murder, we have a new wealth of evidence to use to put Fowler away for good."

Grissom sucked on his cheeks throughout the explanation, leaving large craters on either side of his face, but as Ben finished, he nodded again, just a single time, like some goddamn Roman emperor. *My will be done.* "We'll have to reexamine the evidence to make sure it matches up, but if it does, that's a big break." He stood, and so did the rest of the room, myself included. I nearly spilled my coffee across the table in my hurry to get up. Was this meeting done already?

Before anyone could leave, as if anyone would try without being dismissed, Grissom made one final proclamation. "Knowledge of the events of Detective Capone's evening does not leave this room." He turned his emerald eyes on me. "You have recordings of the conversations, I believe? Agent Turner said you always keep those."

"Already sent them to the team, sir. I can forward them to you as well if you'd like."

"Anything good on there?"

"I'm sure there's something we can use."

"Sergeant Popov, do you trust your detective to keep from doing something like this again?"

Instead of answering right away, Popov turned to Ben. "You trust her?"

"Of course."

"Good. You're officially in charge of keeping your partner on the straight and narrow. If she screws up again, you're both fired immediately. Or as immediately as the union will allow. Understood?"

Ben agreed without hesitation, and I made a mental note to both thank him and profusely apologize later.

Popov asked me, "We clear? You do this again, and he gets fired, too."

"Yessir," I said. "Loud and clear, Sarge."

Popov turned back to Grissom. "I trust her now."

And that was all there was to it.

I left the room in a daze. Somehow, I'd made it out virtually unscathed. No, not somehow. Ben Escobar. He had stuck his neck out for me once again and saved me.

"If you weren't a woman," Ben mumbled as he passed me on his way back to Death Row, "I would kick your ass right here, right now."

THIRTY-SEVEN

An hour later, Ben yawned loudly, drawing my attention away from my monitor. "Why don't you just go home?" I asked. "They have him in custody. You know the FBI has it from here."

"Why don't *you* go home?" he barked.

"Nice to know you're talking to me, at least."

"How am I supposed to make sure you don't do some stupid shit and get me fired if I refuse to talk to you?"

"Good point. But then again, it hasn't stopped me yet."

He grunted.

When I felt the presence of someone new in the office, I looked to see who it was and swore under my breath. Of all the people...

"If it ain't the mob squad," said Detective Towers. He was in his patrol uniform, duty belt and all.

Ben's eyes roamed the other detective's get-up. "They finally demote you back to patrol?"

"You wish. Just picking up a little OT. My wife just told me she needs braces."

It was too easy with him. "Reason number 148 to wait until your woman graduates middle school to get hitched, I guess," I said.

"I'm truly shocked they let you back out on patrol," Ben said. "I thought the sole purpose of promoting you was to keep you from tasing another old lady."

Towers held his arms out from his side like a grizzly trying to look larger than it was. "Don't you start with that again, Escobar. *She* came at *me* with a weapon."

"It was a cane, dipshit. She thought you were a prowler."

"Yeah, yeah. Youse guys don't understand a thing about all that. I was over in Baker. Sector ain't exactly a cakewalk. What sectors did *you* jabronis work in before you made detective, anyhow?"

"Charlie then Henry," said Ben.

Impressive enough, but I had him beat. "Edward and more Edward. We once had an attempted murder-suicide where the shooter blew his jaw off, then realized he wanted to live, so he fled and crashed his car into another car parked on the curb. Ended up killing two men who were trying to break into *that* car, and then he opened fire on us when we cornered him, but not before unsuccessfully trying to blow his head off again. I think that was on a Wednesday night. But you're right; grandmas with canes is some hardcore action. Baker! Phew!"

Towers rolled his eyes. "You Edward shits are all the same. So full of yourselves."

I was a little bummed to lose my only distraction when he turned and left; I could have emasculated him for another twenty or thirty minutes and not grown bored.

Ben watched him leave, too. "Sometimes I marvel that

someone as stupid as him has survived this long, let alone kept his job."

"They seriously shouldn't let him back out onto the streets. I heard he performed a cavity search on—"

A wail from the main hallway cut me off, and we exchanged a glance before we were on our feet, rushing toward the sound.

The source of the cry was easy enough to spot. A stout officer had her arm around a tall, broad-shouldered woman, who whined miserably before erupting into inconsolable wailing again. The large woman's hands flew into the air as if to ask the heavens, *Why?*

"Good lord," muttered Ben. "Whatever she's been drinking tonight, count me out."

"Drinking or snorting," I replied.

He headed back into the office, but I stuck around to see this brief distraction through.

The officer steered the hysterical woman down the hall toward a private room where they could talk. It was clear some sort of victimization had taken place. Probably another mugging just off Sixth Street. It had been a problem for years now that no local politicians seemed keen on addressing and that law enforcement couldn't possibly do anything about without more resources and support. Gangs prowled the side streets, waiting for an oblivious woman on her phone to pass, and then they'd swoop in. Thankfully, it was usually just a mugging and not a sexual assault. But sometimes, it was a sexual assault.

Only as the distraught woman came closer down the hall did I realize that she struggled to walk, limping hard on a bum left leg. The officer wasn't so much comforting her as propping her up. Poor thing.

I recognized the officer from passing her around the station, but I didn't know her name. As she got a few arm's lengths away, I read it on her uniform. Quark.

Officer Quark led the presumed victim my way, and my eyes traveled down to search for the cause of the broad-shouldered woman's limp. No blood, so that was good. But there *was* a massive lump on her left shin. I sucked in air sympathetically, then all at once, it clicked.

Ho-ly shit.

But it couldn't be. The timing didn't work. Unless...

I caught up with them a few yards past me. "Need some help, Officer?"

The victim continued wailing as I slung my arm around to support her on the other side.

Quark failed to hide her suspicion over a detective offering to help out with something like this, but she didn't vocalize that suspicion in front of the victim.

We made it into the room, and I pulled out a chair, where Quark helped the woman sit. "Can I get you some water, ma'am?" I asked, placing a gentle hand on the crying woman's shoulder.

She stammered something incomprehensible, which I took to be a yes.

"Detective Capone. Homicide," I said to Quark. "I'll be right back. Keep her in here. Don't let anyone else speak to her yet. Not even your sergeant. Not even *my* sergeant."

Ben was back at the doorway to the hall when I passed him on my way to the break room. "What's going on?"

"A hunch."

"Is it a hunch that's going to get me fired?" he called after me.

"Fifty-fifty."

By the time I returned to the small room with the assault victim and Officer Quark, the victim had calmed somewhat and was less hunched. Only then did I spot something peculiar about her anatomy. I placed the cup of water on the table in front of her. "Here you go." It wasn't just the woman's broad shoulders that were distinctive, but her Adam's apple. I so frequently encountered trans women in my line of work that their gender would have normally gotten little more than a passing thought from me, but I suspected it might be especially worth noting here. "What's your name?"

"Gwen Masters." She took a tentative sip of the water.

"Gwen, I'm Dana. I can tell you've had a rough night of it."

Gwen chuckled dryly at the understatement. "Could've been a lot worse." Her voice slipped into a lower register only briefly at the end.

"Officer Quark and I want to hear everything that happened if you're ready to talk. I know you've really been through it, so if you need more time—"

"No, no, I'm ready."

Officer Quark pulled out her notepad, but I'd already slipped my hand into my pocket to pull out my phone. "You mind if I record this conversation?"

I could feel Gwen tightening up. "Why do you need to do that?"

"Because I have a feeling that whoever did this to you might have done the same to other women, and I want to have it on record so I can compare the accounts and present the case to my superiors. And listen, I know sometimes recall isn't great. If you miss a detail or don't get it quite right, that's okay. It happens. I'm not gonna nitpick or hold it against you later, okay? I'm going to do everything in my power to make sure your attacker is caught."

Gwen forced a wan smile. "Okay. I believe you. Do you need my legal name, or will Gwen Masters suffice?"

"Gwen is fine. We'll get all the legal stuff later. Someone assaulted you?"

Her eye makeup ran down her face as she said, "Yes. He attacked out of nowhere."

"Did you recognize him?"

"No. I didn't get a clear enough look at him to try."

"Where were you when it happened?"

"Sheep's Clothing. I'd just stepped into the alley for a smoke."

"Sheep's Clothing?" I asked.

"It's a bar," Gwen replied. "A drag bar."

"You're not in drag, though," I said.

She rolled her eyes. "Of course I'm not. I'm a *real* woman, not just one on the weekends." The bitterness was impossible to miss.

"So you're in the alley for Sheep's Clothing. Is that a side alley, back alley?"

"Back alley. There's a door to it the same hall as the restrooms."

Limited visibility. Was he waiting out there already, or did he follow her out? "And then what happened?"

"He just came up on me from behind."

"And you didn't see his face?"

"Believe me, I tried. But he was wearing, like, pantyhose or something over his head. God, I didn't know people actually did that. Shit."

A knot like a clenched fist formed in my stomach. This might not be connected. Everything we knew about the three murders pointed to our unsub *knowing* the victims, possibly even luring them to their murder sites under false pretenses. There'd be no need for pantyhose if that were the case. Here we had a slightly different MO.

I asked, "Any chance you've been hanging around Laugh Attack lately?"

Gwen appeared offended by the mere implication. "That ratty old fire hazard on Seventh? The one for *comics*?" I nodded. "Not a chance."

My head started to pound, and I was about ready to give up on this. It seemed so promising. Or maybe I was still hoping for a miracle I know won't come.

But then I remembered.

"Your shin. What happened to it?"

Gwen's colored-in eyebrows shot up toward her hairline. "What *happened* to it? The psycho stomped it with his redneck boot! That's *what happened*." She raised her leg above the table, and I was confronted with the angry lump again. Officer Quark cringed. "That's not all this dickhead did," Gwen continued. "While I was cursing and asking him what the hell he thought he was doing, he went for my neck and started choking me. I fought him off, but he wouldn't quit. He said, 'I'm not letting you get away, bitch,' and somehow he managed to get a cord around my throat and tighten it." She tilted her head back, and the ligature marks just below her Adam's apple were still angry and red.

"And you fought him off?"

"Of course I did! I kicked back and heeled him right in the jewels. He dropped to the ground, and I ran all the way here."

The air froze in my lungs. "Hold on. You came straight here?"

"As quickly as I could. I knew I was right by the station, and I sure as hell wasn't going to wait around with that lunatic until police arrived. I know how things work, and y'all don't exactly hustle over to drag bars."

"Fair enough," I said, but I meant it more about not wanting to hang around where she was attacked than the assertion that cops didn't help the LGBTQ community like they would anyone else. Okay, *some* wouldn't, but those cops were worthless all around. "You're safe here, Gwen. We're gonna find that guy."

"You said he's been doing this to other women?"

"There appear to be some similarities. How tall would you say he was?"

She considered it. "I'm six foot, plus these heels, and he was a little shorter than me. Maybe five-ten, five-eleven?"

"Could he have been shorter? Like five-eight?"

"Maybe, but that's pretty short for a man. I think I would've had that thought if he'd been so short."

"And his skin color?" I asked. "I know he had pantyhose over his face, but could you see his arms or anything?"

"Oh yeah. White guy. There wasn't a whole lot of light back there, but that was obvious enough."

"Could he have been Hispanic?"

She closed her eyes and tilted her head back. "I mean, I guess so. Sometimes they're light-skinned."

"And his clothes?"

She opened her mouth to speak but hesitated. "I think he had on a black T-shirt. Or maybe it was a polo?" She shook her head. "I'm sorry, I don't know why I can't remember that."

"It's okay. Was he in shorts? What kind of shoes?"

"I don't remember about the pants. Jeans, maybe? He was definitely wearing cowboy boots, I remember that. The goddamn heel of them is what got me."

Goddamn cowboy boots.

I told Officer Quark, "Get some units out to Sheep's Clothing. You need to check the area for any man fitting the description who's limping like he just got kicked in the balls. He probably left, but maybe he hasn't made it far. We gotta catch him. This might be our only chance."

I had muscled her off this interview, but I couldn't make myself feel sorry for it. She could be the best officer in the department, but she was not a detective, and this was officially related to a homicide now.

To her credit, Quark seemed to understand, and she nodded and slipped out of the interview room.

I tried not to let on how much I wanted to sprint out of the room and get going on all the other implications of this discovery. I breathed in through my nose then asked Gwen, "Will you be okay if I leave you here for a bit and send in a medic to check you out?"

"As long as it's a woman, fine. And not a TERF. But I'm pretty much done with men for the night."

"Totally understand. I'll get you set up. Do you need anything else in the meantime? Coffee? More water?"

"Coffee with cream, no sugar."

"Righto."

Once I was out into the hall, I hollered up front for a female medic, then headed straight to the break room to fix up a coffee. My heart was still racing, and my calves felt spring-loaded. A Wonder Woman mug was among the clean communal ones on the drying rack, so I grabbed it for Gwen.

As I was pulling the cream from the fridge, I heard Ben's soft footsteps behind me. "What the hell's going on?"

"I'm getting a victim some coffee."

"From *our* break room? You know there's a Keurig in the front lobby. And disposable cups."

"K-cups taste like shit, and she deserves the good stuff."

I tapped the spoon on the side of the mug and put it in the sink, but when I turned, Ben was blocking my way.

"You need to slow down and explain to me *why* you just inserted yourself into that mugging. You're Homicide, Capone. And she seems very much alive."

"Dylan Fowler isn't our man."

He bowed his head and pinched the bridge of his nose. "Oh, you gotta be kidding me..." I allowed him a moment to mourn the loss of having the killer in custody. He didn't yet see how big of a lucky break this was. "Dana, *you* were the one that gave us the final piece on him. You found the heels in his car, the same ones that convinced the FBI Stephanie Lee was one of his victims. You tied it all together. He *has* to be our man."

"He can't be. Because whoever killed Cheryl and Stephanie and Leslie just tried to kill the woman in that room."

His expression went slack. "What?"

"She fought him off because she's... Well, she's large. Anyway, I promised her a cup of coffee while the medics treat the *ligature marks* on her neck and the *whopping bruise* on her shin. Once I drop this off, we can talk about how the real killer is still out there."

But I didn't head straight back to Ben after checking in with Gwen. I needed a moment alone to think, and the only place for that in the station was the ladies' room.

I flipped the toilet cover down and sat, trying to let the disparate elements swirl into one comprehensive portrait. The pieces didn't all make sense yet. Some of the MO was the same: attempt to break the shin, strangle, possibly use the cord to bind. But it hadn't worked. Perhaps the predator underestimated the strength of his prey. Did he realize she was a trans woman? Obviously, not all trans women were built like a brick house, but Gwen was. And she was also significantly bigger than any of the other victims. Stephanie Lee was only five-two.

Maybe he was feeling more confident in his abilities, looking for a challenge.

Still, whether or not it was an intentional transition from cisgender women to a trans woman victim would make all the difference in guessing his underlying psychology. The fact that the attack took place in the alley of a drag bar seemed to hint heavily toward it being an intentional change of victim profile.

It also hinted that Laugh Attack was merely a location of convenience. He didn't necessarily fetishize bad comedians. Gwen had said she wouldn't set foot in that comedy club. There was something else he was after. Something he was working his way toward.

The image of Dylan in cuffs jumped to the front of my mind, and the throbbing in my head intensified. The shoes might be a coincidence. An incredibly unlikely one, but still. Maybe they *were* his mother's, like he'd apparently told the FBI. Or they could be a girlfriend's. Just because he'd gone out to drinks with me didn't mean he was single.

Now that I thought of it, I'd never asked him about that. I'd just assumed he was available.

I'd assumed a lot. Too much. And now the wrong man was in the FBI's custody.

Probably. Assuming...

There I went again. I needed answers, not theories.

I left the stall and inspected myself in the mirror only briefly. The dark circles under my eyes from years of this job had earned squatter's rights. No more pretending that "I just need some sleep." No. I was officially a woman who always had dark circles. Maybe that was just what thirty-six looked like on the force.

I splashed cold water on my face, and that felt... not exactly better, but it helped ground me. I rubbed away even more residual makeup underneath my eyes with a rough swipe of my thumb.

Five-ten or five-eleven. Could the attacker have been five-eight? That detail nagged at me. It was almost a clue, but it was unreliable. Dylan was five-eleven, but he was in custody, so he couldn't have done it.

Was it related? Could this be another man responsible for Gwen's attack? It wasn't as if the local news had exercised discretion on the gory details of the previous murders, and copycats were a real thing. The pantyhose, the sneak attack—the MO was just different enough for this to be someone else entirely. Maybe the FBI did have the right man.

I tried to tune in to hear what my gut had to say, but I couldn't make it out. My gut had said it wasn't Dylan before. Then I'd spotted that yellow shoebox, and everything turned upside down. No matter the truth, I had misread Dylan entirely at least once.

Wasn't that always the problem, though? You couldn't tell just by speaking with a person. The liars who felt no remorse were undetectable. Why did I keep expecting to spot them? How could I ever trust anyone?

Too far, Dana. Stop it.

I'd looked over the edge of that precipice before, and it was a long way down. I knew better than to take that final step out, where the ground disappeared.

This wasn't in my hands anymore. Whether Gwen's attack was linked or not was entirely up to the FBI to decide. And that decision could free an innocent man or put a killer back on the streets.

I'd find out soon enough.

THIRTY-EIGHT

I didn't waste time uploading the recorded interview with Gwen to the computer. Instead, I set my phone in the center of the conference table and waited until Agents Wicklow and Turner arrived. Popov's eyes were red, the way they always were when they hadn't gotten enough rest from his contacts, and his expression made it clear that this better be good for me to call him in so early.

Ben stood next to me once we were gathered in the closed room, his arms crossed over his chest, staring fixedly at my phone. He hadn't liked what I told him, but he'd agreed that it could be related. Enough to stick his neck out for me in a moment? We'd see.

I set up the context quickly, paying close attention to each listener's expression as it morphed from annoyed to curious to varying degrees of perturbed.

Yeah, I knew the feeling. This new info didn't exactly simplify things, but as I relayed it, I couldn't help but feel a small twist of excitement in my guts.

The recording ended, and no one said a thing. The

impermeable silence played tricks with time as each person seemed lost in the implications, ten steps ahead of where we found ourselves now.

Turner was the one to speak first. "We still have Miss Masters around?"

"Yes," I said. "She's still being cared for in the interview room."

The agent revealed no visible signs of where she fell on the matter. "We'll need to speak with her further."

"Might I suggest you go alone?" I said. "She's not exactly keen on men at the moment."

Wicklow scoffed. "Isn't *that* rich."

Turner glared at him, but if he noticed, he pretended not to care.

Ben cleared his throat, his eyes glued to my phone in the center of the table like it might explode or try to escape. "There are too many similarities in the MO. It seems likely that this is a related incident committed by the same person who killed Scopes, Lee, and Blackstenius."

"I see it differently," Sergeant Popov replied. "I think there are too many differences in the MO for this to be our unsub."

"Copycat?" Turner asked.

Popov shrugged. "That would be my guess."

"Do we know precisely what the media has described from the crime scenes?" I said. Turner's intense expression told me that she was tracking, but Wicklow gave no outward signs of it, so I went on. "If we know everything the media has reported—and anything they've reported incorrectly—we can compare it to the attack on Gwen Masters. If, say, some outlet incorrectly reported that the

Stand-Up Killer wears pantyhose when he murders women..."

"Then we can conclude it was a copycat," Ben finished for me.

Turner pulled out her phone and started tapping away. "I'll get a summary of that information for you."

Maybe the FBI was useful after all.

"If it's not Dylan Fowler," Wicklow said through gritted teeth, "then we go back to only two victims. Scopes and Blackstenius. We would have to throw out the evidence of the shoes, which are what tie Stephanie Lee to the others."

"Or," I said, "we could look at the MO of the attack to link them. Each of the women had blunt-force trauma to one of their shins, just like Gwen reported."

"I hate to nitpick," Wicklow countered, clearly glad to be nitpicking, "but we don't know what happened to Stephanie Lee's shins. The only one remaining showed no clear signs of a boot heel. Also, Gwen said herself she wouldn't be caught at Laugh Attack. That would make her the first victim we know of who has no affiliation with the place." He paused. "There's a lot missing here."

"Have the officers found anyone fitting the suspect description in the area?" Popov asked.

"I heard back from Officer Quark right before this briefing," I said. "They didn't turn up anyone who fits Gwen's description. We think he might have already driven away or slipped off into the crowds by the time they initiated the search. Sounds like they could only free up four officers to look. Too much going on with the Fourth festivities downtown."

"If he had two brain cells to rub together," Ben said,

"he'd be halfway to Mexico by now. When your attempted murder goes south, so should you."

"We could wait and see who disappears from the Laugh Attack scene," Wicklow suggested. "And if no one disappears, we know we have the right guy, and Masters' attacker was a copycat."

"Not necessarily," I said. "If we're dealing with a psychopath, he's unlikely to be a flight risk. They tend to think they're smart enough to get out of any pinch. And besides, he was wearing something over his face. He knew it might not work out like he'd hoped, and he took the necessary precautions. Regardless, what we can't have getting out to the press is that we have someone in custody. Because if we have the wrong guy, *that's* when we're going to see the real killer leave and set up shop somewhere else. He'll change his MO completely, and we'll have a hell of a time ever getting a hold of him."

"Assuming we don't *already* have the real killer in custody," Wicklow said. "Besides all the arguments you've put forward, Detective, the simple fact is that it's highly unusual to see a serial killer switch from female victims to male victims."

I was really in no mood for more of this ignorant nonsense, so I took a different approach. "We don't *know* if the killer realized Gwen was a trans woman. And it's possible that her attacker doesn't mentally distinguish between cis women and trans women—we're in a progressive city, after all. We also don't know that this isn't the direction he's been moving the entire time. We've already seen him switch from an Asian victim to white victims. And it should be noted that the Asian victim was smaller than the other two. I know you might not be able to tie Lee's murder into the rest of this legally, but even *you* have to admit it's clearly part of it."

"I don't have to admit that, Detective Capone." I could sense the rage quivering behind his nonexistent chin. "I only know what the evidence shows."

"Jesus Christ," I muttered.

"Just got a list," Turner said, holding up her phone. "Strangulation, bound by electrical cord, skinned behind shoulder blades, one had a leg missing..." Her eyes remain glued to the screen for a few more seconds as she scrolled. "That's it of the facts. Of the misinformation, it looks like a few news sites reported that all the victims had their ankles bound, one said the women were hogtied, and another said they were gagged." She looked up for our opinions, but I could already tell what hers is.

Just to be sure, I asked, "Nothing about the shins specifically?"

"Nope."

"And nothing about pantyhose?"

"Nada."

"Okay," Popov said after a heavy sigh. "Probably not a copycat."

Ben jumped in. "It said electrical cord? Not mic cable?"

Turner squinted at her phone screen again. "Yeah, just electrical cable is all the analyst sent me."

Ben looked around the room. "Does that matter?"

"It could," I replied. "Gwen just described a cord around her neck. And I saw the ligature marks. They were small."

"Smaller than an XLR cable would make?" said Turner.

"Yeah. Maybe half the size, unless XLRs come in smaller varieties from the ones used on Leslie and Cheryl."

"They don't," Ben said. "But that might not matter. Maybe the type of cable is a matter of convenience rather than preference."

I played it out. "The murderer behind Laugh Attack had XLRs at the ready. The XLR at the Scopes murder on the hike-and-bike trail hints that the killer swiped another one from the club, probably earlier that night."

"Do we know if any went missing from Laugh Attack?" Wicklow asked.

"Yeah, we've already confirmed that they seemed to be short, but they keep a lot on hand. It's irrelevant anyway," I added.

"They're heavy," Ben said. "Maybe he learned after lugging it out to the lake and switched to something lighter."

"Entirely possible."

Turner chewed her bottom lip. "I'm more focused on the shin. VICAP only has one other entry logged for a murderer with an MO that includes a shin injury like these —I've looked—and even that one's a stretch. The victims were Hispanic males, immigrants, and the fractures were all concluded to be a result of a sledgehammer, not a boot heel. I'll speak to Gwen Masters myself," Turner continued, "and see what else she has to say. Ultimately, this will come down to what ASAC Grissom says, but I think everyone in here is on the same page, or close to it."

I couldn't help but sneak a glance at Wicklow, who was supposed to be the one leading this. His cheeks were hollow, like he was sucking a lemon. He'd just been blatantly outperformed by his colleague, and he knew it.

Awesome. I'd take my joy where I could find it.

Turner concluded, "If Grissom decides the attack is related, then we'll release Fowler from custody with our full apology." She turned to me. "Does that work for you, Capone?"

"Seems fair."

"And you, Sergeant?"

Popov's arms were crossed so tightly across his chest that he might have been performing the Heimlich maneuver on himself. His nostrils flared, but he said, "Fine by me. If you do release him, though, just make sure he knows that the FBI was behind his arrest, so he's clear who to sue for this."

THIRTY-NINE

It was just after noon when I lugged my tactical bag out of my back seat, throwing the strap over my shoulder with a grunt. My attention caught on a fresh sign taped to the bricks of the apartment building ahead of me. *Pika. Lost cat. Please contact Serena Villarreal.*

I recognized the cat immediately. It had chased Sadie up the stairs more than once for trying to sniff it. "Goddammit."

Another missing animal.

I hadn't allowed my suspicions around the slain animals to crystallize into a full-blown theory yet, but my intuition was having its say regardless.

If that cat did show up, it wasn't gonna be alive. I just hoped it didn't end up on my doorstep.

The sun leered down from directly overhead as I crossed the courtyard. On my way through, I noticed a few neighbors lounging on a blanket in the sun. A mother and daughter, the former in her forties, the latter probably in her late twenties, each puttering away on their phones. I tossed them a small wave when they looked up, but my mind was elsewhere.

Sadie. I needed to see her. I couldn't put words to it, but with each step closer to my front door, my craving for her gained frightening urgency. My heartbeat became a clock ticking down to zero.

I took the stairs two at a time, and when I finally put eyes on my front door, the sight caused me to miss the top step, and I had to grab the railing to keep from falling forward. My big toe throbbed from kicking the concrete slab, but I didn't have a second thought to spare for it.

The fluffy face of Pika stared back at me from the Lost Cat sign taped to my front door. I confirmed what I'd already guessed when I looked down the row of doors and saw that no one else's had the sign taped to it. Just mine.

As I dropped my bag on my doorstep, Sadie's excited whine coming from inside my apartment hit pause on the ticking clock. But I didn't breathe a sigh of relief yet.

I drew my gun then turned the key in the lock.

Sadie wiggled oblivious circles around me as I then, room by room, cleared my home.

I'd changed the locks myself after finding the door open last time, but if someone could work their way in the first time, they might be savvy enough to do it again. And if that someone was in my apartment, I was sure as shit not waiting for an explanation. The law was on my side in Texas, and at a certain point, a gal has had enough of feeling unsafe in her home.

Nothing seemed out of place, so I relented to Sadie's overeager greeting and tucked away my .40 before scratching her behind the ears. "Come on, girl."

She followed me out onto the breezeway, where I

tossed my bag inside, shut the door, then walked down the row to the Villarreals'.

I could hear Serena chattering away to Miguel just before she answered the door. She wore an oversized white T-shirt and jean shorts, and her son clung to one of her thighs as he stared up at me over a pacifier.

She smiled. "Dana."

"Sorry about your cat," I said in Spanish, "but I just need to know, did you put one of the flyers on my front door?"

She pouted her lips and angled her head to the side. "No. *Por qué?*"

It was clear she was telling the truth, so I told her not to worry about it and that I hoped the cat came back soon.

Not sure what else to say, I left them with the best assurance I could muster: "*Los gatos solo hacen esto a veces.*" Cats *just do this sometimes*. To some extent, that was true.

Sometimes cats *did* just get murdered.

FORTY

July 6th, 2018

30 days since Blackstenius murder

I was back in the kitchen. Not mine, but theirs. The Boudreauxs'. And I was already too late to stop him. There she was on the floor, unmoving in a dark puddle, vacant eyes counting ceiling tiles through a mask of crimson still flowing from the hole in her head.

I let the bastard go (*this time*), allowed him to escape through the back door, across the yard, over the fence. I could still save her. Sarah. I was a sworn protector; this was what I was supposed to do. I knelt beside her, cursing. He'd done to her the same thing that he'd done to Rochelle. If I'd caught him sooner, Sarah wouldn't be on death's door.

I leaned forward to check for breath. And as I did so, her empty eyes filled with rage, locked on to me, and her death-ice hands shot out—

I jolted awake at the touch of something cold around

my neck. Gasping, I reached for my throat but found nothing there. No one.

Just a dream.

On top of yet another nightmare, my sleep schedule, if I could ever claim to have such a thing, had become extra screwy lately. I rolled over onto my side, groggy, disoriented. My guts felt like a thousand pounds of slush as the distorted memory of my shooting five months earlier fizzled away. How much more nightmare fuel was life going to throw my way? I hardly had time for it all.

Bright light penetrated the small crack between my blackout curtains, but it could be eight a.m. or four p.m., and I wouldn't be the wiser. What day was it?

I dredged up what I could remember: Dylan had been arrested Wednesday night. Gwen had come to the station in the early hours of Thursday morning. I'd made it home around lunchtime, taken Sadie for a long walk, slept poorly. Friday, I'd gone into the station for a few hours to catch up on my backlogged cases. But I'd left early when Ben insisted that I get some rest while he followed up on a few of my leads for a recent shooting downtown. So maybe it was still Friday? Or Saturday?

My pulse slowed, and I wiped away the sleep in my eyes as I rolled over to grab my phone. Still Friday. Just after five in the afternoon.

I swiped away the push notifications littering my screen —Washington Post, Twitter, Lyft, an email from my sister that started, *You really owe it to Mom to*—but tapped to open a text from Ben: *Just got word the FBI released Fowler last night.*

I bolted up, causing Sadie, who'd been snoozing

longways on her back against my legs, to flop around until she'd gotten her feet under her.

"Sh-sh-shh…"

Sadie slipped back to snoozing.

The time stamp on the message indicated he'd sent the update hours ago. It felt like I should be taking action, but what was there for me to do? They'd let Dylan go. It was what I'd wanted. The job was done.

I lay back down again, but as I stared up at the ceiling, the initial excitement twisted slowly to dread.

What if I was wrong? Had my ability to make a compelling argument teamed up with my tunnel vision to free a killer?

Raymond used to say I should be a lawyer. I'd convinced the FBI of the wrong conclusion when I called in the high heels in the Prius. Could I have done that again?

You don't have that much power, Dana. Chill out. The FBI knows what they're doing.

I actually chuckled at that. Never thought I'd see the day.

With my eyes closed, I counted down from one hundred. I made it to sixty-five before something seeped in like an ink stain soaking across the canvas of my mind. I couldn't make out the shape yet, but I knew to keep looking.

It wasn't just anxiety. This was a solid shape, one I'd encountered before. Something was off about *all* this. In my haste, I'd missed something crucial. And it was right there.

The pressure inside me grew, the ink stain taking on familiar features. I didn't want to be wrong again. But I also didn't want to be wrong forever.

Dylan had been released. He hadn't murdered Cheryl and Leslie and Stephanie. Someone else must have. This was the simplest conclusion, but it didn't feel *complete*.

"What am I missing?" I whispered.

An hour passed, and I felt like I'd slither out of my skin if I didn't get out of bed. I sat up slowly this time, gently slipping my legs from around my sleeping companion to avoid waking her.

There was only one thing I could do once my mind started spinning in these circles.

The coffee table was covered in debris from the last two days—an empty chips bag, way more remote controls than a TV and soundbar should need, an epic fantasy novel I'd been chipping away at for the last year, two beer bottles, and a few used paper towels, but in no time I had my royal-blue cloth spread out over the cleared surface, and the Thoth tarot deck stacked neatly on the edge.

It was rare that I brought out this deck, but my hand was on it in the cabinet before I was aware of making the choice. A Rider-Waite deck was my usual go-to. I had plenty of them that I rotated between. Those decks were comfortable, familiar, easy to connect with and interpret.

Thoth was different. Not just different cards, but a different history, a different type of person it attracted. Every draw of the damn thing made me uneasy. I had no idea why I'd chosen it.

I shuffled the deck, held the question in my mind, and began the spread. Querent turned Prince of Disks. Crossing turned Hermit.

The subconscious card was next, and the moment I revealed the Moon, the truth struck me over the head like a lead club.

This reading wasn't *mine*. But I knew whose it was.

The swirling detritus that had driven me from bed now formed a complete picture.

How had I missed it this long?

I stared at the Prince of Disks, then back at the Moon, trying to locate holes in this new theory, fighting off the tunnel vision, combing through the facts I knew, but more importantly, the ones I might not know.

But it was futile: the inevitable stared up at me from the spread. I didn't need to keep turning cards. The answer wasn't in the cards, anyway. It was in my mind. It had been there, begging to be freed, keeping me from sleep, a truth pleading to be heard.

The heels. There was no denying he had them in his car. A close match to two of the victims'. We hadn't explained that yet; we just dismissed it in light of other evidence.

Francis Fowler would never wear shoes like that. They couldn't be hers. But they also weren't for the next victim in line. With no girlfriend to speak of, there was only one conclusion to follow.

Those heels were *his*. He was going to wear them. Maybe even later that night once he'd dropped me off at his car. Maybe even to Sheep's Clothing, where Gwen was later attacked.

Dylan wasn't a murderer. What he was, though—and it seemed so obvious now—was a crossdresser.

But why hadn't he just told the FBI that? Why had he lied and said the heels were a gift for his mother? The truth could've gotten him off the hook completely. It proved the whole thing was a misunderstanding, that he hadn't done anything illegal.

I turned the next few cards in the spread and let my mind hover over them.

He was a kindergarten teacher at a Catholic school. His life didn't allow for any so-called deviant behavior. If it got out that he dressed in women's clothing... so long, employment.

And his mother. Good god, I couldn't bring myself to imagine the verbal abuse he'd suffer from her.

But to hide it at the risk of being charged with murders he didn't commit?

Maybe that was the flaw in my theory. Because it would be *crazy* not to spill when so much was on the line. He was facing multiple charges of first-degree murder in Texas. The victims were pretty, young women. The jury wouldn't deliberate for more than thirty seconds on the sentencing for something like that. If he was found guilty, he'd get the needle. But first, years, maybe even decades, of imprisonment with no chance of parole. A miserable end, and he was willing to risk it?

Except maybe he didn't think it was a risk. While Dylan was clearly not the typical Caucasian male, the world saw him that way and had no doubt treated him accordingly his whole life.

In my experience, no one put their faith in the infallibility of the justice system quite like white men. Even guilty white men often seemed confident they'd be let off, let alone innocent ones. It was how Michael Morton spent twenty-five years in prison for a murder he didn't commit. He never saw it coming because *he* knew he was innocent. And now we had the Michael Morton Act in Texas. Ah, nothing got new laws passed quicker than a single instance of a white man being wrongfully convicted.

White women weren't much better in our rose-colored view of criminal justice, no denying that, but at least we'd heard enough stories of dangerous male partners being acquitted to have our faith shaken from time to time.

Our courts were a pretty good system on the whole, but they were far from perfect. I understood the limitations of it all too well—offenders released early when they shouldn't be, and people trying to piece their life together after an overlong sentence for a minor crime. It was a high-stakes game with the ripples from every imperfection carrying on and on.

I pressed my palms into my tired eyes then looked over the cards again. Maybe there was more to be mined.

It wasn't only that he had high heels in the back seat of his car, was it? It went beyond that. The shoes he presumably wore looked just like the one nailed to Stephanie Lee's foot and the pair on Cheryl Blackstenius. Same color. Same basic style. Seemed like more than a coincidence. But if it didn't mean he was our killer, what *did* it mean?

Come on, Dana. You're close.

The tarot spread was complete now, but I still couldn't get a handle on it. Context, that was what I was lacking.

I used an old trick a professional psychic taught me on a burglary call long ago: I flipped over the deck, letting the bottom card serve as an undercurrent.

The Devil.

It was a card that came up frequently in my readings. Not evil, but imbalance, obsession.

My eyes jumped from card to card as I tried to shake free another degree of understanding. *The Moon. Seven of Cups. The Devil.*

My gut twisted. That was it.

Dylan wasn't the obsessive; he was the *obsession*.

And it might already be too late to save him.

FORTY-ONE

Knowing it was essentially futile, I sent Dylan a text asking him to call me as soon as he could. The odds of him responding were virtually zero. I'd gotten him arrested for murder. Granted, I was also the reason he was released, but I doubted that message had been properly conveyed, and even if it had been, it couldn't make up for all those guns pointed at him in his driveway.

Shit. What did I do? I had to keep trying to reach him.

I paused in my scramble, gathered my thoughts. Did I just text him my concerns and hope he would read it?

No, I couldn't risk it. I needed him to confirm he'd heard my warning, actually listened to it. I needed to hear his voice.

I texted him again, this time apologizing for withholding the fact that I was a detective and that, for what it was worth, I didn't think he was the killer.

I hit send.

My phone was at two percent charge—I'd forgotten to plug it in before falling asleep—so I docked it, then took

Sadie out to pee in the courtyard. I waited on the second-floor balcony as she ran down, sniffed the ground, peed on some dead grasses, then continued to nose around.

The complex was oddly silent. The white-noise traffic on William Cannon calmed my nerves enough for me to take a deep breath. Maybe I was overreacting. Even if Dylan *was* the object of the killer's obsession, there was nothing suggesting danger was *imminent*. Predators like this usually stalked their prey for a while before striking. It could be weeks, so long as nothing tipped him off that his time was running short.

Sadie ran back upstairs at the sound of my whistle, and I treated her to a firm head scratch that flopped her little ears around. "Sorry, girl. I know I haven't been much fun lately. We'll hit the lake tomorrow morning."

Back inside, I locked the door behind me and found my phone in my hand a moment later without remembering how it got there. No notifications. I plugged it back in.

What now? Should I let Ben know what I'd come up with? Or would it be wrong to out Dylan like that? Was I overreacting? This *had* all started after I awoke from another nightmare. I was used to them, sure, but I wasn't totally immune to the paranoia they sometimes left me with.

It was a quarter to seven now. Maybe Dylan was watching TV and ignoring me. The odds heavily favored that scenario. He'd had a hell of a forty-eight hours. No one would blame him for vegging out.

My stomach growled, so I headed to the freezer and took out a frozen pad thai.

As it rotated in the microwave, my mind wandered back to my options.

There was one ace up my sleeve for locating him, but I couldn't justify it yet. It wasn't illegal, per se, but it would be yet another betrayal of his trust, that was for damn sure. I wouldn't use it unless I was sure he was in imminent danger.

I ate my food without checking my phone, subconsciously hoping that ignoring it would attract the thing I wanted. After, I let Sadie lick the fork, tossed it in the sink, and returned to my phone. Still no messages. Fine, one last attempt.

I figured out why you had those heels in your car. I'm not judging. I think you might legitimately be in danger. Stay at home and don't answer the door for anyone, even if you know them. Please just text me back to let me know you're okay.

Needing to move, to *do* something, I leashed up Sadie, who wasn't complaining about going out for a second time in an hour, and we were already at the traffic light a quarter of a mile down the street when my phone finally buzzed in my pocket. It was Dylan.

I'm fine. Now kindly fuck off.

Okay, I deserved that. And at least I knew he was safe. For now. Would he actually listen to my warning, though? Was my obligation fulfilled? Or was there a next step before I could absolve myself of guilt, ease my panic, and forget about this whole thing?

Whatever that next step might be, it could wait another fifteen minutes while I battled with the moral implications of outing someone based on a suspicion that I'd gleaned from tarot cards. If I'd thought getting the others to believe my theories before was hard, just wait until the word "tarot" entered the conversation. Jesus. I shuddered just thinking about the look on Popov's face.

By the time we were back at the complex, my sense of urgency had subsided to calm, silky waves slipping up and down the beaches of my consciousness. There was an easy rhythm to it. Best not to ignore it completely, but no fear of it slipping away.

I closed the door behind me, locking the deadbolt in the same motion.

Just because cards hinted toward obsession didn't mean that was the truth. Maybe I'd concocted the whole thing. Maybe he wasn't even a crossdresser.

"You gotta be kidding me," I mumbled as Sadie ran off to slop water all around her bowl. "I'm doing it to myself. I'm talking myself out of it!" Why? Why was this still my first instinct after all these years? *Oh, don't worry, Dana. It's not that terrible thing you think it is. There's a perfectly reasonable explanation for it.*

I worked in Homicide, for god's sake. It was *usually* the terrible thing I thought it was.

I had plenty of people in my life to talk me out of believing my own theories. I didn't need to add myself to the list.

Enough. I pulled out my phone and called Dylan. I wasn't exactly shocked when it went to voicemail. "Dylan. Hi. I know you hate me, but if it's any consolation, I was the one who got you released from custody this morning. I know you didn't commit those crimes. But I really, really need to hear your voice and talk to you. I think you could be in danger from the person who *did* kill those women. I don't want to tell anyone else why you had those shoes in your car, but if I don't hear back from you, I'll be obligated to tell others in law enforcement so we can make sure you're okay. But like I said, I don't want to do that. It's not my place. So just, um, just call me back, okay?"

It was a long message, so I gave him a solid five minutes to decide to check it, listen to it all the way through, and call me back.

But once those five minutes were up and still no call, the urgency returned, and I had all the justification I needed to tap my last resort, to play the ace up my sleeve.

I pulled up the tracker app on my phone.

The small square I'd dropped in his car would give an approximation of his vehicle. I'd take any hint of reassurance I could find right now while my gut was spurring me on so roughly. If he was at home, maybe I could let it go for now. Maybe I could even fall back asleep.

Please let him be safe and sound.

But when the dot appeared on the map, my lungs turned to solid bricks. Assuming the tracker hadn't been found by someone and removed, his Prius was parked on a side street half a block from Laugh Attack.

It was a Friday. There wasn't an open mic there tonight. Probably some headliner instead. Maybe he went to watch. Or maybe he wasn't at Laugh Attack at all. He could have parked there because it was familiar territory and then walked anywhere downtown. Maybe to Sheep's Clothing.

On my laptop, I pulled up the comedy club's schedule to see who was performing. I couldn't blame him for wanting to see some real talent once in a while. But only a matinee show was listed on their website, and I'd never heard of the guy. Didn't mean he wasn't big, though, just because I didn't know who the hell he was.

I looked him up on Twitter. Two thousand followers. Okay, he wasn't big. Dylan didn't even follow him.

There were too many possibilities. I had to narrow them down.

The show would be over by six thirty, maybe seven if the opener ran long. I checked the clock. It was already seven thirty. Maybe Dylan watched it and then headed to the bar after. I could easily drive down there and look around the usual places for him, or I could...

Damn. No. This was how I landed Ben in the unemployment line. I couldn't go off without telling anyone what I was doing. Dylan was released, sure, but that didn't mean the FBI was done with him. I had no clue of the circumstances of his release. Letting him go didn't necessarily indicate he was no longer a suspect. It just showed they didn't have enough to keep him. Or had a strategic reason to risk letting him free.

Time to make this concern of mine official.

Well, official-*ish*.

I dialed the agent's number and waited.

"Agent Turner speaking."

"Agent Turner. It's Detective Capone. Are you at the office?" But the chatter of children in the background answered that well enough.

"No, I'm at home. Calls forward to my cell. What's up?"

"I need a favor. I promise it's important, or else I wouldn't ask it of you after hours."

Her hesitancy was unmistakable, but still, she said, "Go on."

"I need you to track Dylan Fowler's phone for me. There's not a snowball's chance in hell y'all let him go without knowing how to find him at a moment's notice—no point denying it—so I just need you to look it up on your computer real quick."

Turner cleared her throat. "It's Dana, right?"

Uh-oh. "Right."

"Dana, I'm currently tied up cooking dinner for two preteens who eat twice their weight at every meal. Now, I won't say there aren't ways to find where Fowler is, but we released him because ASAC Grissom decided he *wasn't* our man. So, at this point, I'm gonna need a very compelling reason to put down this wooden spoon and track his phone."

"Unfortunately, I have one for you. I think he might be in imminent danger. I believe the killer will go after him next."

I heard the spoon tap against a metal pot before she shushed one of the children in the background. "What makes you think that?"

How to explain without spilling his secret? Hopefully, I could present the pieces of information I'd had to work with to Turner, and she would figure it out on her own. Ethical loophole or not, that was all I had. "Those shoes in his car. They weren't for a victim, and they weren't his mother's. As far as I've heard, he doesn't have a girlfriend. That only leaves one person who would wear them."

"Uh-huh," she said.

"I reckon the killer knows this and has bought matching

pairs for the victims to wear. I'd wager whoever killed those women has been working toward Dylan Fowler as a target."

A second's pause, then, "You think Gwen Masters was a steppingstone."

I shut my eyes to brace against the relief. "Yes. I do. I texted Dylan as soon as I realized and told him to stay home and not answer the door. He ignored my texts."

"Can you blame him?" A high-pitch voice screeched, and Turner yelled, "Jasmine!" away from the receiver.

"No, I can't blame him. He eventually texted back and told me to get lost. But how can I know it was him? I called and left a message, but no answer." I hesitated before continuing, but it was too late to pull back now. "I dropped a tracker in his car when he gave me a ride. Just a little one I had for my wallet."

"It's probably long gone. They searched his car."

"I hid it well. They were looking for instruments of murder, not something smaller than a credit card. I'm pretty sure they missed it, because I just looked up the location on my phone, and it pinged right by Laugh Attack. I can't be sure, but I believe his car is there. I need to know if he's just downtown on a Friday night or if he's at the comedy club."

"Does it make a difference either way?" she asked.

"I think it does."

"Explain?"

"If he's not our unsub, then we're probably looking for someone else involved with the club. There was a show tonight, but it should be over by now. Yet his car is still there. It's possible he caught the show and then hit the town. But if his phone is still with his car, it just doesn't seem right. It's like there's a little nudging in my brain trying to point me toward something important."

"How long you been on the force, Detective?"

It wasn't the question I'd expected. "Fifteen years."

"Then that nudge sounds like probable cause to me. But I'm going to need you to work on articulating it better for the reports." The background noise on the other line faded out—she was on the move. "Let me grab my work laptop."

I fist-pumped the air, though this wasn't the time for any kind of celebration. "Thank you, Agent Turner."

Waiting for Turner to speak again, I paced my living room.

But when she spoke again, it was exactly what I didn't want to hear. "His phone places him right in the middle of Laugh Attack."

"How long has he been there?"

"Looks like he arrived at 19:06, and he's been there ever since. You sure he's not just there for a show?"

"Not unless they have one scheduled that wasn't listed on the website."

He's been lured. Just like Leslie.

"I'll call Wicklow and Grissom," Turner said, "and get some people sent out there."

"It's gonna take you an hour just to convince them to hear you out."

"Where do you live?" she asked.

"Southeast, near William Cannon and Pleasant Valley."

"Okay. I'm in Travis Heights. I'll meet you there."

My mind jumped to the wooden spoon left discarded somewhere in her kitchen. "You don't have to—"

"It's fine. I have a husband. He can tear himself away from the TV long enough to get the kids fed. Just don't go in without me, Capone. You do, and I'll make sure you get suspended. Meet at the edge of the alley behind the club."

"Roger that."

"Be there in fifteen."

It was a seventeen-minute drive to the club from my place, so I'd have to make up the time on the road.

That was what I was up against now. Time. It took on a tangible form in moments like this. You could feel it moving through you as you moved through it.

The phone line for Laugh Attack rang and rang but no answer as I pulled off Seventh Street and parked. It was the second time I'd called. No success. I'd just wanted to be sure, though. Cover all my angles. And my ass.

I made it to the club in fourteen minutes, and that included the time it took me to dress and grab my essentials —badge, gun, cuffs, and, in a rare moment of optimism, Taser.

Turner was already here, dressed in black slacks and a white shirt, no jacket. Too hot for that, and hard to move in it besides. She jogged over. "Located his car on the street out front. He's not in it."

"Anything suspicious?"

"Nothing stood out."

I grabbed my cuffs, my gun, and its holster from the side compartment of my door and tucked them onto my jeans. "Jesus. I thought *I* hustled over here, but you really got me beat."

"Let's just say it's nice to be out of the office and back in the field," she said.

"And out of the kitchen, too?"

A wide-eyed nod. "Lights are off inside. I called Heidi on the drive over. She's in New Orleans but said Scott should be around to let us in."

"He didn't answer the phone when I called the club. We should try his cell," I suggested.

"Already did," she replied. "Went to voicemail both times."

"And is Dylan's phone still inside?"

"It is. I checked again just before you showed up."

We were standing by the side of the windowless building, and I tried to assess which entry point would be best. "It'd be a shame if we had to kick a door in," I said.

She grinned. "Sure would be."

"I guess you're in charge. I'll let you pick which one."

"Back door looks like a good time. It's already half rusted off the hinges."

"Then after you, Agent."

We hurried toward the entry point, taking the corner cautiously. I was half expecting to see another murder scene by the dumpster, but it was all clear.

Turner tried the handle, and it was locked. She didn't even pretend to be sad about it.

There was an explosion of sound as her boot separated the metal door from its hinges. Then, as if in slow motion, the whole thing fell inward, landing with another echoing bang.

If anyone was in there, they'd know we'd arrived. Nothing to do about that but hope we had bigger guns and better aim.

FORTY-TWO

"FBI," Agent Turner announced, entering pistol-first.

I stepped into the darkness of backstage, flicked on my tack light, and followed her lead. Every shadow was packed with potential energy in a location like this, each only a moment away from animating, taking human form, lunging or firing. My pulse beat staccato in my ears as I kept my gaze focused on my beam of light, relying on my peripheral vision to alert me to dangers in the darkness.

Cords dangled noose-like from racks.

I'd cleared buildings like this before, but never in a case this tangled. I should be the hunter, but surrounded by the killer's accoutrements of death, it was more likely that I was the prey. Had we wandered straight into the unsub's snare?

Behind us, I heard a small pop and whirled to cover our six. The building shifting? An old air-conditioning unit? An echo from our steps?

Finally, we slipped free of backstage and emerged into the main theater. Small inset lights glowed dimly, but the corners of the space remained dark, obscured. Rows of tables branched out like spokes in a semicircle surrounding the stage with foldable chairs like little centipede legs along each. No major visual obstructions for us, though.

Turner nodded for us to split up. I checked behind the sound table then scanned for any hidden compartments on the stage, but this wasn't the kind of theater that would need a trapdoor.

What was I even looking for here? Dylan tied up and gagged? The unsub with a knife to his throat? Please. Real life was never that dramatic. Killers may want to show off their handiwork, but the act of killing itself was usually too intimate to be shared.

Agent Turner looked to me for an update, and I shook my head. She met me on my side of the room and led the way around to the front lobby with the smaller stage.

I cued up the image of the bar in my mind's eye as we entered. It would be a perfect place for someone to hide for an ambush, so it would be the first place I checked.

An image of Dylan tied up, his face blue, skin cold, flashed in my mind, and I shoved it away. No point.

Turner made for the ticket booth by the front door as I crept toward the bar, breathing steadily through my nose to keep my wits about me.

Feet from it now. Just one sidestep for full visibility—
Nothing there.

This room was unoccupied, too.

Turner confirmed the ticket booth was clear with a nod. There were a few more places to check—the kitchen, bathrooms, the office, maybe a few storage closets—but this was looking more and more like a flop.

How did that make any sense, though?

Could the GPS signal have been off? We'd already

confirmed Dylan's vehicle was outside, and there was no reason his phone would register here if it weren't somewhere within the building.

A bang from the hallway, like a door slamming.

We whirled toward it and closed ranks. I was closest, and I took the lead this time.

The hallway branched off in two directions—to our left were the bathrooms, to our right the office and kitchen. A sound like a board dragging across the floor directed me toward the office.

Turner slipped to the other side of the doorframe, and I leaned against the wall, listening.

What had sounded like a board being dragged was now clearly a drawer slamming. Then another. Someone was in there, and they were looking for something. Was that Dylan inside?

I met Turner's eyes, and she gave the sign, her gun aimed down at the floor in front of her. For now.

There were a few ways to go about this entry, but because Turner had stuck her neck out for my hunch, I decided to take the more conservative and procedurally sound approach. I stepped to the other side of the doorframe before knocking. "Police." Turner twisted the handle and wrenched the door open, and then we waited for a short count before moving in.

His hands were already in the air, his eyes wide, his mouth hanging open in stunned shock.

But it wasn't Dylan Fowler.

"Whoa, whoa, whoa! Where'd you come from?"

"Oh my god, I'm so sorry," I said, relaxing my grip on my weapon.

Scott Ruiz chuckled anxiously but kept his hands up.

"It's cool, it's cool. You're law enforcement. You gotta do what you gotta do. But Jesus, you nearly gave me a heart attack."

"You didn't hear us come in?" Turner asked, lowering her weapon but not yet holstering.

Scott nodded toward headphones on his desk. "I was listening to music while I worked." He looked at me. "Who's she?"

"Agent Turner with the FBI," she answered, digging her credentials out of her back pocket.

"No need, I believe you." His grin was congenial enough, but I could tell the old hippie was still rattled from the sudden armed intrusion. Why wouldn't he be?

"You can have a seat, Mr. Ruiz." I gestured toward the wooden chair by the desk.

He lowered his arms then, his hands visibly shaking. "Will do. Mind if I get a glass of something strong from the bar first?"

"In a second." I nodded toward the chair again, and this time he sat. Turner took a step back, signaling for me to take the lead. "We're looking for Dylan Fowler. We have reason to believe he's in this club."

His mouth hung open as he stared up at me. "Dylan? What's he done? Wait. You aren't telling me he's—"

"We're not telling you anything, Mr. Ruiz."

"Just Scott, please."

"Has Dylan been in here at all today?"

His mouth continued to hang open. "If he came by, I didn't see him."

"And you've been here all day?"

"Not all day. Came in around the start of the matinee. I

went to grab dinner from Pho King down the street a little while ago. Otherwise, I've been around."

Agent Turner said, "I'll go check the bathrooms and kitchen," and disappeared.

I looked around the rest of the office. The desk was covered in papers. "What's all this?"

"Huh? Oh. I balance the books on Fridays."

"That's why you're here late?"

He nodded.

"All clear," said Turner, and she slipped back.

"Agent Turner called you on her way over and got voicemail," I said.

Scott scrunched up his face and grabbed his phone where it rested facedown on his desk. "Is that who the missed calls are from? I figured it was a robocall."

With my mind back on cell phones, a wild thought occurred to me. The odds of it resulting in anything helpful were slim, but since there was no harm in trying...

I pulled my phone from my back pocket, stepped out into the doorway, and called Dylan's number. I didn't put the phone to my ear. I wasn't listening for him to pick up. I tried to open up my awareness to listen in all directions at once.

Agent Turner shot me a questioning look, but before she could speak, I held up a finger for silence. She moved closer until she could see my screen, then she understood.

Scott looked around, oblivious, until we all heard it.

A vibration.

But not from anywhere by the bar. It was coming from his desk drawer.

I watched him closely as his brows pinched together. "Who...?"

Turner pulled out the drawer as the buzzing continued. She didn't find it immediately—it was buried under a small pile of receipts. But the glow of the screen gave it away.

She held it up for Scott, demanding an answer with a single glare.

He frowned and shook his head. "Do you know whose that is?"

"Where did you get this, Mr. Ruiz?" Turner's voice was a knife ready to cut through whatever bullshit came her way.

"Denise." Scott's voice cracked as he said the name, and he held his hands in the air, the scotch still clutched in one. "She's a server here. She found it in a chair tonight and handed it to Mike Check. He passed it on to me to keep safe until someone claimed it."

There was a lot to unpack in that single explanation, so I started with what caught my attention the most. "Mike Check was working tonight?"

"Yeah. He ran the sound."

"Why would a server hand a lost phone to the sound guy?"

Scott shook his head vaguely, eyes darting between us. "He manages the front of house sometimes. He opened the place this afternoon. She probably sees him as a manager even when he's running sound."

"Excuse me for a minute." I mumbled, "Francis Fowler," to Turner as I stepped into the hall to call the number saved to my work phone.

It was a landline, and part of me was hoping Dylan would answer and put an end to this field trip.

"Hello?" It was Francis, and I could already tell she wasn't happy about someone calling past seven o'clock.

"Mrs. Fowler. It's Dana Capone."

"Who?"

Shit. "Dana Dwyer."

Silence.

"Mrs. Fowler?"

"What do you want?"

Hey, at least she hadn't hung up on me straight away. "Is Dylan at home with you right now?"

"No. He's probably out running around with one of his tranny friends."

Oh, god. She'd found out. I had no clue how, but she had. Maybe she was a more skillful interrogator than the FBI. Or maybe she didn't care to follow the Geneva Convention. "You don't know where he is?"

"Don't know and don't want to know. There are some things a mother should *never* have to endure. Of course, you wouldn't know about that."

"If he comes home, will you tell him to call me right away? It's urgent."

"He wouldn't do that even if I did ask him to. He doesn't listen to me. And it's your fault his life is—"

I ended the call. I wasn't a complete masochist.

Scott was giving Turner the rundown of the club's schedule that night when I reentered the office. She looked up. "Anything?"

"He's not at home. Mrs. Fowler doesn't know where he is."

Scott looked lost standing there behind Turner, scanning his messy desk. "Is this going to take long?"

"I hope not," I said.

"Well..." He patted his pockets and twisted around to look over everything again. "Do you need me for it?"

I was already calling Ben, telling him to locate Mike, so Scott's question took a back seat in my mind. "No, I guess not. You have somewhere to be?"

"Ah, Heidi's out of town, so the dog's been inside all day." He paused. "I guess it's not the end of the world if he craps on the rug. If you need me to stick around, I understand."

"No, no," I said. "Turner, do we need him to stick around, or can he go let his dog— Ben! Hey, I need you to coordinate with Wicklow and see if you can find Mike Check. Dylan's missing, and he's in danger. Yeah, check the footage once that's done. We need to see when he came here and when he left."

Turner grabbed Dylan's phone off the desk. "Mind if we hold on to this?"

"Of course not."

I finished relaying the essential information to Ben and tried to focus my mind on the next step.

"You can call me if you need anything," Scott said. "I'll know it's you this time." He flashed me a washed-out grin, then dug his keys out of the same drawer where we'd found the phone. He paused at the door. "Hey, I know you ladies gotta do what you gotta do and all that. I'm not one of those anti-cop Austin bums—APD's helped me out many times—but if Dylan did anything wrong, I'm sure he had a good reason for it. Maybe just go easy on the kid."

That wasn't how this job worked, but there was no harm in pretending. "Sure." I forced a smile.

"The front door will lock behind you, so whenever you're finished with this, just leave through there."

"Oh, um—" I shot Turner a glance.

"Back door is busted in," she said. "I'll send for someone to fix it ASAP."

While it looked like Scott had a lot of questions about that, he took it in stride and left without asking any of them.

"If he's not here then there's no point in us sticking around, huh?" I said.

Turner held up Dylan's phone. "We technically found what we were looking for. I think the next step would be to head back to the station and help sort through the security footage. We have two angles to look through over a period of an hour or so. The more eyes on it the better. I think it's our only lead to find Dylan."

"You still believe he's in danger?" I asked, as we hurried out of the office toward the back exit.

"More than ever."

"Glad it's not just me."

As the kicked-down door came into view, Turner said, "Oh right," and grabbed her phone, then called in for someone to come fix it. "I'll meet you back at the station," she muttered, just before greeting someone on the other end of the line.

We split off to our own vehicles, and I let my anxiousness carry me the rest of the way to my CRV at a jog. Dylan was somewhere, likely in critical danger if he wasn't already dead, and we were his only chance.

But as I reached for my car door, I pulled up short. My subconscious was shouting at me so loudly that I could've sworn someone else was speaking. *Stop! Look again!*

And so I listened. I stopped, my heart racing on. But what was I supposed to be looking at?

Something I'd missed. It was right there. I couldn't put my finger on it yet...

The Prius. Dylan's car. It didn't make sense that it would still be there when he wasn't, but his phone was. I had to see it with my own eyes.

I changed course and headed back around the corner to where Turner had mentioned seeing it.

It was gone. Not a Prius in sight. She said she'd seen it, though, and I believed her.

Suddenly, none of the scenarios I'd considered made any sense.

Dylan had taken his car and left? When? Why? Without his phone? Maybe he'd tracked it back to Laugh Attack but found the place locked. It would have been after we arrived, though. He would have knocked, and we would have heard him. Maybe he went around the back and saw the door kicked in. That could've kept him from entering. He could've thought there was a break-in and reported it before driving off.

But no, he couldn't have reported it without his phone.

Still stuck in my head, I continued to circle the comedy club. Maybe I was misremembering where Turner said she'd seen his car. Doubtful, but not impossible.

Nothing, though. I didn't see it anywhere. My head buzzed as it spun new scenarios, trying to string together the facts into a cohesive narrative. Turner had already left, so it was just me now as I returned to my vehicle.

Again, I stopped in my tracks.

This time, I hurried around to the street side of the club.

And there it was, parked just a few spots down from the entrance to Laugh Attack.

Not the Toyota Prius. The Nissan LEAF.

I'd seen it before, not only in front of the club, but at

both of the memorial services. It had to be the same one.

I cursed again and again as the data lined up in single file into a coherent explanation, one that made the bile rise in my throat.

I called Ben.

"Haven't been able to locate Mike Check yet," he said.

"Ben. Forget him. I need you to run a plate for me."

"It's a damn good thing I love women ordering me around."

"You have the system pulled up yet?"

"Uh... Now I do. Hit me."

I read it off to him, and a second later, he said, "Twenty-seventeen Nissan LEAF, right?"

"Yep."

"Registered to Scott."

"Scott Ruiz?"

"Right. We saw him in it at Cheryl's and Leslie's memorials, remember? Stupid-looking thing if you ask—"

"Shit, shit, *shit!*" I scanned the Friday night downtown crowd thickening around me. Who did I expect to see?

"Dana, what is it?"

I kept Ben on the line but removed my ear from the phone to free up my hand as I dug out my keys. I heard him shouting more questions at me, but he could wait in suspense until I knew I was in a secure spot.

Only once I was back in my car with the engine running and the doors locked did I put the phone back up to my ear.

"...are screwing with me, Dana, I'm not in the mood."

"Ben. I'm here. Shut up for a second. Just shut up. I'm not screwing with you. It's Scott. Scott Ruiz. He's our unsub. And I think he has Dylan Fowler."

FORTY-THREE

I was backstage at Laugh Attack again. Just me now. The darkness had closed in all around me, but I had to find Dylan. I knew he was near.

But someone else was nearer. Someone who would do anything to make sure Dylan wasn't found.

A clatter to my left and I jerked toward it, gun drawn. Nothing lunged.

But something crawled.

He emerged slowly from the deepest shadow, clawing his way forward.

"Dylan," I breathed. "Are you—" But I choked before I could finish. Emerging into a sliver of light, the true horror of him was now visible.

His legs were missing. Gone. Blood trailed on the floor behind his stumps. "*Help,*" he whined, reaching out to me—

I was jolted awake by the clunk of a ceramic mug hitting the desk in front of me. I looked for the source and found Ben staring down at me with an incredulous but not unkind expression. I blinked and surveyed Death Row to reorient myself. Asleep in my chair. Typical.

"I feel like I'm just enabling you at this point," Ben said, nodding down at the fresh cup. "Coffee can't substitute for sleep forever."

The steam hit my nostrils, and I already felt more alert. "I was just resting my eyes."

"Yeah, yeah." He carried his cup over to his desk.

The analog clock on the wall had both hands raised high in the air. Almost midnight.

The FBI had managed to intercept Scott Ruiz just as he arrived at his home in Pflugerville.

They'd found him driving Dylan's Prius.

My hidden tracker had been to thank for that little trick, not that it would garner me much favor with anyone around here. Seemed like everyone's shit list had my name at the top for one reason or another.

"I reckon he's not talking," Ben said, following my eyes to the clock on the wall.

I sighed and stretched a crick from my neck. "Or he's spilling even more than they hoped for, and it's just taking a while to work through the details."

Ben squinted at me. "Are you... having a stroke?"

"You're right." I sat up straighter and inhaled the scent of my fresh coffee. "Foolish hope doesn't look good on me, does it?"

But there *was* still one foolish hope I held on to, and that was that Dylan Fowler was just fine, wherever he was.

ASAC Grissom had come up from San Antonio as part of the FBI's not-so-subtle move to transition from support to lead. They'd unofficially taken over the investigation, starting with the interrogation of Ruiz. Wicklow had made sure I knew I wasn't invited to the party. I decided not to take that personally, since neither Agent Turner nor Ben had been brought in for the interrogation either. I was in good company.

"Heidi's on her way back from New Orleans," Ben said. "Agent Wicklow asked me to call her and let her know."

"Makes sense. Wicklow's too spineless to do it himself."

"*And* he's currently interviewing the suspect."

I took an exploratory sip of my coffee and found it hot but not scalding. "I can't believe ASAC Grissom trusts him with this."

"I don't know that he does. Grissom's in there, too."

"It ought to be Turner," I grumbled.

"She's definitely the more capable one. But Wicklow calls the shots, not Turner."

I rolled my eyes. "You know why, right?"

He held up a hand. "Yes, I know. You don't need to say it."

"I dunno," I mumbled, cradling the mug in my hands as I leaned back and kicked my feet out. "Maybe I do need to say it. *Someone* needs to say it, and keep on saying it until it stops happening."

Ben let my bitterness go, and I woke up my computer and clicked through the still frames we'd collected from the cameras outside Laugh Attack. It was the kind of evidence that would support whatever theory you were cooking up. I sorted them into a timeline.

3:57pm, front door – Mike Check arrives at Laugh Attack. Lets himself in with key.

5:05pm, front door – Scott Ruiz arrives in crowd of matinee show guests.

6:59pm, back door – Mike Check takes out trash after show.

7:06pm, front door – Dylan Fowler arrives.

7:13pm, front door – Mike Check leaves, not seen again.

7:29pm, back door – Dylan Fowler stumbles into alley, heads toward vehicle.

7:29pm, front door – Scott Ruiz leaves, doesn't lock up.

7:37pm, front door – Scott Ruiz enters.

7:52pm, back door – Agent Turner kicks down door.

There were a few takeaways from it. Mainly, Dylan had left on his own two feet, but barely. Could he have already been tipsy when he entered, pounded a few more shots, and left totally shithoused twenty-three minutes later? Sure, but why? It was clear in my mind, at least, that he'd been drugged.

And then there was the matter of Scott stepping out the front door only a few seconds after Dylan went out through the back. I was sure Wicklow and Grissom were hearing a perfectly reasonable explanation for why he'd done that, probably the same line he gave us about grabbing dinner, but it was all bullshit. Scott had met up with Dylan in the alley, just outside of the range of our cameras. What had he done with Dylan in that eight-minute window before he returned? Hidden him somewhere to find him later? Stuck him on a bus or in an Uber? We had patrol units searching the area, but nothing had come back. I suspected nothing would.

Of course, there was no proof that Mike Check hadn't hung around after he was seen leaving through the front. There were seven minutes where he and Dylan were inside the comedy club together. He could have spiked Dylan's drink, stolen his phone, and handed it off to Scott so Dylan's whereabouts wouldn't be tracked. And then he could have hung around outside for the next sixteen minutes until Dylan left through the alley.

That wasn't what happened, though. Why would Scott have taken Dylan's car if any of the latter story were true?

I pulled up a picture from the Blackstenius murder, the horror that had started this whole mess. Ruiz had done it in his own backyard. Goddamn that bastard. And goddamn us for not seeing it sooner. The boldness was torture in hindsight.

But there was more to it now. Murdering someone on his home turf was the brazenness of a man who'd done this before, and not just once, to Stephanie Lee, but many times. He'd wanted to see if he could pull it off without anyone suspecting him. And until a few hours ago, he'd succeeded.

Heidi had been his alibi. She'd cleared his name off our list right away. We should've pressed her harder. I should've pressed harder. I'd bought the washed-out Austin hippie act he was selling. I couldn't believe it.

And that stupid FBI profile. God, did I loathe it. So close, yet so far. That was the problem with the profiles. They could get just enough of the facts right to make you believe they had all the facts right. But they were always, *always* wrong in crucial ways.

In this case, the age had been a miss, and not just by a little. Scott was fifty-four years old. That was fifteen years outside the initial range. Those who followed the Gospel According to Profilers would automatically disqualify him from the pool of suspects on that alone, barring any discovery of a stunted development earlier in his life—possibly some years were stolen from him in prison or some such that delayed him getting started.

I'd admit, it was rare for a man to wait until he was in his fifties to make his first kill. I could see why profilers would default to that. But we already knew Cheryl Blackstenius wasn't his first kill. Stephanie Lee had come before her. And others, maybe even dozens, had come before Stephanie. I could almost guarantee it.

Where had Scott lived before moving to Austin in the nineties?

Unfortunately, that was a question that would take time to map out and may never be fully answered.

Because as it turned out, my guess about him from that family photo on Facebook had been correct: he was adopted by the Ruizes when he was thirteen. His records before that were a muddled mess of paperwork that I'd only had the time to dip my toes into. Foster home to foster home. Never a good sign for a kid. To make matters worse, it looked like his adopted father had been military, and the next five years of Scott's life were a series of relocations. And then what? A blank space existed on the timeline between when Scott finished high school and when he came to Austin in his late twenties.

What a wreck that profile was. And that wasn't even mentioning the near-miss of the Prius.

The profile had pointed to that make and model in particular. I was sure they'd had their reasons. Something about blending in, looking socially responsible, acting the part of an evolved man in a progressive city. But once again, the detail had only caused blindness to the adjacent truth.

It was a LEAF we'd been looking for, and it had been there in front of us the whole time.

Poor Dylan had the misfortune of being a stereotypical Austinite, and now there was a very real possibility he'd end up paying the price for our myopic mistake.

If he hadn't already.

My wandering thoughts began swirling around him, where he could be, what state he was in, and how someone Scott's size could've overpowered someone a few inches taller. Had Scott refined his technique after the attack on Gwen Masters? She was about Dylan's height but had a few pounds on him.

Loud, precise footsteps approached from the hallway, pulling my glassy-eyed stare away from my monitor. ASAC Grissom stood in the doorway, his arms crossed in front of his chest. "Detective Capone."

"Yes, sir?"

His top lip curled into a scowl like he'd just smelled something rank. "Hurry and finish that coffee. Ruiz wants to speak to you."

It was the last thing I'd expected to hear. *Don't celebrate, Dana. Keep cool.* "Scott wants to speak with me?"

"You and Agent Turner. Yes. He's requested you both, and I guess I'm just desperate enough to try it at this point. Wicklow and I will bring you up to speed while we wait for Turner to arrive."

"Right."

He disappeared from the doorway, and I had to stick the mug in front of my face to hide my excitement from Ben.

This was all probably pointless, anyway. What Grissom had just asked me to do was futile, and on some level, I understood that. Only a psychopath could do what Scott had done, and I knew better than to think I could get anything useful out of a man like that. And yet there was always that hope, wasn't there? Maybe this time I'd learned enough. Maybe this time would be different.

Ben chuckled and held out his hand across our desks. I gave in immediately and high-fived him.

He nodded toward the hallway. "Go get him, Capone."

FORTY-FOUR

Predawn. July 7th, 2018

31 days since Blackstenius murder

Even though I'd just finished one, when Agent Turner arrived at the station with a large McDonald's coffee for me —the only drive-thru open at this hour that would still brew you a cup—I didn't turn down the offer. My sleep schedule had been the very definition of chaos for the last fifteen years. Why start regulating it now?

ASAC Grissom finished briefing us on what they'd gotten from Scott Ruiz so far, which amounted to a steaming pile of nothing. They'd laid out the accusations for him, and he hadn't admitted to a thing. He hadn't asked for a lawyer, though, and I wondered if he believed that would make him look less guilty somehow when this thing went to trial. Or maybe he just thought he could do it better himself.

Heidi was his alibi for the Scopes and Blackstenius murders, as well as the attack on Gwen Masters. That was the story, at least. We'd check on it again once she was safely back in town from New Orleans.

I couldn't wait for Heidi to crack. Wouldn't take much, I suspected. I only hoped to be there when it happened.

"Good thinking on the cars," Turner said as we left the briefing and headed down the hall toward the interview room. "We were so close to missing him. Again."

"You were right, though. There was a significance to it; we just hadn't found it yet."

"And now we have." We reached the door, and Turner paused. "You sipped a little off the top yet?"

"Of course. I'm an addict."

"You still got some left?"

"Of course. I have my problem totally under control."

She removed the plastic lid from hers. "There's better-tasting coffee around, but Mickey D's has the scent appeal down to a science."

I'd interviewed my fair share of criminals, but it was clear Turner had me on experience yet again. Either that or she was a prodigy at torture techniques that fell within the bounds of the Geneva Convention.

I ditched the lid to my coffee, and damn if she wasn't right about the smell. It'd be a struggle not to gulp it all down myself while we were in there.

"Ready?" Her hand waited, ready, on the door handle. "Like we talked about, I take the lead. If he addresses you, I trust you to keep your cool and respond accordingly. If he's really our guy, he's a bad one. And he's a smart one. But not as smart as he thinks." She paused. "I guess I'm not telling you anything you didn't learn a long time ago. All right. After you."

She opened the door, and I entered first.

Inside the small room, a war raged between the dark corners and the two fluorescent lights hanging at the center of the room. Scott sat with his hands on the table, fingers clasped together, wrists cuffed. He watched me closely, fully ignoring Turner, and as I strolled toward one of the empty seats across from him, my double did the same in the reflection of the two-way mirror.

When I pulled out my chair, I dragged the metal legs across the linoleum floor to elicit a grating squeal. I may not know much about Scott Ruiz, but I did know that to carry out the crimes he had, the man necessarily hated women. And yet he'd just requested two of us to come and speak with him. It didn't make sense in the usual way things did, but it made perfect sense for a serial killer. His kind craved and hated in equal measures.

Just by inhabiting this body, I could get under his skin. Every other annoying quirk was a cherry on top.

His gaze was still locked on me when Turner finally broke the silence. "You wanted to see us. Here we are."

"Yes. Here you are." He held up his wrists. "And here I am. I don't get it, though. We were just chatting a few hours ago, and everything was fine. I don't know what's changed since I left. Certainly nothing on my part. Why didn't you arrest me then? And why am I here now?"

He'd made his first move. Not a bad one. Playing dumb worked for a while, and could agitate people who knew you were full of shit, which Turner and I did. The cause for his arrest had been explained in detail when they first brought him in. Grissom had said he showed Ruiz the crime scene photos, and the man across the table from me hadn't looked away, only cocked his head to the side to get a better angle.

I wouldn't let his time-wasting get to me.

"Whatever the charges are, I assure you this is all overkill. Sure, I dealt a little dope back in the eighties, but I'm not *violent*. Anyone will tell you that. They've already searched me more thoroughly than I care to mention. Why the cuffs? I'm not a violent guy."

And still, Turner and I said nothing. The best way to respond to bullshit was always to pretend you hadn't heard it. No point in pretending to be his friend—that might work with a low-IQ killer whose crime was half accident, but it wouldn't work with a man like Scott.

Changing tack, Scott asked Agent Turner, "You said you're FBI, right?"

She nodded once, patiently.

"Then maybe you can clue me in on why the *hell* your friends surrounded my car, arrested me at gunpoint, and threw me in here with these cuffs."

Going for righteous indignation, then. Figured.

Turner wasn't biting. She blew on the top of her steaming coffee and, in doing so, wafted the scent across the table at our interviewee. "*Dylan Fowler's* car. Not yours."

He closed his eyes as if to ask the good lord for patience. But he didn't offer any explanation about the vehicle he was arrested in.

"Where is he?" Turner asked.

"Who?"

"Dylan Fowler."

"I already told your boss, I have no idea."

"You were driving his car, Mr. Ruiz."

"Did your superior not already brief you? Jesus. Dylan asked me to take it. And I promised him I wouldn't say why. I promised him."

"You know you're up to your eyebrows in trouble, Mr. Ruiz, don't you?"

"I don't. Why won't anyone tell me what you think I've done?"

Turner let it drop. Circles. The smart ones could keep mediocre investigators hemmed up in them for far too long. But she wasn't playing his game.

"What do you know about Dylan's life outside of Laugh Attack?"

"Not much."

"Did you ever see him at Sheep's Clothing?"

He rocked his head back. "Ahh... So you know about that."

"And so do you. We want to know how *you* found out."

"I was there with some friends one night and thought I recognized one of the performers. She—Dylan, that is— didn't see me, so I kept it that way. I never told him I knew."

"Why not?"

"A person has a right to some secrets, agent. He tells jokes about being a teacher at a Catholic school. I figured he'd want to keep the whole drag queen thing on the down-low, so he didn't lose his job."

"How long have you known?"

"Is this relevant?"

I kept from rolling my eyes, but only just. This wasn't a goddamn courtroom, and we weren't here for small talk. Of course it was relevant. But even if it wasn't, we still had to ask. This was our home field, not his.

Turner's voice showed no signs of my own impatience when she said, "Yes. How long have you known?"

"Not sure. Must've been last summer. He only comes around in the summers and Christmas break."

Speaking of Christmas, holy shit. If my theory was at all correct, it meant Scott had been obsessing over Dylan specifically for about a year. And we'd only found bodies dating back two months. Even with the *generous* guess that it'd taken him six months of working up to it before his obsession turned to killing, we were looking at four months' worth of murders we don't know anything about. But I wasn't feeling generous. People just didn't wait until their fifties to start dabbling in murder.

It was time to shake things up. Turner would understand later, I hoped. I jumped in. "Tell me, Scott, was it your bio parent, a foster parent, or an adopted one who used to call you a fag?" I hated the word, but any weapon that might pierce below his armor was one I was willing to use. There was more at stake than feelings.

Scott whipped his head toward me like I'd slapped him, and I allowed myself a smile at the sudden flash of viciousness that streaked across his expression. There then gone without a trace. "You think I'm *gay*? Why, because I'm an ally? Detective, you really need to get out more. Austin culture could do your closed mind some good."

Gimme a break. "A foster parent, then? Or maybe more than one?"

He looked at Turner, but if he was hoping for backup, for my ballsy move to split the party, he was left disappointed.

"I don't see what my sexuality *or* my childhood has to do with anything."

"You don't see what it has to do with you attacking a trans woman in a back alley? Or with stalking Dylan Fowler once you realized he did drag on the weekends? You're not stupid, Scott. Cut the bullshit. You claim to be so goddamn sexually liberated, so I'm just trying to figure out why you won't let yourself become a woman. That's what you want, isn't it? Like you said, this is Austin. What's stopping you? Was it a foster dad? Did he catch you trying on his wife's clothing? Was that it? I bet the shaming was bad, but the beating worse."

It was a series of shots in the dark, or at least my conscious mind thought so. But maybe all that tarot was paying off, because what he said next showed just how much I'd gotten under his skin.

"I guess you *would* know all about daddy issues, Detective Dwyer."

Ahh, there it was. Not a confession to murder, but a confession to something even more insidious.

Turner said nothing. Good. If she stepped in on my behalf, it'd make me appear weak.

I kept my voice even, detached. "And here I was praising my skills of deduction. What tipped you off?"

"The stupid wig."

I didn't realize it was possible to hate that wig more, but there I was. "What do you know about Raymond?"

At first, he squinted like he didn't understand. Then his mouth formed a small O. "Wait. *No.* I just meant I knew the Dana Dwyer at the club the other night was you. And now you mean to tell me... Raymond Dwyer? Raymond Lee Dwyer is your *father?*" He leaned back, his cuffed wrists falling into his lap, and laughed. "I just figured you wore that femme fatale wig because you dreamed of being a sex worker. That's all I meant about the daddy issues. But *damn.*"

I would be mad at myself if I believed a word of it. He was lying, of course, jerking us around for the hell of it, playing a complicated game, trying to make it seem like I'd given something important away, had slipped up.

"What do you know about Raymond Lee Dwyer?" Turner said, tagging in.

"Just remember hearing about him in the news. One of Texas's most prolific serial killers."

I didn't correct him on the technicality, but Raymond wasn't just *one of* the most prolific; he was *the most*. And that was before you even added in the women who were never counted.

Turner arched a brow. "The man hasn't been in the news for years, and you remember his name that clearly?"

"With prompting, sure. I didn't at first. You two tipped me off." He gawked at me again. "Really. Raymond Lee Dwyer. This is starting to make sense now. I told Heidi you were too cute to be a cop. You could have done all kinds of other things and made way more money with looks like yours. But I guess you got something to prove, huh? Yeah, now that I think about it, I remember hearing about how his daughter was the one who busted him. Was that *you*?"

"Where's Dylan Fowler?" Turner said.

"I told you, I have no idea."

"Why did he want you to take his car?"

"I can't tell you that."

Turner wouldn't back down. "You're being held on multiple counts of murder, and you won't tell us this simple thing? You're aware Texas allows for the death penalty, right, Mr. Ruiz? This is capital murder. If charged and convicted, you *will* pay with your life."

Scott sighed and brought his cuffed hands up to scratch at a patch of five o'clock shadow on his chin. "A man's gotta have his integrity. I promised I wouldn't say anything, and I stick to my promises. Besides, as Dana Dwyer here will tell you, people on death row can end up waiting for their execution date for decades. I'm fifty-four. I don't have that much longer to go anyway."

He knew too much about Raymond's situation.

It had been a suspicious amount of time, if you asked me. Convicted serial killers didn't usually get so long. But Raymond had. And only someone who'd kept up with the appeals process would know that. The average person who had heard about it on the news back in ninety-six would assume the execution had come and gone in the last twenty-two years. While Scott's knowledge could hardly be used as evidence against him in a court, it was plenty to continue building my case.

Turner asked, "Why did you want to speak with us specifically?"

"I don't trust men." He shrugged. "Maybe Dana was onto something with her little psychoanalysis."

She leaned back, mirroring his nonchalant posture. No innocent man ever looked like that in an interrogation room. It was the posture of feigned innocence and overcompensation.

Turner sipped her coffee slowly, and Scott's eyes flashed to it.

"I think you'll agree," she said, speaking as if this was a casual coffee shop chat, "that it's been a long night for you. It's been a long one for us, too. We'd all like to go home. So will you tell us whatever it is you called us in here to tell us?"

The relaxed hippie I'd met before was impossible to spot in him now. Yes, he was still wearing flip-flops and the ripped tie-dyed T-shirt, but the man *wearing* the clothes had changed. I was certain Turner saw it, too. And I thought he could tell we saw it. But he didn't seem to care. And that worried me. It meant he believed he had some kind of leverage, some card left to play to get him out of this.

Scott set his hands on the table again with a clatter of metal on metal and leaned forward. "I wanted to ask you a question."

"Then stop flirting with me and ask it," Turner replied.

"How many dicks have you had to suck to get to where you are in the FBI?"

Agent Turner stared at him passively, like he was a particularly messy piece of art. She took her time, sizing him up. "You think about fellatio a lot, Mr. Ruiz?"

Scott's face turned to stone.

"Last time," I said. "Where's Dylan Fowler?"

"Dunno. Probably dead."

"We'll find him," I said. "Dead or alive, we'll find him."

Scott inhaled deeply and straightened his spine. "I wish you the best on that. In the meantime, I'm not saying another word, Dana Dwyer, without my lawyer present."

FORTY-FIVE

A silver Suburban laid on its horn, and I honked right back.

"I told you I should drive," Ben said. "Shit, Capone. How many hours you been awake?"

I tried to calculate. Wait, what day was it?

Maybe he had a point. Not like I'd admit that. "I'm fine to drive."

"That soccer mom you almost ran off the road might disagree."

"That soccer mom shouldn't have changed lanes in front of me and proceeded to go fifteen below the speed limit."

"It's not an emergency. We have him in custody."

"It's an emergency to me."

Ben shook his head. "Sounds like the ravings of a cop on the edge of burnout."

"You're starting to sound like a cop on the edge of getting your ass handed to you by a cop on the edge of burnout."

I kept my attention on the highway, but I could feel Ben roll his eyes next to me.

Not a mile later, a Jeep full of teenagers, including one behind the wheel, nearly changed lanes right into the side of me.

I smashed the horn again. "We're in a police vehicle, you idiot!" The Jeep swerved and slammed on its brakes as soon as it realized who it had nearly killed. "This place is a deathtrap."

Ben shot me a look. "Pflugerville? You think Pflugerville is a deathtrap?"

"Of course I do. It's the suburbs. The place is teeming with families, so you end up with a bunch of stress-addled soccer moms and teenagers behind the wheel."

"Stress-addled, eh? You wouldn't know anything about that, would you?"

I didn't want to pick a fight with Ben, but I did want to pick one with *somebody*.

While I kept my composure through the interview with Scott and the debrief after, I'd been itching to punch something since.

I knew it was Scott who'd killed those women, and probably more we didn't know about yet. I knew it in the true sense of knowing, where you could feel it in your bones, and it called you to action.

"We'll know as soon as anyone hears anything about Dylan," Ben said, correctly identifying one of the sources of my anxiety. "In the meantime, this is the best way to find him, and we're both *extremely* lucky that the Bureau trusts us with this."

"That's a fancy way of saying, 'Don't screw this up, Capone.'"

"I guess I'm just a fancy man."

The Ruiz home was in one of the newer subdivisions, where everything had been flattened for the build, and the HOA-mandated trees were still hardly more than twigs, struggling against the brutal Texas sun.

We pulled up and parked across the street from the two-story home, and my imagination jumped ahead to the eventual news interviews with neighbors and friends of friends proclaiming, "Who would have thought a serial killer lived there!" Despite my past, I had no clear picture of what a serial killer's home *should* look like. Then again, I didn't think the knuckleheads who said that sort of thing had a clue either.

For a couple that claimed they only made pennies from their primary source of income, the Ruizes' house seemed lavish. Boxy, with generic red bricks on the front, sure, but some decent square footage and a well-manicured lawn with prickly native plants interspersed among gray pebbles. Then I remembered that this was the kind of wealth that most white late Gen-Xers had amassed by middle age without really trying, so long as nothing too financially catastrophic hit.

I had to remind myself that I could've bought a house like that if I'd wanted to. I just didn't want to. This far from downtown Austin, the mortgage wouldn't be too bad.

But then I'd have to live in Purgatory.

Heidi stepped out onto the front porch wearing a rose-colored tank top and light wash jeans with intentional tears across the thighs.

"Glad to see she dressed up for us," Ben muttered as we unloaded from the car.

"Be nice. She just found out her husband is a murderer."

"*Alleged* murderer."

"For now."

"Good to know you're going in with complete tunnel vision," he muttered, closing the passenger door behind him.

"You heard the interview, Ben. You surprised?"

"Not at all. I was just hoping one of us would keep an open mind. Guess it'll have to be me. Again." He adjusted his belt, sliding his holster further back on it with a small grunt. "Okay, let's go find what we need to lock this shithead away for good."

"You're making this a hostile work environment, talking dirty to me like that," I said, passing in front of the vehicle. "I'm gonna have to report you to Pops."

"Please. Like every shift with you *isn't* a hostile work environment."

When I spoke with Heidi on the phone just an hour earlier, she'd seemed more than happy to comply with whatever we needed for our investigation. But that could always change. And quick. We had a search warrant in our back pocket, but having to resort to that when we had compliance would be a failure of detective work, far as I was concerned. Best not to let her hear us trash-talking each other.

I donned a more serious expression as we crossed the street and approached the house. "Afternoon, Mrs. Ruiz."

She must have driven all night and gotten in early this morning, and she looked it. Or maybe the sunlight just brought out her age where the lighting at the club smoothed it over. "Please," she said as we made our way up the walk from the driveway, "call me Heidi. I knew I never should've taken his last name."

Ben said, "You mind if we come in?"

"Of course not. That's why you're here, isn't it?"

On the phone, I hadn't explicitly mentioned that we would be looking around, let alone bringing Crime Scene in, just said we wanted to speak with her, answer any questions she might have, and that we'd come to her. But of course we were going to do a preliminary search, and the Crime Scene technicians were just a half-hour behind us, as per our instruction.

I would tear this place apart if I needed to, but I had a feeling Scott was too smart to keep anything damning in his home. Any trophies he might have taken from the crime scene—skin from the shoulder blades, say—would probably be kept somewhere off-site, a storage unit, a safety deposit box, you name it.

As we stepped into the high-ceilinged entryway, I immediately felt like something was missing. Then it hit me. "Y'all have a dog?"

"Not anymore. I had one when we got married, but she died about a year ago."

I didn't inquire into the specifics of how the dog died, mostly to spare myself. Maybe it was a standard euthanasia at the vet. Or maybe the dog was savagely beaten.

Or flayed, I thought, trying not to mix the two most troubling situations currently in my life. The dog's cause of death was irrelevant anyway, but Scott's lie to Agent Turner and me back at Laugh Attack about going home to let his dog out wasn't a bad bit of evidence against him.

"I'm making coffee if you want some," Heidi said, leading us into the kitchen. "I didn't get a whole lot of sleep last night. Drove back from New Orleans as soon as I got the call, and, well, you can understand why sleep didn't come easily, I'm sure."

"I understand," I said, taking a seat on one of the stools at a small extension of the countertop jutting out between the kitchen and breakfast nook.

Ben pulled out the seat next to me. "We'd love some coffee. Thank you."

Heidi gazed at us across the white marble countertop. "I mean, I can drink mine first if you want. Just to show it's not, ya know, tampered with."

"That won't be necessary, Heidi," Ben said, beaming warmly. "We have no reason to suspect you for anything."

Except covering for your husband while he murdered women.

But even that seemed far-fetched. She didn't strike me as someone who would do such a thing knowingly, and what she said next only supported that.

"No, I guess my bastard husband's done enough for the both of us." She sighed. "But I know I'm his alibi, and that makes me look pretty damn complicit."

"That's actually one of the things we want to talk to you about," I said. "We have a feeling that if you covered for him, it wasn't on purpose. It was more along the lines of the careless error of someone who assumes, sanely enough, that her husband didn't commit murder."

She nodded solemnly. "And do *you* think he did it, Detective Capone?"

"You can call me Dana, and I haven't formed an opinion one way or another on that."

She chuckled darkly. "I listen to people recite memorized lines every night of the week, trying to make them sound natural. I know a script when I hear one. But I appreciate you trying. At least it sounds like we're on the same page." She pulled coffee mugs from a small countertop display rack, and I was momentarily transported back to the Fowler kitchen, where Francis made me coffee I hadn't asked for. My life had become reduced to vignettes of people handing me coffee.

Once Ben and I had our mugs in front of us, Heidi leaned her elbows on the island and cradled her steaming cup between her palms. The posture put her cleavage on full display, in all its squished and lifted glory, and if Ben remembered a single word of the interview we were about to have, he deserved an award. I didn't believe she even realized what she was doing. Either these poses had become second nature to her, or she was just past caring.

"What can I help you figure out?" she said.

For voluptuous reasons, I took the lead. "The night of Cheryl's murder. We need to straighten out that timeline. Because based on our conversation with you and Scott, it eliminates him."

She conceded with a humble nod, and I ran her through our timeline from start to finish. "Now, as is, there's only a fifteen-minute window between when Cheryl Blackstenius goes out back to smoke and when you and Scott leave the club. It's possible that fifteen minutes is enough time for him to have completed the murder, but that's tight. Going back to your statement, you describe a moment on your way home when a drunk individual stumbled out in front of your car. You both agreed that took place about ten minutes after you left Laugh Attack and that the clock in the car said ten fifteen."

She nodded, her lips pressed together in a tight knot.

"Yeah, I said that. And I didn't mean to mislead you when I did. I just didn't want to press the point with him in front of you. I thought it might make him a suspect unnecessarily."

"Back up. You're saying that *wasn't* the timeline?"

"That's what I'm saying. When I looked at the clock after we *first* got in the car, it said ten fifteen, not when we almost hit that drunk. I didn't even check the clock at that time. Why would I? Some dipshit wandered out in front of us. I'm not looking to see if it's asshole o'clock. Who cares?"

"So, you just went with what Scott said from there?"

"Yeah, I went ahead with it. Partly because I didn't want him to become a suspect, but also because I figured there was a chance I'd misremembered."

"You didn't misremember, Heidi. I don't believe that for a second, and I hope you won't, either. If your gut told you it was wrong at the time, it was wrong, okay?"

Ben flicked me on the thigh below the countertop, and I cleared my throat. "If everything's pushed back, that means you weren't already at home when Officer Tyber called you?"

"No. We were still on the road. I didn't know why he said otherwise, but I figured he was just embellishing. He does that."

"What about the night of Tuesday, June nineteenth?" I said, moving on to the next murder. "You remember what you told the police for that night?" I pulled out my notepad to start scribbling nonsense. I could tell she'd respond better to a little sterile officialness. The anger, betrayal, and loss were all too fresh. Making the conversation more clinical would help.

"That's the night when Leslie was killed, right? Yeah, I said he was asleep in bed with me."

"Do you still stick to that story?"

"Hell if I know where he was. He was in bed when I took my meds, and he was in bed when I woke up the next day."

I glanced up. "Your meds?"

"I got in a car accident a few years back. Still have pain from it, so the doctor prescribed me painkillers. It's the only way I can sleep at night. They knock me out, though. Or, if I wake up, I don't remember it."

"Do you know what time you went to sleep that night?"

"Not exactly. I don't remember anything after about eight thirty. When I actually made it to bed is anyone's guess." She paused. "Trust me; I tried everything else before I hit the meds."

"I believe you."

She hadn't specified which drugs she took, but I didn't need her to. I'd figure that out for myself in a bit. No need to put her on the defensive about something asinine.

"This is extremely helpful, Heidi." I put the pad to the side and took a sip of the coffee. It was good stuff. Small blessings. "Just so we're clear, do you think Scott is capable of doing the things he's charged with?"

I was sure Ben knew what I expected to hear—"Not Scott! Never! You never met a nicer man, truly!"—so she surprised me.

"Of course."

I set my coffee down quickly. "Of course?"

"Yeah, I mean, he's a man, isn't he?" She turned to Ben. "No offense."

He held up a hand to let her know none was taken.

"This is the kind of shit men do. My last husband back in SoCal siphoned off tens of millions of dollars from a nonprofit that helps children orphaned by war. In a lot of ways, that's worse than serial killing. Who knows how many kids died because of it? So, yeah, maybe I'm jaded on men, but I think they're all capable of this. It's in their blood. Women, though," she went on, "we only ever kill out of revenge."

Ben glanced suspiciously at his mug.

"We *always* have a good reason to do it," she continued. "Maybe the guy raped us or one of our friends or our kids. Or maybe he threatened to kill us first. I tell you, I'm just fucking sick of men. Excuse the language, but I'm fucking sick of them. If Scott did this, lock his ass up. Good riddance."

I hadn't expected this from someone whose entire body was sculpted to appeal to the male gaze, but clearly, I'd misjudged her.

"Fair enough." I took a final sip and scooted my chair away from the counter. "Mind if we take a look around?"

"Of course not." She threw her hands into the air. "Have at it!"

"Where is the master bedroom? I've found women generally prefer a female detective for that."

"We don't use the sex toys anymore if that's what you mean. Well, I use some. But he doesn't."

That was, in fact, what I'd meant, but it was nice to know I wouldn't have to use up any energy on discretion with her.

Ben took the downstairs, and I went up. I knew I had the more intricate job, but that was fine. Despite Heidi's low opinion of men, she stuck close to the well-groomed detective as he poked around.

If she was actually complicit in this whole thing, there

was a good chance she'd hidden anything obviously incriminating prior to our arrival. But that was how it went. We'd had to give her a heads-up; the house wasn't technically a crime scene yet.

I had to hope that I could find things Heidi might not even know were evidence. Because even if she *was* complicit, there was no way Scott would've told her everything. That wasn't how men like him operated. They liked their secrets. They were fueled by the power of them.

I gloved up on the stairs and started in the master suite. It wasn't long before I discovered the box of Heidi's toys in her bedside table. No need to poke around too much in there, gloves or no gloves.

It wasn't easy to search a place without knowing what I was looking for, but this was just preliminary, anyway. I checked under the bed—nothing there—then between the mattress and the box spring. Still nothing. Violent porn or some sort of bondage tools would have been a jackpot, but as someone who'd never been overly optimistic, I wasn't expecting this to be that easy.

When I moved into the master bath, I headed directly to the medicine cabinet. The orange bottles of OxyContin caught my eye right off the bat. Three of them, each containing a few dozen pills. I checked the labels, and it was as I expected. Each one had a different doctor's name listed. I didn't doubt her story that the prescription had started innocently enough. No one intends to become an addict.

There was a small box on the next shelf up, and I recoiled as soon as I realized what it was. Fentanyl patches. No need to run screaming, but I was careful as hell when I picked up the box and peeked inside to see how many were left. Just one. I didn't mess with it, closed the box, and set it down carefully. That poison could seep right through gloves like mine. That doctors could prescribe something so easily lethal to a patient for pain while cannabis was still illegal was one of those things I was sure my generation would be absolutely roasted for forty years from now. Maybe ten. Gen Z might even be roasting us on Snapchat *at that very moment.*

Heidi's name was on all the prescription labels, and that lined up—psychopaths, and I was all but convinced Scott was one, didn't generally like being under the influence. They might dabble in the hard stuff early on, but once they realized how little control they actually had over themselves, and got close to exposing their true self a few times, they'd give it up, retreat to a drink here and there, and that was it. They liked power too much to loosen their grip on it.

My mind conjured an image from years ago of my mother passed out on the couch, an empty bottle of cheap gin lying on the floor next to her. Maybe Heidi hadn't been as oblivious to her husband's tendencies as she'd let on. She must have known *something* wasn't right.

Maybe Heidi suffered from physical pain, but I had a feeling that wasn't all these drugs were numbing for her.

Someone ought to have an intervention. But perhaps getting Scott out of the house would be intervention enough, and that was what I planned on doing for her.

I hit the closet next, looking for a scrapbook, a box of letters, a journal—each would be too good to be true, but also not out of the realm of possibility. If he was a cocky killer, he would want to document it. And so long as his wife spent her time at home in a state of moderate oblivion, he might've assumed he could get away with a ballsy move like that. But as I said, unlikely.

And yet, the moment I stepped inside the walk-in, my brain lit up. *Ding ding!*

It was a second more before I realized what had tripped the alarm.

The candy-apple red.

FORTY-SIX

Behind a pair of black knee-high boots, the sliver of red stood out like a spotlight was pointed right at it.

I snapped pictures of the shoes without touching a thing, then I moved the boots to the side and got a better shot. This would be the first place I'd send Crime Scene.

I searched the rest of the closet closely, but I didn't find anything nearly as impressive as the red heels.

Most of the upstairs was taken up by an open lounge area on the landing with a stiff tan couch devoid of any personality and a few plush beanbag chairs facing a television that spanned the opposite wall.

Neither Scott nor Heidi had kids, as far as we knew (small blessings), so who they expected to join them for a viewing, I had no idea. For whatever reason, beanbag chairs and no kids practically screamed "swingers" to me, but I wasn't going to go down that rabbit hole if I didn't have to.

There were two smaller guest bedrooms decorated straight out of a Rooms To Go catalog. I started with the one that adhered strictly to a pastel-pink theme. Nothing appeared out of place. I wondered if anyone had ever stayed here, or if the Ruizes were simply among the millions of Americans who thought they should buy the biggest home the banks would lend them the money for.

There was a sense of denial in the decor, whatever the case. A grandiose delusion of future company. I reminded myself that the whole house and both of their lives were little more than fiction, then I moved on.

I checked the guest bedroom closet. It was bare except for an iron and ironing board and a spare set of sheets. I unfolded the sheets, shook them out. Nothing. The dresser was empty, too, and a framed picture of Heidi and Scott in a tropical setting, perhaps ten years younger, sat on top next to a gold-speckled vase of fake lilies.

Light seeped in through sheer curtains pulled across plastic blinds, giving the entire space a soft, ethereal shimmer. I approached the bed. The edges of the floral quilt were tucked in tightly, like their sole purpose was to restrain the mattress.

I hated to disturb the flawless surface of the bed, but it was necessary. I lifted the mattress from the box spring, but there was nothing there either.

By the time I reached the second guest bedroom—this one more masculine with charcoal, black and white making it feel a little like I'd stepped into a silent movie—I figured I'd already found the best I was going to get with those heels.

But then I checked under the mattress.

The black nylon straps might have gone unnoticed for who knew how long. Maybe forever. The taut comforter certainly showed no signs of these restraints between the mattress and the box spring.

These types of bonds were made to be easily concealed, and this wasn't the first time I'd seen them, which was how I'd known to look. I pulled the nylon straps up and over so they lay flat on the bed, as they would when in use. Two adjustable loops for the ankles, two for the wrists. And let us not overlook the additional hooks to bind both wrists or both ankles together.

I started snapping pictures. A preference for BDSM didn't mean anything on its own, but I'd be interested in asking Heidi about it, since she seemed to be an open book this afternoon.

By the time I made it back downstairs, Ben and Heidi were standing in the kitchen again, chatting casually, given the circumstance. He must have completed his search.

They turned their attention to me as I entered, and I saw the questions behind their eyes right away. Heidi was hugging herself, and Ben was holding his coffee in his right hand, his left shoved into his pants pocket. Both waited for me to speak.

"This is going to sound strange," I said, "but those red heels up in your closet?" Ben's head cocked to the side almost imperceptibly. "What's the story with those?"

Heidi squinted at me. "The red...? Oh! Those awful things. Yeah, never wear them. Kinda tacky. Impractical. Plus, Scott never takes me out to places where those would fit in."

I struggled to think of a place other than a drag bar where they *wouldn't* be conspicuous.

"When did he give them to you?"

She cast a glance at Ben and shifted her weight from one foot to the next. "I think it was maybe a year ago?"

"Special occasion?"

She opened her mouth, then closed it, and her fingertips pressed into the flesh of her arm. "No. I— Well, now that I hear what he's charged with, I don't really know what to believe."

"About what?"

"I found them in his car about a year ago. They didn't seem like something I would wear. I just assumed they were for someone else. So, I confronted him about it. I said if he was having an affair, he needed to tell me right then and there. But he said he wasn't. The bastard was practically in tears that I would even think it. He said they were a gift for my birthday. Of course, then I started feeling like a real bitch, so I let it drop. I lied and said I loved them, but then I couldn't just toss them out after that. They're tacky as hell, though."

"You said this was about a year ago?"

"Something like that."

"Summertime?"

"Yeah, I mean, summer or something near it. Might've been August."

"And when is your birthday?"

She sucked in her cheeks and then sighed. "February."

I felt for her. I did. It just went to show how much people wanted to believe in each other.

"Was he cheating on me, too?" she asked. "Did he tell you that? I'll believe it. I guess I always kind of suspected it from that point on. And now, well, I'll believe anything about him."

"He hasn't said anything about cheating, Heidi. Not to my knowledge, at least." Not much of a consolation, but I'd give the poor woman what I could. "The next thing I'm going to ask you is personal, so I apologize. But I wouldn't ask if I didn't think it was relevant."

"Just come out with it."

"Did you and your husband ever practice sexual bondage?"

She laughed, her eyebrows shooting up her forehead. "Like BDSM? Uh, no. Like I said, I have a bad back now. And I truly cannot imagine Scott planning out a scene. He can't even plan his breakfast."

"Sounds like you have some familiarity with it, though."

She scratched below her bottom lip with the back of her thumb. "Yeah, you could say that."

Neither Ben nor I spoke, and the rest came out shortly. "I did a little porn back in California."

"Any BDSM?"

"No. I didn't need to do that freaky crap with tits like these. I got by with the vanilla shoots."

But sure, the heels were too tacky for her.

"Is it the crime scenes?" she asked.

"Pardon?"

"Are you asking about the bondage because of the crime scenes? Cheryl and Leslie were tied up, right?"

God, had she not even heard about Stephanie Lee? Did she think it was only two? "Right. They were both bound."

"That right there might be the best defense he has. Scott never once showed *any* interest in that kind of thing."

The ties under the guest bed begged to differ.

And, you know, the staged murders.

"Need a reheat?" she said. "There's still some left in the pot."

Ben accepted, but I declined, grabbing my neglected

mug off the kitchen island and taking a sip of what dregs remained. I'd made my peace with room-temperature coffee a long time ago.

Everything we had so far was circumstantial, and I wondered if it was enough. It was enough for me.

"One last question," I said a moment later, interrupting an in-progress conversation about their preferred coffee brands. "Does the name Dwyer mean anything to you?"

A lopsided grin crept onto her face. "Is this a trick question?"

"Not at all."

"It was the name you used when you showed up at the open mic in that god-awful wig."

I'd burn the wig in the courtyard when I got home. Yes, that'd be nice and cathartic. "You knew it was me?"

She chuckled for the first time. "Yes, Detective Capone, I knew it was you. Immediately." Ben hurried to raise his mug to his lips to disguise his smug grin. He didn't do it well.

Then Heidi asked, "Are you one of his fans, too?"

Initially, I thought the "his" referred to Ben, but that didn't make any sense. "One of whose fans?"

"The artist. Scott's obsessed."

My mind jumped two steps ahead, but I struggled to believe it. No, she couldn't mean what I thought she did. "Which artist?"

She pushed off the counter she'd been leaning against. "Come. I'll show you."

When I stepped into the living room, my eyes found it immediately on the wall facing the sofa. My mouth went dry, and a sudden urge to throw up washed through me.

The damn thing was huge, easily eight feet wide.

"What do you think?" she said, then, without allowing me time to reply, added, "I hate it. Always have. I don't mind abstract art, but this one just seems so... harsh, I guess. Scott thought it was *sensual*. That was the word he always used when guests asked about it. 'It's sensual.' Dear god, if he really killed people, if he's going to prison, I'll burn this piece of shit on the front lawn and not shed a tear." I felt her attention turn away from the reds and blacks of the canvas to look at me. "Oh no. You like it, don't you? Shit. You *are* a fan."

"I'm not a fan," I said quickly. "And I think you're right. It's harsh, and there's nothing sensual about it. Burning it would be an improvement."

Heidi appeared satisfied. "Glad to have your blessing."

Ben slid up next to me and mumbled from the corner of his mouth, "I don't know anything about art. What am I missing?"

I found it impossible to tear my eyes from the abstract gore in front of me. "Not much," I said. "It's just a Raymond Dwyer original."

FORTY-SEVEN

Back at the station again, and my head was still swimming from the visit with Heidi. The shoes, the bindings, the absence of a dog. The painting.

Ben and I had debriefed on the drive back, but since then, he'd allowed me space to think.

If, at some point, I stood a chance against tunnel vision in this case, that time had ended. Scott was our killer. I couldn't imagine anything that would convince me otherwise short of a video recording of someone else murdering the victims and kidnapping Dylan.

I'd told Ben that the Raymond Dwyer original on the Ruiz living room wall was the clincher for me, but that wasn't exactly true. I wouldn't admit it to anyone else, but I'd admit it to myself: I'd locked in on Scott the second I saw his LEAF parked out front of Laugh Attack. Since then, I'd only had eyes for him. It was almost romantic, and maybe the closest thing to romance I'd ever get, the intimacy of narrowing in on a suspect. It was a little obsession all my own.

Either way, the painting left no room for doubt in my mind. Normal people didn't own the shitty artwork of an infamous serial killer. But I knew that line of reasoning wouldn't get the prosecution very far in court.

Besides, Raymond had produced over two hundred paintings during what degenerates on the internet had dubbed his "bloody period." Not everyone who owned one was a serial killer. At least, I hoped not. Yes, none of them could be totally right in the head, but there was a long road to travel between serial killer fanboy and murdering for sport.

Before we left and sent in Crime Scene, I'd asked Heidi what she knew about the man who created the painting. As I suspected, she knew nothing about him. She didn't seem to know what he'd been up to outside of his art. It was believable enough; she was in California when Raymond was found out. The sad truth was, there were enough serial killers around to make most people forget the names of all but a handful.

In certain online forums, though, the name "Dwyer" was almost as revered as "Gein" or "Ramirez." Thankfully, I'd given up stalking those corners of the internet a long time ago. One small step for me, one giant leap for my mental health.

When a call from Agent Wicklow came through for me, I already knew what he would say before I tapped the hold button on my office phone. But I let him talk anyway.

"...like getting blood from a stone," he said a few minutes into his petulant rant. "His lawyer is Jared Mansfield."

I cursed—not right into the speaker, but not where I couldn't be heard, either. If Jared Mansfield hadn't popped out of his mother with a position in his father's prestigious firm already lined up, the man might've turned into a serial killer himself. He was an absolute sociopath—vicious, conniving, willing to do whatever it took to get his verdict with no regard for future consequences because, for him, there weren't any. Never had been, never would be.

In other words, he was born to be a defense attorney for murderers. His daddy's firm and paycheck provided him with enough power over others that he'd never had to resort to killing to achieve that supreme high. He could screw people over in a number of other creative ways instead.

Case in point: the asshole had been pulled over for drunk driving three times, and each of those times, the *arresting officer* lost his job not long after for absolute bullshit reasons.

Hiring Jared Mansfield was an acknowledgment of guilt, as far as I was concerned. And how Scott could afford him was beyond me. Probably banking on a hefty civil suit against the city once they got the acquittal they were after.

Wicklow went on, "The DA refuses to file official charges yet."

"Of course she does." I wasn't happy about it, but it made sense, especially now that Mansfield was involved. Taking the wrong man to trial on a high-profile case like this without ample physical evidence would be about as smart as parachuting off the Empire State Building without first checking that you'd packed a parachute.

"We need to find Dylan Fowler," I said. "He's the key."

Wicklow sighed. "We don't know that he hasn't just skipped town, Detective. We have no reason to believe he's in any kind of danger."

Brandolini's Law states that it always takes more

energy to refute bullshit than it does to produce it. And, without fail, every conversation I had with Agent Wicklow proved that law to be true.

I'd been over all of this with him. I'd laid out the obvious facts, and he'd accepted them, or pretended to. And then he just jumped right back to square one. It was like someone kept doing a hard reset on his entire mushy brain.

So instead of stating my case all over again, I asked, "What's the plan?"

"We're going to have to cut him loose."

"Well, obviously." I'd seen it coming. "I mean, what's the *surveillance* plan?"

"Round-the-clock."

"You have agents assigned to him? No breaks between shift change? Are you tracking all the Ruiz vehicles? Got a wire on his house?"

"Afraid I can't give you the specifics, Detective."

"Is that because *you* don't know them? We can't let him out of our sight for a single second, not a man like—"

"Understand that I didn't *need* to call you." His voice was tight, and I imagined his fleshy lips thinning out and going white. "I'm doing you a courtesy here, so I'd appreciate it if you didn't question my competence at every turn."

And I'd appreciate it if he'd *prove* his competence. Even just once.

"I understand that," I said, "and I appreciate the update. But this isn't about me. And this isn't about you. This is about making sure no one else is murdered as a result of our actions. I understand why we have to let him go—trust me, I've seen this before and know how it works—

but Scott Ruiz *is* our guy. And we're about to let him walk back into the public. So, I hope *you* understand why I'm a little concerned about surveillance. Thanks for the call." I hung up before he could. It was a petty power move, but hey, it felt amazing, and it was all I had on him.

I could feel Ben's eyes on me, but I didn't look up from the phone yet.

My mind was a tornado of anxiety, and I needed to take action. But there was nothing I could do, was there? Not yet. There would be soon, though. I could feel it like a coiled spring inside me.

The moment I sat across the table from Scott, I'd guessed it would come to this, that we'd end up here, with him walking free. He was willing to play chicken with the DA; I'd seen that in his eyes. His choice of attorney only confirmed it. The DA had too much to lose, and Scott knew we didn't have enough to confidently slap the official charges on him and get the initial indictment. That was part of the thrill of it for men like him. He wanted people to know his evil but never be able to prove it. That terror, for the world to know killers like him walked among us, was one of his favorite drugs.

Some criminals got tired of having to outthink the cops, and once they were in custody, they'd call uncle before long.

But not Scott. This was his sport. He lived for it. And with the FBI cutting him loose, the game was only getting started.

FORTY-EIGHT

Predawn. July 10th, 2018
34 days since Blackstenius murder

I stared up through the dark at my bedroom ceiling. My eyes had adjusted to the orange glow cast by my digital clock, so that I could make out the individual bumps of the popcorn texturing above me. I absentmindedly created constellations between the points. Had I fallen asleep at all, or had I been awake all these hours since I first crawled into bed? How, *how* could I fail to nod off after so many consecutive hours awake? Insomnia was so damn pointless. That was really what made it excruciating. It served no purpose at all. None.

To say my room was silent wouldn't exactly be true, but I'd stopped noticing the backdrop of neighbors playing the radio nonstop and the occasional whizz of a car racing down William Cannon. My mind had zeroed it all out, faded it into the backdrop.

Then a sudden noise pulled my attention. It registered

as tapping initially, and it was coming from... somewhere inside my apartment.

No, not quite tapping. Something else. Clicking? Rattling?

The pieces snapped together all at once.

Someone was trying to get in.

My training took over, and I whipped my legs off the side of the bed and grabbed my loaded pistol from the bedside table.

Sadie had heard it, too, and she pressed her nose against the space beneath my locked bedroom door, sniffing frantically.

I checked the clock: 4:18 a.m. Whoever was at my front door now had done their research and found the sweet spot between the drunks coming home from the bars and the early risers leaving for their backbreaking minimum-wage jobs. This person knew when they had the least chance of being seen.

I unlocked my bedroom door, and Sadie charged out ahead of me, ready to take out whoever this was at the knees. I hissed at her to calm down, but she didn't listen. She barked once, deeply, aiming for intimidating. She knew this wasn't a drill. Good girl.

But the moment my ears recovered from that loud sound, I heard something else on my doorstep. Something metal hit the concrete, followed by the slap of hurried footsteps.

I rushed forward and flung open the door, gun drawn.

Nobody there. Not anymore.

"Sadie. To me."

She clearly had a mind to follow the trail, but I couldn't have her doing that. That was *my* job. She may be built like a battering ram with sharp teeth, but I had the gun and the training.

I stuck her inside, shut the door, and pursued the suspect down the stairs.

But I'd lost the trail. I couldn't hear the footsteps anymore, which either meant this person was fast or they'd stopped running and were hiding instead.

Realizing that I hadn't locked up behind me, I hurried back upstairs. Sadie was whining on the other side of the door as I spotted something lying on the ground. Just a typical lockpick. I didn't touch it; it was evidence now. As were the fresh scratches on the lock above my doorknob.

I scanned the complex again, down each wing of the breezeway, the shadows of the courtyard, trying to let the corners of my eyes catch any movement.

Was it the same person who'd gotten in before? If so, they must've known I'd changed the lock, or they wouldn't have brought the other tools with them. Guess they hadn't anticipated the double deadbolts I added after their last stunt. They might still have been able to sneak in while I wasn't home, but when I was, and could lock up fully behind me, there was no chance in hell. They'd have to kick the door off the hinges, and that would be bad luck for them, because there'd be one pissed-off Homicide detective with a loaded gun waiting on the other side of it.

I debated putting Sadie on the leash and seeing if we couldn't track down the person together. But that was a little more vigilante than even I was comfortable with, and forcing an off-duty confrontation after the immediate threat had passed was just bad police work. Besides, everything pointed to this person coming back later. They hadn't completed the thing they'd set out to do, whatever that was. I'd get them next time around.

There was only one responsible thing left to do right now. I went inside, bolted the door behind me, and called the cops.

This wouldn't normally be categorized as a high-priority call. People in this busy sector often had to wait an hour or more for an officer to make it over to a situation like this, where the suspect had already fled, and there was no immediate danger. But identifying myself as a Homicide detective sped things up, and fifteen minutes later, red and blue lit up the sooty expanse of the predawn sky as a cruiser slow-rolled into the complex.

I got the first lucky break of my morning when Officer Arthur Bainbridge strolled into the courtyard. Not only did the man love working patrol like no one I'd ever met, but he was one of those rare men with through-the-roof social intelligence. His presence on even the most volatile scene was like injecting a sedative into everyone's veins.

Bainbridge and I had worked together for a few months in Edward sector before I promoted, but it felt like I'd known him for years by the time I moved on. Hell, he'd even been one of the few to figure out my history and former last name, but he'd never turned it into the hot gossip it could have been. His discretion only made me like him more.

As he climbed the stairs up to my floor, I hollered down, "How the hell they convince you to move down to Henry?"

"They didn't. This is OT. I'm sticking with Edward till I die."

"Shouldn't be long."

He was grinning as he reached the top step. "Your lips to God's ears." He leaned against the railing across from my door and tucked his thumbs into the armpits of his vest. He was a white guy in his mid-thirties and had one of those faces that couldn't offend anyone. Forgettable, but kind. "What do we got here, Capone?"

I caught him up to speed, and he nodded along, snapping pictures of the entryway and dustings for prints as I gave him the rundown.

"Any hunches?" he asked.

"Only that I really need some coffee. You?"

He accepted, and a few minutes later, I was pouring us two mugs inside. He sat at the kitchen table, scratching Sadie behind the ears as I brought over our drinks.

"You selling drugs?" he asked.

I didn't respond, simply presented him with my best stink-eye.

"I only ask because I've never seen an attempted break-in at a complex like yours that wasn't related to drugs. Actually, I take that back. But if you're not selling drugs, then you *definitely* slept with someone's girlfriend."

"You think it's targeted."

"Don't you?"

Hell yes, I did. But I shrugged a single shoulder. "Maybe."

He tucked his chin and eyed me with more than a little skepticism.

"Okay, fine," I said. "Yeah, this is... not the first incident on my doorstep lately."

"You didn't report the others?"

"Couldn't. Nothing to report. Well, not enough for a Homicide detective to report it."

"Sure. But when you string it all together..."

"It does seem a little suspicious. I figured an attempted break-in might finally push it into report-worthy territory."

"No kidding." He sipped his coffee and nodded approval. "Tell me about the others. I know you think it's not enough to get worked up about, but humor me."

Finding myself on this end of the interview with Bainbridge, I was starting to understand how he'd talked down so many deranged lovers with loaded guns in the few short months we worked together. But I didn't spill all at once. I tested the waters first.

"Cats have been going missing around here lately."

He leaned back. "Uh-huh?"

I had the feeling he already knew where I was going with this. The context was all there. *I* was the context. "There were a couple of mutilated squirrels, and then someone left a flayed cat on my doorstep."

His calm expression changed with a widening of his eyes, and he paused, his mug steaming and suspended just in front of his lips. He set it back on the table. "A flayed cat on your doorstep?"

"Yep."

"Dana, that's... I don't mean to sound alarmist, but it seems like you're dealing with a real psycho. Maybe even a serial killer in the making. Think this might be related to that big case you have going on right now?"

Though I'd been quietly functioning under that assumption myself, I didn't expect the wave of relief that washed over me upon someone else hearing only the barest of details yet arriving at the same conclusion.

I wanted to reach across the table and hug him, but I refrained for obvious reasons, the least of which was that it was incredibly uncomfortable to hug someone in uniform with their gear hooked to their vest.

"Maybe. Wanna see pictures of the other animals?" I asked. "I have them."

I reached for my phone in my back pocket, but he said, "Just email them to me later. But I take it from the fact that you took photos that you had the same suspicion right off the bat." His gaze was soft but penetrating. "You didn't want to say anything about it. I get it. But rest assured, I don't think you're overreacting here by connecting the dots. It sounds like you're being targeted, and, at the very least, the person is deranged. Leaving dead animals for you is something only psychopaths and cats do."

"Same thing."

He grinned. "You mind if I mention the previous incidents in the report? I think we'd better get all this on paper in case something worse happens."

I stared down at the smooth, dark surface of my coffee. "You speak good sense, sir. Just, you know, maybe don't point it out to anyone. I don't want everyone in the department thinking—"

He held up a hand. "I get it. I'll just slip it in there at the end. I won't mention it to anyone. Totally under the radar. Only there if we need it. And I hope we don't ever need it."

Once we were out on the doorstep again, he turned to me. "I know it's not really my business, but you ever considered moving somewhere safer? Somewhere with more security?" He looked around. "Not that this place isn't lovely in its own way."

It was past five now, and a handful of my neighbors were stumbling around in the courtyard. A toddler took off in only a diaper with his mother hurrying after to scoop him up.

"Nah, I think I'm good where I am. The last thing this place needs is one fewer cop."

He conceded with a shrug, said goodbye, and headed out.

I waited outside a little while longer, taking whatever coolish air I could get before God turned the oven back on this afternoon.

A stout woman on the first floor shoved a shirtless man out her front door, yelling at him in what I'd guess was Vietnamese, and he stumbled into the sun-dried courtyard in shock.

Yep, I was sticking around. I'd been run off from my home before, and I'd be damned if I let it happen again.

Besides, it seemed that evil followed me wherever I went. At some point, a woman had to stop running.

FORTY-NINE

I stood in the lobby of the station with my arms folded, mostly to keep my hands from doing anything stupid before my mind could catch up. Would I like to strangle Scott Ruiz? Yes, I would like that very much. Would it be the best thing to do?

Ah, well, that was where legality and morality parted ways.

So, there I was, watching the FBI finish the process of cutting him loose.

From beside me, Agent Turner, whose arms were also folded, likely for the same reason, leaned my way and murmured, "I made sure the surveillance doesn't suck. Wicklow wasn't asking for nearly enough, so I made sure Ruiz won't be able to empty his bladder without us knowing about it."

"I feel sorry for whoever is on piss observation duty."

I couldn't speak for Turner, but I was treating myself to a little revenge fantasy of him taking one step off the curb outside the station and being plastered by an oncoming Capital Metro bus.

Sure, it would rob a lot of people of justice, but it would *feel good* to watch. So I only half wished it.

Mostly, I was preoccupied with—or, more precisely, worried for—the next person Scott would try to slaughter. Because he wasn't going to stop. He might be able to wait it out until the FBI could no longer financially justify the surveillance of a man who did nothing out of the ordinary, but once he was given an inch, he'd kill again.

Though I suspected that Dylan had become the ultimate target of obsession (for now) and that Scott likely believed his need would finally be sated once he had his way with Dylan, I didn't buy that bullshit. You didn't stop craving heroin after your first hit of fentanyl. You just started craving fentanyl. Scott's wife could've told him that much.

"He's not going to lead us to Dylan anytime soon," I said, and I could feel Turner's eyes on me.

"You never know. He could get cocky."

Scott caught sight of us watching and brooding, and he grinned. Then he waved, a little twiddle of his fingers.

"Oh, he's cocky, all right," I muttered. "But he's not stupid."

"They're all stupid," Turner said. "Stupid enough to get caught eventually."

"Sounds like biased data to me. You're only including the ones you catch. And he's smart enough to be walking out of the FBI's custody right this second."

Fifteen minutes later, I carried a hot cup of coffee—yes, more coffee—with me as I trudged into Death Row. Ben had his head down, staring at a legal pad on his desk as he scribbled notes and recited a litany of "Uh-huh... yeah... and then what?" into the receiver of his office phone.

I collapsed into my chair at the desk across from his and tried not to crash.

Grief, that was what I was feeling. Something about watching Scott walk out those doors a relatively free man had felt like the nail in Dylan's coffin. It was just a feeling, though.

A sudden craving for one of my tarot decks prickled at my fingers, and I couldn't help but smirk as I imagined clearing off my messy desk and throwing down a spread right in front of Ben and the rest of Homicide. They'd think I'd lost it completely, finally snapped under the pressure and trauma.

And they might be right.

I sighed, woke up my computer, and pulled up my running to-do list.

- *Hom 14: Follow up w/victim services*
- *Hom 16: Contact gas station on Oltorf, security footage?*
- *Hom 9: Update supp report, statement from employer*

"Hey." Ben's voice was a welcome distraction a few minutes later. "They let him go?"

"Yep. Watched the bastard waltz right out the door, gloating with a smug-ass grin the whole way."

Escobar looked exhausted, wrecked even, and I wondered how long he'd looked that way without my noticing. Was it just today? Had this case been wearing on him like it had me?

Or was it *me* that had been wearing on him?

"Turner promised me they have him under tight surveillance," I continued, "whatever that means. Well, no, I'll tell you what it means. It means there's zero percent chance he'll lead us to Dylan. Ruiz will know he's being followed and monitored."

Escobar rotated in his chair until he faced me directly. "Can I say something without you getting mad?"

I narrowed my eyes at him. "Unlikely when you have to preface it with that bullshit. Just grow a pair and say what you want to say."

"What if it's not Ruiz?"

I wasn't even angry, just... bored? Was that what I was feeling? A deep, roiling sense of boredom? "It's Ruiz."

"But what if it's not?"

I groaned and leaned back in my chair. "Okay, fine. Who is it, then?"

He didn't have a smart comeback because there wasn't one. The only answer was that the FBI had just cut loose the man who'd killed at least three women, attacked another, and possibly captured and killed Dylan.

"Mike Check?" he said, and I could tell he didn't mean it. He couldn't even pretend. "Dana," he said, leaning forward so he wouldn't be overheard, "I know you *bonded* with Dylan or whatever—honestly, I don't get why you're so attached to him—but can't you see how an argument could still be made?"

"No, I can't. Why don't you explain it to me like I'm stupid?"

Ben didn't appear to be getting any pleasure out of this, which was great news. He shouldn't be.

He pressed his lips together and exhaled curtly through

his nose. "Okay, fine. Let's say that the attacker outside Sheep's Clothing wasn't the same person who killed Blackstenius and the other women. That's a possibility. The FBI could have made their mistake there. So, then they cut Dylan loose, thinking he's not the guy they're looking for, and shortly after, he takes off. He leaves his car, doesn't tell anyone where he's going, asks Scott to look after his car, and makes it look like he's been abducted. He just vanishes. Might be a smart move if he's really the guilty one. You've said it yourself: these guys don't stop killing until they're caught or killed. If it looks like they've stopped, it's only because they've disappeared and reappeared somewhere else with a new identity."

His reasoning was sound... ish. It all hinged on whether the person who murdered Cheryl, Leslie, and Stephanie was the same one who'd attacked Gwen. And while I was fairly certain about that, it was definitely the weakest part of this whole case.

But I had a few more cards to turn. "Then how do you explain the painting in the Ruiz house?"

Ben threw his hands up in surrender. "I can't. I'll admit, it's suspicious as hell, but it's not *proof*. It's circumstantial."

I blinked as it clicked what he was doing. Because I'd seen his expression in the Ruiz living room when I told him about the painting. I'd seen the lights go on in that skull of his. He'd *known* what the presence of the painting meant, known it in that deep way that stuck.

Holy shit. His gut was telling him the same thing as mine.

Which meant he wasn't making this argument in earnest. So, why...?

Son of a bitch. "You're playing the devil's advocate! *Dammit*, Ben." I slapped my desk. "*When* did you find out about this?"

"Just yesterday." He cringed apologetically. "I overheard Wicklow—"

"Of course it was Wicklow. Only he could be thick enough to adopt that theory. *Dylan?* That's really their top suspect *again*? But what about Ruiz driving Dylan's car? What about him having possession of Dylan's phone? How does Wicklow explain all that?"

"You know how," Ben said. "He doesn't. He ignores what doesn't fit in."

I took a deep breath and shoved my palms into my eyes. "How does someone like him make it this far in the FBI?"

"That," said Ben, "is something I actually *can* help you with. I did a little research, and his uncle is a U.S. senator. Also, never underestimate the power of white male privilege."

"I never do."

His tone darkened. "There's something else, Dana."

"Oh god."

"Turner told me about Dylan's... hobby. And so I looked into that, too."

"And?"

Ben hesitated, which told me two things right away: this was going to be juicy, and it was going to make him sound a little crazy. "His stage name is Marie Possa." He tilted his head forward and stared at me with wide eyes, as if I was supposed to know why the hell Dylan's drag queen name mattered.

I waited for him to continue, but he didn't.

Deep in my mind, the answer knocked on a door, waiting to be let in.

"Mariposa," I said. "Butterfly in Spanish. Oh *no*."

The missing skin of the victims just under the shoulder blades. It was wings, after all, but not angel wings or even fairy wings. Butterfly wings the whole time.

Ben nodded. "I already told Turner about it. I had to, Dana. It looks relevant to the investigation."

I waved him off. "I know, I know. Don't worry. I'm not mad." Drumming my fingers on the desk, I thought it over. "And they interpret it as further evidence that *Dylan* is the killer?"

"Yep."

"Damn. Swing and a miss, FBI. They're so close to being useful, but they just refuse to take it a step further."

"Meaning?"

"They suspect someone like Dylan, who has found a way to express his sexuality openly in an environment that supports it, would *also* be compelled to kill women and mark them with a symbol that he uses for his alter ego? No way. He doesn't *need* to. He's already expressing his urges as Marie Possa." God, how did so-called professionals manage to get this wrong? And I thought *I* had tunnel vision. "Whoever is compelled to strangle women, overpower and conquer them, and carve butterfly wings into their flesh is someone who *doesn't* know how to express their repressed sexuality in any productive or harmless way. Ergo, it's not Dylan Fowler. It's Scott Ruiz." I sighed. "If Wicklow is this off the mark, it's clear I'm going to have to do this myself."

Ben's head went immediately into his hands. "Please don't get me fired."

"I make no promises, Ben. So, you might as well back me up if you're going down either way. Someone has to snag this guy, and it looks like it'll have to be you and me."

He scrubbed his palm over the imperceptible stubble of his jaw line. "Okay, sure. Where should we start?"

I opened my mouth but paused. That was a good question.

"Exactly," he said. "We have no leads. Following Scott around would be redundant, and we have no idea where to start with finding Dylan. How about maybe we catch up on some of these other cases for a while?"

I wanted to argue, but damn if it wasn't a solid suggestion. Other people had died in this city recently. Not in as showy of a way, but dead all the same. They deserved justice too, and their killers could also kill again, though it would be in the name of gang dominance, road rage, or run-of-the-mill intimate partner violence. Related, but momentary, not born out of pure malevolence. "Fine, but only until we catch wind of another promising lead on Fowler or Ruiz."

Ben shook his head, the exhaustion showing again. "Whatever you say, Dana. Now can you forward me the affidavit from the Williams case?"

With a sigh, I relented, turning back to my computer screen.

I hated hitting this impasse on Dylan's whereabouts, but that was the nature of the job. Until he turned up dead in our jurisdiction, he wasn't technically one of our cases. And other victims were. I needed to take myself out of this and be objective, and when I did that, I found myself right where Ben already was.

All we could do for Dylan now was wait.

FIFTY

July 13th, 2018
37 days since Blackstenius murder

A week slipped by as I followed up on my other cases.

The trail for Dylan was cold, and even though Wicklow didn't seem to put much credence in the possibility of Scott being our guy, Turner had kept true to her word and maintained round-the-clock surveillance of him. She'd even gone a step further and kept me apprised of it, though I suspected her motivation for that was less out of a sense of teamwork and more to keep me from going all vigilante.

If anything had stopped me from doing that over the last few days, it wasn't Turner, but my workload. The summer months always led to more homicides. Not the planned and calculated kind, but the knee-jerk variety—easier to solve and close, but markedly more frequent. Despite it being Texas, plenty of crappy rental homes and apartments didn't have air conditioning. Or they did, but it was broken, and the landlord couldn't be bothered. Or folks had a single window unit to cool every room against the sweltering temperatures. That meant that even when it was 105 degrees, it was often cooler outside in the shade than indoors.

And when everyone was outside and irritable from the heat, and teens were running around with guns on their summer break, murder happened. It was just basic math.

That wasn't to say I hadn't done a little side investigating what I now thought of as "the Ruiz case" in my insomniac hours. But my investigation had turned up nothing. Just a bunch of dead ends. And the places I'd really have liked to check out—the Fowler home and Laugh Attack—were off-limits to me, for obvious reasons.

Then finally, after days of nothing, there I was: an early-morning meeting at FBI's Austin office that I was, frankly, shocked to be included in.

We packed into a conference room with ASAC Grissom at the head of the table. Turner and Wicklow flanked him while Sergeant Popov, Ben, and I sat across from them as if we were ready to negotiate the terms of a high-stakes divorce.

It was a quarter past five in the morning. I'd received the call to come in around three thirty and had passed Ariadna in the parking lot as she readied her taco truck for the day. I hoped this wouldn't take too long so I could get back to Sadie at a reasonable hour. She wouldn't get out of bed to use the bathroom before I left, and she hadn't been especially interested in a four a.m. breakfast.

"Everyone got enough coffee?" ASAC Grissom asked,

being an uncharacteristically gracious host. The hospitality sounded like it was costing him, though.

Ben raised his compostable cup in confirmation. The whole room smelled like the freshly brewed carafe sitting on the coffee station in the corner. I was on my second cup already.

This wasn't unlike some of the meetings we'd held over at the station, except the FBI didn't use projectors. No, they'd graduated into the twenty-first century. They were *fancy.*

A sixty-inch 4K TV powered on behind Grissom, and Popov appeared determinedly unimpressed. It occurred to me for the first time that Sarge might hate working with the FBI just as much as I did, or very close to it, and simply hid it much better.

An evidence photo appeared on the screen. But it wasn't the usual kind of evidence—a weapon, bloody clothing, bullet casings, a cigarette. It looked to be a sheet of printer paper with handwriting on it. Lots of it. The edges of the paper disappeared into the white table below it.

The slap of a newspaper in front of me jolted my attention away from the screen, and I looked down to see that day's copy of the *Austin-American Statesman* on the table in front of me. Agent Wicklow had dropped a copy in front of Ben and Popov, too. Oh boy, this couldn't be good.

"The *Statesman* offices received a letter in the mail yesterday," Grissom began. "Of course, they waited until about midnight to bother reporting it to us." He dismissed his seething anger with a quick twitch of his right eyebrow. "It appears to be from the Stand-Up Killer."

Ben and I shared a glance at the mention of the

pseudonym, and despite the severity of the situation, I could tell he was struggling not to smirk as much as I was.

Popov was the first to unfold the newspaper, and there it was on the front page. The same photo as on the TV. "This has already gone out?"

"Not yet," said Grissom. "This is the draft. They had the sense to run it by us first."

Popov frowned at it. "You can't stop them from delivering?"

"We don't see the need to."

Sarge's head shot up. "You don't see the need to nip this panic in the bud?"

Grissom shrugged a single shoulder. "The public is already concerned."

A vein bulged on Popov's forehead. "All due respect, Grissom, but concern is a different animal from panic. Concern doesn't put officers' lives in danger."

I hadn't expected Sarge to go toe to toe with the ASAC, but if he was ever going to do it, now seemed like the right goddamn time. This was madness.

Rather than explain himself, Grissom said, "Just read the letter, Sergeant."

We all did. I could guess the nature of it easy enough, so the question I hoped to answer was whether this was a fake or not. It wasn't uncommon for some nut job to claim credit for a psycho's handiwork, to slip into the readymade persona of a local terror and take it for a spin.

Dear Editor,
This is the Stand-up Killer. I'm writing to you in hopes that you will share this in tomorrow's edition. I believe the public deserves to know just how much their law enforcement

community is failing them. I have left a preponderance of clues for them to follow straight to me as well as a wealth of physical evidence. And yet I remain a free man. Because of this, I will kill again. I enjoy killing, and I've long since admitted that I cannot control the urge for long. The final crunch of a woman's trachea beneath my grip, savoring the fear in her eyes, her heaving chest as she struggles to breathe, is too much of a temptation for me to resist ever again. There are plenty of insolent women in this town to keep me occupied for months, maybe even years. The real question you should ask is not who am I, but will Detective Dwyer catch me before I murder as many as her beloved father? The hunt is on.

-SK

After the initial jolt, I read the letter through one more time, numb now—I could feel things later if I needed. At this moment, though, I had a heap of clues in front of me, and there was no time to take it personally.

I didn't need the paper's typed transcription below the image to read every word just fine. It was written in print, not cursive, and the words were clear and evenly spaced. I'd studied correspondence like this before, and the handwriting was usually lopsided chicken scratch in quasi-cursive that started tight and loosened up as the maniac found his rhythm and flow.

Not this, though. This was from a practiced hand. Sloppy handwriting in a letter of this magnitude would be a power move, albeit a subconscious one. It would put the burden of communication on the reader, who had to decipher it *or else*. It cost the receiver unnecessary energy. And that was what killers enjoyed most, taking from others.

When it came down to it, that was all power meant to these people.

This handwriting didn't require that expended mental energy, though. It was clear, easy to read. Almost as if it was intended to be legible to those in the early stages of literacy.

I knew whose writing this was before Grissom spoke again. "We have handwriting samples from Scott. It's not a match. Not even close. We do have a match, though." His eyes were on me, and I met his gaze, challenging him to say it and challenging myself not to show any signs of emotion when he did. "Dylan Fowler wrote this."

"Obviously." No way was I giving him the satisfaction of thinking he'd surprised me with this.

"Obviously?"

"Yes. To start, the person who wrote this singled me out by my former name. While that's not exactly classified information, it rules out the average attention seeker here, narrows the pool significantly. Then you have the lettering. I dunno about you, but I've only ever seen elementary teachers write like this. You know they don't teach cursive in Texas schools anymore? It's true. So, if you're teaching kindergarten, you have to write in clear print. Then there's the spelling. Whoever wrote this has at least a college education. 'Trachea,' 'breathe' with an *e* at the end. Taken together…" I shrugged.

"You agree that this is from Dylan Fowler?" ASAC Grissom said. "That there might be some truth to our theory that he skipped town?"

Easy there, partner. Now he was pushing it. But I'd play along a bit more. "You said it matches Dylan's handwriting, and I don't have the training to argue that point. And nothing I know about him contradicts that this could be his handwriting. So, sure, I'll accept that this is his. You say they received it yesterday?"

Grissom nodded.

I considered the timeline. How old could the letter be? If it was only written the day before, Dylan could still be alive. That was the only bit of good news I could find here, though.

I skimmed the letter again. "Did forensics fail to mention that the longer downstrokes have a visible shake that indicates the writer was suffering either extreme nervousness or low blood sugar? Or did the handwriting analysis include that, but *you've* just decided to omit it?"

Sure, I didn't have formal handwriting analysis training, but that didn't mean I hadn't studied it in-depth on my own, maybe even called a few of the top experts in the nation to ask my questions and strengthen my understanding. When you don't have a life outside of work, you'd better be damn good at your work.

Grissom stared at me passively, and then his eyebrows rose just a millimeter, as if to ask if I was done.

I wasn't. "I won't question whether this is Dylan's writing. I assume your guys compared the samples thoroughly in the short time they had before coming to a conclusion. But even while functioning on that premise, there are *many* possible reasons he would write this letter. Is this shaky downstroke evidence of guilt or duress?"

He'd had enough of my bullshit then. "There is no indication that our unsub would kidnap a grown man, Detective Capone. Even one that dresses like a woman."

"But Gwen Masters—"

"Masters was attacked while we had Dylan Fowler in

custody, and since Dylan is our main suspect now, she can't be related to the case."

I pressed a hand to my forehead. "Jesus. If I knew we'd be asked to do this kind of bullshit acrobatics, I would have stretched beforehand."

"There's no established behavior indicating the unsub is interested in keeping a captive. His enjoyment, as you can see from this letter, is obtained through the act of killing."

There was always a point when it became clear someone was so far down the wrong path that there was no calling them back to the fork and convincing them to take a different route. That was where Grissom was. He wouldn't backtrack as far as he needed to, to follow me down the road I was walking.

And from his perspective, it was likely the same with me. I wouldn't go back to the split. But that was only because it was so obvious what was really going on.

It was Dylan's writing, but those were not his words.

Scott may not have taken a captive before, but he'd never *wanted* one. Not until Marie Possa. If I'd learned anything important, it was that Scott was not the oblivious bum he pretended to be. He was smart. He would know that as soon as Dylan was gone, the fun was over. And he'd be forced to face the fact that the act of killing his ultimate prey *hadn't* quenched his dark desire.

I hoped the tension drove Scott slowly insane. I hoped he was in agony from that need to indulge warring with the knowledge that he could only kill a person once.

As far as I was concerned, this letter meant that Dylan was very possibly still alive. And as long as he was, I had hope of saving him, of fixing my mistakes that had landed him where he was.

Because one thing this letter said was undeniably true, no matter how much it hurt to admit it. Law enforcement had failed so far. I'd failed.

Now it was up to me to make it right.

FIFTY-ONE

July 17th, 2018

41 days since Blackstenius murder

A copy of the *Austin-American Statesman* was sitting on my desk when I entered Death Row. It'd been four days since the publication loosed Dylan's letter upon the city, and just as Popov had expected, panic ensued. I'd done my best to tune it out. It was mostly noise, and that noise was entirely out of my control. I did feel for everyone manning the phones and email at Crime Stoppers, though.

Glancing down at the new copy on my desk, I caught sight of a snippet of Dylan's handwriting above the fold— new letter, same old shit, I was sure—before I scooted the thing to the side to make space in the clutter for my coffee cup.

Ben looked up from his copy, trying to sneak a glance at me but getting caught. "You're not even going to look at it?" he said.

"Let me guess. He made some sort of demand and said more women will die if it's not met."

Ben exhaled deeply. "Are you bored *all the time*, Capone?"

"Huh?"

"I'm just asking, because if I could guess the behavior of the so-called unpredictable, I think I'd be bored all the time."

"I'm bored a lot of the time, yeah. But psychopaths aren't unpredictable. They're some of the *most* predictable people around. They don't have any tender emotions to cloud their judgment at random moments. They do whatever will get them the most power over others. Period. The trouble with predicting what shape that will take occurs on our end, from our inability to separate ourselves from our emotions to see what would be most advantageous for pure power. He has the city's attention now, so the next obvious step is to wield it. Power that goes unused atrophies."

"And when you say 'he,' you're talking about...?"

I glared at him. "Scott Ruiz."

"Okay, so *not* the person who we know is writing these letters, but someone else who's been under twenty-four-hour surveillance and hasn't once visited the *Statesman* offices or a post office or even been all that close to a mailbox?"

I grabbed the newspaper and unfolded it, mumbling, "You're functioning under the assumption that the surveillance is any good."

The front-page headline was about as sensational as I'd have expected, but that wasn't what caught my eye. Just below the top story, perhaps drafting on the public fears of murdered women, was a story of a discovery from the night before.

"What in the *ever-loving hell* is this?" I held it up for Ben, pointing at the headline of *Woman's Remains Discovered in Lady Bird Lake*.

He squinted at it, giving it a double take that told me he hadn't known either. "That was last night? After we went home?"

"Goddammit, Krantz," I said, as his name jumped out at me from the page.

Ben groaned. "He hasn't been placed indefinitely on admin leave yet?"

"They kept this from us intentionally, Ben."

"I don't know if—"

"African American woman, possibly in the lake for months, no ID yet." I could've punched something, but there was no good target within reach, so I settled on cursing again, a long string of obscenities.

Ben grimaced. "She doesn't fit the—"

I pinched the bridge of my nose. "Don't. God, please just don't."

"Fine." He held up his hands in surrender. "I won't say it. But if you're going around claiming this is murder number four for the Stand-up Killer, *everyone else* will say it for me."

"Let them." I read on through the article. No mention of high heels on the vic, but I'd be checking Krantz's report on that. It was likely too much to hope for, though. I doubted even Agent Wicklow was dull enough to ignore an obvious connection like that, should it exist.

When the article turned to quotes from random locals about APD's relationship with "the Black community" as if it was some monolithic thing, I knew I'd gotten all the pertinent details I could from it. I logged into my computer to pull up the actual report.

It was sparse, as all of Krantz's reports were. No doubt he was the kid in school who bitched and moaned at every writing assignment.

I couldn't find anything in the report that directly indicated a connection to the other murders, and whatever photos had been taken on scene hadn't been uploaded yet. Intentional? More likely, Krantz's lazy ass hadn't called in to the admins to have them push the records through.

I disengaged, shut my eyes, and tilted my head back.

Maybe this had nothing to do with Scott. There was nothing to go on other than the location where the body was found, which wasn't exactly a novel dumping ground.

We didn't even have a full ID on the body. Who was she? Did she have a family? Was she homeless? A quasi-transient?

I knew who she was not, and that was a "college student with a bright future." If she'd lived the kind of feel-good life society valued, we would've heard about her disappearance on the news long before the body turned up.

I scrolled through the open missing person records from the last year, but nothing jumped out at me. The transient possibility seemed more and more likely. No one to miss her. Those she might have seen regularly could have assumed she'd moved to greener pastures in another city or under another overpass.

"Hey, you should really read this," Ben said, motioning at the front page. "Something just caught my eye. I won't say what it is yet. I want to see if you pick up on it, too."

I smoothed out the paper and read the latest letter in Dylan's practiced hand.

Dear Editor,
It's me again. The shadow. The lone wolf. The police still haven't found me. If anything stalks this town, it's their ineptitude. Most citizens need not fear. I only have my eye on a few. I don't like doing this, but someone has to cull the herd. I've taken a break, but I'll be back at it again. Tomorrow? The day after? Next week? Every day until I'm caught? Wait and see. Dwyer knows this is not a science but an art. I interpret the natural patterns and reproduce them. Life imitates art imitating life. And my art deserves an audience through the finale.
You'll be hearing from me daily. If you fail to publish what I have to say, another woman dies.
SK

I tossed the paper onto the desk again and sipped my coffee. I knew what Ben thought he'd found because I'd found it, too. The pieces, as deranged as they were, snapped comfortably together.

Scott's games didn't make me angry. In fact, I wanted him to keep talking. He'd slip up eventually. They always did.

And he might have just given the game away.

"He didn't say 'Detective Dwyer,'" I said.

"Damn, you got that on the initial read?"

"Probably for the same reason you did. The first person to come to mind when I see that name isn't me."

"Sounds like the Stand-up Killer is a fan of your father."

"We already knew that from the painting in Scott's living room. But yes, Scott and every other psycho have a real hard-on for the legend of Raymond Lee Dwyer. Prison is the best thing that could've happened to Raymond in that regard. He's built a cult following without meaning to. He's practically the Nelson Mandela of serial killers now." I paused. "Did you notice what SK is called himself here?"

"The lone wolf."

"And then he talks about culling the herd. And patterns. He likes the idea of outsmarting the police and FBI. He gets off on it. He wants to humiliate us."

"He's doing a good job of it, if I'm honest," said Ben.

"He's dropping hints. Big ones. He wants to be able to say, 'I gave you everything you needed, and you still missed it.' That's his game."

That got Ben's full attention.

"Dylan is still alive," I continued. "These letters have to be written in his hand for consistency." It was lining up, bit by bit, and my heart started to race. "Wherever he is, he's alive. Scott can't risk killing him before this game is played out. If he has to change his approach, pivot his message, he needs Dylan's handwriting for that. In Scott's mind, Dylan is the 'finale.'"

"But how? I don't disagree with you, Dana; I just don't know what we're supposed to make of that."

"Surveillance is turning up nothing. We have to meet Scott at that final play and be ready for it."

"Except we have no clue where or when that final play will be."

"Speak for yourself."

Ben's eyebrows shot up. "You know?"

"Of course. It's right here. The lone wolf, the patterns,

Dwyer." There was an elegance to it, I supposed, but it also seemed a bit clichéd. Melodramatic.

"Care to share?"

"July twenty-first, 1996. The day Raymond Lee Dwyer committed his last murder."

The toxic memories threatened to surface like flop sweat. Anchoring myself in the present, I focused my attention on the desk, the file folders, the buzzing overhead lights, Ben's slack-jawed expression.

"You really think that's it?" He laced his fingers together, resting them on his head like he was trying to catch his breath after a sudden sprint.

"I do."

"How can you be sure?"

"I just know."

He wanted to say something, but whatever it was caught audibly in his throat. He exhaled, letting his hands fall into his lap. "Yeah, okay. When you know, you know, I guess."

I eyed him cautiously. "You're on board with this?"

"Seems like it."

"Great. You and I only have a few days to prep."

But then he shook his head resolutely. "No, no, no. If we're going where I think we're going, that location is part of the FBI... Ahh..." He nodded slowly. "It's not anymore."

I grinned despite myself. "Exactly. If they think it's Dylan, then by their logic, Gwen Masters' attack couldn't be related. Dylan was in custody at the time."

"We're Homicide, though. Gwen Masters' attack doesn't fall to us."

I shrugged. "Then we don't go there for *her*. Her attack took place on Eighth Street, right? We still have the unsolved murder of Victor Aguirre that occurred only seven blocks from there. Aguirre was beaten then stabbed to death—"

"Yeah, I remember," he countered impatiently.

"If Gwen isn't technically a woman, as some in the FBI seem to believe, then, again, by their logic, she's a man. Which means we have a *second* man who was beaten up in a back alley within a seven-block radius of an unsolved homicide." I conjured my most serious expression, masking the excitement building inside me at finally, *finally* knowing my next move on this case. "I dunno about you, Detective Escobar, but I'm thinking both attacks could have been committed by the same person. The Back Alley Bandit."

Ben scrubbed a palm over the minute stubble on his jaw but remained silent, staring at his keyboard. Finally, he sighed. "You still have that stupid-ass wig?"

FIFTY-TWO

July 21st, 2018

45 days since Blackstenius murder

It was dusk after a long summer day when I found myself on the doorstep of the Escobar home in a town just south of Austin. Our shift had finished a few hours previous, and for once, I'd left the station when I was scheduled to.

Buda was more of a suburb of Austin than a town all its own, and Ben got a gold star in my book for moving south of the city limits rather than north. Slightly less repressed.

Only slightly, though.

Shopping had taken longer than expected. I'd had to hit three stores before I found what I was looking for. Seemed red wasn't in this season.

A plastic shopping bag around my wrist swung and knocked into the front door just as my knuckles did. Then the door opened, and I was left staring at empty air. I lowered my gaze. Audrey smiled at me. "Hi, Dana."

The little girl looked so much like her mother that no one would've blamed Ben for requesting a paternity test. Especially not after how that woman had run around on him.

It wasn't just the little girl's darker skin that favored her mother, but every feature. She had big, round eyes, a giant smile, and a heart-shaped face—none of which could be traced back to Ben.

"Your dad home?"

"Yeah, he's cleaning up the dishes." The ten-year-old leaned forward and whispered, "He doesn't want you to know we have a dirty house."

"Nothing wrong with a dirty house."

Aubrey nodded emphatically. "That's what I *told* him. I said you wouldn't care." Her eyes dropped down to the bags. "What are those?"

"How about I come in and show you?"

Ben was drying his hands on a dishtowel when I followed Audrey into the living room. There was a clear view of the kitchen from there, and he turned around only after starting the dishwasher. He eyed the bags. "Looks like you got quite the haul."

I set the burden down on the couch. "I wasn't sure what size dress you wore, so I had to get a few things."

He pressed his lips into a thin line and hitched a brow at me.

"I know, I know," I said. "You wouldn't be caught dead. That's too bad, really." I flashed a grin Audrey's way. "Wouldn't you like to see what your dad looks like as a woman?"

Audrey giggled and nodded. "Are you two going undercover?"

"Sort of," I said. "I'm going somewhere that has a dress code to fit in."

"I'm not invited inside," Ben explained. "Dana just wants the attention for herself."

I scoffed. Our planning had had nothing to do with who wanted to dress for the drag bar and everything to do with how stupid and dangerous the operation was, given what we knew.

Though I'd never say it outright, Audrey played a major role in why I'd refused Ben's offer to go in while I hung back. The only person who'd miss me if things went wrong was Sadie, and she would have a good home with Ariadna if it came to that.

Audrey looked up at me wide-eyed. "Who are you going undercover as?"

Ben strolled farther into the living room. "Dana is going undercover as a woman."

I shot him a glare then turned to Audrey. "I'm just dressing up. Bought some new clothes for the occasion."

"You get the shoes?" Ben asked.

I wrinkled my nose. "Sort of."

"Dana."

"I already told you I don't do heels. Now would be a hell of a time to start."

"Are they at least red?"

I pointed at him. "Yes, I did manage that much. And I treated myself to a new outfit."

Ben chuckled. "Makes sense. It's a big day for you."

"Here's hoping."

Ten minutes later, I stepped out of their guest bathroom in the new outfit.

Ben, who was relaxing on the couch, looked over. His mouth fell open.

Good sign. It hadn't been easy to put together a sharp look that would blend in, didn't make me look like a cop, and, most importantly, wouldn't trip me up in a foot pursuit. That was a lot of requirements to fulfill at once.

I'd opted for black because I didn't know much about the other colors of the rainbow in terms of fashion. Except for the shoes. I went with candy-apple red for those. Flats.

"You look *hot!*" Aubrey exclaimed.

I laughed, feeling some of the self-consciousness that went along with putting in a little effort start to melt away. "What do you think, Ben? Do I look hot?" I kicked out a leg, striking a pose.

He'd managed to shut his lolling mouth fairly quickly, and now he said, "Gorgeous. You definitely pass as a woman."

Audrey wasn't allowed to see the next part of the process, so Ben sent her off to play in the backyard.

He stepped up behind me and tried to reach down the back of my shirt first, the battery pack of the mic clutched in one hand. My boatneck tee allowed for a little room, but not enough.

"The bottom," I said. "Just pull it up."

He did, and I shuddered at the sudden contrast of his warm fingers and the cool air conditioning hitting my lower back at once.

"I don't know if this is going to fit on the bra strap," he said. "It's pretty tight back here."

That would be the new bra. I'd treated myself to a black one while I was out but had completely forgotten that it would need to carry some weight. Lace might not have been the best choice.

"The pack's not that heavy," I said. "Keep trying."

He did a few more times before pulling his hands back and tossing the mic onto the couch with a frustrated grunt. I turned to face him. "Give it to me; I'll do it myself."

"Did you have to buy the sexiest bra you could find for this? Are you trying to arrest Scott or seduce him?"

I glared at him. "Easy on the judgment. Almost sounds like you're jealous that I didn't buy it just for you." I reached past him and grabbed the mic clip. "The front will hold it." I pulled my shirt up to access the reinforced and padded cups.

"Jesus, Capone."

"Let me know if you glimpse anything you don't know the name for."

When I got the pack into place, I shimmied my shirt back down and looked up. Ben was no longer averting his gaze.

Blood pulsed loudly in my ears, but it was just anticipation for the plan ahead. Obviously.

"Can you tell it's there?" I realized after I'd said it that I was essentially asking my partner to closely examine my bust.

He stepped closer, cocking his head to the side for a better look. A sly grin danced at the corners of his lips. "Looks good to me."

I shoved him back. "You dog."

He laughed, and I reached in one of the bags and grabbed the final piece of my outfit: a faux-leather jacket to help obscure the shape of the wires and my shoulder holster. No way I was going in unarmed. It was by no means jacket season, but at least I wouldn't be melting under that goddamn wig.

Holster, sidearm, then jacket. I rolled my shoulders and moved my arms to test out my mobility. It allowed for a good bit of it, but I hoped that wouldn't be necessary.

"Hold still." Ben grabbed a tag that I'd missed on one of the sleeves and pulled it off.

"Can I ask you something?" I said.

He nodded.

"I'm well aware that you're putting your job on the line here, and there are exponentially more ways this could backfire on you than go the way we're hoping."

"That's true."

"Why are you helping me?"

He crossed his arms, and his attention fell toward the tan carpet. He was silent, thinking, then looked up again. "I guess I'm just sick and tired of being wrong about you being right."

We were close enough that the tiny flecks of gold in the deep, swirling browns of his irises glistened in the overhead lighting, and a truth about him struck me for the first time.

A knock on the door pulled my attention, and as Ben unfolded his arms to answer it, Audrey came zooming through the living room from the backyard. "I'll get it!"

"Probably the babysitter," he explained. And a moment later, I heard a singsong voice at the door. Audrey showed the woman, who couldn't be more than college age, into the living room.

"Hey, Sabrina," Ben said. "Thanks for coming so last minute. This is my partner—"

"Dana." I stepped toward and shook her hand before grinning back at him. "Ready for the drag bar?"

Then Sabrina looked at him with new eyes.

Ben exhaled slowly. "*Ay dios mio.*"

"Don't want to be late and miss the acts," I said before whispering to the babysitter, "He pouts when he misses the opener."

"That's not— It's work," he spluttered.

Audrey had been following the conversation with an intense expression. "What's a drag bar?"

Ben shot me a glare, then said, "Don't worry about it, baby. I won't be home until you're asleep, but I'll see you in the morning." He leaned down and kissed her forehead, hesitating before finally turning toward the door. As he passed me, he muttered, "Let's get this shit over with."

FIFTY-THREE

The pulse of the club pulled me closer, and I claimed my place in line. Ben had dropped me off a few blocks down, and the bass had cut through the clatter of downtown immediately.

The bouncer, a wide though not necessarily muscular Caucasian man with a long and crooked nose, eyed me with suspicion when I finally arrived in front of him. I ran a quick mental check to see if I might've forgotten some crucial step to looking like your average thirty-something on the town, but before I got very far, he nodded me through without even asking for my ID.

Damn. I hadn't realized I looked that old.

I flashed him a grin, then entered Sheep's Clothing, passing into another world.

The bass from the speakers enveloped me completely. I could hardly hear myself think. Colorful track lighting splashed pink and green and blue down otherwise jet-black walls, and the air carried an oppressive aroma, like someone had sprayed the whole place down with a firehose of old beer and cheap perfume. Maybe a dusting of baby powder to top it off.

It was only a few degrees cooler inside than it was out, and as I made my way deeper inside, the fake leather jacket began sticking to my arms.

The show started at ten, in fifteen minutes, so I only had a little time to get myself set up somewhere before the real crowd packed in.

While Ben drove, I'd refreshed myself on the billing for tonight's show. The lineup was a string of performances by queens with names like Tricky Dixon and Mildred Fierce.

My guess was that the show would draw a sizable crowd.

And in that crowd would be the man I was looking for. The one who'd killed at least three women, but probably many, many more.

I didn't know his exact play, just that it'd be at Sheep's Clothing tonight. His letters had spelled that much out with his mention of the lone wolf and culling the herd. Was he hoping I wouldn't put the pieces together so he could gloat? Or was he hoping I would so I could meet him at his finale?

It was the second option that kept me on high alert as I slipped onto an open seat at the bar.

As subtly as I could, I tried out my small tan earpiece in this louder environment. "Escobar, can you hear me?"

Ben's voice came back through our private channel, but I couldn't make out the exact words.

I leaned casually to the side, plugging my other ear. "Say that again?"

This time I could make out his words, but only just. *"I hear you. Sounds like a party."*

A man and woman, both wearing plaid shirts but in different colors, chatted on the stools to my left. To my right, two men made out sloppily. Seemed a little early in the night for that degree of drunkenness, but I wasn't so much judging as jealous. It'd been a while since I'd had the pleasure of making out with anyone, let alone while drunk in public on a Saturday night.

A sudden longing to trade places overtook me, however pointless that was. I'd only ever end up in a place like this on an investigation, and even then, I'd be there alone. I couldn't keep people around, period.

I tossed a grin the bartender's way. She eyed me appraisingly and must not have found anything especially objectionable, because once she'd finished serving a customer on the other side of the lip-locked men, she headed my way.

The bar was a long oval in the middle of the establishment. There was a dance floor on one side of it and a stage with a catwalk on the other. I'd put my back to the dance floor to have a clear view of the stage.

"What can I get you, love?" I sensed that the bartender's British accent was about as real as the mile-long rainbow eyelashes she was wearing. Maybe if she blinked rapidly enough, I could get a little air circulation in this muggy place.

"Just soda and lime, please."

Graciously, she didn't give me a hard time for skipping the alcohol but nodded, fixed the drink, and slid it toward me. I pulled a five from my clutch, but she waved it away. "Water is free, babes. The bubbles and lime are on me."

I put the cash on the bar anyway. "Then it's a tip. For this one and the next."

She grinned flirtatiously. "Look at you getting hydrated out on the town." And then she winked, the light catching the metallic threads in her eyelashes, and stuck the five into the tip jar closest to her.

Though one of my more reliable informants had already drawn me up a floor plan of this place, this was my first time inside. I would've come myself to scope it out, but I had a feeling Scott would be waiting for that to happen, that he'd somehow find out. I couldn't explain how he'd know that, and according to recent FBI intel (that Ben may or may not have leaked to me), Scott hadn't been anywhere around the drag bar lately. He hadn't even gone to Laugh Attack since being released from custody.

Heidi, in the meantime, practically lived there now. Couldn't exactly blame her. Surveillance said she'd moved most of her essentials to a cousin's condo downtown before Scott was released. Smart lady. Even if she didn't buy that he was a serial killer, she knew those ties under the guest bedroom mattress weren't for her. Whatever got her out from under a roof with him was fine by me.

It wasn't ideal, running an operation in a place I'd never physically been, but it was by no means unheard of. You had to make do with what you had when you were up against a time crunch like this. If Scott had really decided July twenty-first was the day he would make what he believed to be his final play before disappearing, we had to do something. And with Agent Wicklow and ASAC Grissom following the trail of Dylan—perhaps because there *was* no trail and that allowed them to focus on other things—I had no moral choice but to put my career on the line. Again. After all, people got fired all the time. But not everyone had a chance to trap a killer to keep him from taking more lives. For me, the stakes had always been higher than continued employment.

I sipped my drink and oriented myself according to the informant's description, locating the hall to the bathrooms, the emergency exit that led to a set of stairs onto the roof. Only one out of every four or five people in the place was dressed in drag, and the rest seemed to be the typical young Austinites, some from the LGBTQ community, others likely just allies. But all of them fawned over the queens like they were genuine royalty. It was nice. These people had probably spent most of their lives feeling like outcasts, and now that they were out and proud, free to be themselves in their own way, they had become local celebrities. If only there were a place like Sheep's Clothing for everyone, a place where your authentic self was glorified and protected.

Well, maybe "protected" wasn't quite right. Not tonight. Not with a killer on the loose.

I set my empty glass on the counter and motioned to the bartender that I was ready for the second. She dropped it off, but my attention had wandered over to the catwalk lit up in pink and green flashing lights, sitting empty until the first act could take the stage in a few more minutes.

Almost as if I'd summoned her into existence, a woman in a red leather catsuit prowled up the stairs, microphone in hand.

I felt a buzzing in my ear. Ben was trying to say something, but I couldn't make it out. I acted like I was tucking my hair behind my other ear, but plugged it instead. "Come again?"

He repeated himself, but it was no good. The emcee had begun warming up the crowd, and the overwhelmed mic pulsing through the speakers overhead left me no chance of understanding Ben's words. Looked like this communication was a one-way street.

The area by the stage had filled in more tightly with bodies, standing room only. I squeezed the lime wedge into my drink and took a quick sip as the emcee warmed up the crowd. "Ladies and not-so-*gentle*men, kings and *queens*"—the audience went wild at that, and the room became truly electric—"we've got some real glamazons lined up for you tonight."

"You new here?" came a voice from behind me. I turned to look at him, already knowing who would be there, who'd taken the place of the man and woman in plaid.

Beneath my jacket, the hair stood up on my arms. My eyes locked on to the tan, unreadable face of Scott Ruiz.

"Right on time," I said, not bothering with pretenses.

He'd ditched his usual Austin hippie attire of tie-dye and flip-flops and was instead dressed head to toe in black. He flagged down the bartender, and when she noticed him, she grabbed a bottle of whiskey off the shelf, poured him two fingers, and set it in front of him without him having to ask. As his attention was elsewhere, I let my gaze travel down to his feet. There they were. The boots. I was seeing him in his business attire for the very first time. He planned on making another kill tonight; I was sure of it. But who did he have his eye on?

Right now, it was me. His eyes traveled down my body, and a hint of a grin turned his lips when he found my red shoes. "Sort of asking for it in those, don't you think?" He waved a ten in the air so the bartender would see it before slapping the bill on the bar.

"You sure you should be drinking alcohol right now?" I

said. "If I were you, I'd want to keep my wits about me so I could make it out of here in something other than handcuffs or a body bag."

A half-grin tilted the corner of his thin lips while the rest of his face showed no visible signs of mirth. "I have no idea what you mean. You don't have a single thing on me, Dana. That's why *you're* here, and not the FBI or that handsome partner of yours. Speaking of him, have y'all slept together yet? I've been going back and forth on that."

"I know you orchestrated those letters to the *Statesman*, even though they were in Dylan's handwriting. Otherwise, *you* wouldn't be here." I took a drink, eyes glued to him, searching not for confirmation of my suspicions—I didn't need that—but some sign of his plan tonight.

"You may think you know something about me in that dark little heart of yours," Scott went on, "but that doesn't make it evidence. You don't know anything about me."

"I know you're holding Dylan Fowler captive somewhere. That was how you ended up with his phone and keys in your office. That Mike Check story was bullshit. So, how'd you do it? How'd you overpower someone Dylan's size? Where are you keeping him?"

His chuckle was like a jackhammer cutting through the dense cacophony around us. "Holy *hell*. For someone who said she knows things, you really don't have a clue. How could I be 'keeping him' somewhere when the FBI is on my ass night and day? I'll tell you: I can't. It's not possible. You think you got this figured out, but you're way off. You've got the wrong guy with Dylan. The FBI ought to have told you that much."

"You had one of Raymond's paintings in your home," I said, steadying my tone. I couldn't let a man like this find a fingerhold in my emotions, especially when a hairline crack was all he needed. "You must know all about how *that* went down, maybe even a little about my childhood," I continued. "So you should also know better than to think I can't smell bullshit like yours from a mile away. I grew up knee-deep in it."

"Tell me, if you're so sure I have something to do with Dylan's disappearance, how come the FBI isn't here instead of you?"

"You don't know they aren't."

The music continued to blare, and waves of shouted glee from the enthusiastic audience threatened to overpower Scott's restrained voice entirely. Luckily, I was so keyed in on him that I could've read his lips if I had to.

"Oh, yes, I do," he said. "The Feds have been tracking my cell phone. I believe they're tracking my car as well. The in-person tail stopped yesterday, though, so that's been a nice little surprise." This was news to me, if there was any truth to it. I wouldn't have put it past Wicklow to do something so stupid just to double down on his theory, though. "I left my phone at home tonight," Scott continued, "and I borrowed my neighbor's truck. Feds haven't followed me. And from everything I've heard, if they truly believed I would be in this place at this time, they wouldn't have sent traumatized little Dana Dwyer in as their eyes and ears."

"Capone."

He took another swig and swished it around in his mouth. "You change it to sound tough?"

"No. It's my mother's maiden name. I figured if I had to choose, I'd go with Capone. Old Al killed fewer people, after all."

Scott arched his eyebrows. "Did he?"

"Thirty-three, it's said, and most of those were carried out by his cronies. Raymond allegedly killed thirty-eight, and he didn't have any help with that."

"Allegedly? You don't think he did it?"

Applause broke out behind me from the direction of the stage as the first act wrapped up. I let it settle before continuing.

"Oh, Raymond did it. He killed all thirty-eight. I just happen to know there were a whole hell of a lot *more*."

Scott grinned. "He was good at what he did."

"Being evil? Sure, but it's not hard once you commit to it. Being good is the tricky bit."

He tilted his head to the side, inspecting me like I was a lab rat. "I gotta ask: why don't you call him Dad? Denying he's blood?" He motioned at me with his glass. "Or are you hoping that your real nature can be hidden in plain sight behind that badge?"

"Nice try."

"And you're wrong. Raymond didn't do it all on his own. He probably could have, but he didn't. He had help." Scott smirked.

"Jesus. You gonna try to take credit for his murders now?"

"*Me?* Hell no. I didn't know about him till he hit the news. I'm talking about you."

"That's bullshit."

"It sounds like you genuinely believe that. But do you remember every moment of your life back then? Or are there some... blank spots?"

A thick smog wafted through my mind, trapping me in a limbo between the past and the present. I struggled to keep my focus on him while also groping around for proof that what he'd said couldn't be true.

"You were *complicit*, Dana. You found out about your dad's *real* works of art long before you reported anything. And in the meantime, you became his little *apprentice*. The FBI must have taken mercy on you, young as you were. But should they have? I don't know. I see him in you. You like the hunt just as much as he did."

"Fuck you." But as relieved as I was that I'd managed to force out some sort of words, I knew it was too late. He'd more than found that fingerhold—he'd sunk his claws in deep.

"That man you shot back in February. I heard about it on the news. Another cop, even. Your father was proud, I'm sure." He grinned. "You didn't have to shoot him, did you? But you wanted to."

The ugly end to the Rochelle case flashed before me—Sarah's limp body on the kitchen floor, her husband cornered, trying to find a way out, ready to take another life if he had to... "He'd already killed two people. He had a gun and pointed it at me."

"Come on, Dana. You wanted him dead. And you wanted to be the one to do it."

"Nice try. Where's Dylan?" My heart was racing wildly now. He'd found all the ways to get to me, but I had to hold on, to keep focused on the reason I was there. This wasn't about me. This was about Dylan and the women Scott had murdered for sport.

"You know," he said, then paused to take a swig of his whiskey, "from the very first time I laid eyes on Marie, I was hooked. It was right here." He motioned toward the catwalk. "She was up on stage, singing some Broadway song, romancing everyone in the crowd. It was beautiful to see someone so in their element. I couldn't get her out of my mind. She was perfection. Absolute fucking perfection.

"How the hell had she found it? That was the question I got stuck on. Does a man wake up one day and just *know* he needs to put on a dress, fake tits, and high heels? What were the evolutionary steps between Dylan's miserable daily existence that he riffed on at my club and Marie's glowing celebration of life? It boggles the mind. I tried to understand it for months, but eventually, I gave in and accepted that I never could. Not me. I was made differently." His attention homed back in on me. "There was only one thing left to do with her, then. One thing I wanted more than anything."

"Where's Dylan?" I asked again. "Where's Marie?"

Something in his expression shifted, and for a moment, I felt like I was back in Raymond's studio, staring into the true face of evil.

Then Scott's mask slid back into place. "How's Sadie?"

The skin prickled on the back of my neck, and my muscles filled with the need to run. Not away from him, but toward home.

"You thought I didn't know about her?" he said. "About the one thing you care most for in this world? Well, besides Detective Escobar."

"If you so much as—" But I never got to finish the threat. Over the speakers, the emcee said something that tipped all of my mental alarms at once.

"...welcome tonight's surprise guest, Marie Possa!"

I twisted toward the stage, putting my back to Scott just in time to see something large drop like a colorful bedazzled sack from the shadowed ceiling beams. But it didn't make it down to the catwalk before the rope attached to it snapped tight.

The crowd gasped then began screaming.

Oh, god. No. It couldn't be him...

In candy-apple-red heels, a tight sequined dress, and massive silken butterfly wings, Dylan's body swung a foot in the air at the end of the rope. I couldn't see his face, couldn't make out if his eyes were open, if he was still alive when he'd dropped. As long as his neck hadn't snapped.

I only had seconds to reach him, to take the pressure off his neck, to stabilize him if he had any chance of surviving.

"Escobar!" I shouted, hoping he could hear me through the earpiece. "Get in here now!"

Pushing my way through the confused crowd, I climbed onto the waist-high catwalk and grabbed Dylan around the thighs, lifting him as best I could to try to take pressure off his neck. The sequined dress offered me a little textured grip, but this wasn't the best approach.

"We gotta get him down," I said to two people in drag who'd hopped up to help. Both were taller than me, stronger too. One of them took my place, lifting him. That freed me up to dig in my pocket for my knife. How I would reach high enough to cut the rope was anyone's guess.

I turned, scanning the crowd for Ben, and instead my eyes landed on Scott Ruiz. Pleasure flowed from him in unmissable waves.

This was what he'd been working to the whole time, wasn't it? Marie Possa's body on display, the tableau of chaos. Maybe even the decision I now faced.

He'd coordinated it all for this precise moment. And now it was here. The bastard thought he'd won.

Maybe he had.

With every second counting, I grabbed the shoulders of the drag queen beside me, staring her dead in her eyes. "Your only job is to get him down." I handed her the knife.

"Escobar!" I shouted, not daring to take my eyes off Scott to continue searching for my backup. "Dylan is here. On the catwalk. He needs aid *now*."

My job was to protect the innocent, and right then, one was swinging by his neck less than a yard away from me. Did I stay or go?

The image of Sarah Boudreaux bleeding on her kitchen floor came back to me. Maybe if I'd stayed with her instead of pursuing her husband to his death, her kids would still have a mother.

This was my chance to make a different choice. This was my chance.

Which was why it made me sick what I was about to do. Deep in my marrow, this decision had already been made long ago.

Scott grinned at me, winked, and then took off into the crowd.

He'd been right about one thing: I was a predator. And predators hunt.

"Escobar," I shouted, "Ruiz is heading out the back. I'm in pursuit."

FIFTY-FOUR

I burst through the emergency exit after him and found myself facing the brick exterior of the building beside Sheep's Clothing. Down the narrow alley to my right, I could see Eighth Street, and to my left was a set of rusty stairs leading up onto the roof. Which way had he gone?

Then I heard the clatter of metal above me. I drew my gun from my shoulder holster, hoping I wouldn't have to use it, and raced for the stairs.

"Escobar," I said as loudly as I dared, "I'm heading up the stairs to the roof. Radio in for backup."

Where was Scott going? Did he think he could hide from me? Unless there was another set of stairs leading from the roof, he had just backed himself into a corner.

The idea gave me little comfort. Someone like him wasn't made *less* dangerous with nowhere left to go.

I reached the top landing and paused, taking in the surroundings, letting my eyes adjust to the still night. It wasn't completely dark—the moon was large and lights from the surrounding bars and clubs soaked into the atmosphere—but the bright security lights at the bottom of the stairs had impaired my night vision enough to warrant a moment of adjustment before charging on.

The layout of the roof came into focus. It was flat, covered in black tar, but with more visual obstructions than I'd have preferred—large exhaust vents, a wall around the edge that cut in at places, and what looked like a storage shed of some kind. Hiding places.

There didn't seem to be another set of stairs, so unless there was a secret escape hatch, Scott was up there. Only, I couldn't see him.

Maybe he jumped. We weren't terribly high up. He might've made the landing with little more than a sprain, and then he'd be gone. Or maybe he'd land at a bad angle, hit his head, and that would be the end of it for him. And the end of true justice for his victims.

I didn't think he'd jumped, though. If he wanted to escape easily, he wouldn't have taken the stairs in the first place. He had other plans. Plans I was undeniably a part of.

My stealth was gone by the time I'd climbed the rickety metal stairs, so I called out to him. "Scott. I know you're up here. Just come out with your hands up, and we can make this easy."

I waited, creeping forward. Behind the storage building seemed the most likely hiding place. It was also the nearest one to me. The roof creaked beneath my steps as I kept the gun out in front of me. Only a few feet away from it...

I approached it on my left, keeping my breath steady, *expecting* to find him so the surprise of it wouldn't cause me to overreact. He would be there, and I would *not* pull that trigger.

...however much I want to.

I paused. Listened. Heard nothing.

I rounded the corner.

He wasn't there.

Something moved on my right instead.

Scott lunged before I could turn, and there was a sudden slash of heat across the back of my forearm, causing me to lose my grip on my gun. It clattered to the rooftop.

He lunged again. Rather than snatching up my weapon, I deflected his knife strike. I grabbed hold of his dominant wrist, the one that wielded the blade, but his strength surprised me. He shook free.

When going up against someone with a knife, you expected to get cut. There was no getting around it. My goal was to be slashed up as little as possible before I could disarm him.

"I don't want to kill you, Dana."

He sure had a funny way of showing it. He swung again, and I ducked and managed to roll out of the way. I needed distance between us almost as much as I needed to get a hand on my gun again. But Scott stood in my path for that.

"Drop the knife. If you don't want to kill me, drop it."

With his focus entirely on me, he didn't notice the loaded gun behind him. If he had, he could have ended things right there.

His facade could no longer contain the evil rupturing from him like blood from a severed artery. His eyes were black, irises swallowed completely by gluttonous pupils.

"Just say you did it, and I won't have to kill you."

He smirked. "Did what?"

"Killed those four women."

"Four?" He cackled, and I waited for him to deny it. Instead, he said, "Oh, Dana, it was way more than four."

"Where are the rest of them?"

"Around."

His next blow was directed at my side, but I recognized tunnel vision when I saw it. Rather than waiting, I kicked, taking his plant leg out from under him. He swung the knife down. I deflected his arm in time to avoid serious injury, but the blade still found me, slicing across my bicep. I grunted as the night air hit my fresh blood.

Somehow, I managed to get out of the way as his momentum carried him forward. I assisted him with an extra shove, and he skidded face-first across the roof.

No time to gloat. He still had his weapon.

"Drop the knife!"

I rushed forward, crushing his wrist beneath my foot. The pain caused him to loosen his grip, and I brought my other foot around to kick the knife free. It went skittering across the tarred surface.

But that was a mistake. My feet were too close together now.

He chopped at the back of my left knee. It buckled just enough to cede my advantage. He shoved me forward with his free arm, and I went down onto my knees. As I caught myself with my hands, his arm slipped free. *He* slipped free. But he didn't go for the knife. I spun as he rushed for the gun ten yards away from us.

Shit! He had a head start. I couldn't beat him. But maybe I could stop him.

I slipped off one of my red flats and hurled it as hard as I could. It hit him in the back, causing him to turn. Was it enough? I was on my feet again, my other shoe in hand, racing toward the firearm.

He beat me to it, his hand nearly on the barrel when I chucked the other shoe and caught him in the back of the head. He missed his grab. Lowering my body, I hit him from behind.

He tumbled forward, and I hardly kept my feet underneath me.

And then I had it. My fingers gripped the gun, still warm from my touch. "Stay down!" Panting, I leveled it at him as he rolled slowly onto his back.

He stared up at me, his chest heaving.

"Sit up slowly, hands on your head."

He complied.

I was in control now. I knew where he was, and I had the gun. But being able to breathe again also meant feeling, and the cuts on my arms began demanding attention.

"Escobar. I have him on the roof." Who knew what Ben was already dealing with inside the bar? Had he heard my call for backup? Was anyone coming? "I have Ruiz."

Time to get the cuffs on him. I would feel better the instant he had them on. I reached for the set in my jacket pocket but came up empty. Shit. They must have fallen out during the grapple. But where? I couldn't take my eyes off him to search. Too risky with an asshole like this.

"Just do it, Dana." Scott grinned. "Just pull the trigger. Indulge that urge."

"Shut up. You're done. You get to face justice the long and tedious way."

"You didn't have to follow me, but you did."

"I said shut up."

I should have closed in on him, told him to keep his

hands in the air, and shoved his wrists behind his back. I could have held him until other officers arrived.

But something stopped me. I didn't know what. He repulsed me, maybe that was it, but I would have done as well trying to walk through a solid brick wall as close the distance between us.

"You really don't remember," he said, shaking his head pityingly.

"Shut—"

"You were there. You *helped* him." Scott's chuckle was like a wave of automatic gunfire. "I'm telling you, it's in your blood. The department might not see it—"

"Stop talking."

"But others do."

In my ear: *"Capone, where are you?"*

Thank fuck. "On the roof. I've got Ruiz."

Scott grinned. "You so sure of that? Last chance to shoot me in cold blood, Capone. Claim you had to."

"Oh, please, you don't want to die."

He shrugged, his hands leaving his head to rise higher in the air. "I've done all I needed to do. Dylan is dead. No more fun time for me, I'm afraid."

My stomach lurched at his casual words. Had he killed Dylan before ever bringing him to the club? He *had* to have. And I must've known it deep down. Why else would Ben already be looking for me? There was nothing left to do for the victim.

Dylan was dead.

The blood pulsed angrily in my fingertips, and I tried not to clutch my weapon too tightly. "You want someone to make a martyr out of you? Is that it?"

Ben would have his cuffs with him. I could stall until that time.

"This isn't about martyrdom, Dana. It's about nature. Your nature. I want to help you. We all do."

I heard the back door to the club slam, but I didn't breathe a sigh of relief yet. I couldn't do that until Scott was safely tucked away in the back of a squad car. The smug little fucker wouldn't stop trying to get loose. People like him always thought there was a way out.

And, unfortunately, for people like him, there usually was.

Scott's attention shifted hurriedly toward the stairs, toward the sound of Ben's footsteps. I didn't like that at all.

"Stay where you are. Don't move!"

He spared me one last triumphant smirk before he plunged his right hand toward his waistband.

No, please, no.

Drawing a small pistol from the back of his belt, he aimed it right at the top of the stairs.

The choice in front of me was so easy, there was almost no choice at all.

I fired three shots into Scott Ruiz.

FIFTY-FIVE

July 27th, 2018

Six days later

"Looks like heaven, Sean," I said as the bartender slid two pints our way. It was just the two of us, Ben and me—not counting the other guests packed into McNelly's on a Friday night—and that was how I preferred it now.

It would have been ideal if I could have brought Sadie along. Finding her safe and sound at Ariadna's apartment after Scott's insinuations had been one of the biggest reliefs of my life, and I was finding it hard to leave her even for short periods of time. Thankfully, I supposed, I'd had almost nowhere to be for the last week.

I raised my drink.

"The hell are we toasting to?" he asked.

"To you picking up the bill."

"Least I can do for someone who saved my life."

I rolled my eyes. "Stop it with that bullshit."

"It's not bullshit."

"It is. Fat chance that bastard could've hit you from that far away before you got a shot off yourself."

"Stranger things have happened."

I still couldn't believe Scott had stashed a gun in his belt. The only slack I cut myself on that front was that any sane person would assume a criminal with *both* a gun and a knife would go for the gun first, not the knife. But he'd had both, and he'd opted to fight me with a knife. Had he been serious about not wanting to kill me?

Ben's eyes found my bandaged forearm, and his grin faded.

I groaned and sipped my drink before he could ruin it with his somber mood. "I'm fine. Jesus. I've cut myself worse shaving my legs."

"I know you're fine," he said. "You can handle yourself."

I changed the subject. "You gonna give me the scoop?"

The whole point of this rendezvous, beer aside, was to debrief. He'd just come from a meeting that I had *not* been invited to, funnily enough. A side effect of being on administrative leave.

I wasn't bitter about it, believe me. At least I still technically had my job. That wouldn't be the case if we'd been wrong about Scott. Well, if *I'd* been wrong about Scott, since it was my suspicion that had dragged Ben into the shitstorm in the first place.

Ben took a swig and stared absently at something over my shoulder for a moment—I tried to guess if it was a drunk or a busty woman—then began to fill me in. "Popov said it was privileged information I'm absolutely not allowed to pass along. I think he specifically means to you."

"Cut the foreplay. Everyone knows you're gonna tell

me. Jesus, can't you identify a cover-your-ass statement when you hear it? Sarge just had to get that on the books. Now spill."

He rolled his eyes. "They still don't have any strong physical evidence against Ruiz."

I shrugged. "I'm not especially worried about that, now that arresting him is out of the question. It's not like he's gonna be murdering women from the grave."

"The good news," he continued, "is that they've officially dropped Dylan Fowler as a suspect."

"No shit?" I feigned shock. "Wow, the FBI is really going above and beyond on this one. Must've flown in a whole panel of psychologists to piece *that* one together... after Ruiz confessed to the murders right in front of me."

Ben blew by my sarcasm. "I get the feeling their plan is to give it a few months to cool off, then move this investigation forward slowly. They don't want to be wrong again."

"Guess I can't blame them." Confessions had been bullshit before, I supposed.

"As long as no more victims turn up, they'll move forward with the formal charges against Ruiz."

"It's a damn shame he won't get to rot in jail."

"You didn't have a choice, Dana."

He wasn't wrong. But he wasn't completely right. He assumed I didn't have a choice because Scott had pointed that damn gun at him. But I was starting to suspect I'd had no choice but to kill that bastard long before Ben ever set foot on those stairs.

"Any update on Dylan?" I asked. It'd been impossible for me to keep up when I didn't have access to any of my usual work materials or databases, and calling him directly was out—no way he'd want to hear from me, and I shuddered to think what would happen if his mother answered his phone.

Scott had lied to me about Dylan—not exactly shocking. Dylan *had* been alive when he dropped from the ceiling. The reason for the lie wasn't hard to decipher: Scott had *wanted* me to kill him. I hadn't unknotted that yet.

How did Dylan see me now? Little Dana Dwyer, practically an urban legend from his youth, the daughter of pure evil. He found me again, reunited as if by fate, and decided to play with fire.

Sweet Jesus, how he'd been burned. I must be like the boogeyman to him. Or the boogeywoman. Either way, I imagined he'd more eagerly welcome a visit in the ICU from a hooded figure wielding a scythe than from me.

"Released from the hospital yesterday," Ben said. "I read over his statement, and"—he exhaled sharply—"that's some batshit insane stuff."

Sean slid a basket of fish and chips across the counter to us. "Y'all looked like you could use a little something to go with your beer. On me."

Ben waved his thanks, and I nodded mine before picking up the conversation again. "Have they located where he was being kept?"

"Nope. He said he was held in the dark somewhere. A man—Scott, presumably—brought him food and water. There was a toilet for him to use, but it wasn't connected to sewage. Like, it didn't flush or something. A latrine, I guess? Is that the word? The transcript made it sound more like an outhouse than a shed or anything like that."

"Delightful."

"Fowler claims he was lured to Laugh Attack the night he was abducted. An unknown number called him, and when he answered, it was Scott Ruiz. Made it sound like he had something important to talk about. Dylan arrived at the club right as the early show was letting out. The last thing he remembers is having a drink alone with Ruiz, who was offering him Mike Check's emcee spot for open mics."

I sighed. "Didn't have Scott pegged as a poisoner, personally. Shows what I know. What a cowardly little bitch."

In the temporary lull in our conversation, the memory of the final look that had passed between Scott and me before he drew his weapon came freshly to the surface. The damn thing had been looping in my brain for almost a week, and I suspected it would keep on doing so until I could decode its full meaning.

"You okay?" Ben's voice was soft, and I didn't like the delicateness directed my way.

"I'm fine." Before he tried to argue, I said, "What I still don't get is how Scott managed it. The FBI kept an eye on him, at least at first. How did he manage to get to wherever he was holding Dylan without anyone knowing?"

"That's the question, isn't it? And you'll be thrilled to hear it's driving Agent Wicklow absolutely insane."

"I'll drink to that. Have they checked the Ruiz house? No basement or hidden bunker?"

"They've checked. No basement, no attic to speak of. Nothing in the backyard."

I paused. "What about Laugh Attack? Could it have a basement?"

"It *could*, but it doesn't. FBI searched there, too."

"So, where the hell was he?" It wasn't a question I

expected Ben to answer. There was only one person who could answer it, and he was dead. I'd blown his goddamn head off.

From my other side at the bar came a man's voice. "Well, look who it is!"

He seemed to know me, but I struggled to place the man's face, not because my memory was lagging, but because his was an unremarkable face, and it meant next to nothing to me. Finally, it clicked. Those Tom Hardy lips. Ah yes.

"You manage to fuck up the head start I gave you?" I asked.

"Nope. Won first place." He reached in his wallet and pulled out the McNelly's gift card my trivia skills had earned him. "Still got some money left on it. I got your next round." He winked.

"You gonna get my next drink, too?" Ben leaned forward to look past me down the length of the bar. He held up his half-empty beer.

The man's eyes widened. "Oh. I didn't know you, uh... My bad, bro. I didn't know she was taken."

To Ben's credit, he scoffed at that.

"Even if I wasn't taken," I said, "I'm not interested. I wasn't interested before, and I'm not interested now. You know why we're out here having a drink? Because I murdered a man. Shot him through the head, among other things." I grabbed a few fries and chomped off half, then grinned. "You want a woman to wreck your life, there are less lethal ones over there." I nodded toward a booth where a group of women in their night-out attire gathered around a table of empty shot glasses.

To the guy's credit, he took my advice and walked away.

I watched him go with a clinical sort of interest, and when I turned back toward the bar, Sean was staring at me, a cocktail glass in one hand, the soda gun in the other. He stuck the gun in its cradle and set down the glass, placing his palms flat on the bar in front of him. "You, my dear, sound like you're gonna need another drink."

I chuckled. "I wouldn't say no to that."

As Sean returned to making the cocktail, I stared down at my pint. Might as well finish it if there was another coming. I tossed it back.

"Look," Ben said, "I know I'm not your court-ordered psychologist, but how are you *really* doing?"

My attention shifted toward a mounted television behind the bar where Premier League highlights played. "About as good as can be expected, I guess."

"I heard everything he said to you."

I picked at one of the pieces of fried cod. He didn't have to specify who "he" was; I could tell by the tone. "Yeah, fun stuff. Great conversationalists, serial killers."

"What he said... It can't be true. And even if it was, no one could blame you for it."

"And by 'what he said,' you mean the part about me helping Raymond torture and murder women?"

"Yes, that."

I waved it off. "Don't worry about it. Scott was a psychopath. I don't believe anything people like him say."

Ben didn't look even halfway convinced. "You sure? Not even the stuff that feeds your fear of being rotten to the core?"

I jerked my head back. "What the hell are you talking about?"

"You know damn well what I'm talking about." I opened my mouth to argue, but before I could come up with anything, he added, "You made the right decisions at every step. Chasing after him instead of helping Dylan? That was the right choice."

"Was it? Scott wasn't trying to flee. If he had been, he wouldn't have gone up to the roof. He wanted to lure me. If I hadn't fallen for it, we might've been able to catch him alive."

"You don't know any of that," Ben said firmly, "so, for the love of god, just stop guessing. Whenever you start speculating, you always come up with the scenario that makes you look the worst."

I tried to act outraged, but damn if he didn't have my number tonight. "What do you mean, 'always'?"

"The Rochelle case, for one."

"Maybe we should stop calling it that. It was the Rochelle and Boudreaux case, technically."

"I thought you hated naming them after the killers."

"I do. That's not the Boudreaux I was talking about." I accepted the cold pint from Sean, thanked him, then mused, "The Blackstenius, Scopes, Lee, and..."

Ben shook his head. "They still haven't IDed the other woman."

"That's just as well. He said there were more than the four, anyway. Fucking men."

"Hey," Ben said.

"Not you, obviously." I waved him off. "One evil man can do so much damage. I guess it makes sense to name the cases after the killers. For brevity's sake."

"Let's talk about something else."

I arched a brow at him. "Like what? You have something else going on in your life?"

He chuckled darkly. "Good point."

"The Capone case," I said. "One woman, two victims. Well, two *known* victims."

"*Jesus Cristo,*" Ben muttered. "Is this a kink of yours? You get off on taking the blame for shit you can't control? If you're into that, just say the word. I'll blame you for all kinds of things. In fact, how dare you make this summer so hot. How dare you interfere with the election and get *el Pendejo Naranjo* elected. And how dare you make my marriage fall apart." He said it as a big joke, but Ben wasn't the only one with insight here. I'd known *him* a long time, too.

He gulped the rest of his pint and didn't say any more about that. That was fine by me. I flagged down Sean and ordered Ben another beer.

We grazed on the fish and chips, taking in the happenings around us, the soccer highlights on the TVs. It was only as I finished my second drink that he interrupted the silence between us.

"We should do this more often. It's nice grabbing a drink, watching average people do average things."

"Audrey at her mom's house?"

"Yep." He narrowed his eyes at me. "What do you think it's like hanging out with people who aren't cops?"

I shrugged. "Miserable? Infuriating?"

"I was thinking more along the lines of 'refreshing,' but I see your point. Would you be up for it?"

I thought of my sole non-cop friend, Maggie, though she was practically an honorary cop with all the gory details I'd shared over the years. "I'll be honest: I don't even know where to start on making new friends."

"No, not that. Forget about that. Hanging out with civilians is a terrible idea, obviously. I just mean getting drinks together more often."

"Sure," I said. "I might be up for that. Besides, I owe you at least a few nights out on my tab after I nearly lost you your job multiple times."

"Damn right you do." We clinked glasses again. "I'll assume you got this one to start, in which case, I'd better order some more food. Maybe another drink. And dessert."

Biting my lip, I resigned myself to the unfortunate fate of my checking account and gazed down at the pint in my hand. "Fine. What my baby wants, my baby gets."

FIFTY-SIX

August 3rd, 2018

I scooped up water from Lady Bird Lake with my kayak paddle, letting it drizzle off the edge and onto Sadie's head to cool her. It would've been nice to get out there earlier, but that wasn't how my schedule had worked out that morning. Sadie didn't seem to care, though. Always grateful, no matter the timing.

She shook off the remaining droplets before turning her nose to the wind again. Her sense of self-importance, perched at the front of the kayak like some essential sentinel, never failed to both calm and cheer me. No human could ever be as earnest in their emotions as a dog. Once I got to know her, she required no guesswork. She was brave enough to let it all show all the time, and in real time. No waiting until she was in the car to cry. Just for example.

I'd woken up craving the familiarity of the lake, but I'd also overslept and had an eight a.m. counseling appointment with Dr. Edgecraft, who seemed convinced that all I needed to get over the trauma of getting sliced up, taking another life, and, oh yeah, being the daughter of a serial killer was a little EMDR.

It wasn't working. Today was session six of ten, and I hadn't seen any benefits. If anything, it'd made the nightmares worse than ever. Dr. Edgecraft said that was normal, that I had to complete all ten sessions, that, like all things, it got worse before it got better. I wasn't sold. Some things just got worse and stayed that way. Some things deteriorated until they crumbled completely.

I laid the paddle across my lap and leaned back in my seat. The light but constant breeze across the water's surface cooled the sweat on my skin. It was so pleasant, so simple, that for a moment, I almost forgot.

Four women dead. Cheryl Blackstenius, Leslie Scopes, Stephanie Lee, and the Black Jane Doe that no one would officially admit was his. But I knew. Even as the case remained open in our system, I knew.

And how many more? There were always more. Always.

Was it five? Ten? Had we only found the tip of the iceberg? People went missing in Austin every day, people with no close family, no friends. People who wouldn't be missed.

People like me.

No. Not totally true, at least. Sadie would miss me. And Ariadna would at least *notice* if I never came home. It might take days, though, with how flaky I'd been about being where I said I would be and when.

Ben would notice.

My chest tightened with a warm sort of guilt. He

deserved a better partner. Only now, once the hunt was over and my tunnel vision had cleared, could I take stock of how much I'd asked of him this time around. Too much. And he gave it. I could have destroyed his entire life. Why would anyone stick their neck out like that for someone like me?

Not that road, Dana. Not today.

I couldn't let the thought creep in. Self-loathing was hard to come back from. I'd clawed my way out of the pit before, and I had no desire to do it again if I could help it.

Grabbing my water bottle, I squirted a little on my face, tasting the salt from my sweat drip down over my lips.

Sadie had her eye on a small group of ducks twenty yards off as I began rowing leisurely again, watching the water bead off the ends of the paddle with each stroke.

Who knew how many bodies were at the bottom of this murky lake? Without definitive leads for a search, the divers would never go looking for anyone. The lake was too big, the cost to taxpayers too high.

And what no one ever said but everyone knew was that the odds of divers stumbling onto something horrific they *weren't* looking for was also high. We had enough murders to solve without seeking out new ones, I supposed.

By my house growing up was a lake not unlike this one —not actually a lake at all, but a reservoir. Lake Worth was a giant eyesore with weedy vegetation around the banks. Built to store things. Did bones sit at the bottom of it, waiting to be dredged?

Every single body part hidden beneath Raymond's studio had been Caucasian. The ten they'd found in the woods by the lake, too. It was easy enough to conclude that he was only interested in murdering white women. It fit nicely into a single victim profile, and thirty-eight destroyed bodies were more than enough. Why dredge up more?

I understood that now, having been on this side of the investigation. After a certain point, you just want to put an end to it. You think, *This is plenty for us to handle. We don't want any more. Let's lock this guy up and throw away the key.*

What would the sheriffs find if they dragged Lake Worth today? Had Raymond disposed of his invisible victims there? Women who society expected to go missing? Women who didn't fit the prim victim profile?

Two decades and still no remains. Or if any had been found, they'd been attributed to someone else.

Rowing on the waters of Lady Bird Lake, beneath the honest August sun, with Sadie at the helm, I finally grew too tired. I was tired of guessing. Tired of speculating. So, so tired.

I didn't have access to the Tarrant County records, but I had access to the internet and at least one useful connection up there. IDing the Jane Doe down here would come first. Then it was time to stop guessing, to stop wondering, and to start seriously investigating.

That severed finger in my backyard had belonged to someone, after all. I hadn't imagined it.

Black women must have disappeared near White Settlement during the years Raymond Dwyer was killing. Twenty years since, now. The families of the missing were long overdue for answers. And if I wasn't going to seek them out, who would? Somewhere in my forgotten memories, I was sure I held a key, one Tarrant County Cold Case Division wouldn't have.

Raymond hadn't passed down the kind of legacy I wanted, but it was time to stop pretending it wasn't mine.

Whether or not I helped him with his murders, as Scott had said, Raymond's evil echoed through me. It resonated in my bones. Raymond would never lift a finger to fix the harm he'd caused, but someone had to. And the only someone was me.

Was that fair? No. Hardly mattered, though; it was the right thing to do. So, I'd do it.

I'd dig up the past and everything that came with it. By inviting evil into our home, Raymond had also inoculated me against it. That was part of his legacy, too. I could face whatever was waiting to be found in the wake of his heinous acts. I'd seen it all before.

For right now, though, I was going to let the water of this reservoir carry me inevitably toward the shore and watch my best friend sniff the hot summer air from the front of the kayak.

FIFTY-SEVEN

I knew better than to expect a warm welcome from the Fowlers. But after thinking it over on the lake, this had to happen. It couldn't be done over text. What I wasn't sure about was if I owed it to Dylan or if he owed it to me. Maybe we owed it to each other. Either way, I expected nothing less than emotional flogging.

That said, I wasn't looking forward to whatever Mrs. Fowler's neurosis of the week would be. Could do without that completely. After the hospital, mandatory counseling, and too much time off work to think, I didn't have it in me to be polite to a woman so wildly out of touch with anything meaningful in this world.

"Sit," I said once we reached the Fowlers' doorstep. Sadie, panting by my side but dry from an open window on the car ride over, happily complied. Good dog.

Dylan answered the door. I hardly recognized this gaunt version of him. He'd been thin to begin with, and now... Good lord. And this was two weeks *post*-captivity.

How to properly start a conversation like this was

beyond me. I'd even had time to brainstorm, and still, I had nothing. Maybe I should leave it to him, since he'd been the one to reach out to me first, much to my surprise.

I struggled to spit out something, but, torn between a casual greeting and a profuse apology, no words came.

He spared me the embarrassment when he stepped forward and pulled me into a tight hug.

The coiled muscles in my shoulders released while Sadie sniffed furiously at his knees.

Hug him back, you idiot.

By the time I got my arms to comply, he was already stepping away. "Why didn't you respond to my text?"

"Sorry," I said. "I've been busy." Obvious lie. I'd never been less busy in my life. But *I* didn't even understand why I hadn't texted him back. I just couldn't. "If it makes you feel better, I've been radio silent for everyone."

Also not true. I'd answered Ben's messages and even grabbed a beer with him a few more times since McNelly's. And I'd responded to my family's needy check-ins with one-word answers. I'd feel guilty for that bit of terseness if it wasn't so damn clear that my mother and siblings viewed my brief hospitalization and newspaper headlines as a mighty imposition upon them. How dare I end up in the papers again? How dare I lead a life that wasn't guaranteed to be safe and invisible?

Dylan nodded like he understood, and if that were true, I wished he'd explain it to me.

He invited me inside, also welcoming Sadie, who was more than happy to make herself at home, sniffing the perimeter of the kitchen as we entered it. "Where's your mom?"

Dylan grimaced and stared fixedly at the sink. "She moved out."

"Seems like you should be celebrating."

"I will eventually. But for now..." His hollow cheeks filled as he blew out a long exhale.

"Right," I said. "She wasn't happy about Marie. I already know. I spoke with her on the phone when I didn't know where you were, and she— Well, you know."

"Lost her shit on you?"

I nodded.

"Sounds about right. My boss wasn't too happy when he found out either." He stepped to the side and pointed at a stack of empty cardboard boxes on the floor by the counter.

Oh, for the love... "Goddamn bigots. What year are we in again? Leave it to Texas to make it legal to fire a perfectly good teacher for occasionally dressing like a woman."

For some reason, that made him laugh. There wasn't much juice behind it, though.

I forbade myself from thinking about all the ways this could have been avoided if only I'd reacted with a clearer head the moment I spotted those red heels in the back of his Prius. "Where are you going?"

"Not sure. My teacher's certification is only good in Texas, so I'll have to stay in the state. But I'm hoping I can move somewhere... better."

"There have to be schools in Austin that don't care what *perfectly legal* activities their teachers get up to on the weekends."

He stuck his hands into the pockets of his jeans. His pants hung loose on his thin frame and were bunched around the waist where his cinched belt helped them hold on for dear life. "I'm sure there are. But I don't know if I want to stick around. It's... it's hard." His gaze traveled to the window above the kitchen sink, and he stared vaguely toward the overgrown front lawn. "Scott killed those women because... I have to live with the fact that if he hadn't been obsessed with me in the first place..." He held up a hand to keep me from jumping in. "I know I'm not to blame, that I was a victim, too. I get that, *intellectually*. But that's not how it feels. I can't shake it." Finally, he met my eyes again. "It feels like I helped murder Cheryl and Leslie and Stephanie. I know it's wrong; I *know* it is. But it's how I feel, Dana."

"I understand," I said. "Trust me, I do."

He bobbed his head on a deep exhale, and as his shoulders hunched, his collarbone jutted like the blade of a butterfly knife. "Yeah, I guess you do."

"Sounds like moving is a smart choice."

Dylan reached down and petted Sadie's head. She'd been on her way somewhere else, but the contact stopped her in her tracks, and she sat practically on his feet, soaking up the scratches.

"Your mom will get over it," I said.

He raised a skeptical eyebrow in my direction.

"Or she won't," I added. "What does your brother think?"

The mention of his older brother Brady seemed to put him in a stupor, and I regretted having brought it up. But then he said, "He thinks it's... cool? Said he wants to meet Marie Possa sometime." He paused. "And he thinks that Mom's a sorry bitch."

I wrinkled my nose.

"No," Dylan said, "he's right."

"Your words, not mine."

Sadie must have spotted a crumb and slipped out of Dylan's reach. His eyes followed her absently. "I'm gonna go stay with him until I can find a new place."

"That'll be good."

"Eh, I doubt that." He looked up. "You still have your job?"

"As far as I know. IA has a few more private pieces of my life to pick through before they make a final recommendation to the department."

"And your partner?"

There was that subtle stab in my heart again. "Escobar? He'll be fine. Probably. He's a good detective."

"He saved my life," Dylan said. "That's what I was told, at least. He cut me down and started CPR before he went after you. Left Mildred Fierce to take over."

I nodded. Escobar had told me as much about the events that had gone down concurrent to my little rooftop chat with Scott. "Lucky break, having a registered nurse right there."

Dylan chuckled darkly. "Yeah, can you believe it? A kindergarten teacher and a nurse up on stage together. Real wholesome place, that drag bar."

"You laugh, but it's a hell of a lot more wholesome than most of the places I end up."

He narrowed his eyes at me. "I thought I had you figured out, back when I knew you as a bartender. But a Homicide detective? I couldn't make sense of it at first. I mean, part of that might have been because I was so pissed at you for getting me arrested. But mostly, I didn't understand why you wouldn't get as far away from all the gory stuff as possible. Now that I've made it out of that shack where he was keeping me, though, I think I get it."

"Get what?"

"That unfinished feeling."

I didn't need him to explain any further. But his mention of captivity brought me to the other reason I'd come by. "Can I ask you something personal?"

"More personal than all the shit you already know about me?"

"Not more personal, just more specific. This is about what happened to you."

He sighed, his expression sagging. "Should I put on some coffee?"

"No, I don't think this will take long, then I'll get out of your way and let you pack. There's something about the story that doesn't add up for me."

"Haven't you read the transcripts? It's all in there. I must've been interviewed twenty times."

"I have, but it isn't in there."

I had his attention now and wondered if he already suspected where this was going, what I was going to ask him about. It must have been nagging at him, the small impossibility that kept all the pieces from snapping together neatly.

"While you were imprisoned," I said, "you claim Scott came and gave you food and water."

His tired expression tightened instantly. He *did* know what was coming.

And he was dreading it.

Of course he was. So was I. But I had to ask anyway. I

was done letting a desperate need for closure stand in the way of the truth.

"I've checked the logs myself, Dylan. The Bureau bugged his car, his office, hid cameras throughout Laugh Attack. Heidi even let them in to wire up the whole house before she took off. The FBI only lost track of him an hour before he showed up at Sheep's Clothing, and they didn't realize it until my partner called for backup. That's cutting it awfully close for the drive from his home in Pflugerville to downtown Austin, let alone stopping to pick up a captive and rigging the noose and all that."

Dylan looked like he was going to be sick as he slid into one of the spindle-backed chairs at the kitchen table.

Now that he was sitting down, I came right out with it. "I don't see any way that Scott could have been the one who drove you there." The hair stood up on my arms before I asked the final question, the one that would either close the case or open a fissure in the ground beneath our feet, one that could swallow us, and so many others, whole: "Are you sure it was Scott who visited you where you were kept?"

Too late to take the words back. I'd just given voice to the horror, and it thickened the air around us.

Dylan's head dropped into his hands. "They asked me who it was." His voice was bloated with misery. "I told the first guys I didn't know. They kept asking. I kept saying I didn't know. It was dark; I never saw his face. He made me write those letters, but he was sort of whispering it, and he stood behind me and told me what to write. And that was after days. I hardly knew up from down by then. They—the people interviewing me—asked if it could have been Scott Ruiz. I said it could have, but I wasn't sure." I saw where this was headed, and my mouth went dry.

"When the second interview came," Dylan continued, "they asked again, right off the bat. Could it have been Scott Ruiz? I said it could have. By the time the next person came by with questions, they were calling him Scott from the start. I went along with it. I think I even believed it. I don't know. I was tired, confused. It was easier to go along with it."

I took a seat across the table from him. "But?"

He raised his head slowly. "I know Scott's voice. This... It wasn't him."

"But it was a man."

"Yes.

"Did you recognize it?"

"No."

"Think, Dylan. I need you to really think about this. Just one last time, that's all I'm asking. Think hard about it now, and then you'll never have to do it again. Could it have been Mike Check?"

"You think I haven't thought hard about this already?" Pain and contempt left deep creases around his eyes. "I didn't recognize the voice, Dana. I have no idea who it was. None."

I swallowed down the knot of dread in my throat. "Okay, Dylan. I believe you. I'm sorry I had to ask. But you understand why I had to, right?"

He gave the tiniest hint of a nod, and I forced a soft smile with nothing to back it up. Dread, a silent, creeping thing, grasped at my ankles. In this quiet and ordinary home, we'd released it. It awakened, stretched.

Scott Ruiz was still a serial killer. There wasn't a doubt

in my mind that he'd killed at least four women and that he would have killed Ben if I hadn't stopped him.

But now, that wasn't the end of the story.

Because Scott hadn't worked alone. He'd had an *accomplice.*

And I had no idea who it was.

FIFTY-EIGHT

My mind was still swirling from the conversation with Dylan a half-hour before as I lugged the kayak to the bottom of my stairs and leaned it against the metal railing to dig through my waterproof bag for my keys. As usual, the first thing I'd done when I got out of the car was to throw them in my bag, as if I wasn't about to need them thirty seconds later. And also as usual, they'd slipped into some alternate dimension. I cursed at myself under my breath as Sadie ran up the stairs ahead of me, impatient to get into a little A/C. Couldn't blame her. It was well over a hundred degrees.

Finally, I heard the jingle and extracted my keys. But when I get to the top of the stairs, Sadie was nowhere to be seen.

And my front door was wide open.

I dropped the kayak and reached for my hip instinctively before remembering I didn't have my gun on me. I'd left it locked in the glove box for the second trip down once I unburdened myself of the kayak.

Did I go back down and grab it before heading inside? Sadie must already be in there. I couldn't just leave her.

I had a spare shotgun and shells in the coat closet just inside the door. If I could get to that, I'd be good.

Moving as silently as I could toward the threshold, I peeked around the edge of the doorframe and took my first look inside.

The lights were on. All of them. That was not how I'd left things.

Someone had been inside. Had they left yet?

"Sadie," I hissed, scanning for any signs of movement within. "Sadie."

She appeared from behind the kitchen counter on the far side of the apartment, but it wasn't in response to my call. She pressed her nose to the floor, sniffing frantically.

With no visible threats, I hedged my bets. If someone was still in this part of the apartment, Sadie would've found them. That didn't rule out the bedroom or the bathroom, but I'd rule that out myself once I was armed.

I shut the front door behind me and locked the deadbolts. If someone was inside with me, they weren't sneaking out. And I'd be damned if I let anyone follow me inside and turn my home into a trap.

The coat closet by the front door was first on my list. I stood to the side, inhaled slowly, then flung it open. No one there.

I keyed in the code to the gun safe, and in half a dozen more heartbeats, I had four shells in the thing. Buckshot; I was tired of this shit. Tired of the violations of my home. If someone was in there, I wasn't waiting for an explanation.

I cleared the hallway first, then my bedroom, the hall

closet, and the bathroom last. No one there. No signs of a break-in besides the open front door. Nothing ransacked.

I returned to the open space of my living room, dining room, and kitchen.

As I approached Sadie where she was slopping water from her bowl in the kitchen, I spotted it.

A sticky note the color of the wound on my forearm. It was waiting for me on my countertop. Whoever was here had already gone, but they'd left this.

I crept toward the note, needing to read what it said but dreading what my life might be like once I knew.

My hand shook as I peeled it from the countertop and read the familiar handwriting.

Good work, Bear. He had to go. Two down.
xx Dad

END OF BOOK 1

DEATH ORDER
(DANA CAPONE MYSTERIES #2)

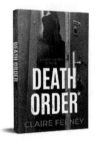

Locked doors won't protect you from the people you invite inside…

Detective Capone is ready for a distraction. So when the report of a murdered stage magician comes in, she's the first to volunteer. But just as she worries the case has hit a dead end, shocking DNA evidence jumpstarts the investigation. Only one problem: the woman it belongs to has been missing for months.

With danger closing in and more bodies turning up, Dana's only shot at solving these serial murders might be throwing herself into the epicenter of evil.

Can Detective Capone find the killer before death darkens her doorstep?

Buy Death Order now

Go to: www.clairefeeney.com/capone2

ACKNOWLEDGMENTS

I wouldn't've had the *cojones* to publish this without the help of my dear, sweet husband, Jack. This book would be nothing without your on-the-job experience and artistic suggestions, like the phrase "suck start my duty weapon." Thanks for reading my books and still keeping me around.

I owe a huge debt to Amy Teegan and Nathan Van Coops, who beta read this book in its earlier stages, back when it was written in third-person past tense POV and then changed to first-person present tense POV and then finally changed to first-person past tense POV. Thank you for allowing me to have *very minor* panic attacks to you about whether I needed to rewrite the whole thing again.

Big thanks to my copyeditor, Julie Strauss, who is not afraid to ask the obvious questions like, "Why would she say this?" and "What the hell is ASAC?" so that I don't get ahead of myself. You make me look good, Julie.

Speaking of making me look good, shout out to Arran McNicol at 720Editing for the keen proofread and making me chuckle (usually at my own typos) in the margins.

To the Citizen Detectives, my advance reader team, thank you for joining up on the first Dana Capone novel to support an author you know little about.

And to every reader who took a chance on this book, thank you. Let's keep on getting our hands dirty together. There's plenty more of Dana's story left to be told. See you in the next book.

ABOUT THE AUTHOR

CLAIRE FEENEY writes gritty crime fiction with dark humor from her home in Austin, Texas.

When she's not consuming true crime or soaking up her LEO husband's work stories, you can find her gardening, propagating indoor plants, playing pick-up soccer, or causing trouble with her two dogs.

pinterest.com/clairefeeneybooks

facebook.com/clairefeeneybooks

bookbub.com/authors/claire-feeney

amazon.com/author/clairefeeney

goodreads.com/clairefeeney

Made in the USA
Coppell, TX
15 February 2023

12862877R00300